(mis)TRUST

Sarah Ann Walker

<u>**Also by Author Sarah Ann Walker**</u>

I am HER...

THIS is me...

We are US...

My Dear Stranger

LOST

Choices...

Copyright © 2016 (071716-1) Sarah Ann Walker
Cover Design: James Freeburg
All rights reserved.
ISBN-13: 978-0-9917231-6-4

Sarah Ann Walker

(mis)TRUST

Sarah Ann Walker

DEDICATION

To Jakkob

You are absolutely everything I love in this life.

Xo
Mommy

ACKNOWLEDGMENTS

James, thank you for another amazing book cover.
To my parents, thank you for not bugging me *too* much for not calling you back when I'm all up in my head writing.
Brennah, thank you for giving me my handsome nephew Zakkary, and my 2 beautiful nieces Piper-Ireland and Teaghan.
Paola, thank you for being my longest, dearest friend.
Silvana, thank you for still making me laugh- the WW is for you.
Sam, thank you for being my BBE- Best Brit Ever. (This Scots for you!)
Amy, I look forward to my ass grabs in Michigan.
Samantha, thank you for our read-alongs, I love our time together.
Rachelle, thank you for being an extraordinary pimping support to me.
Brenda, thank you for still holding my hand. I miss you.

Randi Newman, thank you for your amazing support with this book, and for your constant, beautiful friendship. You are my most special stalker turned dearest friend ever, and I love you and Mike to pieces.
Please tell Mike he finally got an awesome cameo. xo

Katica, thank you for your invaluable input with this story-
Everyone has *you* to thank for the ending.

Thank you Deniro, Kim, Megan, Dawn, Michelle, MTO Diane, Carla, Glenda, Alanna, Samantha, Suzanne, Elizabeth, Raven, Shabby & Laura
Thank you to Darcy, Diana, Amy, Julianne, Jamie and the Twisted Sisters, Lustful Literature, Hashtag Minxes Love Books,
Triple M Books and The Diva's Book Lounge Group
to name a few...

I want to thank all the readers, friends, and bloggers who have supported me these last 3 years and 7 books. I wish I could name you all.

xo
Sarah

Sarah Ann Walker

Introduction

The Past

The Present

The Future

Author's Bio

<u>Music List</u>
Alex Clare- Too Close
Lady Gaga- Bad Romance
Imagine Dragons- Demons
Mumford and Sons- I Will Wait
Franz Ferdinand- Take Me Out
Of Mice and Men- Little Talks
Fun- We Are Young
Lumineers- Ho Hey
Depeche Mode- Somebody
Depeche Mode- A Question Of Lust
Pearl Jam- Rearview Mirror

INTRODUCTION

Feeling Tyler's lips suddenly against the side of my neck, I jump in my chair and playfully swat him away. I have to study and he knows... *Ahhhhh.*

"*Ty*... Oh. Right there," I moan as his hands start massaging the back of my neck. Feeling my shoulders kissed as my t-shirt lowers, I groan when he rubs my tense neck a little harder. "I have to study," I practically gasp when I feel his tongue work back up the side of my neck to my ear.

When he whispers, "I just need 2 minutes, Lovey," I smirk to myself. 2 minutes? Tyler has never been only 2 minutes, but...

"2 minutes?" I turn my head as his hands slide around my neck to hold me close to his mouth. Kissing me softly, Tyler grins an *uh huh* as I open for his tongue. Okay, I can spare 2 minutes I decide as I tug his head down harder to my mouth.

Suddenly pulled from my desk chair with his hand holding the back of my head to the floor, he crawls over me. Moving my legs, Tyler is between them instantly lifting my back as we kiss until my t-shirt is removed when we part lips briefly.

Grinding against me, Tyler takes me from my old, dirty library books to arousal in seconds. Pulling away from my lips, Tyler lowers himself to my chest as his hips continue to grind against me.

Taking my nipple through my ugly off-white bra, I'm sucked in deep through the cotton until my legs spread wider and my back arches closer. Feeling his hand trail down my stomach to the waistband of my track pants I'm already panting. Feeling him slide inside to touch my pussy I'm nearly gasping. When he abandons my chest to move down my body I lift as he pulls my pants and underwear with him as he lowers.

Crying out, Tyler is just shy of too much when I feel a finger push deep inside me just as his tongue lashes at me. "Okay..." I breathe between moans. "You can have **5** minutes," I sigh before feeling him huff a little laugh right against my dampening body.

Closing my eyes, I take in the pleasure. My body has been tight with stress and worry, and my mind has been filled with so much information, I often wonder how I possibly retain as much knowledge as I do. I've been so mentally overwhelmed lately, these moments between me and Tyler are all that seem to ground me. He is always here for me, and he always seems to know when I need to be distracted from the workload and pressure.

Tyler knows me, knows when I need him, and he always loves me harder when I need it.

"I love you," I whisper as the familiar stirring of an orgasm takes me over.

Pulling his hair to keep him tight against my body, I writhe against his face feeling the growing pull deep inside me. I'm not going to take much longer and I'm looking forward to the temporary release of the pressure I'm under.

Working my body, Tyler knows exactly what to do with his tongue and fingers to make me come undone. He knows where to touch me inside and how much pressure to use outside. He knows where I love his tongue against me and he knows what I need to be relieved.

Arching, my body starts grinding back against him as the pressure builds. I'm so close, my words are now muffled, incoherent and nearly pleading. My legs are shaking and my mind is fading as the urgency increases.

Crying out my release against his mouth, Tyler works me a little longer to try to keep me going until I exhale my final groan of pleasure. When my hands fall from his hair to drop on the floor he knows my orgasm is over. He would know anyway, but Tyler always jokes when he hears the thump of my hands on the floor and the physical relief of not having his hair yanked out of his head I'm finally done.

"Your 5 minutes is up," I say as seriously as I can until I look down at Tyler's stunned face. Laughing at his expression, my throat is a little hoarse though I feel so much lighter than I did only minutes ago.

"I. Don't. Think. So," he says laughing as he moves my thighs wider to advance on me. Kissing my mouth, I take in my own taste and scent and pull him harder into me when he makes penetration. Back and forth he enters and retreats until settled in deep we stop kissing for a moment to look at each other with our Tyler/Saige eyes as everyone refers to them.

"I love you," he kisses me slow and softly. "But it's your turn to do some work," he laughs flipping us quickly as I gasp.

Suddenly on top, my hair swings on my shoulders and my hands plant on his chest when I settle on him deeply. Moving and lifting, I know what Tyler likes and I know how to move for him. Tightening my internal muscles as I lean my pelvis back and rise, Tyler always squeezes my thighs with his hands from the pleasure he receives. When I lift slowly off but crash back down Tyler always arches under me.

Opening his eyes, Tyler begs, "Let me get you off again."

"No," I moan. "I'm good," I smile as he groans when I ride him a little harder and faster.

Though I'm very much enjoying this sexy distraction, I don't have time for Tyler to try to coax another orgasm from me. A second orgasm always takes longer to achieve, and an orgasm during actual sex usually takes much time and effort for both of us- time I don't have right now.

"Come here, Lovey," he whispers until I move toward his mouth.

Kissing Tyler, I feel his gentle hands caressing my back and I know everything amazing between us. Tyler is always playful in the bedroom, sometimes even a little adventurous, but he always calms by the end to show me his love with his hands. Tyler's hands are always careful, almost a gentle caress of devotion before he finishes inside me. It's his last act before I know he's ready to release, and I always wait for his hands to pet me softly before I feel everything he doesn't need to say flow deep inside me.

Riding out Tyler's coming storm, I close my eyes, move faster and harder, but feel the softness of his hands on my back telling me he loves me.

Watching his neck suddenly arch as his chest pumps up and down, he breathes in harsh gasps until I know the end for him. Opening his eyes quickly, he stares at me with his hard intensity just as I feel the orgasm leave his body. He is coming quietly, groaning softly, but staring at me like he's giving me every part of himself that he possibly can.

Moving down to rest on his chest during his last pants and thrusts, his arms wrap around me tightly. Tyler is so much larger than I am, I've always loved how tightly he holds me after sex.

Exhaling my tension and the physical exertion of the last 20 minutes, I'm distracted and happy. I know no matter what happens with my exam or my future I'll always have this life with Tyler.

Leaning into my hair, Tyler teases, "You really need to stop distracting me when you have to study, Saige."

Huffing a laugh against his sweaty chest, I ask, "With my sweat pants and ripped t-shirt?" Nodding, he mock glares at me pushing a piece of my hair behind my ear before he kisses my lips again softly.

"When are you leaving for work?"

"Soon. But when I come back tonight I don't want to see you sitting in the same chair hunched over the desk, okay? You need to take breaks, Saige," Tyler says just firmly enough to make me listen without sounding like an annoying parent.

"I will. Thanks for this break, but I really need to get back to it now that I'm all relaxed and calm," I rise on my arms and kiss him deeply once more.

"I can always relax and calm you again tonight when I get home," he grins with the dirty look I love.

"I look forward to it," I kiss him again.

Standing, I look down his body once while he stares at my body with more hunger. "Perv..." I grin as he smiles up at me.

"For you? *Always*..." he laughs as I walk away shaking my ass for him.

*****

Hopping in the shower, I need to get back to my studies. I need to enjoy this release from all the pressure I'm under, at least for as long as it lasts.

"I'll be home around midnight," Tyler says behind the shower curtain before throwing it open quickly to shower. Taking the shower head from my hand, he rinses his body and hands it back to me. Moving me against the tile wall he kisses me deeply one last time before stepping out.

"Love you, Lovey," he grins waiting for my usual goodbye.

"Bye, Ty," I smile before finishing my shower.

Sarah Ann Walker

THE PAST

CHAPTER 1

Leaving for the library, Tyler stops me with a deep kiss in the hallway. Dropping my bag to wrap my arms around his neck, I lean in and take all he can give me. Desperately, I kiss him as he holds my head close and my waist even closer.

After forever, Tyler pulls away with a little grin. "Just thought you needed another distraction."

"I *always* need your distractions," I snuggle in deep.

Hugging me tightly, Tyler asks, "When will you be home from the lecture?"

"Just after 7. Then I'll get down to studying again. What are you doing this afternoon?"

"I'll study a little, then go to the gym before work. But I'll be home by 11 to kiss you goodnight."

"Good. I'm going to need a little Tyler tonight," I say seriously until I notice his smirk and realize what I said. "Not THAT little Tyler," I burst out laughing as he does. "Well, *maybe*," I grin pushing my ass into him when I bend over to pick up my nap sack.

"Enjoy the library," he groans rubbing my ass. "And don't let Handle stress you out. You're going to kill this exam, Lovey."

"Let's hope," I whisper when he kisses the back of my head again before I leave.

*****

Oh, *pleeeeeease.* Why do I hit every red light in the entire city when I'm screwed for time? *Why?* Murphy's Law? The fates? Why the hell am I so hated by the Universe?

Peeling around the neighborhood I can't believe I might be late. I can NOT believe I might actually miss the intro of my final exam.

How the hell could I have possibly over-studied in the library? Isn't that like the lamest excuse any student has ever given since the beginning of time? Well, other than my dog ate my homework, I think 'I lost track of time because I was studying too hard' is the second

1

lamest excuse. No matter what I say though, Professor Handle will only nod and turn his back should I actually attempt to explain, which really, he won't let me anyway.

God, I'm so screwed.

Parking as close as I can to the lecture hall, I run for my life. Professor Handle is a notorious hardass, and he loves closing the lecture hall doors at exactly one minute after. Christ, he even smiles at students running for the lecture hall before he closes the heavy doors in their faces. And god forbid the poor student who doesn't know the rule of the closed door- they're screwed for the rest of the semester. Once they open the door, they are asked their name, then they're asked to leave, and Professor Handle never forgets a name or a face.

Rounding Traynor Hall I'm seconds from the... *NO!!!* Skidding to a stop mere feet from the doors, I'm done. Goddamnit, it's closed.

Leaning against the wall to catch my breath, I can only hope Kyle took notes he'll scan me later. I can hope, and though note-taking isn't one of his greatest attributes it's my only option for the pre-exam lecture notes for my final tomorrow. Looking down the hall, I see one other girl I recognize from class leaning, nope, actually banging the back of her head against the wall like I want to right now. *Shit.*

Walking back to my car totally nauseous, I feel freaked out but refuse to stress any further, or worse yet, burst into tears from the pressure. I screwed up, but I need to focus on studying and wait for Kyle to get home so I can beg for his notes. I have to relax and go home and cry on Tyler's shoulder until he makes me feel better. That's all I can do.

Exiting the building I see another late student suddenly stop running when he recognizes me.

Giving a pitiful, you're totally screwed face, he shakes his head and huffs, "The construction on Kennedy Street?"

"Nope. Over-studied," I practically groan.

"Shitty..." he nods solemnly.

Giving each other a last sad smile, we acknowledge we're screwed and walk in opposite directions from the Traynor building.

I can't believe I did this. I can't believe by studying for the most important exam I'll ever write I've missed the most important pre-exam lecture to the most important exam I'll ever write in my life.

• • • • •

Stopping for a coffee on my way home, I need the caffeine so I'm sharp while studying tonight. I need the buzz and I need the clarity. This exam is all about memorization which means I need to remember all the little cases and the obscure legal facts and dates Handle threw at us all semester. God knows he would never put the famous Roe vs. Wade on the final- he'd consider that an insult to our collective intelligence.

Coffee in hand, almost home, Tyler told me he'd be studying a little for his own exam in a few days before leaving for work, and I really hope I see him before he's left- I *need* to see him before he leaves. Once he's gone, I know I'll have our apartment to myself to pull a semi-allnighter before I wake up after 5 hours of sleep to review before the biggest exam of my life.

This is not a tragedy, I have to keep telling myself. This is a little hiccup, and Tyler will say something wonderful and supportive to make me calm down, and then I'll get down to studying. Things could be much worse, I know that. I just need to focus and adjust to my exam cram reality, and hopefully to Kyle's decent notes in a few hours.

Man, having your entire future mapped out based on one exam percentage is way too stressful.

*****

Walking in our door I'm surprised by the loud dance music playing in the living room. Tyler said he was going to be cramming until he left- not that our definitions of cramming are the same. But still, blasting music throughout our whole apartment seems a little counter-productive.

"Ty?" Calling out he doesn't even acknowledge me over the music. "Tyler?"

Probably studying at our desk, he usually listens to classical music before an exam. He once read classical music makes you retain more information, so this techno pop crap is not his usual choice, nor mine for that matter.

"Tyler? You'll never guess what I did. I..."

I freeze.

3

Gasping, I can't even move.

With my hand still holding our bedroom door, all I see are his hands on her back. Watching her ride him, I'm stunned staring at his hands gently running up and down her back.

What the hell is happening?

He doesn't see me, and she's too busy grinding on him to notice me. She's actually holding MY headboard while she rides Tyler completely unaware of me watching.

And I still can't move.

Leaning against the doorframe, I don't know what to say, or do, or even how I make this stop.

I don't know anything as I watch him rubbing her back gently like he rubs mine when I'm on top. He's touching her the way he touches me and moving under her the way he moves under me just before he finishes.

Barely breathing, I can't understand what he's doing with her.

Absurdly, I wonder if this is how crimes of passion occur. Is this how a murder starts? Is this the disassociated seemingly abstract feeling that takes over the perpetrator before they commit a murder?

Oh my *god*...

I don't know what to do, and my body won't move. I don't even have a voice while I'm stuck still watching a nightmare unfold.

Feeling tears pour down my face, my eyes stay glued to Tyler's big hands gently touching her back as he caresses her like he caresses me.

"I love you, Tyler," she moans as she leans down to kiss him. Watching her ass rise and fall on top of him I wait for his voice.

She *loves* him?

My heart is actually pounding harder than the bass beats I no longer hear.

Everything has faded to a dark tunnel of disbelief.

The music has faded and my eyes have narrowed to focus only on the horrific scene in front of me as it continues.

It's like I'm watching one of Tyler's porns. I'm completely unaffected by the sex itself but mesmerized by the people as they move.

I don't know what to do until I'm suddenly overwhelmed with the need to punch her in the back of the head so I can strangle him before she recovers.

"Lovey..." Tyler moans between kisses and I finally snap out of my painful trance of disbelief.

Gagging loudly, my hand just covers my mouth as a cry bursts from my chest.

Lovey?

That's what Tyler calls *me*. And though I absolutely hate it, he has always called me Lovey since the moment we met. During tender moments, moments after sex, or even during late nights watching the news together. Tyler would say such sweet things to me- and he would call me Lovey. And though I always hated that annoying term of endearment, it was mine. It was Tyler's claim on me because *I* am his Lovey.

When Tyler finally opens his eyes from sucking on her nipples he suddenly sees me and seems to suffer his own moment of utter disbelief.

"Oh, fuck. Get *off!*" He yells trying to push the woman off his hips.

Watching, I actually start crying louder and laughing a little when I see her bare down on him harder and faster while Tyler tries to push himself out from under her. Shitty for him, I think she clearly misunderstood which *get off* he actually meant.

"It's okay. You may as well finish," I yell over the music before covering my mouth as I spin away from this nightmare finally.

Sprinting from my bedroom, I make it to the living room grabbing Ty's iPhone from the speaker base to turn their awful music off.

Holding myself together tightly, my body finally reacts as the sudden silence deafens me. Throwing and smashing his phone on the ceramic tiles in the kitchen, I collapse on the couch gasping for breath.

Crying *and* laughing, Tyler rounds the corner wearing only boxers on his body and a frantic expression on his face.

Stopping all movement, we stare at each other for an eternity.

Looking at my future crash down around me, I honestly feel like I hate him in this disgusting moment between us.

"Are you done?" I ask before bursting out laughing again.

I think I've gone mental over this and all I have is my laughter because I don't know what else to do. Sadly, it appears the moment for head punching and strangulation has passed for me.

Walking toward me, I push back into the couch as he sits on the coffee table to stare at me. Looking every bit as confused as I feel Tyler tears up a little as I wait for something from him.

Shaking his head he eventually pulls in a big breath before speaking. "I'm so sorry. I, uh, don't really know what to say here. This is, um..."

Turning quickly, we both look over at his slut moving toward us in only the long Ramones t-shirt I bought Tyler last Christmas. Wow, did she actually go through my dresser drawers?

"What's going on Ty?" She asks glaring at me like a possessive whore.

"Yes, what IS going on, Ty?" I ask in such a distorted voice I mock both of them at once. "Actually, I saw what was going on in *my* bed. But what's actually going on?"

"We're in *LOVE!*" Who-the-fuck-ever suddenly yells at me causing that potential crime of passion rage to build to nearly unmanageable. "Tell her, Tyler. You may as well tell her now. Her exam is tomorrow, right?" She reasons with him and glares at me like a bitch.

Holy shit. She knows about my exam like she actually knows about me. What the *hell* is going on?

"Kaitlyn, you should leave, okay?" Tyler says softly. Listening, I feel such hurt by his soft voice for her I gasp another little cry when he turns back to me.

"Yeah, *Kaitlyn*... Get the hell out of my apartment!" I suddenly yell when my shock fades completely. Watching Tyler turn back from my outburst to Kaitlyn almost in apology, I see everything very, very clearly suddenly. "*Wow,*" I choke. "I guess you better go with her, too. This is clearly more than a one-time thing."

"We're in *love,* Saige. And I'm NOT a one-time thing. *Right,* Baby?"

Absolutely stunned that this strange woman in my own home knows my name, and is talking back to me to almost intentionally provoke me, I close down and stare between the 2 of them in silence.

Tyler of course looks like he's freaked out and struggling, but *she* doesn't. She's wearing a satisfied smile that screams everything she's saying is the truth. The fact that Tyler hasn't told her to shut the hell up or even attempted to deny anything gives all my unspoken questions the answers I didn't want to know.

Exhaling a long breath as I try to get my head together I really don't know what to say in this situation. Truthfully, I never thought I'd ever *be* in this situation. Especially with Tyler.

"You smell like dirty sex," I gag and start laughing again.

Okay, not a profound statement, but true nonetheless. He smells like sex and sweat and someone else's perfume. He even has her nasty sex scent on him.

Oh *god*... Hunching over my own body, I can't handle this right now. "I can't even go lie down," I say to no one.

Standing in front of Tyler he reaches for my hand as I flinch away. "Don't touch me. Could you please just go now? Take Kaitlyn with you and go live your life."

"*DON'T* tell him what to do, *bitch!*" She has the nerve to yell at me which makes me finally snap out of my devastated calm.

"GET THE *FUCK* OUT OF MY APARTMENT!" I scream before turning on Tyler. "Get her out of here before I lose my *fucking* mind! Take your whore and GET. THE. FUCK. *OUT!*" When Tyler does actually grab me, I fight his hold and whip around and out of the way. "Listen you fucking whore, I'll call the police if I have to. So get the fuck out before I have you thrown out!"

"You can't tell me what to do!"

"Now! Get the fuck out *NOW!* Tyler, I swear to god if you don't get out and take her with you I'll fucking kill you. *NOW!!!*" I scream so loudly I swear the windows rattled before I suddenly closed my mouth the second his whore jumped and ran for my bedroom.

She better be getting her shit to get the hell out of here or I'll kill them both with my bare fucking hands.

Holding myself still, I feel pain pulsing in my head from yelling, and a deep agony ripping through my heart from Tyler. I know I'm not even capable of truly crying yet because a dazed numb has taken me over.

"You need to calm down, Saige. This isn't you," Tyler pleads beside me and again I'm stunned and shocked and pissed that he still thinks he can soothe me. *Christ*, he lost the right to soothe me the very second he caused this nightmare.

"Leave, Tyler. I don't care where you go but just get the hell out. I have my exam tomorrow and I need you out of here."

"Um, this is my apartment, too. And I'm not leaving," Tyler says and I can't hide my disbelief again as my jaw drops. Staring at him with my arms holding myself tightly together, I'm simply stunned by his behavior right now. "We need to talk, Lovey-"

Losing my mind completely, I laugh, "*Lovey?* Are you *fucking* kidding me? I HATE that name- I *always* have. But you said it was me. You said

7

I was your lovey, but now you call some other woman in my own bed Lovey while fucking her and you're *not* leaving? How can you be so cruel to me? *Seriously?!* How can you hurt me this way? I've done nothing to you, ever. I've been the perfect girlfriend and you were-"

"Except when you worked and studied and went to school all the time," he huffs in my face.

Wow. Well, that was as close to a slap across my face as Tyler's ever given me. Pausing to stare at the man I love, there is nothing left for me here anymore.

He has always supported my schooling and wanted me to do well. He helped me study and he was proud of me always. Tyler was the perfect boyfriend to me, and I loved him so much, I actually thanked god for him in my life.

Shaking my head, my heartache quickly turns to anger. "I can't believe you just said that. I *truly* can't believe you said that to me. Talk about mixed messages. You've supported every single thing I've done to get where I am so I can get where I want to be. You have always known why this was important to me, and you said you understood why I needed to do this. But *now* you throw it in my face?"

"I'm not throwing it in your face, I'm just saying there's more-"

"Tyler are we staying or leaving?" His whore suddenly asks and I can *not* believe the nerve of this bitch.

I can't believe she was just caught screwing a man in another woman's bed and she's acting like *she's* the injured party. Looking over at her with her trampy clothes, long legs, and sexy dark hair, I'm embarrassed for her. And really, for myself as well.

When Tyler turns back to her without anger or embarrassment I have my answer to absolutely everything between us.

And our 4 year relationship is over.

"Stay," I say simply as I walk past the woman actually glaring at *me* again. "I'll leave tonight, but you better be out of here when I return at 1:30 tomorrow. You better be gone or I *will* call the police and have you removed," I explain to the whore. "This may be your place, too," I seethe at a silent Tyler, "But it isn't hers. So get her the hell out of here!"

"Listen *Saige*, I'll stay wherever the fuck Tyler want me to stay."

"*TYLER!*" I scream over her bitchy voice so he finally snaps into action. Walking to his whore Kaitlyn, Tyler begins speaking quietly to her as I watch horrified. Feeling like I'm going to be sick, I leave them for my disgusting bedroom.

Opening my closet I can still smell their sex and I want to scream and barf and kill them at the same time.

The urge to kill is so sudden I actually have to take a deep breath before I do something I can never walk away from. I have to breathe away the violence coursing through my veins, and I have to breathe away the urge to ruin my entire life.

Yanking clothes from my closet, I realize I handled myself fairly well considering. Though honestly, it's not very satisfying right now.

"You were supposed to be at your tutorial."

"What?" I pause turning to look at Tyler in the doorway.

"You weren't supposed to be home for at least 2 more hours," he huffs. "I never would've had Kaity here if I knew you would be home. So-"

"It's *my* fault? Are you actually trying to suggest I caused this by coming home early to my own home? That somehow I ruined everything between us because I missed my final tutorial?" I ask incredulously as he starts shifting uncomfortably on his feet.

"No. I'm just saying I wouldn't have let this happen the night before your exam," he mumbles as some kind of pathetic excuse or lame-ass justification.

"*Awww*, thanks, Tyler. I appreciate you looking out for me. Thanks for trying not to screw with the most important exam of my life. The exam that sends me to Law school on full and partial scholarships and allows me to complete my dream of becoming a lawyer. Thanks for thinking of the timing when you screwed another woman in our bed. I'm really sorry *I* screwed with your plans."

"I'm just-"

"You know what? I missed Handle closing the doors. I was studying so hard I screwed up the time, busted my ass to get to the lecture, missed it, and nearly lost it in the hallway. But then I pulled myself together enough to leave before I threw open the door anyway. I kept it together, trying to move past my screw-up, and you know what I thought?" When Tyler doesn't speak, I ask again. "Do you?"

"No."

"I thought about you. I actually thought *thank god* for Tyler. Thank god Tyler will say something wonderful and loving. Tyler will make me feel better before I get down to studying my ass off. But instead of love and support I got to see you fucking someone else in my own bed."

Laughing as I shake my head to clear it again I grab a large tote bag from under my filthy, tainted, disgusting bed, catch another whiff of them accidentally and contemplate walking to the kitchen for a lighter so I can set my bed on fire.

"We need to talk," Tyler steps toward me until I stop him with my hand raised.

"We really don't. It's over. But I'm telling you, you better go with her or get her the hell out of here because someone's gonna die if I catch her here tomorrow when I return. This is done, Tyler. Tomorrow I'm going to talk to the Super about ending our lease early, unless you'd like your whore to co-sign with you?"

"We should talk about this," he pushes again and I almost start to cry.

Tyler is using his let's be reasonable voice and it's breaking my heart. God, this is the voice I thought he'd use on me when I returned. This is the sweet Tyler I needed today.

Looking at his beautiful dark eyes, I honestly can't believe he did this to me and to us.

"You've hurt me so badly, I don't think I can explain it to you in a way you'll ever truly understand. You've broken my heart in a way I don't think *I'll* ever truly understand. You were my last chance, Tyler. And you had the last piece of my heart that was left."

"Saige... I-"

"Is she still in my apartment?" I head tilt to the living room like he needed clarification.

"Not right now. But-"

"After I leave she's coming back? Holy *SHIT!* You are the tackiest, most insensitive asshole I've ever met in my life," I cry a little. Grabbing my pounding heart, I can't understand his behavior anymore. "You're actually going to have her back to *our* home as soon as I leave?"

"It's my place, too, Saige. And-"

SLAP.

Unintentionally, or maybe unconsciously, or maybe by necessity I've slapped Tyler and potentially ruined my entire life.

If he wants to be a dick he can call the police and ruin me with a domestic abuse charge. He can press charges and ruin my future life with just one phone call. He can absolutely destroy me but I don't really care at the moment.

Snatching up my bag from the floor I leave him still standing in just his boxers holding his cheek looking totally shocked by my sudden anger.

Grabbing toiletries from the bathroom I need to get out of this apartment, and really, from my life before there's no turning back for me.

Taking my laptop off the coffee table and my backpack of books from the floor I'm ending my life...

with Tyler.

"Can I just explain what happened?" He asks when I throw open the hall closet for another purse and a different jacket.

"Nope," I answer, calmly ignoring him the closer he gets to me.

"Please? I'm not a total prick here, I'm just-"

Okay, I honestly can't believe him. I can't believe he still thinks he can talk himself out of, or maybe *into* this situation.

He sounds like he almost regrets it, but then he still wants Kaitlyn so I guess he doesn't regret it enough to want me or my forgiveness more than he wants her.

Trying to clear my thoughts while battling the heartache tightening my chest, I explain everything to him as clearly as I can.

"Tyler... I was your girlfriend for 4 years. We live together and we planned our entire future together. And we had a *good* future," I add when he attempts to speak. "I'm an awesome girlfriend and I *thought* you were an amazing boyfriend. We supported each other always, or at least I thought you did. Now, with what you said earlier I don't know that you ever did. Maybe you thought you did, or maybe you just pretended-"

"I did support you!" He interrupts, but I'm not listening.

"We had an amazing sex life so you can't claim you were sexually neglected, and we had a wonderful friendship so you can't claim I wasn't there for you. I'm not a bitch, so that's no excuse, and I'm not some woman who was ever using you in this relationship, because I contributed if not equally, actually quite a bit more than you did financially," I throw in a little dig.

11

"So there is absolutely NO excuse for you not only straying and cheating on me, but to be such an obnoxious piece of shit as to have sex with someone else in our home together. There is nothing worse, and no greater insult to me. You have disrespected not only me but our entire 4 years together. So NO we don't need to talk about anything. Your actions just explained absolutely everything without you having to say a word."

"You *were* awesome, but I needed-"

"Did you use condoms?" I suddenly ask as nausea settles low in my gut. "I never thought I couldn't trust you with my health, but here I am suddenly. Did you use condoms with her?"

"Yes," he huffs.

"Always?"

"Yes. *Okay?*" He replies somewhat pissed off which is hysterical under the circumstances.

"Well, at least I don't have to worry about that," I kind of laugh.

"Look, we need to talk because I don't want you upset like this before your exam. I didn't mean to-" Cutting off his pathetic attempt to soothe me, I end us. Officially.

"You know, there was *nothing* in the world you could have ever needed or wanted that you couldn't have asked me for," I say simply. "Or that I wouldn't have given you in a heartbeat. I loved you that much, Tyler."

Hearing him moan a little as his hands start shaking, I know I just smacked him across the face without the physical replay of earlier.

His silence as he stares at my face tells me I not only won this argument, but that he's actually hearing and seeing what I just laid out in front of him. And it's all true. There is *nothing* I wouldn't have done for Tyler for the rest of our lives together.

"I'll return after my exam tomorrow, and I really hope you at least respect me enough to not have that woman back in *my* home again until I can move out. I think that would be the last tiny show of respect from you that I feel I've earned after all the love and support, and *monogamy* I gave to you."

"Lovey, *please?* I-"

Shaking my head, I feel such betrayal at that word remembering her getting off on him as he called her Lovey in my bed.

"That is the last time I ever want to hear that word from you," I snap.

"*Ever*, Tyler. I'm not your Lovey, I'm just the woman you said you loved more than anything in the world but who you disrespected and attempted to destroy. You've broken my heart, Tyler. And I will *never* forgive you for this."

Finally exhaling, I pick up my bags, purse, and my laptop off the kitchen table and walk away with his face looking almost as hurt as I feel.

Walking away I realize the urge to kill has faded to a pain so deep I can barely breathe, and my heart is broken beyond anything I thought I could survive.

Exiting my life, I'm actually proud of myself for one quick moment for making my closing arguments without bursting into the tears I'm emotionally drowning in.

"Bye, Ty..." I whisper dramatically for the last time ever as I close our apartment door in his sad face.

CHAPTER 2

Driving to the University library, I have to think. My hands are shaking and my foot is shaking on the gas and brake so uncontrollably, I keep slipping off the pedals.

Gasping in quick bursts from my chest, I can't believe how painful this is. I actually feel like my heart is truly broken, like I'm dying inside as my heart shatters in my chest.

My chest is pounding and my head hurts so badly, I need Tylenol, or alcohol, or sleep maybe. I need *something* to erase the last hour of my life completely.

Trying desperately to focus on what I'm doing I realize my options are severely limited, and tragically my life has just become very small all of a sudden.

My mother lives hours away and my father isn't an option. I have Selena, but she has her own shit to deal with plus too small of an apartment for me. I have Mike I guess, but I don't want to ever make our friendship or work relationship awkward, which leaves only Kyle from class.

Texting Kyle from the library parking lot, I've let him know I'm here and ready to grab his notes as soon as Handle's lecture is over. I've texted him and have just over an hour to wait, because amazingly the entire end of my current life took place in less than an hour at home.

Pulling out my books while I wait for Kyle's reply, I again try to focus. I need to get studying, and I need to ace this exam so I *have* a future- a future without Tyler by my side apparently.

Suddenly crying out, I don't know what the hell happened. Why did Tyler cheat on me? Thinking back, I honestly can't believe what I saw.

I can't figure this out or make sense of it, even though I'm desperately trying to understand what happened and what I did wrong. No matter what I think or remember though I don't see a single thing that prompted or provoked this.

Just last night we made love on our bedroom floor when he playfully tugged me from my desk. And the sex was good, and normal, and satisfying between us.

After he came home from work I stopped studying and we watched an hour of TV and crawled into bed together. This morning we even had our coffee and toast together before I got back to my books when he left for his own final class of the semester.

Not wanting to cast him as the villain always, I'll admit Tyler has always been supportive and caring and he never hid his affection for me ever. He was funny, and loving, and good looking, and just an amazing partner for me. Everyone in University has always known us as a couple, and I've always taken pride in our wonderful relationship around others.

Christ, we think the same, want the same things, like the same music, laugh at the same jokes, and love each other the same. We were so together, it was hard to know who thought what or experienced what in our relationship after all this time together.

Unless that was the problem?

God, if he gives me the dreaded, 'it's not you, it's me' speech I'm going to throw up. If he gives me the cliché 'I love you, but I'm not IN love with you' lecture I'm going to lose my mind.

If Tyler says anything other than 'I'm so goddamn sorry, Saige. I screwed up,' I'll never forgive him. I'll never go back to him regardless, but hearing he at least feels sorry will help me forgive him eventually.

Trying to calm myself, I reaffirm what I've always said. If Tyler ever asks me to give him a second chance, I'll never go back. I can't. Or rather, I *won't*.

I've seen what happens to a woman who has been cheated on. I know the craziness and desperation that takes over their whole lives. I know the paranoia, and insecurity, and the madness that takes shape in their eyes after they've been cheated on.

Tyler has always known cheating was the one thing guaranteed to destroy us forever, but unbelievably he did it anyway.

After all our years together from the first week of school when we met, seeing my single mother a couple times a year, and meeting my happily remarried father twice, Tyler understood my hang up about cheating and he always promised me he never would.

I even begged him to give me the hypothetical, 'I'll break up with you first before I cheat' promise, which he did. Though he swore he would never cheat on me regardless of the promise I made him give me. So what the hell happened?

Looking at my phone Kyle's text comes through.
'Meet you at blue entrance of library. What the hell happened?'
Yes, what the hell *did* happen?

Holding in my tears I don't know if I should just have a complete breakdown now in my car alone so I can get back to studying, or if I should hold it in hoping the anger makes me stronger so I can focus.
Laughing, I realize I must still be in shock because I have no idea what to do, and I can't believe how much this hurts.
Truly, I had NO idea how much Tyler could hurt me.

Hopping out of my car 35 minutes later, I'm sure I read 2 chapters of my textbook but I've retained absolutely nothing. My mind keeps going back to what I saw in my apartment and the shock of it hasn't faded at all.
She was riding him in my bed.
She was attractive with a nice body, but it was her hatred toward me that shocks me still. I can't even fathom why she hated me so much. I'm the totally innocent here- *she* was the woman sleeping with a man in a relationship in the girlfriend's own bedroom.
God, they're both so disgusting, I can't believe the insult of what they've done to me in my own home.

*****

Seeing Kyle leaning against the blue doors I pull myself together as best as I can as I approach. "Thanks for meeting me," I try to smile.
"What happened? I couldn't believe it when you weren't there. I swear even Handle was frowning at where you usually sit when the attendance sheet was passed forward."
Kyle is a friend of my own friend and boss Mike so I have to be careful here if I don't want everyone to know what's going on. "Something came up and I was maybe one minute late, but the doors were closed," I roll my eyes to fight off the upset I'm facing. "I knew I was screwed so I went home to study while waiting for you. Can I *please* photocopy your

17

notes?"

Nodding, Kyle's looking at me a little too closely so I turn to look out across the campus gardens while he gets the notes from his bag.

"Of course you can. I even wrote *extra* good notes for you in case you asked," he says like a dork, which makes me smile briefly.

Watching him go through his backpack I mumble, "Thank you." Accidentally making eye contact with Kyle, I feel the tears fill my eyes and I want to kill again.

This is so embarrassing, but I feel like my chest is going to explode if I don't release the pressure soon. "Um, I'm struggling a little here," I say sitting down on the steps.

Waiting, I think I made a mistake not having a breakdown in my car. I think I could've moved on somewhat if I hadn't held all this in.

But I'm suddenly here, and I can't really function if I don't cry this out.

"What is it?" Kyle asks in a gentle voice as he sits down beside me.

Gasping a quick breath I explain, "Kyle, I'm about to lose it. So if you don't want to see this, you better run." Moaning, the pressure affects both my voice and my breathing.

Looking back at me Kyle says softly, "Just let it out if you have to," which opens up the pain. Taking another quick breath, my lungs explode as the upset bursts from my chest.

Crying my eyes out while covering my face, I sob uncontrollably. Intense pain and sadness are all I know in this moment and I don't know how to make it go away.

I can't believe Tyler did this, and I can't believe I had no idea this was happening. I'm in shock that I made love with my future last night on our bedroom floor while he was having a *not* one-time thing with someone else.

When I feel Kyle against my side I soak his warmth into my skin. Leaning into him, I cry until the storm of upset fades to just a gentle rain of sorrow.

Pulling myself together again I reach in my purse for a napkin to wipe up my mess of a face.

Breathing in shallow quick bursts, I know I have to say something to salvage my dignity. "Please don't tell Mike, or *anyone* about this. Please?" I beg turning to look at him.

"I won't. But what's wrong? You have to tell me something cuz I'm thinking all kinds of horrible things right now. And I feel like I should call

Tyler for you," he says looking honestly concerned for me.

"Do NOT call Tyler. He's the one that did this to me. Um, I just caught him in bed with another woman."

Not even hiding his shock, Kyle replies with an almost funny, "Fuck *off*," then quickly recovers to ask, "*Really?*" And like me, he seems to be as shocked as I am from this.

"Yes, really. In my own bed. After I missed Handle's lecture I walked into my apartment to some bitch *Kaitlyn*," I sneer, "riding him in my own bed," I burst out laughing again. How I can say that sentence out loud absolutely astounds me.

"Kaitlyn?" He questions with a weird look on his face.

"Do you know her?" When Kyle looks almost uncomfortable, making eye contact then just as quickly turning away from me, I think he must. "Who is she?" I ask barely above a whisper.

"What does she look like?" He asks instead.

"I don't know. Taller than me, brunette, long dark hair. I don't know, I was a little distracted from watching them screwing to really take her in," I bitch sarcastically. "Do you know her?"

"No," he says shaking his head. "I was just curious if I'd ever seen her around. I don't know who she is, but *wow*, Saige- I feel awful for you. What are you gonna do?" He asks leaning against my shoulder.

Unsure, I say all I can. "I have no idea what I'm going to do. I know I have to find somewhere to stay tonight. I have to study my ass off, and I have to ace this exam tomorrow. But that's about the extent of what I know right now. Um, this has blindsided me and I'm not sure what to do. I don't know, but..." Fading out I really am at a loss for words.

What the hell *am* I going to do after tomorrow?

I know I'll talk to the Superintendent, but besides that I don't know what I do or where I go if Tyler wants to be an even bigger prick about this.

"Okay. Well, you can stay at my place tonight-"

Shaking my head I can't possibly. "No, I-"

"Yeah, you will. We'll go over my notes, and you'll take better notes. You'll probably even find the obscure case studies I can't figure out on my own. You'll help me study for this, and then you can crash on my couch."

"Kyle, I don't know."

"Look, this must suck for you. Actually, I can't even imagine what you're going through. So you're going to borrow my couch tonight, and *me?* I get a Brainiac kicking me in the ass when I want to give up too soon. Then we'll get up tomorrow, grab breakfast, cram some more, and you'll get my ass to the exam on time," he smirks.

Looking at Kyle smiling, I'm overwhelmed by his kindness toward me. "Thank you. I wasn't sure what to do tonight. I'm just so stunned I can't think straight. And my heart is broken," I mumble shutting down totally embarrassed.

"It's cool. And trust me I'm getting way more out of this than you are. My couch is uncomfortable, and my place looks like a frat house. Probably smells like one, too," he grins again as I finally smile a little.

"Thank you. But I have to beg again that you don't discuss this with anyone, especially Mike. I don't know what's happening right now and I don't want anyone hearing about it before I can figure out what I'm doing," I beg as Kyle nods.

"I won't tell anyone anything, I promise. This is *your* nightmare, Saige," he says sadly and again I lean into him a little for just one more moment of comfort. This truly is one of my worst nightmares come true, and I'm completely unprepared to handle it.

"Just follow behind me. I'm going to stop quickly to grab some Micky D's on the way home though. Do you mind?"

"No. I haven't eaten all day, I'm stressed, and I've had 4 coffees, so I probably should grab something to eat."

Standing, Kyle extends his hand to pull me up and then he side hugs me. It's the first hug between us ever, and though I'm a little uncomfortable with it, I'm much more willing to soak up some support from him right now. "I'm really sorry, Saige," Kyle whispers like *he* cheated on me.

"You have nothing to be sorry for. Honestly, at this point you're like a Knight in shining armor for me."

Grinning, Kyle says with a laugh, "Cool. Brownie points to cash in later."

*****

Arriving at his house I can't hide my laughter when we enter. Ugh, frat house is right. On every surface there's an empty beer bottle or can, and I see socks everywhere, *ewww,* and one pair of boxers in the kitchen hanging off a chair.

"Yeah... sorry. My roommates don't tidy up much until we have a huge fight over it, then we let the place go to shit again for another month after we clean. I think we're due for a fight any day now," he laughs not even a little embarrassed by this funny gross hovel he calls a home.

"Where are your roommates?" I ask biting into a McNugget.

"Doug and Sam went home for the week, and Ramez is working then staying at his girlfriend's tonight."

When I suddenly feel very nervous alone with him, I think Kyle sees my discomfort so he quickly jumps in. "Saige, I would *never* take advantage of you. But especially now. I promise I'm only going to use you for your brain tonight," he smiles a little as he squeezes my hand.

Mumbling, "I'm sorry," I'm embarrassed I felt nervous and jumped to conclusions. "I'm not myself right now, that's all. But I really appreciate this," I try to apologize.

"Don't worry about it. If anything, I should be nervous you're going to jump me tonight with a baseball bat when I frustrate the hell out of you studying," he pouts and I relax totally. "Let's finish eating so we can start the torture, okay?"

Nodding, I eat my fries quickly, and enjoy my 6 McNuggets slowly. I love McNuggets, though thankfully I don't indulge too often. For me McNuggets are like a strange little memory of happy childhood yumminess I hold dear because of my father before he left us.

Before all the bad, and before the nightmare began for us all with Alec there were Saturday afternoons and delicious McNuggets with my father after dance class and karate. McDonald's was a special secret we kept from my mum, and I've never forgotten it.

*****

"Kyle, *look* at the rhyme I made. Look at the first letters and remember the cases. There's no other way to do it. Trust me. All the information is right there in the rhyme, so if you remember the rhyme, you'll remember the cases. Sing it if you have to," I huff.

"*Fuck!* This is so brutal," he practically whines.

Almost bashing my own head on the table I'm so frustrated with him I wish I could leave. "Of course it's brutal. Handle is our last hurdle before our acceptance letters. So he has to be brutal to weed out the people who can't handle the pressure."

"I can't do it, Saige," he actually does whine sounding totally defeated.

"Yes, you can. Look, you've already memorized my rhymes for the 50's through to the 80's, so you only have 2 1/2 decades to go."

"I can't handle-"

"I'm going to study on the couch. Read and memorize my rhymes and come get me when you're done. I'll quiz you and then you'll be as ready as you possible can be. I just need to look over my highlights," I repeat rising from the table with a sore ass and a tense neck again. God, I could really use a neck massage from Tyler.

Nearly choking up, I realize I haven't thought of Tyler for about 8 minutes now. After sitting at Kyle's table for the last 3 hours, I can't believe 8 whole minutes finally passed when Tyler didn't enter my mind. I almost want to think that's progress right now considering it was only 6 hours ago that he broke my heart and ruined my life.

When I hear Kyle walking around I yell, "Get memorizing," to a mumbled *fuck off* from the kitchen. Smiling to myself, I'm pretty sure Kyle and I have bonded over this intense stress.

He's funny and a total smartass, but he's seriously trying and I know he really wants to do well. If Kyle just learns my pathetic rhymes and the years attached to them, I know he'll do fine. And after his kindness towards me today I really want him to do well suddenly.

Rounding the corner, Kyle looks like shit. "Saige... It's 1:00 in the morning and I'm going to bed. I've learned the rhymes and I'm sure I'll have nightmares about them for the next 5 hours. But I'm crashing anyway."

Handing me blankets and a clean looking pillow, I stand as he lays out a blanket on the couch and takes back the 2 others to leave at the end for me. "You need to sleep, too."

"I know. I just keep thinking I missed something, or overlooked a highlight from my books because I didn't notice it."

"You didn't miss anything. You're a fucking genius," he laughs at my stunned face. "Yeah, I know most people say you're hot, but for me it's all about your huge brain," he laughs again. "Go to sleep. I'll set my alarm for 6 and we'll study until we leave at 10:30. Sound good?"

Nodding, I know he's right. If I study much more tonight I'll have complete brain-fry, and quite frankly I doubt I'll sleep much anyway with everything going on in my head. I should at least try to sleep a little before I write the 2 hour exam tomorrow though.

"Thank you, Kyle. For today and tonight," I choke up as another heavy wave of emotion threatens my chest. I don't know if it's sadness or shock or just exhaustion, but I feel like crying my eyes out suddenly and I can't do it in front of him again.

Hugging me tightly, Kyle says a very heartfelt, "You're welcome," before releasing me with a squeeze on my arm. "Go to sleep, Saige. Tomorrow is gonna suck ass," he groans as I nod.

Watching Kyle climb the clothes covered, beer bottle strewn staircase, I plop on the couch, lie down and pull the blankets up. Settling in, I turn off the lamp and adjust to the darkness I'm not used to. I watch the DVD clock change minutes, and I start to cry.

Crying over Tyler, my heart just aches from the pain of his betrayal. Hearing myself moan, 'Tyler...' in this strange living room, I'm absolutely heartbroken.

I love him so much, I honestly can't imagine my life without him in it. Choking on my agony I whisper to no one but myself *why did you do this to me* in the unbearable silence of my darkness.

(mis)TRUST

CHAPTER 3

"Good luck, Saige," Kyle says picking me up for a huge hug at the doors. Smiling at him, he even kisses my forehead quickly and says, "Let's do this," as he places me back on my feet.

"Good luck, Kyle. You're gonna rock this," I grin using the expression he repeated all morning while we crammed.

Turning for the doors, my student I.D. is scanned and the guard allows me to enter followed closely by Kyle. Walking to the first available seat in the second row, I settle in nervously. Once seated no one moves or really even looks around at each other as the auditorium slowly fills to capacity.

When Handle eventually enters like he owns the place, I almost smile at his arrogance. He really is a pompous ass, in probably his mid-40's only, but considering all his past experience in the courtroom I respect the hell out of him.

"This exam is 2 hours long. You may not cheat, sleep, cry, pass out, or throw up. If you do anything other than sit silently writing your exam it's over for you. Your exam will be graded from the moment you are asked to leave," he says so seriously most people aren't sure if he's joking or not. I know he isn't though- I've heard the horror stories, and I've seen the posts about him on the University blogs after his exams.

"Begin," he says loudly and there is a collective swooshing of paper as we all flip our exams over.

Writing my name and student I.D. quickly, I immediately flip back to the last empty page and right down the anagrams of my 12 rhymes. They'll make sense to no one but me (and hopefully Kyle) but they're my lifeline today.

And then I begin.

Crying midway through, I try to get my shit together.

I'm losing it, and suffering, and stressed, and just looking at my 70's anagram/rhyme T.y.L.E.R. K.I.LS. E.M. E.V.E.R.y. D.a.Y nearly makes me lose my mind.

Focusing as hard as I can on the 16 cases and torts, I keep seeing his name only. 'Tyler kils em every day' is just so brutal right now because he killed *me* anyway.

He broke me and threw me away. He didn't love me and he killed us. He kills 'em, or at least he kills *me,* and I can't stand all this heartache anymore.

Casually wiping my dripping tears, I'm scared shitless I'm going to get caught losing it and have to stop. I'm scared someone will see me and I'll be done.

I know Handle strips students of their exams if they lose their minds because he feels if you can't handle a simple test you'll never make it in a courtroom. I don't actually know if it's legal, or even an acceptable examination technique at school, but I'm not about to question him.

Forgetting Tyler, I write for my life. Forgetting everything but this test I write for my future. Forgetting what the 2nd 'R' stands for in my 90's anagram I nearly panic but force myself to move on quickly.

With only 14 minutes left, I'm finished. I could probably look it over and obsess, but I did that at the end of each question and answer so I know nothing is going to change suddenly.

Thinking, I wrack my brain for that illusive 'R' from the 90's but I still can't remember it. I have a total mental block where that 'R' is concerned, but if that's my biggest mistake today I feel pretty good about my exam. Besides my little breakdown over Tyler's name, I'm as happy as I can be under the circumstances.

Rising from my chair when Handle announces there are only 10 minutes left, I walk to the front and hand him my exam. Not smiling or acknowledging me at all, I hand him my test papers and turn just as he speaks quietly to me.

"I was surprised I didn't see you yesterday, Miss Masters."

Responding, I say just as gravely, "I was late by 1 minute, Professor Handle. I was studying at the central library and lost track of time."

Smirking at what he probably assumes is a lie he only nods. "Did I see you crying in the exam?" He asks, and I figure what the hell? It's not like he can rip up my test now.

"Yes. But it had nothing to do with the exam. It was a very private matter, and I recovered quickly," I defend myself before he can question me further.

"Yes, you did. I know about your brother so I'm sure that played a role in your upset?" He says as a question and I'm absolutely winded. Gasping my shock, I shake my head with a nearly inaudible *no* and wait for more. When there isn't any more though and many students are waiting behind me I walk away quickly.

Finished with Handle forever I hope, I pull open the heavy doors and burst into stress tears in the hallway.

I can't believe he said that! I can't believe he knew and brought up my brother. I wonder if he had known what the last 18 hours of my life had been like if he still would've brought that up.

Jesus, I'm so out of my depth here fighting all these upsets one after another, I'm nearly panicking.

Trying to control myself, I look to my left and see a couple hugging as the guy leans into the girl because he's crying. Further down the hall, I see a guy I know named Mark actually throwing up in a garbage can.

Wiping my tears, I'm thrilled to see so many others walking away looking shell-shocked and numb. I don't want anyone else to suffer, but at least it means I'm not the only freak having a major adrenaline dump in the hallway.

"Holy *fuck*..." Kyle moans leaning beside me. Laughing at his expression, he moans again, "I feel like I'm gonna puke."

Blinking my eyes, I reach in my backpack for a Kleenex and wipe up my face. "So...?" I ask hopefully.

"I think I actually killed it." Turning to me, Kyle looks so excited, I feel excited for him. "And it was all your shit that did it. I remembered every goddamn rhyme and every anagram of yours, and when I'm working at the best Law Firm in Manhattan in 4 years I'm going to tell everyone about the cutie little redhead who saved my life," he smiles as he side hugs me again.

"With the huge *brain*," I add fake scowling.

"With the *amazing* brain," he says almost awestruck which feels pretty great right now.

"Kyle?" I ask seriously.

"Yes, Saige?" He grins.

"What the hell was the second R in my 90's anagram?"

Bursting out laughing together, Kyle says simply the 'IIRIRA' and I almost smack my own forehead with my palm.

"The Illegal Immigration Reform and Immigrant Responsibility Act...

Shit! I *knew* that, but I couldn't remember it to save my life," I laugh again as all the adrenaline fades from me completely.

Leaning against the wall while others hang around talking to each other, some yelling, others whispering and crying, I feel so exhausted suddenly I can barely move.

"Are you going home now?" Kyle asks quietly.

Pausing without answering, all the air leaves my lungs just thinking about it. Going home is the absolute last thing I want to do though I have no other choice. I need to finish this with Tyler, and I need my clothes for work later.

Nodding, I can't speak. Just the thought of walking into my home makes me want to cry all over again.

"You can call me later if you want. I'll just be home tonight totally piss drunk," he grins as I turn to him. "Seriously. I know we're not good friends or anything, but I'm here if you need anything or just want to talk, okay?"

"Thanks," I squeeze his wrist. "And thank you again for last night."

"Thank *you*," he cuts me off. "Seriously, Saige... you saved my life in there," he says again sincerely as he hugs me tightly.

Not pulling away as quickly as I usually would I kind of hold onto him for a minute longer than necessary. I don't want this easy banter to end, and I don't want to walk away to face Tyler today.

"I should go," I mumble in his chest before pulling away finally. "Enjoy getting piss drunk tonight," I smile walking away.

"Saige," he calls out to my back. "Will you at least call me later to let me know you're okay? You don't have to tell me anything, and I'm not trying to get in your business. But I would like to know if you're okay tonight."

"I'm sure I'll be fine. But I'll let you know," I smile one last time.

Walking away quickly I can't stand the thought of Kyle seeing me cry again. I'm not a crier by nature and I barely know Kyle which just adds to my discomfort and embarrassment. And right now, I feel the stress and tears wanting to burst from my chest again before I face Tyler.

*****

Walking in my apartment I take a huge breath opening the door and exhale like I've been punched in the stomach the second I see Tyler looking at me. Staring at me he rises from the couch then stops.

I'm sure he doesn't know what to say, and I have *nothing* to say. Though I do need to know, "Is she here?"

"No."

"Good. Why are *you* here?" I pause in the little hallway by the door.

"Well, I *live* here," he says so sarcastically I want to punch him in the face.

He was never sarcastic with me before, but now when I feel like he should be all somber and apologetic, he's a smartass? I really don't know or like this new Tyler at all.

Still standing in the hallway, I want to go to my room but I can't. I don't know if it's been cleaned and I don't want to smell their sex again.

Like he read my mind though Tyler finally shows some embarrassment when he says, "I changed the sheets and made the bed for you."

"Such a gentleman," I mumble to myself walking past him.

Entering my bedroom, I don't actually smell anything anymore, though psychologically I may be screwed for a while thinking I still smell her nasty and Tyler's filthy over every surface of my room.

Sitting down on my bed when the weight of my exhaustion hits, I jump back up immediately remembering what happened on my bed last.

God, I'm a mess.

I can't be in here anymore but I don't know where else to go. Walking back out, Tyler's moved to the bedroom hallway so I have to squeak past him for the living room. Almost shoving his chest, I fight the urge to hit him though admittedly it's hard to hold back.

"We have to talk," he says taking my arm as I pass.

"Let go of me," I growl and he does but not before I had to make eye contact with him for a second.

Christ, I don't know what to do anymore.

I'm trapped in my apartment with 2 1/2 hours to kill before work. I'm exhausted and all I want is to forget the last day of my life for an hour so I can rest. I barely slept last night, constantly waking in Kyle's filthy frat house, sometimes scared, sometimes crying in my sleep. Plus, my brain is mush at this point so I could cry just from the mental fatigue alone.

I know I'll sound desperate if I beg but I just don't care anymore what Tyler thinks of me.

"Can you please go out or go away for 2 hours? I need to sleep a little and there's nowhere for me to sleep but on the couch. And I can't stand looking at you," I spit watching him cringe at my harsh words. "I don't want you near me and I won't sleep with you sitting here."

"Saige, I'm really sorry for this," Tyler says with so much emotion I almost lose my mind.

The part of me that loves him wants to comfort *his* upset suddenly. But the part of me that recognizes he's a cheating, lying asshole thankfully holds out. "I don't want to hear it."

"But you have to," he actually begs.

"I really don't. Not now, and maybe not ever. This is NOT the time for a conversation, Tyler. I'm raw, and depressed, and exhausted. I'm hurt and so friggin' angry I really can't do this with you right now. Just please leave me alone for a few hours. Go to your whore's place or wherever."

"She's *not* a whore," he defends so quickly I'm nearly sick to my stomach from the intensity he just defended her with.

Deciding any further comments about his whore might not get me what I want, I try to hold in my rage. "Are you moving out or am I?"

Actually shaking his head, Tyler says the unimaginable. "Um, neither of us can unless we want to break the lease totally, lose our huge security deposit, and have only 12 days to move out by the end of the month," he huffs.

"What? *Why?*" I really wish Tyler had left this to me to deal with but since he didn't I need to know what the hell this means for us.

"I guess there are so many students canceling their leases right now, Kevin's pissed and inflexible with us. I explained it wasn't that we were skipping out but that we just wanted to make changes, but he wasn't interested. He told me the consequences and told me to give him our final decision tomorrow at the latest. Either way though, he's not giving us the security deposit back."

"So why don't you and your *whatever* live here? Just pay the rent and I'll go away," I huff again when he seems like such an idiot suddenly. Looking down quickly instead of answering I know instantly what the problem is. "You can't afford this place without me paying all the bills and half the rent." So I give another dig, it's the least he deserves.

"Not really," he replies quietly and I almost laugh that *this* embarrasses him. Tyler doesn't seem embarrassed by what I walked in on yesterday, but unable to pay the rent embarrasses him? What an asshole.

"Can't she chip in? I mean she looked pretty cozy here," I sneer as the memory of her riding Tyler makes me want to rage again.

Waiting for him to reply I realize I'm being almost flexible with this and I don't have to be. I'm not a pushover, and he did this. So screw him.

"Okay, here are your 2 options, Tyler. One, get the hell out right now and I'll cover everything. Or 2, move your girlfriend in here and figure it out. But I want a decision now, otherwise I'm leaving tonight and I'll be back for my things in a few days."

Looking at me, I know Tyler hates it when I get demanding with him but too bad. In this situation he gave up his rights to decisions as far as I'm concerned.

"How will you pay for everything?"

"That's none of your business anymore," I snap to shut him up and then realize I actually don't want to live here anymore. "You know what? I've changed my mind. Figure it out or leave. I don't care, but I'm leaving here."

"But the security deposit?"

"What about it? *I* paid it- you didn't. So why do you care? It's my loss, just like everything else is suddenly."

"But where will you go? You don't have anyone here and your mom is too far away. What will you do?"

Huffing, I need to shut this down. The longer he speaks the sadder I become. He's using the voice we always spoke to each other with and it makes me so sad and heartbroken, I want to beg and yell and ask the obvious question- *why did you do this to me?*

"It's none of your business where I go or who I stay with anymore. I'm leaving, Tyler, which is what you obviously wanted so don't act like you give a shit now."

"I DO give a shit!" He leans toward me.

"Did you give a shit when you were cheating on me?"

"Of course I did. Do you think this was easy for me?" He whines and again I'm nearly floored by him trying to rationalize what he did.

"Was it hard to get a woman to ride your dick in my bed? I doubt it. You're very attractive. But you know that already, don't you, Tyler?"

"It's not about being attractive, Saige, because you are way better looking than Kaity. You're also smarter and you'll be way more successful than she'll ever be. Everything about you is better than her. *Fuck...* you're way better than me, too."

When Tyler takes a much needed breath after that outburst I see everything he has never shown me before. For the first time I understand he was insecure, or is insecure, or whatever. He never acted that way when he was with me, but maybe he hid it. Either way, it's not my problem anymore.

"I'm leaving. Good luck with all your insecurity but don't you dare put that shit on me. I *never* treated you poorly or made you feel like you were less than me."

"I know, but that actually made it worse. I always knew I'd take a backseat to you and your career, and yet you didn't seem to care about that."

Nearly laughing in his face I have to know, "Who the hell *are* you? No, better yet, who *were* you for the last 4 years? You keep telling me I've done nothing wrong, I'm better looking, smarter, etcetera. You're saying things about me I've never said or even thought, and you're making them the excuse for the inexcusable. I *loved* you, Tyler. I loved everything about you and I *never* thought of you in terms of better or less than me. I thought of us as partners *together*."

"I know. I'm sorry, I just-"

"Cheated on me, Tyler. You chose a less attractive, less intelligent woman who can't even help you with the goddamn rent so you feel better about yourself? You're pathetic!" I snap.

Shaking my head for the hundredth time since yesterday, I end this. "I'm leaving. But I'll be back Sunday to get all my stuff. Please don't be here when I return. It's only 3 days away, and I need to never see you again," I say finally understanding everything and nothing at the same time.

Walking back to my former bedroom, I pull some of my clothes from their hangers aggressively and toss everything on the desk chair. Grabbing my suitcase from Tyler's side of the closet, I toss it on the floor and cram my clothes inside.

"Where are you going? Back to *Kyle's*?" He asks angrily.

How the hell did he know I was there? I trusted Kyle when he said he wouldn't tell anyone anything, and I thought I made it fairly clear that meant everyone, *especially* Tyler.

"It's none of your business where I go."

"I know, but really, Saige? *Kyle's?* Don't you think that makes everything a little awkward for me and Kaitlyn? I get that you hate us right now, but this is totally beneath you."

Shocked again at his passed-off tone with me, I have no idea what he's talking about. "I'm not sleeping with him. I'm not YOU, Tyler. So why would it be awkward for either of you? She gets to have you all to herself now with me gone, and you're free to do whatever," I almost sing song my words.

"Oh, I don't know- because he's her *brother!*" Tyler yells like I'm an idiot. "Yeah, talk about awkward when he called- *What*? Why do you look like that?" Tyler asks reaching for me when I stagger back a little against the closet door. Her brother? *WHAT?!* "You didn't know? I thought Kyle would've told you last night. Um, that's how she and I met. At his house," Tyler says a little quieter while my hands grab for my nauseous stomach.

I studied with him and slept on this couch. I'm the cutie redhead who saved his life, he said. He was so kind to me last night and he didn't tell me about his sister? Holy shit, I don't understand *anybody* anymore.

"I'm sorry, I thought you knew," Tyler says sadly still holding my arm.

Looking up at his dark eyes, I'm absolutely numb again. Every time I think this shit storm is over it crashes over me again and washes away a little more of me in its wake.

"Is that true?" I ask in the most pathetic voice I've ever spoken in my life.

Nodding, Tyler doesn't need to speak the words. "I thought you knew," he says again while I stand still with my head spinning.

I actually trusted Kyle. In a moment of desperation I leaned on a friend and thought he cared about me. God, he even asked me to check in with him later knowing it was his own sister screwing my boyfriend. His own sister who met Tyler at his house, and his sister who talked to me like I was the piece of shit here. Kyle was kind and funny and he made me feel a little better. I didn't like him romantically, but I definitely thought we had forged a solid friendship since yesterday.

Wanting to collapse on the floor I realize quite quickly I won't be able to hide this agony from Tyler much longer. I don't have the strength, and I can't find the reserve needed to get out of here without sobbing.

So I let it take me.

Finishing my clothes scramble, I toss everything into the suitcase and when I run out of room I reach under my bed for Tyler's huge duffle bag he never uses. Filling his duffle, I keep going on autopilot. I move around, grab my little jewelry box and my mementos box, and keep going. Walking past Tyler I rummage under the bathroom sink for everything I left last night and return with my arms full to dump in the bag.

Sobbing uncontrollably, I wipe my eyes when I can't see, and wipe my nose when I'm disgusting.

"I'm so sorry, Saige. Please don't cry," Tyler moans behind me wrapping his arms tightly around me even though I try to fight him off.

When I push and try to pull away he holds me tighter and I literally have no strength left in my body to fight him off.

Crying harder, Tyler says the unimaginable in a voice dripping with his own tears. Calming in his embrace, I don't want to look at his face, and I don't want to see his sadness while I drown in my own.

Whispering in my ear, Tyler explains everything in just 3 sentences between us. "This was never about me not loving you, Saige, because I still love you so much it's killing me. There was just something about *her* I couldn't resist. And I'm so sorry you were hurt because of me, Lovey."

Lashing out at the words and the feelings from his own upset, I smash my head backward against his throat and chin, and as he jerks backward in pain I find my escape yelling, "DON'T *CALL* ME THAT!"

Diving for the suitcase I jump on its fullness and zip around my legs totally ignoring Tyler. Grabbing for the duffle I reach and pull and struggle with the weight of it until slinging it over my shoulder as best as I can I grab the suitcase to leave Tyler, my life, my home, and my everything else behind.

No words are needed, and no dramas need to be played out. I won't give him any more of me or my soul.

He can go fuck her and fuck Kyle for all I care. I don't need a friend and I don't need a boyfriend anymore.

This is the new Saige, and I have to make my life and my heart better than this.

"Goodbye, Tyler," I breathe calmly his full name before closing the door behind me for the last time.

CHAPTER 4

After checking into an affordable motel for the next 3 days at least I realize driving to work this has been one of the top 3 worse experiences of my life. And quite frankly, if I could tell everyone to piss off and die right now I would.

If I didn't need to keep a pleasant face, or a hostile-less presence at work, I would tell everyone to stay the hell away from me. Instead, I have to plaster on my pretty face and serve people happily for the rest of my shitty day.

Entering the back doors, I walk past Selena wishing I could ask her to cover for me again tonight. I would love to beg her to work a double, but I can't. I did that yesterday and she looks exhausted. Plus, if I'm really honest with myself, I would never do it for her 2 days in a row so I'm totally screwed.

But I hate this place today. I hate everyone, and everything, and basically, I'm just a hot friggin' mess wrapped up in anger and agony. And this really isn't me. Or wasn't me. Or wasn't who I thought I would be 6 months ago, or really even yesterday morning before I left Tyler at home with a kiss.

Checking my hair and makeup one last time I look like I should look; professional but attractive. My black and white tuxedo-like blouse has only a tiny bit of cleavage showing, and my skirt reaches my knees so it looks nice but not slutty in the least.

Actually, we're never supposed to look slutty at work which is good. Honestly, I refuse to appear like a slut without the bed-hopping to earn the title.

Inhaling and exhaling deeply this last time for the next 5 hours, I think I might be able to pull off tonight without stabbing anyone. Then again I should maybe tell Mike to keep sharp objects away from me tonight just in case.

Getting a grip, I walk to the boards to see I'm in the Bar/Lounge area which is the best area for tips but also the best area for idiots. And between Tyler, Kaitlyn, Kyle and even Handle this morning, I've had my fill of idiots the last 24 hours of my life.

Wrapping my little black apron around my waist, I take one last look at myself in the hallway mirror and I'm relieved to see I don't look nearly as homicidal as I feel inside.

"What's up, Saige? You look totally pissed off," Mike pauses rinsing a glass. Damn, maybe I don't look as mentally sound as I thought I did.

Turning to face Mike at the bar I realize how easy it would be to take out my devastation on him. If I didn't adore him as much as I do I would lay into him simply for being a man, for being friends with a liar, and for knowing my piece of shit ex and probably even his whore Kaitlyn. But I do adore him, so I bite my tongue and breathe through my anger instead.

Turning over a fake smile, I lie. "I'm not pissed at all. I'm good. Ah, is everyone covered?" I look around at the booths and tables while reeling in my temper.

Smirking at my lie, Mike chooses to ignore it instead of forcing me to talk like he usually would suggesting he really doesn't know what's going on with me and Tyler yet.

Getting the lowdown on my tables, I turn from Mike. "Perfect. Okay, 1, 4 and 6. Got it." Pulling my ponytail tighter I smooth out my black pencil skirt once again. Preparing for my night, I decide to forget last night and today until tomorrow when I'm less angry and more clear.

My brain is fried at the moment, and I'm exhausted and pissed off, which is the best thing for me right now. I know tomorrow, however, the pissed is going to turn into devastation mixed with probably some anxiety and tears- like many, *many* tears.

Walking first to tables 1 and 6, I smile for the couple and start my game of happy and pleasant. Introducing myself, I give out menus and take drink orders quickly while they decide what they want to eat. Moving to table 4's add-ons, I start all over again.

"Hi, I'm Saige, and I'll be taking over for Selena tonight." Looking at the couple without drinks I continue. "Would you like to order a drink while I get your menus?" I smile at both the nodding man and to the woman beside him giving me dirty looks for whatever reason.

"Honey?" He asks his wife maybe, yup, wedding rings, while placing his hand on hers which she noticeably grabs tighter.

Not even looking at me she demands, "I'll have sparkling water and the menu. Now. We've been waiting forever," she tacks on with a nasty glare. Before I can apologize for her supposed wait however the other woman quickly jumps in.

"You haven't been waiting forever, Linda. You've been here 2 minutes," she says with an apologetic smile at me.

Nodding, I know why she smiled- she's attractive- unlike Linda, who is average looking, slightly heavy, oh, and a total bitch. Attractive woman however is just that- attractive- therefore she doesn't have to be a bitch.

"And for you, Sir?"

"Heineken, if you have it?"

"Certainly. I'll be right back with your menus," I nod before turning on my heels.

Linda already hates me. Why? Did I flirt with her husband? No. Did I call her names or make her feel like shit about herself? No. I did nothing but be pleasant and she wants to be nasty to me because acting like a bitch will increase her attractiveness? Nope. It never does.

I can't stand women like that. I've done nothing wrong but she feels better about herself by being nasty to me for some unknown reason- which is totally unfair and ridiculous, especially in light of my current circumstances.

I have never whored myself or used my looks to get ahead, and I never will. I may be attractive to some, but that's not who I am. However, it's fairly obvious UNattractive is who Linda is.

Standing at the bar while grabbing the menus I check on the other tables. 12 tables alone in one section is far too many for one waitress on a Friday or Saturday night, but on a Thursday it's doable because we're never filled to capacity.

"2 house white for 6, and a sparkling water and Heineken for 4," I exhale again as Mike walks to me for my drinks list.

"I gotta go," Selena pipes in as I turn to her. "What's wrong?" She asks as soon as she looks at my face.

"Nothing," I repeat my words to Mike, essentially confirming something IS wrong.

"Don't lie. You suck at it. Was it the exam?"

"Nope. As far as I know that went really well."

"But?"

"No but. I-"

"Ly-*ing*..." Selena sings. Damn, she's good.

"Can I talk to you about it later?" I beg quietly as Mike pours drinks blatantly trying to listen to us at the same time.

"Call me first thing in the morning. You know I'll be up," she says squeezing my hand which makes my upset harder to fight.

Trying to stop the potential tears Selena sees, I get my shit together as she watches. "Thanks again for yesterday," I smile still blinking like a cow.

"No problem. Exams are exams. I remember how stressful they were when I went to school," she fake shudders. "Anyway, I have tomorrow morning off so I'll relax with Griffin- *after* your phone call," she smiles referring to her young son before hugging me quickly.

Still looking at me silently, I have to change the subject before she makes me breakdown in the lounge. "I'll put your tips in the zippered jacket in your locker, okay?"

"Perfect. That's kiddo," Selena nods walking around the bar for the back employee lounge.

Selena is only 6 years older than me, but I'm always kiddo to her, which I guess I would be in her world. I don't have a child to care for, and I don't have an asshole ex-husband to deal with. I just have an ex-asshole. As of yesterday.

God, I can almost feel the anger changing to despair too quickly to reel in again. Blinking my teary eyes I smile at Mike who places the drinks for both tables in front of me.

Nearly choking up, I see him reaching for me so I pull away quickly with my tray. I swear any human contact right now will make me bawl my eyes out.

"I'll talk to you later. Promise," I walk away before he can push any farther. I can't do this now, and any kindness will open up the flood gates to sobbing. And though he means well, I doubt Mike could actually handle a hysterical woman crying her eyes out.

Returning to table 6 I give them their drinks and agree to come back for their order when they still aren't ready to decide.

Walking back to 4, I gently place the drinks on the table and hand the menu to the husband before Linda allows hers to drop out of my hand onto the table. Fighting the urge to pick up the menu and storm away, I swallow my anger and say politely, "I'll be back in a few minutes to take your order," but I'm cut off immediately.

"We're ready," Bitchface snaps. "I looked at their menus while I waited for my drink," she glares.

Taking a second to breathe calmly, I'm grateful this isn't the way most Diners behave. Thankfully, it's not even the norm. Bitches like this one only come out to play maybe once a month, which is good for Servers everywhere. There wouldn't be a waitress left who hadn't inadvertently stabbed a customer with behavior like this.

"My sister and brother-in-law should start since they've been *waiting* the longest for someone to serve us," Linda says again with such venom, I swear to god I'm either going to burst into tears or I'm going to stab her- that's like the only 2 options I see at this point.

Smiling at the sister, I can guess why Linda is extra nasty. Who the hell would want to be (presumably) the older sister to the younger gorgeous sister? Not many.

"What can I get you?"

"Can I have another water and he'll have another beer," she smiles adorably at her husband before they each order their meals.

Watching them, they're just so cute together, I find an instant sadness settle behind my teary eyes I quickly cover up blinking again. God, Tyler and I were cute like that with each other.

"And for you?" I turn to smile at Bitchface.

"I'll have the house salad with a light vinaigrette on the side," she replies totally miserable and defeated. Well at least now I know why she's a moody bitch- she's on a diet.

"I'll have the New York steak. Medium-rare with the baked potato," Linda's husband orders as I smile one last time before leaving them to their drinks.

Entering the orders on our computer I move quickly to the surrounding tables. One after another I ask how their meals are, if they would like another drink, and if desserts are desired before table 1 finally places their order with me.

*****

Tidying up an empty table I watch a group of 8 men enter 20 minutes later and I'm instantly stressed again. I don't like large groups of men to begin with, but my day has been horrible and Linda made my mood worse.

Looking over I make eye contact with the group, signal I'll be with them in a moment, and give myself a little pep talk before turning for Mike to help set up the tables. I know I can handle the addition, especially with the bitch's table nearly being served and the other tables starting their meals or just finishing up.

Ignoring the slightly loud group while Mike and I arrange the tables, I move quickly but purposefully. I never lean over the table to give an inadvertent ass shot, nor do I lean over so they can see down my blouse. I know how to move to be the least sexual and flirty, especially among 8 men who I think have already been drinking based on how loud their multiple conversations are.

When Mike returns from the bar to place the menus around the table I walk back to the waiting group with my most professionally detached though warm personality.

"Hello, welcome to D'Vecseys. If you'll please follow me..." I turn already catching one guy staring at my ass like an idiot.

Waiting at the end of the table, Mike quickly fills the water glasses for me while they each sit down. Introducing myself, I continue, "Would you like to order drinks to begin?"

"Sure. We'd like separate bills as well please," a pleasant looking guy from the end says as I nod.

Separate bills typically means larger tips which I need desperately right now since I have to scramble to find a place to live. Plus, no one can pull any shit when each customer is served and billed exactly what they ordered. It still amazes me how many people try to imply they didn't order what they ate, or didn't buy as many drinks as they were charged when a joint bill of a few hundred dollars is suddenly placed in front of them on the table.

"Certainly," I say as usual, which is kind of my catch phrase in the restaurant.

Waiting, each guy begins ordering and thankfully I remember all the drinks, down to the last guy, though I'm sure they're all secretly waiting to see if I screw up their drink orders like most people do. What most don't understand, however, is remembering drinks and dinners is easy-remembering antiquated laws in Latin is not.

"I'll give you a few minutes to decide what you'd like to order," I announce before turning for the bar just slightly faster than a walk.

Placing the drink orders with Mike, I walk back to check on my remaining tables. Table 6 has been taking forever to eat which means they're probably on a second or third date, delaying the obvious departure while they figure out if tonight's the night for sex. And table 1 and 7 are just finishing their coffees.

Bitchy Linda and her table are nearly finished with her scarfing down the last of her dressing on one limp lonely piece of lettuce, so I think it's almost dessert time, I grin.

Cashing out table 7, I wait a few more minutes when I see the large table is still talking and haven't even picked up their menus yet.

"How was everything?" I ask removing each husband's plate from Linda's table.

"It was okay," Linda shrugs. Of course... here we go. "But the salad wasn't very fresh," she sneers though she's just shy of licking her plate.

"Oh? You should've told me before you ate the entire meal. I would've gladly had the chef prepare another salad for you." Take the hint, Bitch.

"Well, I didn't want to cause a scene," she replies so seriously I almost start laughing. Cause a scene? She seems like her entire life is causing a scene, but whatever. I'm going to kill her... with kindness.

"I'd be happy to comp a dessert for you. Anything on the menu. We have New York cheesecake with a delicious dulce de leche, or a chocolate explosion volcano cake," I smile as she starts frowning. "Or our delicious homemade chocolate marble bread pudding with a sweet vanilla glaze that practically melts in your mouth. And last but not least, we have our *to die for* warmed caramel apple blossom," I smile sweetly knowing my words are absolute torture for her.

"Oh! I'll have the chocolate explosion cake," attractive sister grins as her husband nods he'll have one as well. Even Linda's husband gets in on it when he announces he's dying to try the Cheesecake which leaves poor, nonscene-causing Linda to either cave for dessert or hate everyone around her who'll be eating it.

"Just coffee for me," she exhales totally defeated which makes up for the nasty glares she's been giving me all night. "But you can comp my husband's dessert," she barks.

"Certainly," I nod walking away with a *fuck you* smile.

After entering the dessert orders and checking on table 7 who are finally leaving, I walk back to the bar for the 8 drinks Mike has already placed on a heavy tray for me.

Stepping up to the table, I begin where I started. Walking behind each man I place his drink to his front right side listening to the first table talk about a baseball game they saw. When I make it down to the other end of the table I listen to 3 men discussing some local married politician who was caught cheating on his wife. Of course he did, I almost sneer.

Throughout the drink delivery they were all polite and thanked me so I think it should be okay for me tonight. Though you never can tell how well or poorly behaved a group of drinking men will be long term.

"Would everyone like a little more time, or are you ready to order?" I ask just loudly enough to stop the first table from talking as they all look around at each other.

"Probably a few more minutes," a large, intimidating guy in the middle suggests as they all begin speaking to each other again.

"I'll be back in a few minutes then," I nod walking to the bar for the bills for tables 1 and 6 just as another couple are escorted in by Kelsey to my section holding hands.

Greeting the new couple, they tell me their drink and food orders immediately because they're on their way to a late movie. I love these tables- they're less work and the tips are typically the same as when I have to spend 2 hours with them.

Looking around, 7 and 1 finally leave, 6 is finishing their coffee stillllllll, my new table 2 has drinks, and shitty table 4 are finally standing to leave with Linda looking as miserable as ever.

Walking over to wish them a wonderful night, Linda's husband slips another $20 in my hand which is weird considering he already left me a large tip on the bill. Then again, with his smirky smile I know he's apologizing for his wife's behavior. Even hot sister smiles warmly at me and wishes me a good night when Linda leaves the side exit quickly.

Good riddance. Though I did just make a fortune in tips from the rest of her table, it still wasn't worth dealing with the death glares all night. It definitely helps though, I smile to myself.

Placing my new table's drinks, I walk back to table 6 and ask finally if there's anything else I can get them. I've been working for over 2 hours, and they were there before I even began. I mean, you don't have to eat and run, but seriously, is the quiet, darker, soothing atmosphere here that nice, that you have to spend a few hours of your life here? Ah yes, actually. I know I feel much better than I did when I started.

"What's going on with you? Did you tank your exam?" Mike asks with a grin knowing there's no way I would ever tank it.

"Can I talk to you later? Now really isn't the best time for anyone," I beg forcing myself to keep it together at work.

Looking at me sadly, Mike reaches over to squeeze my hand. "Later," he nods. "Go take orders and in an hour you should be good to wind down," he nods toward my big table.

"I'm okay," I sigh turning for my big table.

Think of the tips. Think of the individual bills. Think of the *tips*, I inhale deeply as I walk over.

"Are you all ready to order now?" I ask from the head of the table once again. Speaking a little louder than usual to hopefully shut them up I pray they'll order this time.

When middle of the table man nods, he speaks louder than I did and gets all their attention for me... and 8 orders later I'm done. Relatively painless and with few pauses each of the 8 men ordered, asked for another drink, and were perfectly polite to my professionally detached.

One thing I will say about men ordering meals is they typically want exactly what's on the menu. There are no dips or dressings on the side, no alternate swaps of one vegetable for another, and no questions about baking versus frying. Generally, a man points to an item and moves on which makes my job easier.

Walking back to the bar, Mike scooches over so I can input all my orders into the computer. "Are we celebrating tonight?" He bumps shoulders with me.

"Nope. I'm crashing," I answer too quickly which gives me away.

Bumping my shoulder a second time, he keeps going. "But you always celebrate after a big exam. That's the *only* time you usually celebrate," he grins because it's a joke around here how little I drink or party.

Tyler never said I was too serious but apparently he must've felt it. Was I too boring? Was that what made her so attractive to him?

43

After entering the last order in the computer, I pull the drinks chit for Mike and lean into his side for a little of Mike's much needed kindness.

"This one is huge and I'm trying to keep it together tonight."

Pulling the slip from my fingers, Mike gives me a little side hug and relents. "Okay. I'll stop asking for now."

Grabbing the 4 beers ordered for the guy table, Mike starts the mixed drinks in silence as I wait. Looking around the bar area, I know I can kill time bussing the empty tables but my earlier angry adrenaline is fading fast and I'm becoming slower and sadder as the minutes pass. The weight of my reality is starting to settle in and I'm feeling totally overwhelmed by it.

Once Mike finishes the drinks, I thank him and grab my full tray to continue knowing he's watching my delivery to make sure everything stays professional for me.

"Go take a break," Mike tosses his head to the back when I place the empty tray on the bar. "Table 2 is eating and your men are settled in for the food wait. Go now before their orders are up."

"Please don't call them *my* men," I groan. "I can't stand one man right now, never mind 8 of them. But I'll go freshen up quickly," I agree already turning for the employee lounge and bathroom.

Sitting on the couch, I realize my mistake immediately. Here in the quiet alone of our employee lounge, my thoughts are too loud. I keep seeing Tyler having sex and I keep hearing why he did it.

I believe I did nothing wrong, as confirmed by Tyler, but I can't seem to take comfort in that. Maybe I should, but it's still too new and raw for me. I can't find comfort in my blamelessness because I'm the only one hurting and alone.

They have each other, and I'm essentially homeless, loveless, and I feel such pain in my chest, I swear I can't take a deep breath without my ribs feeling as though they might crack under the strain.

Sadly, I realize I'm totally alone for the first time in 4 years, and I ache with loneliness and despair.

*****

44

Walking back into the bar area I prepare for the final hours of my night knowing afterward I'll drive to the motel I rented and crash for 12 hours if I need to. I'm not scheduled back at the restaurant until 4 tomorrow afternoon which leaves me plenty of time to cry out this shitty reality I'm drowning in.

With Mike's help from the kitchen, we each grab 3 plates for the men's table. Starting from my beginning end, I set down my plates carefully to thanks and pauses in conversations, point Mike to who gets which plate, and make my way back to the kitchen.

Gathering the last 2 plates for my table, I just lean slightly around the 3rd man from the right when I feel a hand suddenly up my skirt grabbing the lower part of my butt and upper thigh as I drop his plate with a loud crash on the table and a frightened yelp.

Gasping, I practically throw the last man his plate of food before I turn on the asshole.

"If you touch me again I'll have you arrested for sexual assault. Got it?" I seethe barely holding myself back as I spot Mike moving quickly from behind the bar.

"Calm down, Cherry. Don't talk to me-"

"*Cherry*? Who the hell is Cherry, *Dickhead*?" I yell before I can stop myself.

"*Dickhead?* Get the manager!" Dickhead barks as I smile wide. Good luck asshole. I think Mike saw him touch my ass so he's getting nowhere with the manager tonight.

"Holy shit, Keith. Stop being such an asshole!" The guy from the end yells as another man across from us stands up quickly from the table.

"She swore at me!" Dickhead says like a baby.

"And you grabbed her ass *under* her goddamn skirt. I'm so sorry, Miss," intimidating man says with standing guy nodding beside him while all the others take in the show quietly. "If you'll permit us to stay, I promise this *dickhead*," he grins at me, "will be on his best behavior."

When Mike is standing beside me, I suddenly feel a little less rattled. Actually, I really feel like slapping this asshole across the face but thankfully my intelligence wins out.

"I have a question before I decide," I state trying to calm my nerves. "For him," I point right at Dickhead's face who is so red he's either super pissed at me or totally embarrassed- it's hard to tell.

45

After speaking the standing good looking man agrees immediately. "Go ahead and ask him whatever you want. And again, we apologize," he adds with a kind smile while all the others either nod silently, or agree out loud.

So turning to Dickhead I ask my question. "Do you have a mother or sister?" And there's the look instantly. This always works and I always enjoy the immediate discomfort of an asshole looking like a deer in headlights. At least this one has the balls to man up though.

"Yes. *Both* actually," he kind of smirks like he knows where I'm headed with this.

"Okay... so your sister is working her ass off through school, paying her bills, paying huge student loans, fighting hard some days just to stay afloat, and she comes to you to explain her days." Pulling in a big breath, I know every single person at the table is staring at me, and I even feel Mike lean in a little closer to offer me support, I think.

"Your sister explains to you that in doing her job, a perfectly acceptable form of employment, not that it should matter what she does... Anyway, she tells you that in the course of her days, men- complete strangers- feel as though they can sexually harass and sexually assault her whenever they want to."

Suddenly crying, I wish I had held in the tears but sadly they're unavoidable. "Your sister tells you that though she behaves professional, dresses well, and invites NO sexual attention whatsoever- again, not that that should matter- but men feel like they can slip their hands up her skirt, grab half her ass and her thigh on her bare skin, scare the hell out of her and make her feel physically violated, and that's just the way it is?"

Wiping my cheeks with a quick sniff I try to finish this. "As her brother would you not find that horribly inappropriate, disgusting, and totally demeaning? Would you not want to *help* your sister? Maybe even punch a dickhead in the face who assaults her because *he* thinks it's funny, or cute, or whatever the hell he thinks? When in reality it makes her afraid of men and nervous of their behavior."

"Listen, I didn't mean-" Cutting him off, I quickly revise the question with my deeper, crying voice.

"Now tell me how you would feel if your own mother explained the exact same thing to you? If your mom came home, called you crying, and told you men touch her without asking, grope her without feeling,

46

and then laugh at her when *she* feels violated, hurt, and frightened by them. How. Would. You. *Feel?*"

Looking quickly at Mike, I know I could be fired for this, maybe I even will be fired for this, but I couldn't stop myself. We're told when we start to take all sexual harassment incidents to the manager to deal with, but I don't care. And judging by Mike's angry face glaring at the dickhead, I don't think Mike thinks I'm wrong to ask my questions either.

After a moment of collective silence, when not one of the men begins eating, it's actually the big intimidating guy who stands and leans over the table toward me extending his hand even though I step back a little nervously.

Nodding sadly, he lowers his hand before speaking. "Please accept our apologies. Keith is leaving," he looks at Dickhead. "But if you'll permit the rest of us to stay, you'll have no more trouble from any of us tonight. We'll just eat and leave. You have my word."

When Dickhead looks like he's going to protest, the man whose food I practically threw at him says, "Fuck off, Keith. Leave her a *huge* fucking tip, pay for your food, and get the hell out of here. You've embarrassed not only yourself, but all of us tonight."

Taking a step back again, Dickhead rises, looks down at his plate, tosses some money from his wallet on the table, and does turn to me just as Mike steps in closer.

"I'm really sorry, Cherry. I-"

"Saige!" I snap angrily as someone else bangs their hand on the table.

"*Saige,*" he repeats turning a little redder. "You've given me much to think about, and a call to make to my sister this evening," he nods soberly causing me to huff a little of the tension from my chest. "Please forgive my drunken behavior," he finishes before walking towards the restaurant area out of the lounge.

"And take a cab," one of the men yells as Dickhead nods his head but doesn't turn back toward us.

Looking around the table at all eyes on me, I feel so emotional suddenly I need to get the hell away from everyone, Mike included.

"Ah, if there isn't anything else, please enjoy your meals," I gasp as another cry bursts from my chest.

Practically running for the employee lounge I collapse on the couch and just bawl my eyes out. I haven't acted so emotional in all my life,

47

and I haven't cried like such a psycho ever.

Then again, maybe that's another problem Tyler had with me. Maybe I was too calm for him- usually making all my arguments without any drama.

Remembering Kaitlyn going at me in my own home, I imagine she's a very different kind of woman than I am. She's much more aggressive and loud, I learned firsthand. So maybe the drama is what Tyler was missing with me? I have no idea anymore what it was.

All I do know is *no* man but Tyler has touched me in 4 years, and it scared the hell out of me when I felt that Dickhead's hand on my bare skin.

CHAPTER 5

"Manager or friend?" I'm asked by Mike standing in the doorway.

"Friend," I cry a little harder.

"Are you okay?" He begs plopping right down on the couch beside me. Lifting my hand from my knee, he warms it immediately in both of his own and waits for me to speak.

Wiping my nose, I need to know if we'll be interrupted. "Who's watching the bar?"

"Hailey. And Sheila was just finishing up her section, so she's covering yours for now. What's going on with you?"

"Tyler cheated on me yesterday," I pause as Mike breathes a long *fuuuuck* beside me. "Actually, I caught him yesterday in my own bed, so I assume it's been going on for a while. And it's Kaitlyn-"

"*Murphy*?" He asks shocked.

"Yup. Kyle's slutty sister. Well, I want to assume she's a slut because it makes me feel better."

"She is," Mike agrees so seriously I gasp a quick laugh.

When Mike waits for me to calm my crying giggles, I tell him everything. "He said he still loves me and he said it wasn't about me at all. Tyler broke my heart but told me she's not as good looking as I am, she's not as intelligent, and you've confirmed she's a slut. But it doesn't really matter. I'm still suddenly heartbroken and homeless because 'There's just something about *her*,'" I sneer quoting Tyler. "So how can't it be about me? If I was as great as he says I was, he wouldn't have even been attracted to another woman, right?"

"Not really. Most men are dicks, Saige," Mike shakes his head. "And they're always kind of looking even when they're not. So Tyler had this perfect girlfriend at home, but then someone new came around, flaunting, teasing, making him feel like The Man again, and that's about how it happens. Men always want the new woman, but then always regret it and want the good woman back. It doesn't mean anything was wrong with you- it just means Tyler's an idiot who's thinking with his dick right now. I guarantee he'll come back for you though."

Exhaling hard, Mike leans back and pulls me right up against his side as I start crying again. It's only been one day since everything imploded so I don't think it's completely irrational to still be crying all the time over a 4 year breakup with the love of your life. I just wish it didn't make me feel so weak and exhausted all the time.

"I had no idea Tyler was such a stupid asshole," Mike says making me laugh again.

Jesus, I've been crying and laughing back and forth since yesterday. It's like I'm completely incapable of holding on to just one emotion right now I'm so confused and hurt by all this.

"It keeps getting worse," I mumble. "After it all went down yesterday, I needed Kyle's notes after the exam lecture I missed so he met up with me at school and I broke down in front of him. He was very nice and kind to me and we went back to his place and-" When Mike stiffens against me I'm shocked. "*Nothing* happened. God, Mike, do you really think anything would've?"

"No... It's just you know, vulnerable woman, payback, revenge fucking. Whatever," he shrugs. "But no, I know you're not like that. Sorry," he says rubbing my arm a little.

"*Anyway...* at some point I described her, he said he didn't know who she was, then we went back to his place and studied our asses off before I slept *alone* on his couch. This morning we went to our exam, he thanked me for helping him pass, and then he asked me to check in with him to let him know I was okay after seeing Tyler this afternoon. Then Tyler told me about her and I was so hurt again that Kyle kept that from me, or maybe I was mortified that I cried and vented to him and he could tell her everything I said and felt, or... I don't know. I just feel so shocked and betrayed by everyone I thought I knew right now."

"*I'm* still me," he almost pleads pulling me tighter to his side.

"I know. You and Selena are the only 2 people I feel like I can trust right now," I admit sadly.

"Not to be an asshole," Mike says after a minute of silence between us, "but I can't believe he cheated on you. And with *her*," he grimaces with such disgust in his voice I love him even more. "And I can't believe you caught them. No wonder you were so off when you arrived today."

"Yeah, I've been a little messed up since yesterday. I'm just so hurt I don't know what to do, or even what to think anymore."

"Of course you're hurt. That was a shitty thing for anyone to go through, especially when you were writing the exam of your life at the same time," he says angrily.

"I probably should've called in but I need to be distracted with work instead of crying in my car. Then that asshole groped me and I just freaked."

Pulling me in tighter, Mike leans his chin on my head until I calm. "Don't worry about him. You had every right to call him out, and you did it beautifully. Fuck, you could've hit him and it would've been appropriate for what he did to you. Look, before I came in here a few of the guys asked if you were okay and even apologized again asking me to pass it along. If anything comes of this though, I'll tell Hershal exactly what happened."

Listening to Mike, I feel much better. Hershal, the owner is a kind old man, but he's a little old school. He doesn't like aggressive women, but he also doesn't like anyone 'getting fresh with his girls' as he calls all of us, which though fairly sexiest is also kind of sweet, too. I wasn't worried too much about Hershal, I'm just nervous about my job overall.

"I need this job, Mike. I'm even going to tell everyone that I'll take extra Friday and Saturday shifts if some of the staff want nights off. I need the hours and I need the weekend tips now more than ever."

"Who's keeping your apartment?" Mike asks quietly, like it won't hurt me as much if his voice is soft.

"I assume Tyler will try though there's no way he can afford it without me," I sigh again before I suddenly yawn. Feeling the weight of everything sinking into my bones, I swear I can't even drive tonight I'm so tired.

"What can I do to help? What do you need?"

"Don't tell anyone what's going on. I'll talk to Selena in the morning, but I'm pretty embarrassed by all this."

Lifting up from the couch to look down at me, Mike shakes his head. "You have nothing to be embarrassed about. Tyler should be shot and Kaitlyn just proved what we all knew about her. You're amazing, Saige. And I guarantee Tyler's going to figure that out very soon and come crawling back begging like a pathetic loser."

"I'll never take him back though. Cheating was the only rule I ever had between us and he did it anyway."

Smiling at me, Mike kisses my forehead before rising. "I'm glad to hear that because he honestly doesn't deserve you. You are way too good for Tyler, which he just proved. I'm so sorry, but I have to go back out there," he says looking conflicted until I shoo him away with my hand. "Take your time if you want. You're covered, and I don't think you should have to deal with any more dickheads tonight," he grins.

"Thank you," I hide behind another yawn.

"Why don't you lie down for a bit? You look exhausted. But I'll come get you when everyone's ready to close up."

"I will. Thanks," I smile kindly to Mike when he leaves me again in my sad silence.

5 minutes later I realize I'll never sleep or relax here. My mind seems to turn over everything much more vividly when I'm alone, and I need to finish my night before I have a total breakdown in the motel after work.

Checking my face, I tidy it up and add a little makeup to hide the dark circles under my eyes. Wiping away the mascara I smeared crying, I powder my red nose and cheeks, add a little lipstick, and fix my ponytail.

Opening the door, I pull my shit together and start for the bar/lounge area and Mike. Acknowledging Mike who stops drying glasses to look over at me, I nod I'm fine. "I'll never relax, so I figure I should just finish up tonight."

"You're sure?"

"I'm okay," I grin when he gives me a skeptical face. "Okay enough to finish anyway."

Walking back to the men, I notice they all stop speaking immediately when I approach. Ignoring their silence and stares though, I pretend I'm fine.

"How is everything? Would anyone like another drink?" I ask to 3 of them nodding they would. The rest decline drinks but let me know everything is good.

Smiling once, I walk to the bar before anything happens for me, or really *to* me again. At this point I can't trust my emotions anymore and I'm not risking another public meltdown tonight.

*****

Waiting out another 15 minutes, I notice all the men finished so I stroll over for the customary would you like coffee or dessert, but they all decline. Grabbing 3 finished plates, I walk back to the computer to print off their bills, grabbing the debit machine as I turn.

Looking over at the table, the 7 men are still seated which I appreciate and actually need right now. I'm feeling fairly vulnerable and I don't want 7 men standing over me or too close to me when I cash them out.

"Hi again," I continue to the end of the table I started with. "I hope you enjoyed your meals?" I ask prompting most of them to nod and a few to actually speak out loud they did while I lean far behind them and place their bills on the table beside them.

Leaning away as much as possible, I keep my face pleasant, but I know my body language tells them I'm trying to avoid getting physically close to them as well.

"Does anyone need the debit machine?" I ask to all of them nodding, so I start back at the first man.

Entering his amount, I wait silently behind him to the side as he cashes out. Once approved, I move on to each man in turn. None of them are speaking to me, but they're all polite when I hand over the debit machine pausing in their conversations to cash out.

One by one, I eventually notice I'm not getting any tips added to their totals. The fifth man confirms it again when I'm handed back the debit and pull his receipt, and by the 6th man I'm starting to feel very sad and teary-eyed again. I guess they really didn't appreciate me telling off their handsy friend.

When I'm finished, a few of them stand so I step back, suck it up, and thank them for joining us this evening.

Turning, the middle handsome man calls my name just as I'm about to walk away. "Saige? This is for you- to help with your studies, and to apologize once again for Keith's behavior earlier." Leaning toward me, he hands me a piece of paper wrapped around some money I can see along the edge.

"If we didn't know he was drunk before we came in we would've killed him for his horrendous behavior with you. He was very drunk though, and he doesn't normally act like that, but I promise we'll definitely mention what a *dickhead* he was when he's sober tomorrow," he smirks at me as I fight smiling back.

"Thank you," I nod. "I hope you all have a wonderful evening."

Walking back to the bar, I hold my makeshift envelope and watch them leave together, grabbing a mint or toothpick at the receiving desk, laughing and talking among themselves.

Carrying away another 3 dirty plates, I stop at the bar for a rag when Mike leans into me. "So?" He asks pointing at my money.

"I hope it's worth dealing with their friend," I grin pulling out the bills. "Holy shit," I mumble counting twenties and fifties. "Um..." *Jesus Christ!* "There's $400 dollars here. What- "

"Fifty bucks a guy?" Mike blurts out as I stare for a moment before moving quickly.

Rounding the bar, I run through the family side and just make it to the main doors when I see a taxi pulling away. Throwing open the doors, I see 4 of them still walking and yell, "Wait!" as they turn to me. "Wait! I can't accept this," I huff approaching them.

"Yes, you can. And if it makes you feel better we'll beat the money out of Keith tomorrow," the quiet guy from the end says laughing.

Not sure what to say, I kind of freeze staring at the four of them. "I really can't. This feels too weird. Like I'm being paid for being groped or something," I mumble embarrassed.

"No, you're being paid for doing a good job tonight considering how uncomfortable Keith made you feel. You earned a huge tip from all of us tonight for not only kicking Keith in the balls verbally, but for kicking the rest of us in the balls as well." When I laugh and cover my mouth, another one continues.

"Saige," the intimidating man says, "You handled yourself amazingly well, and you have nothing to be embarrassed about. I hope my own sister handles herself half as well with dickheads," he grins at me, "as you do."

"Take the money. It's a gift toward your schooling," the good looking man from the middle says with another one nodding beside him.

Looking at the four of them, I feel like crying again I'm so stunned by their kindness. "Thank you very much. You have no idea what this means to me, especially right now. Um, thank you," I babble again.

"You're welcome," the suddenly *less* intimidating guy says. "You should go back inside though. It's not safe out here alone," he waits until I nod. "Good luck, Saige."

"Thank you," I repeat like a dumbass turning to walk back to the door of D'Vecseys. Looking back as Mike opens the heavy wooden door wider for me, they're still watching me so I wave once and step inside.

"So?" Mike asks beside the door as I enter.

"So, they said I was amazing for handing them all their balls," I laugh as Mike does. "They said the tips were for school, they wished me well, and told me to go back inside where it's safe. Um, they were very nice and they insisted I keep the money."

Leaning against the wall with his arms crossed, Mike smiles down at me. "They sound like real good guys. And they're right, Saige. Even I want to call Silvana later to make sure men don't treat her poorly after what you said," he grins referring to his own sister.

Walking back inside, Mike and I separate to start the cleanup of our section. He has to supervise the restaurant side as well, but it's fairly quiet so he always returns to the bar/lounge side with me to help.

Waiting for the 11:00 official close down, the loud music begins as all of us from both sides start cleaning and tidying. Thinking about my kind table of men, I catch myself smiling often, shaking my head frequently, and giggling from time to time. But when I start scrubbing tables my mind immediately goes back to missing Tyler.

Thankfully, I made a killing tonight in tips and I can breathe a little easier about everything else right now knowing I'm in the motel for the next 3 days. So between my tips tonight and the little money in my savings account, I have more than enough money for another security deposit on a new place.

My exam is over, my conditional acceptance to school should be lifted within weeks, and I can finally start moving past this shitty day and a half of my life... And past Tyler.

After the clean-up when I attempt to leave work at quarter to 12 Mike asks where I'm sleeping tonight. He asks with sensitivity and concern. He asks as a dear friend. He asks because he loves me and is concerned for me. He asks, and then he freaks the hell out on me when I tell him.

Demanding I go back to his place As. A. Friend. We have our first real argument since I started working at the restaurant 2 1/2 years ago.

When I tell him its fine, he yells it isn't. When I say I'll be safe, he tells me I won't be. When I tell him I don't have any other options right now, he tells me I'm being a stubborn ass.

When I eventually burst into tears, he stops yelling at me, gives me a huge hug, and demands I wait for him so he can follow me to the motel.

(mis)TRUST

CHAPTER 6

Parking in the spot right outside the door of my motel room I wave at a totally unamused Mike motioning for me to get inside. Opening the door with an actual key I know a text should come any minute now from Mike, and it does before I've even locked the door.

'I can't believe you're staying there. It's not a rent by the hour but it still sucks. It's not safe. Anyone can break in that window and kill you.'

'Wow. Did you just text that?' I ask stunned.

'Sorry. Will you please come to my house?'

'No. But thank you again. I NEED to sleep.'

'I'll let you sleep.'

'I'm going to cry all night.'

'I don't care.'

'Are you driving and texting?' I ask to change the subject.

'Talking and driving. My phone is texting for me. Are you sure Sage?' Looking at the text I see talk to text always spells my name wrong.

'I'm sure. I won't get murdered tonight. I'll text you tomorrow.'

'In the morning.'

'Yes, Sir.' I grin.

'Does anyone else know you're there?'

'No.'

'Good. Don't tell anyone. Does Selena know?'

'Not yet.'

'She's going to be mad at me for letting you stay there and for not telling her. And she's going to be super pissed that you stayed there. Call me if you need anything.'

'Okay. Good night, Mike. Thank you for caring enough to make me cry when you yelled at me ☺'

'You're welcome 😬'

Looking around my room, it's actually fairly nice. I picked a cheap motel, but its right outside the University neighborhood, so it's a better cheap motel. I think they rent to visiting parents maybe, so they keep it clean and somewhat modern. Besides, I'm okay here for only a few days I hope, because after that I plan on having a plan.
For tonight though I just plan on sleeping. Immediately.

Hopping into the bed after I change, I snuggle in and feel cold instantly. I haven't slept alone in 3 years since Tyler and I moved in together. A few nights he came home very late after a game or concert out of town, but other than that I've slept beside him always.
And I miss him.
Reaching for my phone when another text comes through I hope it's only Mike. I saw earlier I had a few texts from Tyler I didn't read, and I don't want to know who else texted me in case it's Kyle.
'Look outside the window.' Shit. Really?
Crawling back out of the bed, I shiver from the cold room but look anyway and almost jump out of my skin when Mike has his face plastered creepily against the window. Laughing at my reaction as I grab my own chest with a scream I quickly throw open the door.
"I can't do it. I can NOT leave you here alone. So you either come with me or I'm staying here. Your choice," he says seriously though still laughing a little at how much he freaked me out.
Panicking I look around my small room. "But there's only one bed."
"I'll sleep under just the comforter, and you sleep under the sheets and comforter. No touching. No nothing. Just sleep. And in the morning we'll fight about where you're staying tomorrow night," Mike walks in jumping on the far side of the bed I hadn't turned down for myself.
When I watch him settle in I can't move. We're just friends and he even said as much but I feel very awkward having him share a bed with me. After a few tense seconds though he seems to understand my trepidation.
"It's not like that, Saige, I promise. And even if I felt like that about you, I wouldn't do anything about it the day after your huge breakup. I'm just keeping you company tonight, I promise."
"Okay..." I agree feeling totally awkward still.
Walking over, I crawl back in, feel Mike turn the opposite way, and try my best to relax when I flip off the lamp.

This is so strange and unknown for me I feel a little childish, but I'm really uncomfortable if I'm being honest. I actually do trust Mike, it's just I've never shared a bed with anyone other than Tyler and that makes me think of Tyler and ache for Tyler, and just lose it.

Crying as quietly as I can, I wipe the tears sliding over the bridge of my nose, and sniffle as gently as possible. I try to hide my upset, but when I feel Mike slide a hand over the covers to gently pat the back of my leg the tears pour from my chest harder.

Sobbing, I realize I love *and* hate Tyler almost equally, and I don't know how to move past this.

When I feel my tears dry up a little, I reach for the plastic glass of water I filled earlier and swallow it down along with all the resentment and agony I feel in my heart.

"You okay?"

"No," I cry feeling Mike's body move on the bed like he's nodding.

"You will be. Good night, Saige," he whispers before I repeat it with a heavy heart and heavier eyes.

*****

Waking, I'm alone again. I know Mike left early because he made me get up and lock him out but I fell right back to sleep almost instantly. Wanting to text Mike, I look at my phone and realize it's almost 10:30.

'Thank you for last night. You've been a very good friend to me always, but especially now. Could you please not tell anyone at work what's going on, or that you stayed with me. Or basically anything at all to Kyle so he doesn't tell THEM anything. Thank you. I'll see you in a few hours. ☺' Almost immediately Mike texts back.

'You're welcome. Of course I wouldn't discuss anything with Kyle or ANYONE else. See you at 4. You mumble when you sleep. 😬'

Reading Mike's text I laugh to myself. Tyler always mentioned I talked and mumbled all the time when I slept. He also said it drove him crazy because he could never make out actual sentences. Instead he could only pick up random words that didn't make any sense to him.

Deciding to finally check my other texts I find myself holding my breath as I pull up Tyler's text from 7:12 last night- hours after our showdown.

'I really am sorry for all this. And I want you to know I still love you very much. I hope we can talk about this soon and maybe be friends? I've decided to keep the apartment if you really do want to move out. I guess I'll see you on Sunday afternoon? There's no rush. Let me know when you're coming. Call me if you ever need anything.'

Thinking about Tyler keeping my apartment with his whore pisses me off. I'm the one who painted our place and decorated it. I made it a home for us, a very happy home I thought at the time. Just thinking about her living there now enjoying all my hard work *and* the furniture I paid for pisses me off even more.

Before I can stop myself I text, **'Don't be there Sunday after 1:00. And I need nothing from you. So fuck off.'** Hitting send, I feel almost giddy. I don't swear often at people, and I never really needed or wanted to swear at Tyler before all this. It feels pretty good telling him off under the circumstances though.

Pulling up the next text from Tyler at 10:02 it only reads,
'I hope you're okay?' So I figure what the hell?
'Fuck. Off.' covers everything this morning.

Next I see a text from Kyle last night as well, so I mentally prepare for more bullshit.

'I know you know about Kaitlyn and I'm very sorry I didn't tell you. I wasn't being an asshole I just didn't know HOW to tell you. You were so sad and I felt so badly for you. And yes she's my sister but I don't approve of what they did at all. I didn't even know she was sleeping with Tyler until you told me. If you ever want to talk I'm still here for you.'

Three for three? Finding this all so amusing suddenly I text **'Fuck off'** and send it back to Kyle.

And finally, there's a text from Selena from not long ago.

'You were supposed to call me first thing this morning. But its 9:30 and you haven't called and you're not answering your cell. Call me kiddo. I didn't like the way you looked last night. Luv ya. 🖤'

In the meantime, a text beeps through from Kyle again.

'I'm really sorry for all of this. Thank you again for helping me study. You're still the cutest red-headed Brainiac I've ever known. Take care.'

Nope. I'm not engaging Kyle again. He can go away like the rest of them as far as I'm concerned.

Going to the washroom, I have a quick shower and settle in for my phone call. Selena will probably demand I come over when I tell her everything but I don't want to yet. She'll make me cry when she hugs me and when Griffin sits in my lap to play I'll feel bad crying around him.

Using the little coffee maker and the one comp cup of coffee I settle in for Selena to make me feel better...

... And 45 minutes later I do feel a little better.

Selena's home is open to me as of today she offers. Her mother has a huge garage for my things, and she can get me into a little bachelor apartment in her building. She thinks she may even be able to convince her Super to let me rent it monthly with a security deposit so I can move out when I leave for school in a few months.

Oh, and Tyler is a fucking asshole.

Selena hates Tyler and thinks he's a total douchebag who she insists is going to beg me to take him back within weeks. Selena says she knows women like Kaitlyn, and she knows woman like me, and apparently I'm the type of woman men want a forever with 'once they get their rocks off' with women like Kaitlyn.

Selena admits she actually met Kaitlyn once at Mike's New Year's Eve party last year when I was working. She also knows Tyler was there that night which naturally drives me mental wondering if that was the night things started between them. Just the thought of them dating, or screwing, or whatevering for the last 16 months makes me want to scream, and cry, and kill them all over again.

Finally, Selena gives me hell for renting this motel, and says she would have given Mike shit for letting me stay here alone if he hadn't spent the night with me. She also makes me promise I'll check out today and either stay with her or at Mike's starting tonight, which I promise I'll consider so she stops bugging me about it.

When I eventually hang up I realize Tyler broke my heart on Wednesday in a way I'll never get over, even if I eventually move past it. My exam was yesterday and I've set myself up for my future. It's now Friday and a plan is slowly forming for me.

I've lasted 2 days without Tyler and though it aches unlike anything I've ever known, I'm proud I'm still functioning. I'm doing this, and I know I'll continue to do this without Tyler moving forward.

*****

Walking in the back I prepare for a long shift. Friday shifts are 8 hours, but they're so much busier the time flies for us though the exhaustion settles in quicker.

Entering the employee lounge, I put my purse in my locker and turn for the mirror one last time. Smiling at Kelsey, I notice she's looking at me strangely but I don't know her well enough to question the strange look.

Kelsey's behavior suggests she knows what's going on in my personal life, but I honestly don't know how she would. Selena would cut out her own tongue before betraying a confidence of mine, and I doubt Mike would either. Besides being my good friend, he's also my boss, so Mike has to tread carefully with me around the other employees so everything looks fair with no favoritism between us.

Finishing my makeup and hair, I decide to ignore Kelsey. I feel a little hyper-sensitive right now so probably a little paranoid that everyone knows what Tyler did. I'm emotionally off definitely, I can tell by the way I even allowed Kelsey to get under my skin.

Checking the boards, I see I'm in the bar/lounge again, but this time Sheila is working it with me. Eventually trading off with Selena who worked the 1-6 she hugs me tightly and whispers to keep my chin up. And after a 20 minute overlap, she finally leaves demanding I call her later to let her know where I'm sleeping because she hasn't dropped the motel thing.

Watching Mike mix a drink I still feel a little awkward regarding last night, but I think we should be fine. Between him hearing me cry in the night and sleeping beside him I do feel weird though.

"Stop thinking so much, Saige," he grins like he's reading my mind. "Nothing is different between us. We just had a slumber party. And if you crash at my place later you get to do my toenails tonight."

Laughing, I feel better instantly. "Sorry... But you're only the second guy I've ever slept with- *oh!* Not like that," I blush. "Oh, actually like that too," I laugh totally embarrassed.

"Well, I'm honored," he teases.

Laughing when Sheila walks up to us with a grimace and a pout I reach to help her quickly. Dabbing her shirt with club soda to get the dark line of ketchup off her, Mike takes her tray of dirty dishes to the kitchen. When she's significantly wet around her stomach, I laugh again and raise her apron higher on her stomach to hide the mess.

"You could never do this with your scrawny hips," she laughs lifting the apron a little higher to cover more of the mess across her stomach.

"It's not my hips that are the problem, it's my short torso. If I raised my apron any higher, it would rest right under my boobs."

"It totally would," she bursts out laughing already in a better mode then when she pouted her way over to us. "There's a couple at 4 who asked for you," she head tilts over as I look.

Oh, *shit...* Dickhead. Pausing, all the air leaves my lungs and my discomfort is obvious to Sheila. When Keith waves and the woman across from him smiles at me like I know her, I'm totally confused.

"Do they need anything right now? Like could you walk over with me to refresh his coffee or something?"

"Ah, sure. I was just going to pour him another. Why?" Sheila asks already straightening her spine beside me.

Turning my head so he can't read my lips I give her the quick facts. "He was a total handsy pig last night. But he left okay so I doubt he's here to cause a problem."

"Got it," she nods grabbing the coffee pot as we walk over.

When we approach, Keith immediately stands up. Stretching out his hand, he offers it to me with an embarrassed smile.

"Saige..." he smiles politely. "I didn't think you'd talk to me, but I should've known you would," he adds as we shake. Dropping his hand quickly he continues, "I'm here to apologize once more for my lewd, offensive behavior last night, and I'd like to introduce you to my *sister* Michelle," he says with a smirk.

"Hi, Saige!" Michelle, who looks close to my age smiles warmly. "My brother mentioned what a *dickhead* he was last night, so I thought I'd apologize as well. What you said to him was awesome," she grins, and I can't help my own. Nodding, Sheila is silent and Keith blushes deeper.

"Thank you, but it's not necessary. You apologized when you left."

"Well, my friends thought I should maybe say it again. Sober," he adds sheepishly. "I really am sorry for touching and scaring you. I was being obnoxious, and I'm not usually such a jerk when I drink. I promise you I won't be like that in the future."

"Or I'll send him back here so you can kick him in the ass again," Michelle laughs as I smile.

"Apology accepted. And thank you," I smile shaking his hand once more. "I'll leave you to Sheila now. I hope you enjoy your meals."

Walking away before he apologizes again, I round the bar to Mike just stepping behind from the other end. "I made sure he wasn't here to start shit when he came in."

"Thanks. He was good and his sister is super cute," I add.

"Yes, she is," Mike agrees looking over at her and for some unknown, unbelievable, completely inappropriate, totally irrational reason I feel a twinge of jealousy, or anger, or something ridiculous like that stir deep inside me.

Shocked by my own feelings, I look back over at Mike stocking the liquor shelves not looking at Michelle any more, but I still feel a weird possessiveness toward Mike.

What the hell is that? Maybe I'm just possessive because of what Tyler did. Maybe I'm being oversensitive and irrational? Oh god, I hope so. I don't think of Mike like that and I don't want to think of Mike like that. He's just my friend, and I need his friendship right now.

Watching a new group of 4 being brought in by Kelsey, I try to ignore my strange feelings for now.

Greeting my newest table, I play the part of happy friendly and continue on. Glancing over at Keith and Michelle from time to time, I notice him looking at me way too often which feels almost creepy. I also notice Michelle looking at me once in a while which feels different after the Mike comment. I don't want Keith to look at me or apologize, or really to acknowledge me at all. And I really wish Michelle was a little less cute suddenly.

By 8:00, both Sheila and I have our 6 tables seated, eating, or waiting for orders. There's a 3 table wait, our hands are full, and the last 2 hours have absolutely flown by.

Standing beside the bar, I notice Michelle leave for the washroom and that's when I accidentally make eye contact again with Keith. Motioning for me to join him, I almost roll my eyes before acknowledging him but just catch myself. I get it, he's sorry. But this is a little overkill.

Deciding to get it over with, I motion one minute, wait to deliver my drinks to the table beside him and then fake smile as I turn to Keith.

"How was everything?"

"Delicious."

"Good," I nod. "Well, if there isn't anything else I'll have Sheila bring over your bill."

"I wanted to know if you'd have dinner with me?" Keith suddenly blurts out to my obvious shock. Shaking my head no before even speaking, he looks down quickly then back up to focus on my eyes again. "I haven't stopped thinking about you, Saige. And I talked to my sister and she thought you sounded great, and I knew you were great after I left last night," he says almost pleading with me.

"Keith-"

"Just dinner. I can't stop thinking about you, and I'd love to prove to you I'm not really an asshole."

Nearly flinching away from Keith, he has NO idea how much the thought of dinner with him repulses me. Not just because I think he's probably an ass every time he drinks, but more importantly because I still love Tyler.

Right or wrong, I love Tyler.

Not that I'll ever do anything about it with him, but the very thought of having dinner with another man feels like I'm cheating on Tyler somehow. Admittedly, it's not the case, but I can't shut off my love for Tyler in only 2 days just because he shut off his love for me.

"I'm sorry, but no. Thank you for the offer. Have a good night," I throw in as I quickly spin around.

"You don't forgive me, huh?" Keith asks loudly.

Turning back I'm angry and annoyed and a little embarrassed when I see the man at the table beside us watching me listening. "Keith, I do forgive you. But I'm not interested. Have a good night," I say with just enough tone to end this conversation.

Walking back to the bar, I wait for my next table to finish browsing the menus and purposely busy myself away from Keith and his sister. After a few minutes I finally see in my peripheral Keith and his sister leave.

"Got a love note for you," Sheila grins handing me a business card of Keith's as I huff. Flipping it over I read, "I'll make you forgive me eventually... I'm very persistent. Have a good night."

"*Persistent?* Try obnoxious..." I mumble as Sheila laughs at my face of annoyance. Throwing out his card in the garbage under the bar, Sheila raises an eyebrow to me groaning, "Ugh. Never," as I turn for the kitchen.

Grabbing desserts I quickly realize Sheila must know what happened between me and Tyler otherwise she never would've questioned me keeping Keith's business card for even a moment. I've received hundreds of business cards before and no one ever questioned why I quickly threw them away when I was with Tyler. Sheila just did though, I realize feeling hurt and humiliated all over again.

By 11:00 the last table settles in for Sheila and I'm looking forward to my night ending. I may have slept like the dead last night but I'm still exhausted. My feet are killing me and the sadness I feel constantly thinking of Tyler keeps making me tear me up, which depresses me further.

God, I can't stop thinking about Tyler, wondering where he is, and what he's doing. Then just as quickly I think of *who* he's doing and I want to burst into tears again.

Like a mantra I tell myself I only have to get through 2 more hours and then I can cry. I only have one hour of service and one hour of cleaning. I have 2 hours before I lie to Mike and say I'm on my way to Selena's, and 2 hours until I lie-text Selena I'm crashing at Mike's.

I have only 2 hours until I can release all this upset from my chest because of Tyler.

*****

Rounding the bar again for table 3's last drinks, I just lift my head when I hear a deep voice I vaguely recognize.

"Hi, Saige," the intimidating guy from last night says and my reaction is immediate. Jumping as I spin around I almost lash out at him. Not because of him necessarily, but because I'm just fed up in general, I'm tired, and I'm not in the mood to make small talk with another man tonight.

"Hi." Acknowledging the other man I remember with a nod, I continue pouring the wine for table 3 and try to ignore them when Mike walks over to take their order.

Leaving the bar, I don't look back so I don't have to entertain them at all. I hate that they know my name, and I hate that they've returned presumably to talk to me since I've never seen them here before last night.

Tidying up the mess left by my last table, I scrub a little harder than usual. I'm not exactly sure why I feel irritated, but I do. Between the sadness, exhaustion, and irritation, once again I look at the clock and wish this night would end already.

After dumping the used dishes in the kitchen, I have to pass the end of the bar again and that's when we make eye contact. Looking at intimidating guy, he smiles and tilts his head to motion me over to them.

Pausing for a moment I weigh my options on the bitchy front. I could blow him off but he was very kind to me last night- well, they all were after Keith left. He wished me well and even told me to go back inside where it was safe. Overall, he was a total gentleman, as was his friend.

Deciding I can handle a little small talk I walk to them but it's the attractive guy who speaks first. "We didn't get a chance to introduce ourselves last night. I'm Dan Ciccone and this is Malcolm MacNeil."

"Hello... officially," I smile politely before stalling out. I can't think of a single thing to say to these guys and that's usually not like me.

"Tell me lovely, Saige," intimidating man named Malcolm breathes in a delicious Scottish brogue, "Are ye a wee Scottish lass, or an Irish Miss?"

"Scottish," I smile. "Me mum's a MacTavish from Dundee," I say in my best Dundonian accent, not to be out-brogued by Malcolm.

"Aye," he grins. "Well ye certain'ly do the Scottish colorin' prrrroud," he laughs rolling the 'r' in proud way longer than necessary which naturally makes me laugh as well.

"Thank you. If my round face and green eyes didn't give me away, my red hair certainly does," I smile as he nods. "Enjoy your drinks gentlemen. It was a pleasure meeting you both. An a fellow Scot no less," I finish in my mother's native accent.

Smiling to myself, I return to tidy tables next to Sheila while waiting for the last of our Diners to finish. It's nearly midnight, we're almost closed, and though I still feel all the Tyler sadness weighing on my soul, Malcolm did make me feel a little lighter with his teasing.

Sneaking a peak from the side booth near the bar, I realize Malcolm isn't so much intimidating as he is just overwhelming. He's tall, maybe

6'4, but he's built like a brick shithouse. He definitely has large muscles, but with his height the overall effect is one of a huge man with a stern, harsh-looking face when he isn't grinning or laughing.

"Saige..." Malcolm breathes nearly touching my back with his body, startling me so much I actually drop a wine glass on the table as I jump. "Sorry," he adds grabbing my arm to steady me.

Turning on him, I practically yell, "What IS it with you guys?"

"I apologize for scaring you," he replies quickly releasing my arm. "I wanted to ask if you'd like to have coffee with me some time."

"I'm not interested, okay?" Glaring up at him I'm so over all this shit. Moving to leave I just catch his slow grin before turning away. "What's so funny?" I snap again. "Never mind. I don't want to hear it."

"I can't stop thinking about you," he smiles stunning me for a second.

"Look, Malcolm," I exhale slowly. "I'm not interested, okay? And quite frankly your other buddy Keith used that exact same line on me earlier."

When Malcolm looks confused or maybe angry by my statement, I walk away. Leaving him standing alone by the booth I round the bar for the kitchen with my hands full to get away. Nearly tossing the plates in the dirty bins for the Busser, I take a second to calm my racing heart.

Leaning against the wall I wonder why Malcolm thought it was a good idea to sneak up on me. Honestly, why the hell would he practically corner me against the booth if not to scare the shit out of me? Christ, men are such idiots sometimes.

Waiting them out, I notice Sheila walking towards the kitchen, so when she enters I have to know, "Are the 2 at the bar still here?"

Laughing at my irritated face I assume, she asks, "You mean your other admirers? *Jesus*, Saige... Are you producing extra pheromones today or something?"

Surprised by her comment, I burst out laughing with her. "Not that I'm aware of," I giggle.

"Well, you're doing something. Did you see the shorter one? He was *gorgeous*," she fans her face and I assume she means Dan who was both shorter and better looking than Malcolm. "Wanna tell me your secret?"

"Um, I yelled at the earlier asshole last night, and apparently that was a huge turn on for the rest of his friends. Who the hell knows?"

"Huh. Whenever I yell at men they think I'm a bitch. Next time you have to let me watch so I know how it's done," she adds grinning.

"No problem. Have they left?"

"Yup. But they did leave you another love note on the counter. Can I read it?"

Exhaling as I walk back out to the lounge I mumble, "Go for it," as she walks over to their empty glasses on the bar and another business card underneath. "'I hope to see you soon... Malcolm,'" Sheila reads his phone number as I shake my head.

"Not likely." Taking the business card from her, I read Dan's name on the front and see he's a contractor at Ciccone's Contracting, either his family's company or his own before throwing out the card with Keith's in the trash.

God, men are irritating me tonight. Well, this whole week actually, and I really wish everyone would just leave me the hell alone.

Eventually closed and cleaning up I think of Tyler often. Between his life with me, and his ending of us, I'm still shocked by how it all went down. I never saw this coming, and I can't stand how it happened.

Almost laughing out loud when my mind suddenly focuses on a MasterCard commercial, I think my sadness has made me nearly delirious.

4 years of love and devotion.
2 minutes of sex and ruination.
55 hours of sadness.
Eternal heartbreak...
Priceless.

(mis)TRUST

CHAPTER 7

Escaping the back doors before Mike can follow, I make my quick getaway when he locks himself in the back office to put the deposit in the safe. Typically, 2 people have to close out and lock up together but with the other staff and Sheila leaving as soon as the place was cleaned, I knew I had to make a break for it when he was busy.

Running for my car, I'm almost giddy over my escape. I didn't want to lie to Mike, but I just couldn't deal with another argument over staying at the motel again.

Rounding the driver's side, I gasp when I see someone jump at me.

Screaming, I feel myself falling when I'm suddenly hit and tackled to the ground by someone waiting.

Instantly my face explodes against the ground and everything is so dark, I don't know what's happening.

Gasping, I try to scream again but a quick fist to the side of my face shuts me up as the pain bursts through my head stunning me silent.

Fighting as hard as I can, my arms are held tightly behind my back by a hand as my skirt is yanked up to my hips. Twisting and gagging on the blood in my mouth, I try to fight him. I cry-scream when I can, and I close my legs as tightly as possible when I feel his hand trying to pry them open.

Ahhhhh... Feeling fingers tear and push through my underwear from behind I cry out scraping my face against the ground until a knee digs so hard in my back I'm instantly winded.

I can't breathe, but I can suddenly feel his fingers pushing inside me hard and fast.

Oh my *god!*

There's so much pain as he thrusts into my body in both my front and back as I fight to get my hands free. Trying to scream again I can't pull in a breath with his weight on top of me.

Gagging from the pain, I hear a belt buckle jangle and the sheer panic of that sound freezes me in place. I know what that sound means, and I know what happens after that sound.

I know what's happening, but I can't stop it.

"*Noooooo...*" I slur from the side of my mouth before I'm hit so hard in the side of my head, my eyes lose focus and my mind blanks around the stars and darkness swallowing me up.

Fading back in I beg, "Please d-don't do this," but there's nothing but a grunt in reply.

Ignoring all the pain in my body and the feel of being torn apart by dirty hands, I know when my hips are lifted because the pressure on my chest and back suddenly eases.

My face scrapes against the ground again and my arms suddenly thump down to my sides when I'm released.

With one long last cry, my completely illogical mind suddenly thinks of Tyler.

Tyler always said he loved me and he always laughed after my hands thunked on the mattress or floor after he made me come. Tyler thought it was funny and sexy when my arms suddenly fell away from him because I was too weak to hold him in my post-orgasmic haze.

Tyler is the only man I've ever known this way, and I can't stand the pain ripping through my chest at the thought of this man taking that away from me.

Screaming again when I feel fingers tear apart my ass I try one last fight before it's over for me. Pushing back against the body behind me, I rise on my hands and twist and slam myself into my car door before he grabs me again hard by my hips and thigh.

Ripping my flesh and squeezing me so tightly I scream, he lifts me back into position.

"*Saige?*"

Gasping a quick breath, I scream as he slams me against him to penetrate me once quickly before I'm released and thrown forward on my face again.

And then it's over.

"I'll see you soon," he says and I freeze instantly.

Gasping, I know that voice. And I know him.

Feeling him stumble against my legs he quickly stands but kicks me in the side before I hear Mike yelling closer to me.

"I'm... *here...*" I moan grabbing my own ribs.

Inhaling on a gasp, the pain is unbearable. My lungs won't pull in another breath, and my head hurts so badly I'm nearly blinded by the pain throbbing through my skull.

"Saige! Oh, *god...*" Mike cries slamming down on his knees beside me. "Oh *fuck,* honey," he babbles touching all over my body with shaking hands as he turns me over on my side. "Oh, god. Okay. I'm calling the police. *Shit,* Saige..."

Listening to Mike freak out, my mind fades in and out. Gasping for breath, I try to stay with him but I hurt too much. When everything inside turns hollow the night becomes too painful and dark around me to stay awake anymore.

"Saige? Listen to me... No, she keeps passing out. Fuck, she looks so bad. *Saige?* Can you stay awake for me? The ambulance will be here in just a few minutes. Please, Saige? I don't *know!* But her face is really bloody and she's breathing weird and there's blood around her thighs- Not more than 5 minutes!" Mike yells choking on tears beside me.

Leaning toward me Mike gently brushes the hair off my face with a shaking hand when I finally look at him. Flinching, my face is on fire, and his hand though I'm sure gentle feels like sandpaper scraping me harder.

"Don't touch my face," I moan before choking on the blood in my mouth.

"Where are you hurt, Saige? Can you tell me?"

Thinking of what he's asking, I blank again.

Everything hurts.

There isn't a part of my body that *doesn't* hurt. From my knees to my head, all I feel is intense pain.

Suddenly crying, I gag on my sorrow and choke on my blood.

"Don't look at me," I croak realizing my skirt is still lifted and Mike can see my body and everything that was done to me. "Please don't look at me," I beg trying to move my hand lower until he quickly moves my skirt lower for me and squeezes my hand softly.

"I hear the sirens, Saige. And you're safe now, I promise," Mike says so sadly, I focus on his eyes still dripping tears down his face. Absurdly, I find myself nodding to reassure him.

"Did you see h-him?"

Shaking his head, Mike groans, "Not really. He was big in dark clothing with a hood but I heard you scream so I ran to you instead of chasing him. I'm so sorry," he moans.

"So'kay," I mumble again as the pain in my head starts thumping so hard and fast, I feel like I might actually have some real damage. "I know him..." I whisper before the darkness takes me finally.

*****

Waking in the ambulance, the paramedic starts asking me questions I can't answer. I hear him, and I even understand what he's asking me but I can't find my own voice. My lips are moving I think, but no sounds will come out of my mouth. Focusing on a silent, horrible looking Mike, I feel silent tears fall from my eyes.

"I'm so sorry," he breathes softly, and all I want to do is shake my head to let him know he shouldn't be sorry, but my head won't move. I want him to know I'm okay, but I still can't speak.

Mike saved me, and he took care of me. He's not the bad guy here, and I don't want him to feel bad for any of this.

*****

Waking in the ER, I feel the surgical scissors cut away my clothes as a mad panic sets in. Moaning, I feel my hands thrash against the hands touching me before a nurse talks me calm. I'm reassured and soothed and eased by medication as others surround me. I'm foggy and unsure of my reality as lights pass overhead.

I'm awake, but unconscious in my head.

And I'm terrified.

*****

Waking in a room, I agree to a physical exam before I fade to darkness once more as the medication soothes my broken soul.

I wish I could feel Tyler holding me warm.

But Tyler is gone.

*****

74

Waking in a room, I'm not alone. Feeling a man's presence, I look quickly and open my mouth to scream.
Screaming inside from the pain, I stop the fight and look to the woman beyond and know I'm not going to be hurt again.
She won't leave me alone.

*****

Waking, my head is pounding and my face hurts so badly, I cry out before I realize where I am.
Touching my own skin, I'm shocked by the feel of my face. I'm swollen and bumpy, and I throb and ache everywhere.
I am nothing but pain.

*****

Waking, I hear the whirling sound moving around me and feel the closed walls tightening around my chest in fear.
Lashing out, I flail and kick until I'm stopped by a calm voice soothing me back to sleep.
Calmed, I am darkness.

(mis)TRUST

CHAPTER 8

"Saige?" Opening my eyes again, I see Selena smiling beside me. "Hey kiddo... welcome back," she says squeezing my hand.

Gasping my relief, I burst into tears. Feeling my body hugged, I sob in the safe arms around me. Selena is like my big sister. She's my best friend and I love her so much she's just everything good in this moment.

Holding my head tightly, I'm astounded by the pain. Moaning in agony, she gently leans me back on my pillow wiping her own tears away.

"I don't know what to say, Saige," she breathes so sadly in my ear I huff a last cry. I don't know what to say either. I have no words, and I can't think of anything that will make this better for her.

"The police need to speak with you as soon as you can. Mike's already given a statement, and we're both just devastated by what happened to you. I wish I knew what to say to make this all better for you but I don't," Selena whispers softly as another tear slides down her cheek.

Watching her tear fall in slow motion, I realize my brain isn't functioning right. I'm delayed, or damaged, or destroyed maybe.

"I'm not concen- th-thinking right. Like in my head, Sel-ena. There's s-something wrong," I panic.

When she takes my hand again I relax a little as the minutes pass.

"Listen to me," she leans closer until I open my eyes again. "You have a bad concussion with a little brain swelling I was told by your doctors. You're in for at least the rest of today and tonight and maybe even tomorrow night while they monitor you. They explained what might happen to you and confusion was one of the symptoms. But you're going to be okay, so don't worry about that big brain of yours," she soothes. God, if my face didn't hurt so much I might actually smile back at her I'm so relieved. "You're also heavily mediated right now, so that's why you're confused. Oh, and Mike told the police and hospital staff I was your sister if anyone asks."

Bursting into tears again, I slur, "You *are* my s-sister," before I feel her hug me back asleep.

*****

Waking, I realize one thing with such certainty, my heart starts pounding as the fear freezes me still.

"I know him," I cry out loud as Selena gasps beside me.

"How?" She whispers at my side. "How do you know him?"

Thinking of the sounds, and the smells, and the weight of his body and hands, I search my brain but come up empty. "I don't know. But I know I do."

"Okay. We'll tell the police that and they'll find him, Saige. They said it was probably a personal attack because your purse was still on the ground beside you."

Crying, I ask, "Why personal?"

"I don't know."

"He didn't rape me all the way," I suddenly choke then gag when I remember his fingers inside me. "Um, but he touched me bad, Selena. Really bad and painful and it was so awful. He put his fingers in me in both places and I still feel them," I cry as she nods beside me.

Not speaking, she lets me barf out the gross memory to her.

Choking a little as the fear constricts my lungs I tell her all I can. "He hit me, and hurt me, and he was going to rape me, but Mike called my name. He kicked me and punched me and tore my clothes and hit me and he actually *kicked* me, Selena!" I yell angrily.

"And when I heard his belt buckle I knew what he was going to do and I was so scared, and I don't want that, but Mike called my name." Nodding at me, I continue.

"Mike called my name so he could only thrust in me one time. Then he kicked me and stopped, but I was so scared and I didn't want him to do that to me. But then Mike saved me before he could rape me all the way I think."

"Saige, you *were* raped and-"

"No. It was just the one time he was in me, so that's not rape," I find myself desperate for Selena to agree with me, until she nods slowly with another tear falling from her sad eyes.

Sobbing, I try to wash all the filthy memories away. I need to make this stop, and I need to forget this happened.

"God, my head really hurts, and I feel confused and kind of sick."

"I know. Just take it easy for now. The police said they'd be back in a few hours, so you have time to sleep again. I'll be here, and Mike is waiting to see you whenever you can."

"He saved me..." I moan again remembering him fall on his knees beside me. Crying, he was so gentle and kind to me when I needed him.

"I know he did, honey."

"Where's Griffin?" I panic. "He's too sweet for all this ugly. I don't want him to know anything about this. I don't want him to see me like this, Selena. You shouldn't be away from him for me," I freak out desperately until she stops me.

Patting my arm Selena lets me know, "He's with Dave right now, and then he's going to my mom's in the afternoon."

"Dave?" I choke thinking of her asshole ex-husband.

"Yup. He came running in the middle of the night to help me as soon as I called him," she nods. "So he's staying at my place with Griffin until he takes him to my Mom's later. Griffin is safe at home. And Dave manned-up for once," she smirks to my relief.

"Thank you for coming here," I squeeze *her* hand.

"Of course I'd be here." Inhaling deeply, Selena's gearing up for something hard I can tell. I've seen that expression of hers, and I know when she's struggling to speak. "I have to know... do you want us to call Tyler?" Actually whispering his name at the end, it still stabs through my heart.

Shaking my head, I feel the tears start again, and honestly, every part of me wants to say yes. I want Tyler to fix this so badly I'm almost desperate enough to beg for him. But he can't fix me or what he's done, so instead I say, "Never."

"Honey, you've been moaning his name and crying for him all night."

"*Never,* Selena," I glare so she knows I'm serious. "He didn't want me more than her, and I don't want him like this. I'll never know why he really came for me, and I don't want to know if it's only guilt or sympathy. Don't ever call him or tell him because it's over for us. *Please*?" I beg until she nods.

"Okay." Watching her eyes fill up, I know she won't ever tell him.

Thinking of Tyler, I start to cry again from the pain and heartache, and from just missing him loving me.

Tyler always made me call as soon as I left work, and if he wasn't home before I was I had to text him the second I walked into our apartment.

He was always concerned about me, especially at night, so he would've known something was happening when I didn't call him from my car. He would've known something was wrong and he would've saved me.

Leaning on my side, I don't hide my tears from Selena, I just get comfortable so the pain of my loneliness can take me away from this brutal reality.

*****

Waking again, I'm alone until a doctor and nurse begin speaking to me. Telling me about my injuries which are superficial though quite painful they acknowledge, I'm told what to expect and what I'll feel in the coming days and even weeks.

I'm told of my vaginal and anal tears which repulses and humiliates me to the point of sobbing uncontrollably until they stop speaking while I lose it. Then after my breakdown I'm told I've been given dissolvable stitches between my vagina and anus in my perineum and antibiotics to prevent any infection from setting in.

I'm told about the various stitches in my face, my black eye, the swelling everywhere and about the 3 stitches inside my mouth from my busted lip, which honestly, hurts like a bitch.

I'm told of the physical discomfort I'll be given medication for, and I'm told of my concussion and what I need to watch out for, including headaches, slurring, and more confusion.

After they're finished speaking my brain spins and turns over the events so clearly, I can still feel him inside my body. I start to freak out again thinking of his fingers, until I'm pulled out of my gross nightmare by the doctor who insists they need to take photographs of all my injuries. So standing with help, the nurse takes pictures of my naked body, front and back, concentrating on my face and mouth, and then she helps return me to my bed when my full body shivering becomes uncontrollable.

Once they leave my room when I have no further medical questions to ask I'm eventually introduced to a rape counsellor. I'm given additional reading material, phone numbers of an offsite free counseling clinic, and then I'm wished well when I ask the counsellor to leave me alone for a while so I can rest.

*****

Alone for maybe an hour, Selena walks back in my room with flowers and my favorite chocolate bar which makes me smile until I gasp when I feel my lips split back open.

Grimacing like she felt it herself, Selena tries to distract me with facts. "The police are outside and really need to speak with you now. I guess the doctors said you were much more coherent and able to speak about everything that happened, so they gave the police the go ahead. Um, do you want me to stay if they'll let me?"

Nodding, I whisper a desperate sounding, "Yes, please," as she sits down in the chair beside me. Taking my hand again we wait silently until the police enter.

After introductions are made, I tell them everything I remember. I explain what happened, how it was so quick I didn't have a chance to see him, but that I DID recognize his voice. I explain I know him, I just don't know *how* I know him.

Throughout they each ask questions or need clarification from time to time, but otherwise they stay fairly unmoved and dispassionate which I appreciate. Having no reaction from either allows me to graphically detail what was done to me, and finally what was said at the end about 'seeing me again soon,' in a voice I know I recognize.

After I tell them all I can, they ask me to explain my history, past and present lovers and who I've recently met or engaged with. I tell them about the 8 men- Keith in particular, and explain somehow, though I have no idea how and I'm not trying to make any false accusations, but *somehow* I feel like they're involved in what happened to me.

I can't explain further why I think that when I'm pressed by the police but some kind of knowledge or intuition is sitting strangely on my chest. I keep coming back to that group of men either from his voice or the warning itself, or maybe just because I saw 3 of them so recently, and all the others just the night before.

I don't know if it was his voice, or his hands, or what it was about him- but I know it was one of them who hurt me.

I *think.*

When I finally shut down after thinking myself in circles, the police tell me they'll search the garbage bins out back for the 2 business cards and Selena offers to have Hershal pull up the credit card and debit card receipts for the group of them.

Finally, I'm asked to walk through the last week of my life because something might jump out if I think of my week step by step. They ask me to try to remember if anything strange or unusual took place, or if any restaurant patrons gave me a particularly hard time recently.

They ask if I felt like I was being watched, or if I noticed anyone suspiciously around me, which I didn't. With the exception of Keith getting handsy with me, which I also tell them about, I can't think of one single thing that was off this week, except *everything* for me personally.

Thinking until my head nearly explodes, I explain what I did all week, which was study and work until Wednesday when my world imploded. Then I explain I haven't seen anyone outside of the restaurant, with the exception of Kyle, and Mike the night before.

Waiting out any more questions I'm sore and tired and desperate for them to leave. I know I have one more night in the hospital, and I really can't wait for it to begin. I want to take the pain meds and I want to sleep away all this pain and sadness.

"So, you slept with 3 men in 3 days, and you can't think of *anyone* who would want to hurt you?" The younger cop suddenly asks in such an accusatory tone I'm stunned. When my mouth falls open, I grab my bleeding mouth again and can't even reply I'm so shocked.

Selena does however.

Standing up she lays into him. "Three fucking days ago, she slept with her boyfriend of 4 years, who she lived with and had a committed relationship with, who she already told you was the *only* sexual partner she's ever had. Then the next day HE cheated on her in her own home," she spits at the cop. "And she was devastated but she had her final pre-fucking-law exam to write the next day."

"Pre-law?" He asks looking a little shocked himself.

"Yup. Saige isn't a fucking slut, and she isn't fucking stupid either!" Selena yells again. "Then she met up with her study partner Kyle and they *studied* most of the night until she crashed *alone* on his couch before their exam the following morning. And when that was done, because her piece of shit EX boyfriend refused to leave their apartment she had nowhere to go so she rented a motel. So that night Mike- her boss and good friend- the guy who stopped the assault in the parking lot from being any worse than it was last night- *that* Mike stayed at the motel with her On. The. Covers so she could finally sleep a little after the 2 horrible fucking days she suffered before. And then last night she was attacked, beaten up, and raped. So yes, she slept with or near 3 goddamn men for the last 3 nights, but it sure as fuck wasn't sexual, and even if it was HOW *DARE* YOU?!" Selena screams as we all seem frozen in place by her fury.

When the second officer tries to speak, she continues over him glaring at the asshole cop. "Have you ever heard of victim's rights?! Well, let me explain something to you- even if Saige had fucked half the city this week alone, that doesn't mean a goddamn thing! It doesn't mean she caused this and it doesn't mean she deserved to be knocked out and raped in a fucking parking lot! I can NOT believe you just implied her actions caused this and I will definitely let your superiors know that you did!" Selena yells actually lifting her shaking hand to point at him she's so angry.

"I apologize," he breathes heavily. "I didn't mean to imply anything. She just didn't seem like the type to-"

"Okay! *Enough*," his older partner suddenly barks stopping him just as Selena is about to start yelling again. "Get out of here," he points to the door as his partner stares for the longest seconds of my life at me before moving for the door without speaking.

When the door closes behind him there's a collective exhale by all three of us before I burst into tears again by what he implied, what happened, what I'm feeling, and basically because I'm so fucking stressed out I can't do anything *but* cry at this point.

"I apologize. *Deeply,* Miss Masters. I will make a complaint myself and speak with our superiors about Officer Anderson's behavior, but please feel free to make your own complaint."

"She will," Selena snaps as the officer nods.

"Understood. Before I leave however, I need to know if there's absolutely anything else you can remember. I know you've suffered a major conclusion and I know you're in a lot of pain so I won't keep you much longer. But I'd like to write down absolutely anything else you can think of while it's still fresh in your mind." Gently patting my face with a tissue I don't know what to say as he waits. "Big or small. A scent, an accent, clothing, anything? I know you say you didn't see his face, but maybe you did for just a split second? Like when he ran away, or when he first attacked you at your car? Did you see his reflection in the window of your car? Anything?"

Thinking, my head starts shaking before I can voice the words. "I swear I didn't. Believe me I'd tell you."

"Oh, I believe you. I'm just giving you ideas to think about. Sometimes even visualizing what you were doing or thinking, like when you were walking to your car before you were attacked will produce a memory. We have so little to work with physically, I'm looking for anything more specific so we can find your assailant since he was apparently dressed in dark clothing with a hood." Shaking my head again, my headache is so intense it's hurting even my neck.

"Alright. I'll leave you today, but I'll be in touch with you tomorrow. I have your cell phone, and I understand you'll be staying with Mrs. Heart once you leave," he glances over as Selena nods. "Again, I apologize for my partner's behavior, and I will collaborate any complaint you'd like to file against him for his insensitivity and inappropriate comments."

Tearing up a little at his kindness, I whisper, 'Thank you,' as he nods and approaches me slowly.

Extending his hand, he says gently, "Take care of yourself Miss Masters. I've very sorry you were hurt last night but we're working very hard to find out who your assailant was. If you think of anything, or would like to discuss anything at all, you have my card. Mrs. Heart," he nods before leaving me and Selena alone in my room.

*****

When Detective Mathers leaves, Selena plops back down into the chair beside me and takes my hand again. Huffing a huge exhale, she smiles at me before resting her head on the side of my bed.

"Go home, Selena," I mumble out the side of my mouth. "Go get some sleep and go see Griffin."

"It's only 4:00. You'll go stir crazy and feel lonely if I leave too early. Trust me."

"I won't. I'm in so much pain, I want to take more drugs and sleep for a while. I'll be fine," I squeeze her hand back.

"Okay. Would you like me to call your mom?" Selena again nearly whispers so I won't lose it.

"God, no... my mother will freak out. I'm fine, I promise. Don't you have to work tomorrow?"

"No. Sheila's covering for me, and Kelsey offered to work my Monday."

84

"But-"

"Look, Hershal is beside himself over this, but he's covered all your shifts for at least the next 2 weeks. He even covered Mike's shift tonight. I'm going home to Griffin, and my mom is watching him overnight tomorrow so you can settle in without the little monster hanging off you all night. I have to make sure you're okay and monitor the concussion the first night home especially the doctors told me. So I won't argue with you about calling your mom, but that means I get to mother you. Take it or leave it."

"Thank you. I'll definitely take it," I smile sadly thinking of my mom and all the shit that comes with her.

"Good. Now give me a hug goodbye and text Mike soon. He left the hospital to clean up, but he's been bugging me all day to give him updates and to know if you want to see him."

"I'll call him," I tear up a little. "It's just hard because of what he saw."

"It's really hard for him too, Saige. And he needs to physically see you're okay now, or at least that you're going to be okay."

Pushing down a little lower on my bed, I try to get comfortable and I try to ease all my aches so I can sleep. Really, I just want to rest so I don't have to think anymore today.

"I'll call him when I wake up, I promise."

Leaning in, Selena kisses my bandaged cheek before she leaves me alone.

*****

Once the door closes behind her I realize how lonely I suddenly feel. Nobody knows how I feel, and they can't imagine what I'm thinking. That police officer wasn't too far off base in his assumptions, though he may have worded his supposition wrong.

I did this to myself.

Not because I was slutty or because I asked for it. I did this because I wasn't strong enough to fight, and I wasn't smart enough to know better.

Crying, I know Alec would've understood what I'm feeling, and he would've seen me. Before he left, he was the only person in the world who saw me.

(mis)TRUST

Alec was everything to me until he was nothing anymore.
And this is just like the dark loneliness I felt before.

I feel dirty and ruined.
I feel hollow and empty.
I feel disgusting and neglected.
I feel unnecessary and insignificant and just unworthy of everything around me.

Crying, my body feels as broken as my soul is right now.
And I'm all alone with this darkness.

Gagging on my newest reality, I didn't realize there could be anything darker than the loneliness of being left behind.
But I was wrong.

Gasping my way through this storm, I know I loved with everything I had, but it wasn't enough for them.
I fought with everything I had, but it wasn't enough for me.
But I loved.

I loved Tyler until he held the same place in my heart as Alec did. Tyler may have been my boyfriend and lover, but I loved him as honestly as I loved my sweet brother.
I loved each of them but they're still gone by choice.
I am alone without either, and I feel my heart dying away without them here.

God, if my past has shown me anything it is this; I didn't love Alec and Tyler enough to keep them. And they didn't love me enough to stay.

CHAPTER 9

Joining Selena on her balcony with a glass of wine, I come clean once Griffin is down for his nap. "I've talked to Mike, and I'm starting back to work tomorrow. I-"

"But you-"

"Will work the day shift for the foreseeable future, 1-6, same as you. But I'll stay on the family side. I've also decided to rent the bachelor on the 3rd floor. Dennis agreed to let me rent it in 3 weeks, and he also agreed to let me terminate the lease at the beginning of September provided he has a tenant, which he doesn't think should be a problem."

Turning away from the sunlight, Selena really looks at me. "Are you sure? You really don't have to leave. Griffin loves you here, and I feel like I'm enjoying my mid-twenties like I didn't the first time around," she grins raising her glass of wine in a salute.

"I'm sure," I smile before lounging beside her in the sunshine. Listening to Alex Clare's 'Too Close' I inhale the sun into my skin.

"You'll burn in like 2.3 minutes out here."

"I know. This damn coloring of mine is good for nothing but-"

"Looking sexy as hell? Looking vampy? Looking cute and demure? Looking however the hell you want to look depending on your make-up?"

"*Pasty*, I was going for," I deadpan as she bursts out laughing.

"Saige, I don't mean to be insensitive here, but your face still looks really bad. And people will know something happened at the restaurant as soon as you walk in."

"Selena..." I interrupt rolling my eyes dramatically. "I've seen what you do to Griffin's face at Halloween with make-up- are you saying you're not up to the challenge?" I frown knowing she'll be totally on board if I mention make-up.

"I'm up to the challenge, brat."

Enjoying the sunshine before she leaves for work, I need her to understand what's going on with me. I need her to understand why I want to do this, and why I have to do this.

"I *need* to start doing something again. I'm all up in my head, and with the exam results being posted in a week I'm obsessing about what happened and what's going to happen. I can't sleep properly and I want to cry all the time. I'm a mess, Selena,"

"You're not a mess," she reaches over to squeeze my leg but I pull away quickly which kind of accidentally proves my point.

God, I remember her face when I had a shower the day we returned to her apartment from the hospital. I remember exiting the bathroom wrapped in a towel, thinking about nothing but the relief of finally feeling clean after I was attacked until she moaned, *oh god...* staring at my thigh.

I remember yelling *what* as I jumped back in the bathroom to the mirror, then I remember the shock I felt seeing the absolutely perfect black hand print bruise on my thigh. I remember dropping my towel, completely oblivious to the fact that Selena stood there crying silently while I inspected my naked body beside her.

I remember looking myself over, turning this way and that, shocked over and over again at all the bruises and scrapes. But it was the perfect, deeply indented, long finger shadowed black bruises on my hip and my thigh that made me lose my mind.

In a moment of complete disassociation, I lifted my own hand to the bruise on my hip and watched as the black shadow surrounded my own small fingers like they were being crushed. Forever, I stood there staring at my pale skin, broken and blackened, unable to look away, and unable to feel anything.

I was in a catatonic shock until I was suddenly covered in the towel and yanked out of my headfuck by Selena's arms holding me tightly.

But I still stared.

Over her shoulder I saw my huge lips cracked and broken, my black right eye with the stitches under and over my eye. I also saw the pale shock of the woman in the mirror who could no longer cry.

I saw the dark bruises, bloody scrapes, and the nasty dark stitches around my eye and across my right cheek. I saw it all, but it was with someone else's eyes.

And now I never see myself the same as the woman I was before everything changed for me 11 days ago.

"What are you thinking?" Selena asks quietly as I turn to her teary eyes.

"Nothing. Everything, I guess. I wonder if I'll ever be able to be touched again by anyone but my Griffin," I smile thinking of her sweet little boy. "I'm thinking about how my whole life is totally different than it was less than 2 weeks ago which still shocks me. I can't believe it's been 11 days since everything changed and I changed, and my whole life changed so completely."

"Yes."

"But I don't even cry anymore."

"Maybe you should?"

"*Why?* I know the expression crying doesn't solve anything, but I never realized how true it was until I was in the hospital. Yes, there may be a temporary release of physiological or emotional stress and pressure or something, but there are other ways to gain that same release. There are other things I can do. Crying may be a temporary release, but it really doesn't do or accomplish anything long term. Tyler still left me. And I was still attacked whether I cry or not. So why bother?"

"Because you've been through a lot and-"

"I should continue doing what I'm doing? Which is nothing really. This whole week I sat in your living room when you and Griffin were here, and I sat in your living room when Griffin was at your Mom's, or with Dave when you were at work. I took pain meds and I sat lifeless.

"I just sat here waiting for the police to tell me something, which they can't because there isn't anything to tell. They have no leads, and with my *innocent* past as Detective Mathers calls it, they want to say it must've been random, though they know that doesn't makes sense either because I recognized his voice. So I'm scared to leave your apartment in case I'm attacked again but I'm scared when I'm just sitting here in case someone breaks in to attack me. When Dave drops off Griffin I meet him in the hallway because I'm afraid to be in your apartment alone with him though I know he's like family and would never hurt me," I make sure she understands.

"Anyway, I'm afraid to see Mike in case he hugs me because just the thought of anyone touching me right now freaks me out. Oh, and I feel like my intelligence is fading away along with my rest of my life because I can't stop obsessing over what I did wrong with Tyler, what I did wrong with Alec, what I did wrong that night, and-"

Grabbing my leg past my startled flinch, Selena lays into me. "*Jesus*, Saige. It's only been a week and a half. Give yourself a fucking break, would ya? You had your heart broken and you were physically and *sexually* assaulted 9 days ago. Most women carry the pain of either of those situations for months, or years, or even a goddamn lifetime. But you had both within 2 days of each other. You lost your home, your boyfriend, and your physical security within days of each other less than 2. Weeks. Ago," she glares at me. "Never mind all the physical pain you've been dealing with along with all the mental shit."

Nodding, I know what she's saying, but I also know if I don't snap myself out of this depression now, I never will. I barely survived Alec, closing myself right off to any emotion at all until 2 years later when I met Tyler and opened myself up to love again.

But here I am suddenly, 4 years later feeling the same loss, multiplied by my own sense of fear and humiliation, and I'm fading away before my own eyes.

"Tyler has been calling my cell," she says annoyed with him, and again I appreciate and cherish her loyalty.

"I figured he would after I changed my cell number."

"He knows what happened, kiddo. He knows because the police asked him where he was that night. Then he went to D'Vecseys and someone on staff told him what happened to you. And apparently he freaked out and Hershal had to ask him to leave when he refused to give Tyler my address."

"I don't care. I'm not talking to him. What happened to me after doesn't change what happened to us before."

"I agree, and I've told him as much. But he's quite persistent that he talks to you."

"It doesn't matter."

"Okay. But you do still need to get in there to pack up your things." Exhaling, I dread going there but know I have to eventually. "Mike and Dave have both offered to help, and I'll be there so between the 4 of us we can get all your stuff out in one day, okay? I'll even arrange it with Tyler so he's not there."

"Thank you. I guess I better do it soon so his whore can officially move in," I cringe again.

God, I hate her. Which is totally unfair I know. Logically, I know she's just the other woman in this horrible break-up. I know in my head Tyler is actually the bastard here, but I loved him so much it's easier to hate *her* for all this. It's easier to hate her, but it doesn't actually lessen the hurt I feel from Tyler's betrayal any.

Clearing my head, I change the subject. "What else do I need to know?"

"Um, Kyle's calling because he was also asked his whereabouts that night or if he could think of anyone from school who might want to hurt you. He called Mike who confirmed what Kyle knew anyway from Tyler and he desperately wants to talk to you as well. Oh, and Kelsey called."

"Really?" That one is a surprise.

"Yeah... I think she was both scared by what happened to you at work, and maybe feeling a little guilty because she's always been jealous of you and Mike."

"Really?" I ask again as I try to figure out why.

"Yup. It's that classic attention-seeking bitch thing. You had the boyfriend, you're going places, you're beautiful, you have me," she smirks, "and Mike loves you. As a friend," she quickly adds when my head turns back to her. "Anyway, she probably wanted bad things to happen to you, but wasn't prepared to feel so guilty when they actually did happen to you."

Exhaling a nearly silent *wow,* I need to know, "How do you know that?"

"Because before Griffin was born I was a classic attention-seeking bitch," she says laughing.

"I doubt it," I grin unable to imagine Selena a bitch for even a second.

"No, I totally was," she pushes. "Ask Dave. He may be the prick now, but I was the bitch first. The only difference is I changed and grew up when Griffin came along, and Dave didn't. He wasn't always an asshole though- I kind of made him like that," she sighs.

No longer speaking, I watch Selena finish her drink, and shake her head a little as she takes in the memories of her own past.

After forever, Selena again asks, "What are you thinking?"

Lifting my face to the sun I'm already feeling my skin turning pink which makes the cuts sting a little. "Why do you always ask me that?"

Grinning, she replies, "Cuz I'm a nosey bitch. And if I don't ask, you never tell me. You rarely cry, and you never spill your guts if you're not drunk or if I don't make you."

Laughing a little, I turn my head back to her and reach for her hand.

When she does the same, we stare at each other silently.

Loving Selena and Griffin is the only love I'm ever going to give again. And I figure it's well placed. She's so beautiful and kind and loving not just with me, but really to everyone I've ever seen her interact with.

"I'm never going to love anyone but you and Griffin again," I sigh. Almost tearing up, I fight the sadness until it passes. "I'm done, Selena. My love didn't serve my brother well, and it didn't serve Tyler at all."

Shaking her head she practically moans, "You're too young to think like that, Saige. Things change from one day to the next, and you never know what'll happen for you. You might meet the man of your dreams, or the father of your children in a year from now, or next month, or even tomorrow," she continues trying to persuade me from my fatalistic thoughts.

"I really don't think so. I know what I'm destined to do, and I'll do it. But that doesn't mean I have to ever give my love to anyone again." Admitting that truth is hard, but I know without a doubt I will *never* love again.

"So what will you do?" She whispers so sadly, I feel the tears threatening me again.

"I'll rent the bachelor downstairs, and go back to work. I'll keep fighting this physical pain and sadness, and I'll wait for September to arrive so I can start fresh in a new city, unknown and unhurt."

Sitting up, she blocks the sun from me when she leans closer to my face. "Saige, you're always going to be hurt, no matter what you do or accomplish. You've been hurt in a way that never goes away."

"It doesn't matter."

"It *does* matter," she insists.

"Okay, then I'll make it NOT matter anymore. Starting tomorrow."

Standing to walk back inside, Selena gently touches my shoulder and says only, "You're making a mistake letting this stop you from living or loving again, Saige."

Squeezing her hand on my shoulder I disagree without having to say it. Selena knows I'm stubborn, and I know I'm right.

So I'll start again tomorrow.

*****

After a restless night of fear and nervousness I'm ready for work. Selena helped me cake on make-up to hide the residual bruising around my eyes and cheek, and my lips are still puffy but they no longer bleed if I pull them when speaking.

The stitches above and below my eye are now a weird beige color from the foundation, and though Selena is worried the make-up might somehow cause an infection, I don't care.

I hate the dark medical sutures that were used, and honestly, I find it a little weird there isn't a less obvious alternative the hospital could've used on my goddamn *face*.

Taking a last look, I realize from a distance you really can't see anything specifically though my face is definitely still swollen and misshapen because the scratches and injuries haven't healed enough.

Taking in my nonstandard uniform of black dress pants and a long sweater over my tuxedo blouse, I'm as secure as I can be. My clothing isn't the standard uniform, but it's the best I can do emotionally. I won't wear another skirt for easy access, and I need the long sweater to cover up my body.

Looking at myself one last time before we leave, I know no matter how bad it looks my face doesn't actually tell anyone what happened which is exactly what I want to project to others. I figure if I ignore what happened, they will too.

*****

Walking in together, Selena sets out for the employee lounge with our things and I walk to the family side so I won't be cornered by anyone in the back.

Our shifts begin and end the same time so I don't have to walk in or out of the building alone which was a major fear I couldn't admit to anyone. Selena drove so I don't have to walk to my car in the back parking lot when we finish. And Selena also parked at the side lighted alley, so I don't have to fight my nightmare memories by walking my previous steps from that night in the dark.

Barely acknowledging anyone but Mike with a smile and thumbs up, I look at the boards, see Kelsey hostessing, Hailey and Aileen in the family side and I begin with Hailey and my casual trade off of Diners.

And my day passes.

People clearly see my face but no one asks. My clothing hides the bruises on my body, and truthfully, I play the part of a car accident victim in my head. I have the lie ready and available if anyone does ask outside of my fellow employees, but thankfully no one does.

I know the Diners see my face and want to know what happened. I even have a few repeat customers blatantly stare, looking at me like they're wondering if they know me well enough to ask. Fairing on the side of caution though, no one asks and I ignore the questioning eyes, extra sympathy tips, and the pauses in conversation when I approach.

I ignore what happened because it's in the past.

But I *am* careful.

I no longer joke or smile with men, and I watch myself walking past their tables. I didn't ever really flirt before but I was friendly, which can be misinterpreted as flirting by some. So I've cut it out completely.

I'm not going to be touched by men, and I'm going to make sure I avoid their attention as much as possible. I don't engage in conversations, but I stay polite if it's required.

By 5:00, I'm exhausted and my feet hurt so badly, I almost laugh. After only 10 days off work, it's like my trained feet have turned wimpy. My right shoulder which I didn't realize actually hurt before, has changed from a mild discomfort last week to an actual throb as the hours pass without painkillers. And I'm tired.

Laughing at Aileen who's drooling over a man in her section, I find it a relief I can still joke and laugh a little with the girls like I used to. Besides seeing Mike bringing drinks into the dining room much more frequently than usual, and Selena standing in the galley between sides to sneak peeks at me with encouraging waves or smiles, nothing seems too different for me or unnerving and frightening right now.

It isn't dark outside, I'm surrounded by people, and no one gets close enough for me to fear them physically.

Today has actually been fairly uneventful. We were slow this afternoon and its finally picking up as the dinner crowd begins seating. I may not trade off easily at 6:00 but I really don't mind. Selena and I were just going home to Griffin returning at 7:30, and a movie night later after he's put to bed.

*****

Once home, cracking open a bottle of strawberry Zinfandel, I pour both of us a glass and toast my first day back to work. Feeling the one stitch that didn't completely dissolve in my mouth between my lip and the wineglass, I ignore how annoying it is to suck back my drink.

Moaning when I lift my aching feet on her coffee table, Selena follows suit and before I know it I actually feel somewhat, if not happy, at least not completely *un*happy.

No one bothered me at work, and I wasn't attacked afterward. There were no creepers or bogeymen, and I'm safely locked away for the night with my best friend, a bottle of wine, and soon my little Griffin, who always makes me feel better... Unless he's making me watch back to back episodes of the super annoying, oh my god I HATE this show, Bubble Guppies on the kids network.

Feeling myself almost instantly buzzed, Selena laughs at what a light weight I am drinking and before I know what's happened, I'm covered in a blanket, snuggling with Griffin, watching Bubble friggin Guppies with him asleep in my arms happily.

I'm still sad- *horribly* sad actually, but I can already tell my heart is mending a little sooner than my body is.

I think of Tyler nonstop, but it's not quite as painful as it was even a week ago. Thinking of Tyler is becoming almost soothing, now that I'm remembering all our good times, which was *all* the time before our tragic ending.

Feeling the tears fall down my cheeks once Selena takes Griffin away for bed, I realize my mistake immediately. I'm drunk and lonely, which is turning Tyler into an awesome boyfriend I miss, instead of the asshole boyfriend who hurt me.

Crying softly in the dark, I lie down on my temporary bed- Selena's couch, and ask Tyler what I desperately want to know.

Whispering to take away the intensity of my loneliness I ask him, "Did you ever really love me?"

But when I'm surrounded by more lonely silence, I know I have the only answer that matters anymore.

Silence.

(mis)TRUST

THE PRESENT

(mis)TRUST

CHAPTER 10

Walking into work with Selena, I feel a little less frightened than the day before, though I'm still nervous. It's like I'm afraid something's going to happen, I'm just not afraid of what *already* happened as much.

Actually, I can't understand what I'm feeling because my emotions are still all over the place from one moment to the next.

Entering the employee lounge with Selena, I've decided I'm not going to avoid my coworkers today. If they ask how I am I'll tell them because I doubt they'd ask anything more specific than that anyway.

Wearing a work skirt because my black dress pants were dirtied yesterday, I still cover my upper body in my long sweater. Admittedly, wrapping a huge sweater around myself makes me feel a little less female, and covering up makes me feel a little more comfortable in my body.

Checking my ugly beige makeup one last time, Selena glances over my shoulder. "It's getting so much better," she says about my face. "I already see the stitches over your eye dissolving, and the ones under will be removed on Thursday anyway. So, not too bad."

"But the bruises-"

"Are fading. The cuts are almost completely gone, and with the makeup on your eye it looks like it has dark bags under it, not really bruises anymore. You look more tired now than beat up, Saige," she cringes like that sentence was hard for her to say.

"Okay," I smile to relieve her while placing my purse in my locker before turning back to the mirror.

It's funny, but I was never vain before. I didn't wear much makeup other than mascara and lipstick, but now I seem to stare at myself constantly.

Days used to go by with my long hair tied up in a bun, or tied back in a ponytail with only mascara on my light eyelashes. Tyler never had to wait for me to get ready when we went out because I was pretty much a what you see is what you get kind of woman. I never wore much makeup unless we were going out out and I really did it up.

Now however, I'm always looking at myself, fixing what I can, and hiding what I can't. I'm turning into a woman obsessed with looking in the mirror, and I hate it. But I can't stop myself while I look and feel like this.

Turning from the mirror, I walk to the doors and beg, "Selena? Will you pull that one stitch out of the inside of my lip tonight? It's really annoying and it hasn't dissolved on its own."

"Ah, no problem," she agrees looking totally grossed out as I laugh leaving the employee lounge with her following.

Walking past the bar I wave and smile for Mike when he pauses mixing a drink. Watching him raise an eyebrow, I know what he's asking, so I walk over and hug his side for the first time since that night to show him I'm doing better. We spoke earlier on the phone and he's aware I'm doing better, but he's still freaked out by what happened so I know a hug will ease his mind a little.

Mike has been an amazing friend this past week and a half. Well always actually, but especially after he found me in the parking lot. He's been so attentive, almost big brother like, and I really appreciate it.

I kind of need Mike right now because as insane as this is to admit, Mike's kindness keeps me from hating, or rather *fearing* all men in general after what happened.

Mike reminds me with his actions, and even with his kind words and funny texts that not all men are cheaters, or liars, or even rapists.

Mike reminds me to keep living. And truthfully, Selena and Griffin remind me to keep loving.

Settling in on the family side, Hailey and I trade off smoothly and I start my happy-happy for my customers. On autopilot, my day slowly passes without incident or drama though I still feel a little scared and unnerved from time to time.

Flashbacks still hit me often, and knowing the police have no leads makes me fear everywhere outside of this busy restaurant which feels safe, or Selena's locked and alarmed apartment which feels safer.

I'm not scared here, and my Diners have all been either very polite, or ridiculously helpful when they stack their own plates like I'm an invalid, which is almost too funny to me under the circumstances.

*****

"Hi Saige..." He says behind my back as my world collapses around me.

Dropping my tray of drinks I spin around jumping backward into a table chair and even a Diner before landing on my ass.

"What *happened?!*" He yells reaching for my arm as I scream loudly to get away.

Scrubbing my heels in the carpet I push myself back and away from him quickly until I smash into a booth stopping my movement with a hard snap of my neck.

Crying out, I raise my hands to stop him from hurting me again, screaming so loudly I feel my own face pull and tear the remaining stitches.

"*Saige!*" Mike yells entering the family side at a dead run while Malcolm eases down in front of me on his knees. With his hands outstretched, his face is one of shock and sympathy until he's abruptly knocked aside by Mike shoving him to get to me.

"Leave her the fuck alone!" Mike yells as I stare at Malcolm sitting back up from the floor.

Taking me in with wide eyes Malcolm moans, "Oh, *Saige*..." as he lifts a shaking hand toward me again.

Staring at his sad eyes, hearing his sad voice, I look at his face of horror and realize instantly, "It wasn't you..."

Bursting into tears, I hang my head as the fear constricts my lungs.

God, I didn't know it would be like this. I didn't know I would *feel* like this. I've been so sheltered- just Selena's apartment and work I didn't know what the outside world would feel like when I was finally faced with my fears.

I didn't know I could feel such panic, and I didn't know I would feel such madness so quickly.

Collapsing in Mike's arms pulling me close to him, I fight the panic I felt seeing Malcolm again. Sobbing, I hold onto Mike's sleeve and breathe him deep in my lungs. Mike is safe, and he doesn't sound like the man, and it wasn't him.

And it wasn't Malcolm I understand with such surety, my head clears.

Eventually pulling away from Mike when I feel Selena kneel on the floor beside me, I'm horrified to see everyone in the restaurant watching me lose my mind.

Looking for and finding a still silent, unmoving Malcolm, I let him know, "It wasn't you..." before the panic and fear hit me again when I see Dan standing behind Malcolm.

Realizing I look crazy, screaming and crying with my legs up and spread to cover my face and chest, I notice my skirt hiked up high and the hand print bruise in clear view. Glancing back at Malcolm I see him staring at the outside of my thigh and I know he sees it too by his fixed stare.

Moaning, I feel like such a piece of trash suddenly among all the watching eyes I quickly close my legs to fall at my side.

Grabbing my chest, I try to take in a breath but I can't. My lungs won't work, and my mind is panicking again from the pressure on my chest.

Oh *god,* I remember the knee in my back, and I remember the weight of him holding me down.

"I can't b-breathe cuz his knee is s-still in my b-back," I gasp loudly shaking my head to focus on this reality. "Let me g-go!" I scream trying to push Mike and Selena away from my face.

Pushing them away, I close my eyes to get myself together. Trying to slow down the fear, my adrenaline overload makes me gasp even harder. I can't breathe. I can't move. And I can't get this to stop.

"*Saige!* No one is holding you down again!" Selena yells at me as she grabs my upper arms. "Stop! Breathe slowly and stop panicking. I'm right here with Mike and *no one* is going to hurt you again," she yells loudly in my face.

Nodding, I know what she's saying, but my lungs still won't slow down. My chest is pulling in quick hard breaths without taking in any air. Feeling like I'm suffocating, Selena forces my head down as she starts rubbing my back.

Breathing in shallow bursts, I start to feel better slowly. My lungs aren't as tight, and my head isn't as confused. Feeling her hand on my back, my breathing starts to mimic the slow circles she's rubbing against me until I slowly feel calmer. Her hand is clearing out the panic, and her little shushes and whispered cooing sounds are bringing me back to the present.

I'm not in the parking lot, and his fingers aren't tearing inside me anymore.

After forever it seems, I finally raise my head to Selena's sad eyes waiting for me to surface. Watching my face, she doesn't move, and she doesn't speak.

"I need to get out of here," I whisper when I find my own voice.

Nodding, I stand with Selena's help as she wraps her arm around my shoulders. Exhaling deeply a full body shudder, I turn my face into her chest for a second when I try to find my footing.

Looking around at all the faces in the lounge, I'm mortified. Aileen is standing with a freaked out looking Hershal, and no one else is moving. All the restaurant patrons are unmoving, and even Mike looks like he's sitting in a trance on the floor. I'm mortified until I look back at Malcolm being helped up by an angry looking Dan.

"I'm sorry everyone," I cry as I turn on my heels with Selena holding me tightly. Stepping forward Hershal moves toward me but when he suddenly goes for my face I flinch away shocking us both I think.

Hershal always takes our faces in his hands when he's saying something kind. It's his thing. Hershal holds our cheeks in his hand when he speaks to us like a kind grandfather would. It's what he does, but I panic anyway.

Looking at him in apology, he drops his hand quickly and says softly, "You go home now, honey. But you come back whenever you're ready."

"I'm so sorry. I thought I was ready," I whisper between gasps.

"*I'm* sorry," he shakes his head at me. "You're a good girl, Saige," he sighs not trying to sound like a sexist pig I know, so I accept his words with a nod. "You just call me or Margie when you're ready to return, and we'll be glad to have you back." Taking just my hand in his cold old wrinkly one, Hershal smiles so kindly my tears are immediate.

"I'd like to drive her home," Selena speaks softly and I'm almost soothed into a trace by the quiet around us and the soft voices they use.

Everything has slowed right down for me, I feel almost weightless as I stand here silently.

"Let's go, Saige," Selena pulls me away from the entire restaurant still quiet and unmoving.

Leaving everyone behind us, I don't look back as Selena drags me forward. Bumping Kelsey out of the way, I see actual tears in her eyes and I want to die from the pathetic look of sympathy I receive from her.

This so sucks right now, I giggle crazily until Selena squeezes me tighter into her side.

*****

Plopping back down on our employee couch, I finally exhale fully. Selena is already at our 2 lockers opening and closing them while I wait out the loud banging noises.

Sitting here, I feel completely hollow.

I think my freak out cleared out most of the tension I felt and now I'm not much more than empty inside. I find my mind clearer and my chest lighter than it's been for days.

Maybe I was wrong about the crying thing. Maybe I did need to cry out some of the stress I've been under.

"Can you stand?" Selena asks kneeling in front of me.

"Yes," I sit forward when she opens her arms to hug me. "I'm so sorry," I choke up a little before I get her funny, dirty look.

"Shut up, Saige. Don't be sorry, and don't feel bad. You're just fine. And so what if you freaked out in the middle of the restaurant? I would've too. And I'll kill anyone who says anything about it. Let's just go home, okay? Griffin won't be home until 7:30 so we can talk or drink or cry or just chill out until he gets home."

"Thank you."

Standing with her, Selena hands me my purse and exhales herself before walking back to the door. Taking my hand she just grabs the doorknob when we both freeze hearing the yelling outside the door.

"How badly was she hurt? Who the *fuck* hurt her?!"

"We don't know! But it was *really* bad!" Mike yells back.

"Dan, I swear to god if I find out who touched her I'll-"

"Was it *you!?*" Mike yells as I cringe behind the door.

Leaning against the door listening Selena breathes, "Holy *shit...*" as we hear Mike yell right before there's a loud bang against the wall.

Jumping, Selena and I both scramble to throw open the door to Malcolm holding Mike by the throat against the wall.

Shocked, I scream, "What are you *doing!?*" Which makes them both freeze before Malcolm let's go of Mike instantly and spins around to look at me.

Oh my *god!* Malcolm looks murderous until he quickly changes his expression to one of total calm before my eyes.

Looking at Mike rubbing his throat I'm stunned by what I've seen in the hallway. How the hell are Malcolm and Dan even *in* this hallway?

"Saige, go back inside," Mike demands as Malcolm looks quickly at him then back to me and Selena.

"Can I talk to you for a minute?" Malcolm asks in a gentle voice. Almost begging me with his eyes, he doesn't move and I *can't* move.

Finding myself standing behind Selena, I'm embarrassed I'm using her as a shield. I'm actually hiding myself behind her like a coward and using her body to keep me away from everything that could hurt me again.

Eventually finding my voice, I croak a pathetic *why* as Selena stiffens in front of me.

"Hershal's calling the police," Mike huffs.

"Good," both Selena and Malcolm say at the same time which surprises us all I think.

"I just want to talk to you for a minute. I promise I won't hurt you," Malcolm says with such emotion in his voice my eyes fill immediately.

"I know," I cry before quickly covering my mouth.

When Selena turns on me her eyes are wide, almost imploring me to either stop talking, or to explain myself. I don't know what she wants, and I don't know what to do I'm so confused.

"Malcolm didn't hurt me," I whisper for her only. I might not know who hurt me, but I do know who didn't. And Malcolm didn't hurt me any more than Mike did.

"*Please?* I just want to know what happened to you," Malcolm repeats calmly again. "Dan and I aren't here to hurt you, Saige," he says so sincerely I glance over his shoulder to a silently nodding Dan leaning against the wall behind them.

"Why are you here? Are you following me?" I beg desperately while we all still stand in the hall and doorway frozen.

"No. Well, yes," Malcolm says quickly. "We play basketball every Tuesday, so we came here last Tuesday for dinner. But yes, I was hoping to see you again. You weren't here last Tuesday though, so before the game tonight Dan and I decided to come back for the food and maybe to see you. But I didn't know you were..." he stops speaking suddenly like he can't finish his thoughts. "Can we please come in and talk to you for a minute? We'll leave the door open, and he can stay," Malcolm gestures toward Mike still just standing against the wall like he's as confused as the rest of us are by Malcolm's insistence.

"Um..." Feeling so awkward suddenly, I don't know what to say.

"Yes, you can come in for a minute. Mike go tell Hershal we're going to talk to them briefly, but I'll call the police so fucking fast your head'll spin if you scare her again. *Got* it?!" Selena barks.

"Yes," Malcolm grins briefly at Selena before his eyes turn serious again when he looks at me.

Stepping behind the door with Selena covering my body, Malcolm slowly walks inside followed by Dan.

"I have to go check the bar, but I'll be right back," Mike adds staring at both Dan and Malcolm who don't move from their positions.

Waiting for something, Selena doesn't move from the doorway, and I stay right to the side kind of behind her.

After Mike takes one more assessing look, Malcolm crosses the room near the bathroom door and Dan leans against the wall furthest away from me and Selena.

"What happened to you, Saige?" Malcolm asks just above a whisper.

"Why don't you know?" Selena asks instead. "The police were supposed to question you both."

"They didn't," he shakes his head just as Selena moans *fuckers* beside me. Nodding at her, Malcolm looks at my face again and asks, "Why were they supposed to contact me?"

"All of you," Selena continues. "Saige was attacked the night after you and him," she points at Dan, "And that Keith asshole stopped by the restaurant."

"Last, last Friday?"

"Yes. After work," Selena speaks for me still as I watch the interaction playing out. "She doesn't know who did it, but she thinks it was one of you," she growls which makes Malcolm flinch in front of us.

"It was NOT me or Dan, I promise you. After we left the bar I dropped Dan off and I went home."

"How do *we* know that?" Selena questions again what I'm thinking about Dan.

"You know it wasn't me. Don't you, Saige?" Malcolm asks with both a sincere and a somewhat desperate sounding voice.

"Yes."

When my body starts shaking uncontrollably, I hold onto Selena's arm. When my teeth start chattering, I quickly become almost light-headed or something. I don't know why I'm suffering like this when everyone is so calm around me, but I can't stop my body from freaking out suddenly.

"Sit down, Saige," Dan says making me jump at his deep voice. "You need to sit down for a minute. You're coming down from the shock and fear, but you'll be okay in a few minutes."

When Selena quickly moves me back to the couch, I see Mike watching us from the doorway again. Sitting, I see my face in the mirror across from us and I instantly cover up as I panic.

All my makeup is smeared, and the bruises are showing, and even the dark sutures are visible under my eye. Though not half as bad as I was right after it happened, I still look pretty friggin' awful right now.

Pulling over a chair, Malcolm sits 3 feet from us and inhales deeply before speaking. He seems to almost be calming himself before he looks back at my face which is both embarrassing and kind of painful for me.

"I know I look terrible," I moan self-consciously as he flinches again.

"Aye," he replies in his brogue which naturally makes me smile for a split second. "You do look terrible and I can't stand it," he speaks in a horrible emotion-filled voice leaning closer to us until I unconsciously move further away from him. Straightening back up and away, he continues, "I can't stand seeing you look like that, or imagining what you went through. So why don't you tell me and Dan what happened so we can maybe help you?"

"How?" Selena asks. "The police know everything and they said they were investigating. And you should have been at least asked where you were that night after you left here." Shaking her head, she huffs, "I don't understand why they didn't talk to you guys. They talked to everyone else," she says almost like an accusation.

"I really don't know. But I didn't see Saige after we left the bar that night, and I did go straight home after dropping off Dan around midnight."

"And I was home for the rest of the night with my wife," Dan adds unmoving from the wall.

Listening to Dan's voice, I'm almost one hundred percent sure it wasn't him either. I think I would recognize his deep voice as the man who spoke to me that night.

"Where were you hurt?" Malcolm asks and my whole body starts shaking again.

Where? Like what part of my body? Wanting to cry I'm so humiliated, I can't believe he's asking me where I was hurt.

"Was it at home, or somewhere else?"

"*Oh!* It was here after work. In the parking lot."

"She was attacked walking to her car at ten to one in the morning. After everyone had left, she snuck out before Mike could follow her to the motel, and she was attacked until Mike came outside and saved her." When Selena says everything so matter of fact, I feel almost absent from the emotions behind the conversation itself.

"Why were you going to a motel?" Malcolm questions.

"None of your business," Selena jumps in. "Why are you sitting here interrogating us? It should be us questioning *you*. And especially that asshole Keith," she seethes.

"Oh, I'll be questioning my friends later. And believe me if anyone I know hurt her they'll pay for it," he growls so angrily I can tell Selena feels the same fear I do hearing his voice.

"I think we're done here. Can you please leave? I'm going to call the police and rip a piece out of them for this bullshit 'investigation'," she quotes. "They're not investigating at all apparently."

"Okay, we'll leave," Malcolm agrees standing slowly and kind of away from me. "Can I please drive you home?"

"*What?* No!" Selena yells again even as I shake my head no.

"Then we'll follow you to make sure you're okay," he continues and I'm just stunned by his pushiness but also by how determined he seems. "Look, you can't stop us from following you to make sure you're okay, Miss...?" He stares at Selena basically asking her name but she sits still and glares back instead of answering.

"Look, Malcolm, we appreciate this chivalrous thing you're doing, but we'll be fine. No one is going to hurt her with me so-"

"You're like 10 pounds heavier than she is! What the hell are *you* going to do to protect her?!" Malcolm yells as we all silence for a second until Selena finally bursts out laughing.

"*10* pounds heavier than *Saige*? Why thank you, Malcolm. Um, are you single, honey?" Selena suddenly teases and I can't hold it in.

As the two of us howl with laughter at his inadvertent compliment and stupid guy inability to understand women and their weight, Selena holds my hand until we eventually settle. When we see Malcolm's *what the fuck* face as he turns to Dan and Mike then back to us, I exhale more of my tension and Selena laughs all over again.

When she finally stops laughing Selena stands over me in front of

Malcolm. "Please don't follow us home. Saige doesn't need any more fear or upset right now. And being followed by a stranger will scare her even if you mean well, right?" She turns to me and waits for my nod.

"Fine. Will you at least take my number? Here," leaning closer to the table at the end of the couch, Malcolm quickly scribbles his number on a napkin and hands it over to Selena. "Please use it if you need to. For anything at all," he huffs like he hates leaving us like this.

Looking around her to me, Malcolm squats down on his haunches and reaches for my hand before I quickly pull it away. Exhaling deeply, he doesn't try to touch me again. "Saige, please call me if you need anything at all. If you get scared, or think someone is going to hurt you again. *Anything*, okay?"

When he just pauses a foot away from me I'm totally confused and somewhat overwhelmed by him. He's acting like he knows me or cares about me, or likes me or something. He's done nothing but be kind to me all 3 times we've met, but it really doesn't feel right, or normal, or I don't know... I'm confused by his intensity and his attention on me.

"*Please?*" He practically begs and I find myself nodding for some reason I can't explain. "Thank you," he sighs before standing.

Walking up to Mike, Malcolm extends his hand and apologizes. "I'm very sorry I grabbed you in the hall. And thank you for saving her," he says heavily as they shake. "Please call me if she gets into trouble again?" He begs Mike and again I'm just stunned by his intensity.

"Take care, Saige," Dan says in his deep voice before smiling at Selena and shaking hands with Mike in the doorway as well.

"Holy *shit*." Selena seems to feel the same way I am when she drops back down on the couch beside me. "Well, that was intense," she deadpans as we both start laughing again.

"Can we pleeeeease go home now?"

"Of course," she rises immediately as I do.

"Call me when you get home," Mike adds walking to me for a hug. "Are you okay?" He asks in my ear.

Pulling away, I smile a little for him before answering. "I'm okay. Just weirded out."

"Are you sure about the other guy?" He asks as Selena steps in closer.

Nodding, I'm sure. "Yes. There's something about him, or I guess *not* about him that tells me it wasn't him. I think I would've noticed that

deep voice. I don't know, but I'm really sure it wasn't either of them."
"Okay. Good."
Walking past Mike together, I squeeze his hand and Selena gives him
her own huge hug. "We'll call as soon as we get home. Have a good
night, and tell Hershal I'll be in tomorrow," Selena says as we leave.

Quickly leaving the restaurant through the side lounge doors, I see Dan
immediately at the end of the alley by the sidewalk. Lifting his phone to
his ear, he actually smiles and waves at us.
"Come on," Selena huffs as we round her car. "Do you think they'll
follow us anyway?" She questions starting to pull out quickly.
"I think so," I agree watching Dan jump into a big dark SUV pulling up in
front of the alley as we pass.
"Wanna have some fun?" Selena asks grinning.
"God, yes," I grab onto the dash as she peels down the street crazily.
Turning on the radio, Lady Gaga's Bad Romance is playing, so Selena
cranks it loud and throws us into 4th gear before I even know what's
happening. It's only 4:32 in the afternoon, and though not quite rush
hour, the traffic is definitely picking up.
Buzzing around cars, and even swerving through the bicycle lane once,
I can't stop my laughter while Selena keeps her focused intensity as she
drives.
"If you get arrested, I'm running away with Griffin," I giggle when she
turns right so quickly I actually slam into her shoulder. "McDonalds! I
need McDonalds," I scream when I see the Golden Arches.
"You're so weird," she laughs. "Most women eat ice cream or
chocolate, or get drunk when stressed out. You eat fucking
McNuggets," she laughs again with me as she pulls into the drive thru.
Slamming on the breaks behind the 4 car line up, we both look behind
us to see the SUV idling beside the restaurant waiting.
"Dammit, I've lost my edge," she laughs. "When Dave and I were
younger and fighting, I could always lose him in my car." Pouting, she
adds, "I'm getting old. Oh, and I think I really like this Malcolm guy."

Finally pulling up to her spot near the side entrance, we watch the SUV
drive by slowly with one honk as Selena laughs and gives him the finger.

CHAPTER 11

Answering my cell on the second ring, Selena speaks immediately. "Everyone is concerned about you, and Tyler stopped by again to harass me. Hershal officially told him he wasn't welcomed back, and after his initial surprise, he left totally pissed off. But he did ask Mike again to ask you to call him though."

"Okay."

"And there's something here for you. Um, a gift box was dropped off by courier and it says it's from Malcolm MacNeil. *Fuck*, Saige... I want to open it so badly. But I won't," Selena groans almost begging for permission to let her open it.

"From Malcolm?" I ask unable to hide the excited surprise in my voice.

"Yup. I'll be home in 2 hours and Mike's got tonight off, so he's coming over for a drink with us. Oh, and Griffin is staying with Dave overnight."

"You didn't tell me that," I pout.

"Dave just called and asked me if he could keep him. His grandmother is visiting, and Dave and his mom want to show off Griffin. He promised to bring him home in the morning though."

"Okay," I agree like I have any say in what she does with her child. *Seriously?* "Sorry. I just miss him when he's not here," I admit pathetically.

"Awwww... That's sweet. He loves you too. Have you eaten?"

"Not yet. I was going to order pizza for us when you got home."

"K. I'll see you soon," she giggles obviously excited to bring me my whatever the hell from Malcolm.

Waiting for Selena and Mike, I can't stop thinking about Malcolm. Actually, I think about him constantly, always followed by thinking about Tyler afterward. I think about Malcolm with a slight excitement, then my brain counters that excitement with sad thoughts of Tyler.

And I don't understand either of them.

Tyler's behavior and what he did still shocks the hell out of me. Tyler changing so significantly makes me weary of my ability to understand or even trust men. And Tyler's actions make me angry still.

I don't know why he keeps looking for me, and I don't understand why he keeps calling Selena acting like he gives a shit about me. I know he said he still loves me, but he wanted her more. So go then. I haven't contacted him even once since we broke up, yet he's still hovering around me for some reason.

In contrast, Malcolm's intensity scares the hell out of me. I don't know why he was so intense, and I don't understand why he keeps coming around. Yes, we laughed a little before everything happened 2 weeks ago, but that was it. We shared a laugh and a Scottish accent. Once. But he's acting like a concerned friend, or like an over protective big brother to me. And honestly, I don't need either in my life.

"Open it!" Selena yells throwing open her apartment door. Not even dropping her purse, she runs to me in the kitchen and practically tackles me with the box.

"Okay," I laugh. "But calm down, would ya? Pour a drink or something," I smile pulling out the huge bottle of Zinfandel from the fridge.

"Did you go out today?" She asks calming instantly. Nodding, I don't even speak before she's hugging me. "Good for you. Were you scared?"

"A little. But it was daytime and I walked with my hand on my phone and my car keys ready." Stopping, she's looking at me so motherly, I feel kind of stupid. "You know when I go away to school I'm going to have to go out alone all the time."

"I know. But that's 4 months away, and you're doing so well for only 2 weeks since you were hurt," she says as we call that night.

I hate the words attacked, raped, sexually assaulted, beaten up, or basically anything else that describes that night. So in reference we all seem to say 'when I was hurt' which feels less specific and more abstract. Without a definitive term, my memories of what happened aren't quite as vivid and painful as they could be.

"Can you open the box now?" She grins bouncing again.

Taking the box, I walk to the couch and place it on the coffee table. Splitting the tape along the edges with my nails, I lift the tissue paper to...

"Wow. What the hell is- *oh.* Pepper spray?" I realize turning over the little canister in my hand. There's also a little knife shaped almost like brass knuckles so it stays in your hand. When I push the little button on the handle making it snap open we both jump laughing.

"Is that a whistle?" Selena asks blowing into it gently but nearly bursting our ear drums it's so loud. "And that's a...?"

"I don't know."

Turning over the necklace it has a cool black stone pendant dangling from it. Flipping it over I scream when an alarm blares so suddenly my shaking hands can't put the black pendant back on the rope chain. When Selena rips it out of my hand she has a hard time putting the pendant back in the little slot on the chain too. Until she finally does.

Christ! The silence afterward is so quiet and my ears are ringing so loudly, I feel like I'm hearing the alarm still.

"That was so loud!" She yells as we both start laughing. "What's that?" Looking at the last item, it looks like an old school flip phone. It's basically the same shape, though it's bulkier with weird antennas or claws at the end.

"Holy *fuck!* It's a Taser. Look," she points to the wide button in the middle as I drop it back in the box quickly. "Push it," she prompts and when I do we both jump again. The electrical current flashes blue so quickly from between the claws I drop it back in the box as soon as it charges the air between us.

Absolutely stunned by my gift, I lean back on the couch and exhale slowly. I don't know what to think, but I do know half this shit is illegal to have. And just *wow.*

"Well, if that doesn't say lovin' I don't know what does," Selena muses to my silence. "Are you going to call him? I still have his number."

"I don't know. What the hell would I say? Thank you for the weapons of mass destruction? Jesus, this is so out of my comfort zone. I mean Tyler bought me flowers sometimes, not this shit."

"It's really kind of sweet- in a Terminator *I'll be back* kind of way. He obviously cares enough to send you this, and he did look really bothered when he saw you were hurt. I know he called D'Vecseys on Wednesday and asked Mike if you were okay, and though he could've asked for your number, he didn't. Mike was surprised, but I think I know why he didn't- he saw your reaction to him so I think he's keeping his distance for you. He could send this stuff to show he cared without making you feel awkward if he called though."

"*This* is awkward," I point to the box and the note I see before reading.

Hi Saige

I realize this gift is probably awkward for you, and as far as gifts go probably a first as well. I just couldn't think of anything else I could give or send you that was as helpful as these things are. The taser and pepper spray are technically illegal to carry on you, but not illegal to have, however that works. So if you don't keep them in your purse, then they aren't considered 'concealed weapons.' I suggest hanging both from your key chain so they're in plain sight and no longer concealed.

I would like you to know I'm very sorry you were attacked that night. I did NOT have anything to do with that, nor did Dan, I know for a fact. We have both spoken to the police, and I believe they didn't ask us any questions because Dan has a brother on the police force so they assumed we weren't guilty. We did ask our friends from the night we met, and almost all of them have solid alibis. Keith says he was with his sister well after he left the restaurant but we're looking into that. We're also aiding the police in any way we can, I promise.

I'm not sure when you're going back to work, so I'm not sure when or if I'll see you any time soon. But here's my number again. Please feel free to use it for anything at any time. I would still love to grab a coffee with you when you're ready.

Please stay safe,

Malcolm

P.S. Your friend is awesome. Dan and I haven't had so much fun tailing a woman in years.

"Wow," I exhale.

"Um, Saige?" Selena asks pulling her arm through my own when I look over. "I think I'm a little in love with this guy," she smiles and I can see why. "He thinks I only weigh ten pounds more than your one hundred, *and* he thinks I'm an awesome driver. Can *I* call him?" She asks teasing.

Leaning against the back of the couch with her, I'm at a total loss for words. Glancing at the box again I actually do see how sweet his gift is. *Strange* but sweet. Somehow I don't even think having coffee with him would be so bad. But I'm just not there.

"I'm not ready for coffee. I'm messed up, and scared, and Tyler is-"

"Fucking someone else," Selena says so abruptly I'm nearly winded. Feeling the sadness settle in deeply again, I'm hurt by what she said.

"I can't believe you just said that." Pulling away, I need to get out of here for a while. I need to get out but I'm not sure where to go.

"I wasn't trying to be mean, I was trying to help you move past Tyler. He's an asshole, Saige. But Malcolm seems like a really good guy, and maybe you should-"

"Maybe *you* should shut the hell up! You have NO idea what I'm thinking and you have no idea how I feel about Tyler. He was my boyfriend of 4 years, Selena. And 4 years doesn't just go away in a few weeks, no matter *who* he's fucking!"

"It should!" She yells back.

"Okay. I need a break from this. You've been an amazing friend, and I don't want to ruin our friendship over this so I'm going to go out for a while." Walking through the living room, I grab my purse and keys headed for the front door.

"Saige, this is just a fight. People fight, you know? It doesn't mean you have to leave, and it doesn't mean *I'm* leaving you," she says so emotionally I'm stunned for a second.

"Do you really think I'm so weak and fucked up that I think that way?"

"Sometimes, yes. You're a good person, Saige. But you've been left too many times at your age and I think you're a little emotionally messed up over it."

"Are you talking *abandonment* issues?" I kind of laugh at her.

"Between your dad and brother, and now Tyler I think you just assume anything bad between you and someone else means they're going to leave you. But it doesn't mean that. We're having a fight, Saige. That's all," she says again so emotionally I don't know who she's more sad for.

115

"I'm well aware of fighting, Selena. But I feel hurt and sad and I don't want to take the last few weeks out on you if I stay right now. That's all I'm doing. I'm leaving before we make things worse."

"Mikes coming over soon. Look, I'm sorry if I upset you."

"It doesn't matter. You *did* upset me, but I just need a break. Can I come back though?" I ask desperately.

Staring at Selena, I realize I really am at a loss without her. Oh, and I think she may be right about me. I never really thought about it, but yes, I do think like that sometimes. And so far it's always been true.

"Of course you can. You better," she grins walking toward me. "Where are you going?"

Huffing, I say all I can. "I don't know. Just out, but I shouldn't be long."

"K. I'll leave some wine and pizza for you," she smiles before hugging me tightly. Whispering in my ear, "I'm sorry I hurt your feelings," she holds onto me tightly.

"It's okay," I squeeze back.

"I just want something to go right for you now, and I feel like Malcolm is kind of right. I don't want you sad and lonely forever because of a douchebag," she says as I huff a laugh against her.

"2 weeks isn't forever, Selena. It's nothing. And I *am* getting better."

"Will you call Malcolm? If for nothing else then to thank him for his very thoughtful, albeit intense gift?" She smirks.

"I'll call him later to thank him only. I'm not ready for coffee or anything else right now. Christ, I'm not even back to work yet."

Nodding, she watches me leave for wherever I'm running to as I hold in the tears I want to cry over everything suddenly.

*****

Deciding I need a long drive, I find myself unbelievably on the turnpike to New Haven. Thinking of my mother and what she felt when my father left us, I don't know if I'll tell her about Tyler or not. All I do know is I want to see her suddenly.

Whether because the way my mum is will force me to move past all this bullshit with Tyler so I don't become like her, or whether I just want the sympathy of a woman who knows what it's like to be the one who wasn't wanted, I'm not sure.

CHAPTER 12

Pulling into my mum's driveway 2 hours later I hope to hell she's home. I learned an hour ago when I was going to call to give her the heads up I forgot my cell on the side table at Selena's, so my mum doesn't know I'm coming, and I don't know if she goes out on Friday nights now.

I know she didn't, or actually she *couldn't* when she was drinking herself stupid after my father left us. But that was a few years ago now and she tells me she's still sober, so there's a chance she does have actual plans on a Friday night. She may even be going out with one of her 2 girlfriends from the Scottish Rite where she's maintained her membership since she arrived here 26 years ago to follow my father.

Knocking on the door there's a long pause which makes me nervous until I hear her high voice yell 'comin' through the door. When it's thrown open, her shock turns to a huge smile followed by a sharp look.

"What in the bloody hell happ'ened to yer face?" She asks opening the screen door widely.

"Car accident," I lie quickly.

Turning me this way and that so she can stare she asks, "Were ye no wearin' a seatbelt then?"

"No. Ah, Selena and I had just sat in the car when we were hit from behind, so I hit my face on the dashboard." Shiiiiit. I hate lying in general, but with my mother it's nearly impossible. She has a freaky sixth sense for lying she picked up when my father was cheating on her.

"Well, ye lok like a dog's arse," she mumbles making me laugh. "Did ye no think ta tell me?"

"It's no big deal, just a fender bender. My face took the worst of it."

"Well, come in then. Are ye stayin' or letting the air oot?"

"I'm staying. Would you mind if I spend the night?"

"Aye, of course. I'm fetchin' to hae a date at 8 on the time, but I'll be home after the cinema. Would ye like to come wee me and Mary?"

Feeling a little disappointed she won't cancel going to the movies for me, I smile through it. "No, I'm good. I'll just watch TV til you come back. When are you leaving?"

"Quarter past 7. Come in wee ye," she tugs me toward the kitchen. "Ye dunna hae a bag?"

"No. This was a last minute visit." Flinching, I realize I screwed up instantly. I don't visit my mother except on specific holidays, and I've never come without Tyler.

"Ah, so you and the fella hae ended it, no?" Blushing, I look down quickly at the table before she continues. "What did the dirty, rotten scoundrel do?"

"*Scoundrel?*" I laugh. "Mum, you've been here for twenty five years. Don't you think it's time to drop the old school Scottish vocabulary?" I grin at her quick outrage.

"I'll hae you know, its people here who canna speak. We from the ol' coun'try started yer language, but it was YOU folk who slauuuughtered it," she shakes her head with a laugh turning for the kettle on the stove.

Remembering Alec, I laugh with her. Alec used to tease her mercilessly about her accent and words from 'the old country'. Alec would get her so worked up she was barely coherent yelling at him, smacking his arse with a spoon while he laughed and ran around the kitchen taunting her.

Alec would tease her until she would end up yelling in a weird Scottish kind of unintelligible gibberish with barely understood words and sentences as I watched them both laughing my ass off when she chased him through the house with her spoon. It was usually after 5 minutes of her completely losing her shit that Alec would finally grab me and throw me at her so he could run upstairs to his locked bedroom for safety.

And that's when she'd yell with her spoon raised up high to the gods, "That wee bastard will be the death o' me," with a smile.

And he *was* the death of her, I realize.

At least in part.

Finding myself crying at the table, my mum sits down in the chair beside me. "Drink yer cuppa," is all she says because that's all there is with her. My mum thinks anything can be fixed with a cup of tea.

"You know I hate tea," I grin wiping my eyes.

"Well, that's half yer problem, no?"

"I guess."

Patting my hand she prompts me. "Tell me, love."

"I miss Alec," I say accidentally which effectively ends our first night together since Christmas.

"Aye." Rising from her chair, my mum is out of the kitchen before I even finish my sentence or thought.

Exhaling deeply I realize talking about Alec is out, cheating is out, the attack- *forget* it. So that leaves... why the hell did I come here?

Taking a little sip of tea, I spit it back in the cup without getting caught and cringe. I *hate* tea, but I always try to like it because 'There's no a good Scottish lass without tea in her blood,' my mum always says.

Sitting in my mum's old fashioned kitchen of blue wallpaper with big white roosters I almost laugh at how ugly it is. I mean, I guess rooster wallpaper was in style once upon a time, for like a week. But *really?* After this many years, she hasn't changed a damn thing in this house. Alec's pictures are exactly where they were beside mine on the mantel, his room is the same as when he left it, and I bet if I checked, my father's leftover clothing would still be in his half of their old closet.

She's in an absolute time warp, and I don't find it comforting like some people would. I find it horribly stifling. Almost angrily, I want to rip down the ugly blue valances in the kitchen windows, and I want to scrape off the goddamn rooster wallpaper I've always hated.

God, I don't know what I thought I'd find here, but I haven't found it. My mum is exactly the same, and this house is exactly the same. It's just me who isn't the same anymore.

Everything here is cautious, unchanging, and inflexible.

"There's bread from the Scots shop in the fridge if yer hung'ry," she says from the doorway.

Dressed impeccably, my mum may not change her home decor or even her perfect blonde blunt hairstyle, but her clothing has always been very modern and elegant. She's actually a very attractive woman at 46 when I look at her objectively.

"Mum? Can we redecorate your kitchen tomorrow?" Looking around, I see her eyes widen as a slight panic sets in. She's never changed anything for them. "They're not coming back," I whisper staring at her beautiful green eyes as she nods slowly.

Breathing deeply, my mum stares at me like she's thinking, but it isn't until she tears up a little that I realize she's never thought about her kitchen before. "I'm well a'ware thur no com'in back, Saige."

"So can we? I'll pay if you want?"

"Dunna be stuuu'pid," she growls. "I can pay for some paint. I've always hated bloody cocks any'way," she says so seriously I pause for one second before I burst out laughing.

Cocks? Oh my *god!* I'm dying, and as she blushes deeply I see the exact moment she realizes what she just said.

"Per'vert," she shakes her head laughing at me.

Trying to stop my giggles, I look at the clock and tell her to get going.

"Ye know... I always want'ed a modern black and white kitchen. Do ye think ye canna pull that off this week'end?"

"Sure, I can!" I jump up excited. Looking around at all the white cupboards, I don't think it'll be that hard once all the cocks are gone, I start giggling again. *Seriously?* So not a word I ever thought I'd hear my mum say.

"I'm ootta here. I'll be back by half past 10 I'm sure."

"Have fun," I giggle one last time as she grins and kisses the top of my head before pulling my hair.

"Yer gonna be bald by fort'y if ye dunna stop with these tails, Saige," she says walking out of the kitchen like she has since I was a little girl.

Looking around the hideous kitchen of my childhood, I lean to the left of the table and pick at a seam with my nails. Pulling off a small piece of wallpaper starts a manic ripping of anything I can reach, and within minutes I have sections and pieces all over the table and floor. Standing on the chairs, I've never been so happy to throw cocks to the floor as I am right now. Laughing again at my mum's terminology, I rip off my hoodie and get serious.

2 hours later, I have the whole full wall and all the wallpaper above the counters removed. The brown wallpaper backing is still there, but I'll buy a steamer tomorrow to get it off as well. Thinking of a black and white kitchen, I'm not sure what to do about the flecked greenish blue countertop, but I'm sure Lowe's can help with that as well.

Satisfied that I can't get any more wallpaper off, I tidy the counters, table and floor of the bits of wallpaper and settle in with a gross cup of instant coffee- the only kind my mum has in her house for us *heathens*. And after toasting some Scottish soda bread which is delicious in my empty stomach, I'm ready for bed.

Wandering around my mum's sterile, ugly home, I realize how little I've actually thought of Tyler today. I do still, but not as much, and somehow I almost find that sad in its own way.

I'm a little more comfortable, or maybe ready to let our past go. It still hurts like a bitch realizing the one person you loved beyond all others is gone. And it's sad to say goodbye to the entire life you had planned, but I think I'm almost ready to face it now.

The attack right after our breakup gave me the reason to focus on something else. The attack also allowed me to suffer physically what I was emotionally suffering both by Tyler and his actions and by someone else that night. Now that I've had a little time though, I think I need to prioritize myself and what I want for me from now on since things have changed for me so drastically and completely.

Tyler doesn't have to change anything anymore to be with me. He's kept our apartment, he's already enrolled in our current school for next year, and he has the woman he wants to be with.

So now I have to change my plans, and I'll do it alone. I'll finish law school away from my current life in a different school in a different city away from my current self and my old boyfriend and my old friends. I'll set out on a new course that I make on my own. It's what I did the first time I went away to school anyway, so I'll just do it again.

When I left for University 4 years ago I hadn't planned on meeting Tyler my first week there, and I hadn't planned on being a couple for the next 4 years of my life. At the time I started school I was 18, single, and young. I was also scared but determined.

So I'll do it again. Not as young, just as determined, and single once more.

After this last escapist weekend, I'll go back to work for the money I desperately need, and I'll go back to Selena's for 2 more weeks. I'll move all my shit out of Tyler's place next weekend for a storage locker, and I'll rent the little bachelor for a few months until I leave for good.

And I know it's for good this time. I'll always visit Mike, and Selena and Griffin, but Midland isn't my home any more than Cambridge will be. But maybe I'll make it become my new start.

Maybe Boston can be my new home for good, and my fresh start forever.

(mis)TRUST

CHAPTER 13

After a hilarious drive to Lowe's, followed by Home Depot, I've learned new and interesting ways to swear at passing motorists using everyday words in unimaginable ways. My mum is hands down a horrible driver, but according to her it's every other motorist on the road. Oh, and apparently I'm old enough to hear her swear now, which is funny, and a little scary actually. Honestly, she's got the most messed up potty mouth I've ever heard in my life.

Returning to her home, she's so excited about her new kitchen, I feel it with her. Someone from Home Depot should be by this afternoon after 3 to measure and order the new sleek black countertops she splurged on, and in the meantime she and I are steaming the hell out of the walls before painting the walls and cupboards bright white hopefully first thing tomorrow morning.

After Home Depot we stopped at a kitchen outfitters and she bought new canisters, placemats, dish towels, curtains, and bowls in bright red to have as an accent color to her new black and white kitchen. She was lucky her fridge, stove and floors were already white because I have a feeling she would've bought new appliances too.

As it is my idea to rip down the hideous rooster wallpaper has cost her thousands, but she doesn't seem unhappy about it at all.

"This is so ex'citin'," she says for the hundredth time when we pull into her driveway. I can't wait to see what her new kitchen will look like, especially in 3 weeks when the countertops are installed. I've even promised to come back sooner than later so I can see it all completed.

Grabbing the bags of supplies and stuff, we enter her house and walk straight to the kitchen. Running to change, my mum is almost childlike with her excitement which is awesome to see- especially when I follow her jumping every second step up the stairs to change into the new clothes I had to buy for myself this weekend.

Thinking about her life, I spent years watching her quiet insanity, and previously her drunken hostility, so this fun version of her is amazing.

*****

"Would ye like ta talk, wee Saige?" My mum suddenly asks from the doorway. Pausing with a bag in my hand, I feel strange, and sad, and just unsure of everything at the moment. I don't know if she means talk talk, or just casual talk, because my mum rarely does emotional or heavy conversations if she can help it.

"What did the fella do?"

Exhaling as I turn, I say the unimaginable to my mother. "He cheated on me in my own home, and broke my heart."

"Aye. Go on then."

"That's it. He shocked the hell out of me, and I've been having a hard time dealing with it," I say without emotion so she doesn't get weird with me, or maybe *on* me. I don't know with her where she'll go from one minute to the next discussing cheating.

"Can I give ye a wee bit of advice?" Nodding, I mumble sure but brace myself for the coming storm. "Sit down," she drags her own chair from beneath the table as I place the bag on the counter to sit across from her. "Are ye lis'nin'?"

"Yes."

"Nev'er ev'er give yer heart to a man, Saige. He won't apprec'iate it, and he won't value it. No man does. Its thur nat'ure I think. They may love ye but they dunna know what to do wee a heart that's been giv'in to them. So they break it."

"What?" I ask because that's the extent of my vocabulary all of a sudden.

"I've loved three men in me life. My father drank him'self deed, yer father left, and Alec did what he did. Not one of them loved me back, and not one of them didna break the heart I gave 'em. So let this be a less'en to ye."

"But- *what*?" Shaking my head I try to find something to say, but really I have no argument because they did the same thing to me. My father left, Alec did what he did, and Tyler cheated then left me. "But aren't you lonely?" I question desperately.

"No. Why would I be? I go oot if I want ta. I hae friends I like. If I fancy a date I take one. And if I wanna get wee someone, I do. I'm not lonely *and* I get to keep the litt'le piece 'o my heart I hae left."

"But I want to have children one day," I gasp kind of freaked out.

124

"Well, ye no need a man for tha. There's ways to avoid tha altogether now."

"I know but-"

Cutting me off she says what I didn't want to ever hear. "That fella of yers had lust in his eyes, Saige. I saw his lust for ye, so I knew it would be for someone else as well. Ye canna have lust with someone that lasts for'ever. It just dunna happen. I know," she shakes her own head before smiling. "But yer a good lok'in lass, so ye can find some sex if ye want ta but ye dunna have to give anyone else yer heart. Why bother?"

"I don't know... because it's natural to want to be loved?"

"Says who? What has love ev'er given ye back, Saige?"

"Ummm..." Well, this is bizarre. And awful.

Love has given me nothing back. But I feel like I'm supposed to protest what she's saying, or at least *try* to protest. Love should be important somehow though if I'm really honest, I'm leaning more toward what she's saying.

Holy *shit,* what a messed up conversation.

Desperately thinking as she waits patiently, I throw out the ridiculous. "I just met a man who seems like kind of a good guy, at least from what I've seen so far. Oh! And he's Scottish," I add hoping she'll say something positive now.

"Ah, so he'll be good in bed but he'll eventually drink him'self deed or leave ye for a diff'rent lass. He'll no love ye enough to be sober, or he'll no love ye enough to be kind and true to ye. That's the Scotsmen I know."

"But daddy wasn't Scottish!"

"Aye. And he was nev'er good in the sack. He's not who I was ref'errin to, though it applies ta him as well."

Bursting into tears, I almost laugh too. Fuck, my mum's a trip. And I *really* didn't need that information about my father's bedroom skills.

"Well, shit mum... You're like the worst pep-talker ever," I laugh cry a little more. "Why can't you be all supportive and shit?"

"I am support'in ye. Go to school. Be a lawyer. Work yer arse off like ye always have. Just dunna love, and ye should be good," she pats my hand like she's said the right words suddenly.

Even smiling at me, my mum rises from the table and grabs the bag of red ceramic bowls from the floor to place on the table. "Now, how do we get this crap off the walls?" She asks lifting the wallpaper steamer and water bottle in the air.

And that's it for soul-defining pep-talks apparently. My mum starts moving around, lifting and shuffling until I stand to help her. I don't know what to say, and though I really do think she's wrong about love, there's a part of me that thinks she's really right as well.

*****

Sitting down to eat my mum's delicious Scottish steak pie, I'm done. Looking around the kitchen I'm excited again by all the gleaming white and red everywhere. Admittedly, it doesn't look that great with the ugly countertops, but I know it'll look awesome in a couple weeks.

For being 46, my mum's in really good shape having done just as much work as I did while cooking and baking and singing as well. She stayed up scraping walls as long as I did last night, and she was up before me this morning preparing the paint cans and drop cloths.

It's actually been kind of fun with her, and I definitely like my sober mum much more than the old angry drunk one. She even seems much more relaxed than she used to be before my father left her.

Other than torturing me with her old Scottish crooners all bloody day, we got along well, laughed often, and planned another visit in 3 weeks. Christ, she even made my favorite steak pie in the middle of painting the walls and cupboards.

*****

During dinner when there's a knock on the door, she swears an interesting twist on frogs and Scottish sheep I've never heard before as she rises for the door. Laughing at her she grins and pulls my ponytail as she passes mumbling something about *balding* again.

"Saige? Saige, come 'ere!" My mum yells strangely as I topple my chair to get to her.

Staring at the police officer in the doorway, I have a horrible flashback tackle me as I stop dead with fear. "What's wrong?" I croak with my suddenly dry throat.

"We're investigating a missing person's report as a courtesy to the Midland PD."

"For me?" I ask dumbfounded.

"Are you Saige Masters?" The officer asks as both my mum and I say yes. "An official report was made yesterday at 4:00, 24 hours after your disappearance, but from what I understand due to recent events concerning you, an active search was underway before that."

"What recent events?" My mum asks looking between me and the cop. "What does tha mean?"

"I'm not missing," I change the subject desperately. "I've just been here at my mum's house since Friday night." Holy. Shit. "I didn't realize, um, maybe I should've called. Was it Selena Heart who made the report?"

"I really don't know," he looks down at his notes. "Can I see some ID Miss Masters, then I'll be on my way. I'll let dispatch know you've be found and they'll relay the message to Midland PD."

Nodding, I can't move until my mum actually shoves me. I never thought to call anyone, and I'm so fucking dead for this. God, Selena's going to kill me.

"Here," I hand over my ID to the cop talking in his shoulder radio my name, date of birth, and my driver's license number. Listening to the reply squawking, my mum is silent but her stare is deadly.

"Okay. That's it then. Have a good night ladies, and maybe you should call home to let everyone know you're okay in case Midland PD doesn't relay the message quick enough."

"Thank you. Um, I'm sorry, sir," I mumble embarrassed because I really don't know what to say in this situation.

"Have a good night," he nods walking away before my mother shuts the door.

"Well, that was ex'citin'. Kidnappin' me own daught'er," she laughs. "I guess ye bet'ter make that call on the telly, no?"

"I'm so dead," I mumble walking to the living room phone.

Dialing, my mum leans in the doorway and watches with amusement in her eyes. We'll see how amused she is in about 10 seconds.

"Hello?!"

"Hi, Sel-"

"You. Fucking. *Asshole!*" She screams and cries at the same time. "Are you alright?!" She keeps yelling.

"I'm fine! *Sorry.* I'm at my mum's."

"Your *Mom's?* All the way in New Haven? What the *fuck* were you

127

thinking?" She keeps screaming and even when I try to explain she keeps yelling over me. "What the fuck have you been doing?"

"Taking wallpaper off the walls," I say stupidly with a flinch knowing she's going to freak again, which she does.

"*Wallpaper?!* I thought you were *DEAD!*" She screams loud enough that my mum actually laughs before walking away.

"I'm sor-"

"I thought you were dead, Saige. I've been crying for 2 fucking days thinking you were dead. I imagined the worst goddamn things and I thought I was going to have to identify your body," she cries in a big sob. "Everyone we know has been looking for you. And I- She's *alive!*" She suddenly screams again.

"Who's that?" I ask quietly but the phone is being muffled like she's holding it against her chest. "Selena! Who are you talking to?"

"Mike says he's firing your ass tomorrow when he sees you," Selena says hopefully joking.

"I'm so sorry. I just ended up here and my mum and I redecorated her kitchen and it's been fun," I smile just as my mum plops down on her couch to listen with her plate of food in her lap.

"And you couldn't call?"

"I forgot my cell at your-"

"No fucking shit," Selena cuts me off again. "By the way, I love that Grif is your password," she says calming down a little. "Why isn't your mom's number in your phone? When are you coming home? We've been going *crazy,* Saige."

Trying to speak I finally jump in when she takes a breath. "Ah, I was leaving in about half an hour, so I'll be back like 9-9:30."

Exhaling deeply in the phone, Selena says sweetly, "I love you, kiddo. But if you *ever* scare me like this again, I will never, ever speak to you again. Got it?"

"Yes. I'm really sorry. I just started driving and I didn't think to call. I didn't think you'd be worried-"

"About you? *Really*? You're living in my house, we have a fight, you leave for a little break you said and I don't see or hear from you again for 2 goddamn days. And you don't think I'd freak out a little? *EVERYONE* freaked out!" She screams.

"I'm sorry," I mumble again because that's about all I have in me at the moment.

"Get your ass back here so I can yell at you in person. Mikes waiting here for you and I have some calls to make."

"Okay. I'm-"

"*Sorry.* I know. Drive carefully but hurry the hell up!" She yells one last time before slamming the phone down in my ear. Shiiiiit.

Looking at my mum, she's so amused by all this I want to be mad at her for something. Instead, I exhale slowly and try to fight the adrenaline coursing through my veins.

"Ye didna tell anyone where ye went? Yer a daft cow, Saige," she laughs shaking her head. "Well, come on then. Finish yer supper and get goin'," she rises walking toward her kitchen.

"I'm not really hungry anymore," I call to her back headed for the stairs to get my clothes.

"Get yer crap, then yer finish'in yer supper before the drive," she yells up the stairs.

20 minutes later after a very uneventful goodbye with the promise that I'll be back in 3 weeks, I'm driving away from my mum's.

Still a little overwhelmed by Selena's reaction, and the police, and by the 'everyone' she mentioned, I'm driving a little faster than usual, and I'm thinking a little too much.

But once on the highway, I crank the radio and sing along to Demons by Imagine Dragons to block out thoughts of the impending explosion I'll feel once I enter Selena's apartment.

God, I'm just desperate enough to hope Griffin is home so I can grab and hug him like a shield from his angry mom when I return.

*****

Pulling into the closest spot to her building, I'm only about 15 car lengths away from the front doors in the dark but that's when I realize I'm still *afraid* of the dark.

I didn't know I was scared still because I've worked my few shifts in the afternoon, and I haven't really left to go out at night before.

But here I am suddenly- scared to get out of my car.

Wishing I had my cell phone to ask Selena to meet me, I work up the nerve slowly with my hand on the door handle. Holding my purse tightly with my keys, I breathe in a quick burst of energy, throw open

129

the door, hit the alarm and start running when I see no one else walking out front.

Running for my life, I see a huge man step onto the sidewalk and I stop so quickly my runners actually skid for a second as the air leaves my lungs on a strangled scream.

"It's just me. It's Malcolm!" He yells with his hands raised and out in front of him. "Saige, its Malcolm," he tries again as I slowly shake my head to clear it.

Looking up at him, he's huge. He blocks out whatever moonlight there is, and he seems to devour the street lights around us.

Shaking, I can't find my voice and he doesn't speak or move toward me. Standing 5 feet away, Malcolm looks like the intimidating bastard I remember and he's scary as shit like this...

Until he smiles slightly and says, "Welcome back."

Whoosh... I lose my air once again.

When he smiles he looks so different. Kind of good looking, but more like safe or something. All the huge and intimidating that goes with his stern face and body disappears to be replaced with a kindness I feel in my soul.

"I'm afraid of night now," I say so suddenly I cringe in my own skin at the confession.

Nodding as his smile fades he asks softly, "Is that why you sat in your car for the last 20 minutes?" *20?* I thought it was like 2 minutes while I sucked up the bravery to get out.

"Why are you here?" I ask instead of answering.

"Selena told me you'd be home between 9 and 9:30, so I was waiting on the steps of her building since 9 in case you were scared."

"I'm afraid of night now," I whisper again to his knowing nod.

This is so weird suddenly, I feel like I'm confessing my sins, or taking comfort in a counsellor as I speak. He doesn't seem surprised by anything I say, and he isn't reacting or saying meaningless platitudes like most people do. Malcolm hasn't even said 'you'll be fine' like everyone else does.

"Would you like me to walk you inside?" He again asks so gently, I'm immediately relieved but saddened for some reason.

Tearing up, I nod my head but don't move.

I feel trapped in the fear of darkness but also completely safe with Malcolm. Stuck in this moment, I don't know how to move forward.

"You're so big," I mumble stupidly.

"Yes," he replies calmly.

With a quick grin he turns sideways and extends his arm toward the walkway of Selena's building but otherwise doesn't move forward. He's waiting for me and I still can't move into his huge shadow.

Staring, I ask all I can. "Why are you here?"

"I was worried about you, and I wanted to make sure you got home safely."

"How do you know I was away?"

"Selena called me yesterday morning when you didn't come home."

"Do you know why she called you?"

"She was scared to death so she was calling anyone she could think of," he says in a calm voice again mirroring my calm questions. "She wondered if I had heard from you about the gift I sent, and when I told her I hadn't she started to cry. So I pushed her for information and that's when I learned you were missing- we *thought*," he adds with a huff and the first sign of any emotion other than calm.

"I wasn't missing," I mumble again.

"But we didn't know that, Saige," he waits until I nod silently.

"Um, I should go in. I'm really sorry for this." Walking toward the doors, I add, "I'm sorry you were involved in this."

"No problem," he speaks beside me as we advance on the apartment walkway. "But you definitely owe me a coffee now. I'll pick you up tomorrow after you're finished work."

"But-"

"It's the least you owe me, don't you think?" He grins again and I don't really have an argument for coffee.

"I'll smell like the restaurant," I say so stupidly as an argument against coffee I blush like an idiot.

"That's okay," he grins at my embarrassment.

Opening the main door, I use the key Selena gave me and when I turn to Malcolm he nods me further inside.

"I'm taking you to her door," he continues walking to the elevator.

Once inside, pushing myself against the back mirror wall, I glance at him looking down at me. "You're not afraid of me, Saige," he says as a statement I actually agree with.

When his phone rings, he answers just as the elevator opens. "We're in the hallway," he says as Selena's door is flung open and Malcolm hangs up. Still holding the elevator doors with his hand, Malcolm nods toward Selena to make me move.

"See you tomorrow, Saige," he says as he lets the door close.

"Wait!" I yell at the closed door before I hear Selena call my name.

Turning quickly around, I'm engulfed in a hug so tight I'm nearly suffocated. Looking around her, I see Mike standing in the doorway leaning with a scowl on his face.

"You are such an asshole. I want to beat the shit out of you and hug you, then beat the shit out of you again," Selena moans against me pulling me towards her apartment.

"Hi," I mumble to Mike who hugs me as well.

"I'm glad you're okay, Saige. But wow, you scared the hell out of us."

"I know. I'm sorry. I just didn't think about calling when I was with my mum. We were so busy and time flew by."

Being pulled to the couch by Selena, Mike walks into her kitchen as she stares at me. Not speaking and feeling totally awkward, I attempt to apologize again but she cuts me off.

"I get it. It was just so intense here. You didn't come home after a few hours so Mike and I stayed put waiting. Then night came and we started calling you only to realize your cell was vibrating on the table. Then nothing still. So by 3 in the morning I was freaking and Mike called Tyler to see if he'd heard from you."

"Why Tyler?" I gasp.

"Who else would you go see if you weren't with us? It's not like you have other friends or another ex-boyfriend," she replies like I'm an idiot for asking. "So Tyler drove around for a bit, called me all the time, and Mike called Kyle just in case, though I doubted you'd be with him."

Watching Mike walk toward us with drinks, I gratefully accept mine and chug half the vodka and orange while they drink their own.

"Why did you call Malcolm?"

Huffing, Selena moans, "There was no one else to call. I really didn't think you would, but I wanted to see if you maybe called him to thank him and told him where you were going. I didn't know, but I was desperate, Saige. The police were called at midnight, but they wouldn't do anything about it until 24 hours had passed, even with what happened to you just a few weeks ago," Selena growls. "Anyway, Malcolm hadn't heard from you either, but he was very concerned. He asked questions and kept me updated and tried to find you himself."

"How? He doesn't even *know* me," I cry out feeling so confused by all this suddenly. Between calling three of the four men I kind of know what the hell did she think I was doing? "I don't understand this. I mean I get you were worried, but why the hell did you get Tyler, Kyle, and Malcolm involved? Where did you think I was?"

"I didn't have a fucking clue, so I called whoever I could," she says angrily. "Tyler, the useless dick, couldn't remember your Mom's maiden name, and I know she changed it after your parents divorced, so unless we drove to New Haven to an address Tyler only vaguely remembered how to get to, we didn't know what else to do. It was this morning when I was talking to Malcolm again that he questioned your family so I mentioned your mom, and he remembered her maiden name was MacTavish right away. It was actually Malcolm who called to tell me the police were contacting the New Haven PD for him as soon as possible."

"How did he know?"

"He knew *nothing*, Saige- that's the point. No one did. But his friend is a cop so once they figured out who your mom was they sent in the call to the New Haven police. And that was ALL Malcolm. I wouldn't have known what the fuck to do after you didn't come home again last night," she huffs before taking another breath for more. "I was so scared you were hurt again," she cries, gulping back her drink as I reach for her.

"I'm so sorry. I literally just started driving, forgot my phone and ended up at my mum's. I didn't even think to call you because the only person I've ever checked in with was Tyler, and he doesn't care anymore."

"He cares, Saige. Tyler was frantic to find you, too. He called Kyle and together they called some of your old classmates to ask if anyone had seen you. But no one had and there was nothing to do but wait. God, he's such an asshole it was really awkward with him on the phone all the time," she huffs for the hundredth time. "Anyway, I'm glad you're okay. And please don't ever do anything like that again."

"I won't. I just never thought to call, but I will from now on, okay?"

"Okay," she nods taking my hand.

"Where's Griffin?"

"With my mom again."

"I'm so sorry, Selena." Looking at Mike, I apologize as well.

"It's okay. I'm gonna get going though. I'm working the entire 11-11 tomorrow. Have a good night," he leans over to hug me. "And *you*, get some sleep," he pushes hugging Selena.

"I will," she nods standing but I shake my head for her to sit. Walking Mike to the door, I don't want to apologize again, but other than an 'I'm sorry for all this' I don't know what else to say.

"Are you working tomorrow at 1:00?"

"Yes."

"Okay. I'll see you then."

"Thank you. For everything," I smile as we hug before he leaves.

Closing the door, Selena rises and says simply, "I'm going to bed," in a tired, almost sad voice I don't recognize from her.

Feeling totally uncomfortable with her suddenly, I ask the only thing I can think of. "Are we okay?"

"Of course. I'm just tired, Saige. This has been a shit weekend for me. But DON'T apologize again or I'll go mental. Sleep well, kiddo," she adds walking away for the bathroom.

Holy shit. My brain is spinning and I feel so badly for everyone. I really didn't think when I left Selena's without a word.

Thinking of Malcolm suddenly as I finish my vodka and orange I'm so overwhelmed by him, I don't really know what to do anymore. He was so sweet to be here and to help and to just be whatever he was being.

I'm sure having coffee is just coffee, but I don't feel ready for coffee. I mean what's the acceptable timeframe to have coffee with someone after a 4 year breakup? I don't know. But I kind of want to have coffee with Malcolm even though I kind of don't.

CHAPTER 14

Back at work, no one is talking to me about anything concerning me, which I'm both grateful for and weirded out by. Selena was only slightly grumpy with me today before work, Mike was normal-ish when I walked in, and Hershal touched my cheek gently when he welcomed me back. Even Kelsey smiled and said hi only, which again is good, but so weird for her I don't know what's going on.

No one is asking anything, and I'm grateful enough to try to be normal around everyone so they *don't* start asking.

"Are you excited about your coffee date?" Selena giggles, suddenly much less grumpy with me.

"No. *Yes,*" I admit with an embarrassed grin. "I haven't had coffee with someone since I was 18, so I'm definitely nervous."

"Don't be. Just remember coffee means coffee. He didn't ask you to dinner which means more, and he didn't pick you up at home at 8:00, or for dinner and a movie which means more. He's meeting you here to take you for coffee."

"I know, but-"

"Don't over think, Saige. He's a really nice guy and Its. Just. Coffee," she glares until I nod my head. "Good. Only a half hour to go," she reminds me making me nervous all over again.

"Thanks for the pep-talk. You're as bad as my mum," I groan when she skips away like a teenager.

Finishing out my last table, my stomach is in knots. I'm sooooo nervous, I'm afraid I'll look like an idiot. I'm sooooo nervous, I'm afraid I'll *act* like an idiot. *Jesus,* I'm nervous.

"Ready to switch off?" Mike asks with a grin he can't hide. "When's he picking you up?"

"I don't know. Now, I guess. He said he'd take me for coffee after my shift which he seems to know all about. So now? Can I go? Aileen's here, and I want to change quickly."

"Go," he smiles. "And have fun, Saige. It's just coffee," he reminds me like Selena did and I almost ask if they practiced that line together.

Turning back to the family side, I walk right into Aileen as she grabs my arms to steady me. "Are you okay?" She asks with the whispered concerned voice everyone uses around me now.

"Yeah. Ah, table 4 and 3 are set up for the food wait, and table 2 hasn't ordered yet, so it's all yours."

"Got it. Have fun," she says brightly and I don't know if she knows or if she just means in general. Then again, I'm being a nervous idiot, almost paranoid over my first coffee date in forever.

Turning back for the lounge, I move quickly. It's 5:55 and though I didn't see Malcolm in the restaurant waiting, I need at least 10 minutes to change and freshen up.

Throwing open the door, I run for my locker and strip down right there in plain sight of anyone walking in. Pulling on my loose dark jeans and a black turtleneck overhead, I finish with a big black sweater overtop.

I may be a little over-dressed for the warm spring weather but I feel safe in my clothes. And I need to feel safe today.

Not that Malcolm doesn't make me feel safe because he kind of does which he shouldn't. He's a stranger to me and I need to remember that before I allow his presence to be a comfort to me.

In the bathroom mirror, I take in my face. It's no longer bumpy or swollen and all the sutures have either dissolved or been removed, but there's a little darkness still below my right eye, and the cut above my eye is still really noticeable.

Using the foundation Selena bought me, I dab around my eye darkness and blend around the scars. The rest of my face is super pasty but that's normal for me. Even the scraps on the opposite cheek from the pavement are all healed up a pale pink now. So I'm basically back to being a pasty bog person, Tyler used to tease.

Shaking my head, I effectively toss Tyler from my mind. I'm not going there, and I'm not doing this today. Tyler is gone and he'll stay gone, I've decided. No matter how much he stalks Selena for updates and information, he's done for me.

Adding a little lipstick, my lips are fuller than they used to be, but that's actually the scar line I now have just below my lip line. When my teeth were knocked through my lips, the placement was perfect, I laugh unexpectedly. Wow, what a sick thought I grin again pulling out my eyeshadow. Adding just a little purple color in the crease, my green eyes always look so much greener with purple. Finishing up with a sweep of mascara, I'm ready.

My hair is in my standard ponytail, and that's it. Looking again, I feel so nervous still, I'll probably clam up instead of talking. And really, Malcolm has seen me yelling, crying, beat up, freaked out on the sidewalk... and that's about it. Jesus, it would be nice if he actually saw my real personality, or that I even *have* a personality, I burst out laughing again nervously.

Walking back into the lounge, Malcolm stands as soon as we make eye contact. Blushing, I try to quickly get my shit together, especially after he grins like he knows I'm freaking.

"Saige..."

"Um, hi Malcolm." Looking at the bar I see Mike smiling at a mixed drink, and even Selena standing just to the side of Mike grinning at the same mixed drink like idiots.

"Would you like to have coffee here, or would you rather go somewhere else so your friends won't be smiling at us the whole time?" Leaning a little closer to me Malcolm groans, "They're kind of freaking me out."

Huffing a quick laugh, I'm unable to answer. I'm not sure if leaving for coffee means more than staying for coffee here. I'm not sure what to do until Malcolm makes the decision for me.

"Just coffee. I'm not taking you out for dinner or on a date, and I'm not keeping you out late. We're having coffee only."

"Okay, but-"

"Blended down on Market Street. It's like a 5 minute drive," Selena interrupts us. "Just thought I'd help," she smirks walking away when both Malcolm and I laugh at her.

"Okay. So Blended? Shall we walk or drive?" Ugh. Another pause as I over-think and freak a little. "Saige, I would absolutely *never* hurt you, and you can trust me in my truck for 5 minutes. You have my word."

"I know. I'm sorry, I'm just new to coffee. It's been a long time for me." Fading out I sound like an ass so I shut up, pull my shit together, and say all I can. "Lead the way," I start for the doors.

Turning just once I see Selena back with Mike and both are smiling with a head tilt to get going before I walk smack into Malcolm's back and bounce off him.

"You look like you're walking to the gallows," he grins.

"No, I don't. I was just checking she wasn't actually following us," I lie quickly as he shakes his head grinning at me.

"Yer blethering, Saige," he calls out my lie in Scottish before opening the doors for us.

Seated in his truck as he walks around to join me, I make a quick decision to stop the shit. He seems perfectly harmless in a brick shithouse sort of way, and he's never been anything but nice to me. I'm not socially awkward normally though my head shakes and pauses suggest otherwise, so I'm going to try to be a little more normal.

"Small talk?" He asks sitting in his SUV. "Or should we wait until we're seated with coffee to get to know each other?"

"Coffee. Everything is better with coffee."

"Does your mom call you a heathen for drinking coffee?"

Laughing quickly I nod yes. "Every chance she gets. Are both your parents Scottish?"

Glancing at me then back to the road, he explains, "No, just my father. He met my mother abroad when she was vacationing in Britain with her parents. They met, had 4 days and 3 nights together, exchanged information, and my dad moved here to be with her a year later. He said he knew he loved her the moment they met- even though she was a Limey," he adds referring to the Scottish slang for an English person. "And your parents? Both, or just your mom?"

"Actually it's almost the exact same story. My father was touring Europe and Britain before finishing his Doctorate on linguistics and he met my mum on the way to the mythical Stonehenge- or the Devil's trap, as my mum calls it now. They met, she fell madly in love within *one* day, and then she followed him here a few months later."

Turning to me in the parking lot of Blenders, he asks, "The Devil's trap?"

"Yeah. My mum thinks the Druids and pagan myths are just a way to hypnotize normal people into being daft fools. She's not a big believer in love so she thinks the Devil messed with her mind at Stonehenge."

"Huh," he exhales before opening his door.

Waiting for more I think, I don't really want to give it. My parents' love story is ugly at best, and pretty devastating at worst. It's definitely not first time coffee conversation.

Joining Malcolm outside his truck, we walk inside Blenders silently. Finding a corner booth, I'm relieved it's a little quieter in the back with soothing instrumental music heard around us so we don't have to yell our conversation.

"What can I get you?" Malcolm asks absolutely towering over me and the booth.

"A large cafe mocha with no whip cream and an extra shot of espresso?"

"Wow. You don't mess around with the coffee do you?"

"Nope. It's my only vice," I say lightly, but he looks like he read more into it. I don't know him well enough to read his expressions yet, but there was definitely an expression before he turned for the counter.

"Here you go," he places my coffee down as he scooches not so easily into the booth across the table from me. Actually pushing the round table away from him a little, he eventually gets comfortable.

"Thank you." Warming my hands on the pretty teal mug, I'm not sure what to say now.

"Q&A?" He asks with a grin and I nod. "Me first, or ladies first?"

"You. No, me!" I jump in quickly. "How old are you?"

"31."

"Wow, really? I didn't realize you were so old-er," I quickly amend.

"Nice catch," he grins. "Okay, how old are you?"

"Almost 23."

"Wow, really? I didn't realize you were so young-er," he replies cheekily.

Ignoring his reply, I continue. "What do you do?"

"I work for Dan. I'm an electrician by trade, but I home renovate and build up or tear down homes as required. What are you going to school for?"

"I'm going to be a lawyer," I admit quietly.

Pausing for a moment to look at my face Malcolm asks, "Why do you seem uncomfortable admitting that?"

"I'm not. I'm not embarrassed or anything, it's just people always have weird reactions to hearing that. Either they're shocked that I'm smart enough based on my looks and small frame. Or they're surprised I would go to law school because of my looks and small frame. So I usually find myself either insulted or defensive most times."

"I think it's amazing that you have the intelligence and determination needed to be a lawyer. Is there a reason?"

"Um, I watched someone close to me convicted of a minor offense because he couldn't afford a private lawyer. He was defended by a half-ass Public Defender who didn't give a shit about him. And because of that he was convicted of a crime he should have at worst had a major fine for, but instead was given a hefty prison sentence over."

"What happened?"

"The asshole Public Defender didn't remember his name. At one point he called him the wrong name and even after I cried out his real name in court, he just shrugged like it didn't matter. But it *did* matter. And if he had put forth as much time on his client as he did brushing his teeth that morning everything would have turned out so differently."

"What did he do? What was he convicted of?"

"DUI... *barely.* He *just* blew over the limit on his 18th birthday that very night. He had 3 celebratory beers in 3 hours, reacted completely sober when the police did a field sobriety test, and he even walked a straight friggin' line when he was asked to."

"So what happened to him?" Malcolm asks quietly like he understands this is tough for me.

Inhaling, I tell him the truth. "As the State's average sentence, he should have received maybe a license suspension for 6 months with a recurrence warning, and maybe had to fulfill alcohol awareness classes and then it would've been over for him. Instead, he was sent to adult prison for a term of 6 years."

Tearing up quickly, I hold them in as Malcolm stops speaking and asking questions like he knows I need to recover.

"So you decided to become a lawyer? How old were you?"

"16. That's when I decided to become a Public Defender. Did you know financially disadvantaged people, minorities, and immigrants are sentenced to prison more than twice as often as white, middle class people are?" Not waiting for his answer, I keep going. "And you know it's not because the middle class white guy is less guilty, or less responsible for his illegal actions- it's because he could afford a lawyer who knew his goddamn name," I huff. Looking quickly at Malcolm I'm embarrassed to be so loud and I'm pissed that I let this affect me again. "Sorry," I add grabbing my coffee to calm the hell down.

"Don't be sorry. It sounds like that kid was important to you. And I think your anger is probably what makes you so determined." Calming slowly I ignore his last comment until he says in a delicious Scottish brogue, "It's quite sex'y," further calming me as I smile a little at the tease.

"He was important."

"What happened to him?"

"It's my turn," I cut him off before he can ask more. "Siblings?"

"3 brothers, one sister. And yes, my home was crazy and my mom was crazier. She yelled a lot at me and my brothers, but my father was the one to tame us. With just the quick flick of his belt coming off we would scatter and behave for the rest of the night. As far as I know he only ever used that damn belt once on my oldest brother, but we all saw it come out and panicked. We actually stood listening at the closed door until we heard it whipped down and my brother scream bloody murder. And that was it. The threat was cemented," he smirks at my open-mouthed upset. "It's okay. We think they put the whole thing on, though neither my brother nor my dad will admit it to this day," he laughs as I exhale my breath of outrage.

"Are you close to them?" I whisper thinking of Alec again.

"Yes. Well, my 2nd oldest brother lives in South Africa, but the rest of us are still nearby. My sister was the middle child of us 5, so she was protected by her older brothers, and adored by us younger ones. Your turn. Siblings? And would you like another coffee?"

"No, to both. Parent's names?"

"Carrie Havers and Malcolm MacNeil. Yes, I'm a namesake," he grins. "Malcolm MacNeil the second. Your parents' names?"

"Collin Masters and Rena MacTavish," we say her last name at the same time.

"Rena MacTavish? You can't get much more Scottish than that," he smiles when I agree.

"I'm out of questions," I admit before finishing my lukewarm coffee.

"Really? I have hundreds still. Favorite color? Favorite food? Favorite Music?"

"Green -"

"Like your gorgeous eyes," Malcolm says sweetly.

Blushing, I continue. "My mum's Scottish steak pie. And too much music to name. I'm very musically eclectic."

"Favorite CD?"

"Um, an old school Depeche Mode album."

"Depeche Mode?" He asks shaking his head in disgust. "Like before you were even born?"

"Yup. Way before I was born. Have you heard the Black Celebration album? It's my favorite."

"Ah, no. Never. I know a few of their songs from the nineties I think, but nothing older than that."

"Well, you should listen to their older music. It's really- *what*?" I ask grinning at his snarly face.

Shaking his head Malcolm says, "If Dan or my buddies heard me listening to Depeche Mode they'd strip me of my man card and beat the shit out of me for sport."

"*Really*?" I giggle.

"No... to the beating me up part. But my man card would be gone for life," he laughs at my outrage again. "I'm still up since you have no imagination," he keeps teasing me. "Best friend?"

"Selena, then Mike second."

"Boyfriend?" He asks then pauses as I go wide-eyed.

Well, isn't this a complicated question. Or not, I guess. Looking at my empty mug I finally answer, "No boyfriend."

"Since when?"

"Just a few weeks ago. The day before I first met you actually. Ah, that's when we broke up."

"How long were you together?"

"4 totally pointless years," I say bitterly before stopping myself.

Leaning against the back of the booth, Malcolm gives me space before asking, "Not mutual?"

"Oh, the ending was all me. But the pre-ending was *all* him. He did something unforgivable. So though I had to leave him, I never would've left him if he hadn't done what he did." After my sentence I realize by avoiding the reason for our breakup I ended up sounding stupid so I quickly explain. "He cheated on me, so I had to leave him. And it was a shock. Still *is* a shock actually."

"I can only imagine after 4 years together. Do you still love him?"

"Yes."

Looking over at Malcolm, he doesn't look mad or anything he just nods like he gets it without judging my answer. Glancing past the other people in the cafe, I realize the sky is darkening and I need to get home before it's completely dark.

"It's getting late so I should probably get going. Thank you for the coffee."

"You're very welcome. How are you getting home from the restaurant?"

"Selena said she'd come back to get me."

"Let me drive you to your door. I'll make sure you get in safely."

"It's okay. I'll just call Selena."

"Why?" He sounds confused as he pauses for my reply.

"Because I feel a little nervous still and I like the routine of Selena and I walking in together," I admit pathetically.

I need him to understand so he lets this go. He is NOT driving me home because then it feels like a date or something. And it's not a date. It's just coffee.

"You're very stubborn," he says like I don't know that already.

"I know."

"I'm stubborn too, Saige. So I promise you I'll be driving behind you to make sure you both get in safely before I leave."

"Isn't that called stalking?" I laugh just a little uncomfortably.

"Nope. Not if I tell you I'm doing it. Stalking is about being sneaky, but I'm blatantly telling you I'm going to follow you home. Therefore, I'm *following*, not stalking," he counters with a smug grin I can't help smiling back at. "Can I ask you one more question?"

"No. I'm exhausted," I groan playfully.

"It's about the night you were attacked." Flinching, I'm shocked he would bring that up so suddenly. Breathing in deeply, my chest is tighter and my hands start shaking almost immediately. "Just one question?"

"God no," I almost beg holding my breath until he relents.

"Okay. Another time." *Never*, I think to myself. There will never be a time to discuss that night with him. "Are you ready to go?"

"Yes," I nod already rising.

The playful Q&A is over, and my mood has shifted totally. I was starting to really like him, and now I'm back to feeling awkward and self-

143

conscious. I don't even want to get back in his truck with him now I'm so uncomfortable.

"On second thought I'll just call Selena to pick me up here."

"Why? What changed?"

"Nothing, I'm fine," I smile as best as I can stepping out of the booth.

Already dialing Selena she answers on the first ring with a dramatic, "*Sooooo*?" But I cut her off before she can really start grilling me.

"Can you come get me at Blenders? I'm ready *now*," I say with inflection hoping she understands and drives quicker.

"I'm on my way. 15 minutes, tops. Are you okay?"

"No. See you then," I smile so Malcolm doesn't know I'm freaking out.

Completely caught off guard by his question I wasn't prepared for all the fear and insecurity, or just the ugliness of that night to hit me. I wasn't thinking of that night and I wasn't prepared for it to suddenly smack me in the face again.

But now I'm thinking about it with this huge guy standing over me and I feel so small and insignificant again. I feel like someone could hurt me now, and though maybe not Malcolm, it doesn't seem to matter. The fear is always inside me and now it's surfacing as well.

"Are you okay?" He asks in a soothing voice that doesn't work this time. "I'm sorry I upset you. That wasn't my intention," he leans a little closer to me.

Stepping away from his big everything a little, I want to get away from him. Looking at the others around us, I want to run away from this place so badly I start physically shaking trying to calm the mental overload of memories I'm suddenly remembering.

"Would you leave me alone now?" I whisper afraid he'll say no but afraid he'll say yes. I don't want to be alone right now, but I don't want to talk to him either.

"Why don't we stand out front together? I'll just wait for Selena to arrive and then I'll leave you alone."

"No. I c-can't go outside when it's d-dark," I panic shaking. *Shit!*

Trying to stay calm, I'm shivering, and panicking, and basically I look like an idiot. I'm still so afraid of outside I can't stop my reaction. I keep feeling that night again. And though tonight it's only starting to darken, I feel like its closing in on me too quickly to get away from it.

"Saige, listen to me," Malcolm says softly. "I'm going to hug you and-"

"No!" Looking around, I panic thinking others can hear and see me

144

freaking out. Raising my hands out front of my body I'm trying to protect myself but I know it's no use again. I know I can't fight Malcolm if he wants to hurt me. "Please don't hurt me," I beg confused.

"Saige, I'm going to warm you only. Look, honey, look at my arms. They're open so you can lean into me. I won't touch you at all, but you can hug me." Still speaking in a calm quiet voice, Malcolm is huge, but he seems sincere. "Lean into my body for a little warmth only. You need to get the chill out of your skin so the panic goes away."

Standing still with his arms open, I look up at his nice Scottish blue eyes and he still doesn't move. Not smiling, he has his intense, like craggy face on, but his arms are still wide open in the cafe, looking very weird to anyone else watching us I'm sure.

"Go on... *You* hug me for some warmth," he whispers again waiting until I suddenly move.

Leaning into Malcolm slowly, I wrap my arms around the inside of his jacket and suffer a full body shiver as I make contact with his warm chest. Feeling Malcolm slowly lower his arms to his sides, he doesn't hug me back like he said he wouldn't, and I'm so relieved my tears start before I can stop them.

And he's just so warm.

Getting closer, I find myself hugging him around his middle as I cry out the last few weeks of my life.

Crying out the pain, the sadness, and the constant fear I didn't realize keeps me constantly mentally aware and always on guard, I shudder. Leaning against his huge body, I suddenly let go of everything.

Bursting into tears, I wish I was embarrassed, but I don't have the ability to feel it right now. I wish I had the strength to walk away and apologize for my behavior, but I can't.

I'm warm, and I'm not afraid for this one moment in time.

When another shudder takes over my whole body, I cry a little more wrapped around his huge body. Listening to his heart pound against my ear, he still isn't moving and he isn't hugging me back like he promised. Exhaling another shudder I suddenly realize I *do* feel a little better.

But I still can't pull away from his warmth.

When I feel Malcolm move a little like maybe he's shaking his head, I snuggle in deeper until all the everything scary goes away right now. I know it'll come back and I know this is just a temporary reprieve from

145

all the shit in my head, but I need it right now.

For just these few minutes I want to be calm and unafraid.

"Saige...?" Malcolm whispers snapping me out of my calm warmth. "Selena's here waiting for you."

"Already?" I ask breathing in his scent and his warmth for just a second longer before I slowly pull away.

"Aye," he grins, transforming his face once again from stern to handsome. "Can I walk you to her?"

"Thank you," I shake my head pulling out of his warmth. Standing a foot back, I see the couple beside our table is different, and turning quickly to the front I notice the sky is no longer dusky but dark. Selena is sitting at a raised table close to the door with a coffee, and everything feels so strange, I look back at Malcolm confused.

"I didn't realize."

"I didn't care," he whispers back.

"How long did we stand there?"

"Awhile," he flashes a quick grin.

"I'm sorry."

"Don't be. Why don't you get home now and I'll follow to make sure you're alright. Then maybe you'll call me tonight?"

"Okay."

Turning back to a waiting Selena, she hops from her chair and gulps the last of her coffee. She even extends her hand like I'm a child, which is both offensive and humiliating.

"I'm not a little kid," I snap closer to her but close enough for Malcolm to hear walking behind me.

"I don't think you're a little kid," Selena says defensively. "I just wanted to hold your hand, Saige."

"Oh... sorry." Turning back to Malcolm, I say all I can. "Thank you for the coffee. Um, sorry I lost it a little back there. I didn't mean to be-"

"Scared?"

"Yes," I huff.

"I don't care about scared, Saige. I'm just happy you weren't afraid of me. Will you call me tonight?"

"Yes," I nod.

"Okay then. Let's go." Smiling at Selena, Malcolm leans around the 2 of us and walks to the doors to hold them wide open for us. Waiting, he stands there until Selena takes my hand pulling me for the doors.

On the sidewalk, I have one moment of night fear quickly replaced by the beeping of Selena's car right out front with her 4-ways flashing.

"Have a good night ladies," Malcolm waits until we both climb in before he jogs around the side of the building to the parking lot.

"What happened?" Selena asks with concern shutting off the radio.

"I freaked out when he wanted to ask me a question about that night." Turning her head to me, she asks, "He didn't?"

"He did. But not in a bad way. Not like specific details or anything but it didn't matter. I lost it and started shaking and panicking, then I was crying and he just let me hug him until I was warm. He didn't touch me at all," I choke up feeling such relief, almost like the shit in my head is cleared out right now. "He was really nice. And warm..." I hear myself whisper to her silence.

"He's also right behind us," she smiles looking in the rearview mirror as I turn to see his SUV only a few feet behind Selena's little civic.

"He told me it's not stalking if he tells me about it. Um, because he's not being sneaky, it's just blatantly *following*," I actually laugh a little when she does.

"Huh. He's got a good point. And I *really* like this guy," she tacks on.

Finding myself nodding as well, I really do like this guy. Malcolm seems so patient and nonthreatening for being the most menacing looking man I've ever personally known. There's just something about him, almost a quiet calm to him I really like. There's a comfort he projects not just because he seems like the type who could keep me safe, but because he seems like the type who *wants* me to be safe.

*****

Sitting in Selena's room for my quick call, I dial nervously.

"Hello?" His deep voice breathes like a warm caress. Inhaling deeply, I attempt to speak but he does it for me. "Saige?"

"Yes. Hi."

"Hi, yourself. Are you all settled in for the night?"

"Yes." Pausing forever, it's both uncomfortable and kind of nice. He's just waiting, breathing in the phone calmly, and I'm calmed again.

"Thank you for your patience tonight. I'm sure I seemed like a freak to you."

"You didn't seem like a freak. You were a woman taking a moment to calm down when you were afraid." That's exactly what I was doing, but I didn't think he'd understand that at all. "Are you okay?" Malcolm asks and I don't know what to say.

Thinking of Malcolm in the cafe with me all my embarrassment and fear quickly resurfaces but when he stays quiet waiting for me to speak everything is replaced again with calm. I feel like I should say something or do something so he understands this isn't really me, or *wasn't* me before everything happened.

"I was a boring student and totally normal 3 weeks ago, and I think that's why Tyler cheated on me." Flinching quickly, I try to cover up how pathetic I sound. "You wouldn't even recognize me if you had met me before that night."

"It's okay, Saige. I'm not judging you and I don't think there's anything wrong with you after what you've been through."

Like he's looking right into my mind, I'm left overwhelmed by his kind words, and I'm feeling pretty transparent with this guy suddenly. "I'm not a freak at all in my real life, I promise." God, just saying that makes me feel exactly like a freak.

"This IS your real life now, Saige. This has happened to you, so you need to accept it and keep handling it as best as you can." Picturing his smile, he whispers in his soft brogue, "An fer wha it's worth, I think yer a fine wee lass."

With a quick grin I whisper back, "Thank you," just as Selena stands in the doorway to check up on me.

"I should go. I, ah-"

"What's the rest of your week like? When are you working?"

"Um, tomorrow. Then I have Wednesday off but I have to do something all day."

"Are you working Thursday?"

"Yes, until 6."

"Can we try coffee again? Just coffee."

"I guess," I agree sounding almost pained.

"You really have to stop exhaling like I'm leading you to the gallows, Saige. You're gonna give me a complex," he laughs. Grinning, I apologize again. "I'll see you at 6 on Thursday?"

"Okay. Um, good night, and thank you again, Malcolm. You've been very nice to me."

"It's my pleasure, Saige. Good night," he says before hanging up.

Holding my cell in my hand, I look at Selena grinning and smile myself. "We're having coffee again on Thursday."

"Sounds good. And I'd like you to know I think Malcolm is awesome. And he's hot as hell," she adds surprising me.

"I don't think of him like that. He's just a nice guy to maybe get to know a little. A friend like Mike is."

"Uh huh. So you haven't noticed when he's not growly serious, he looks like Gerard Butler?"

"*Really?* No, I haven't." *Gerard Butler?* Oh, I guess kind of. He's bigger but he has the whole dark hair, Scottish blue eyed thing going for him, and when he smiles he does look totally different. "I didn't notice, but I guess," I look at her grinning again.

"He's fucking huge, and good looking, and I've never met someone so intense and caring about a woman he just met before in my life. It's nice to see for you."

"Tyler was like that," I defend.

Actually laughing at me Selena argues, "Ah, no he wasn't. He loved you, yes, but he was always a little too comfortable with you. Like willing to be cared for, or have everything cared for. Tyler was a bum, Saige."

Absolutely shocked she would say that, I'm about to tell her off when she continues over my outrage. "You paid for everything, did everything, and he sat back and let you. Don't get me wrong, you weren't a doormat or anything, but you had to lead and parent your entire relationship because Tyler wouldn't. Or maybe couldn't."

"No, I didn't."

"Yes, you did. But not in a bad way, just in the Tyler/Saige way. So it's nice for me to see a man wanting to be there for *you* now."

"Tyler and I weren't like that. And Malcolm and I won't be like that. He's just a friend, Selena. A nice friend to have right now with everything else going on. And it really doesn't matter anyway, I'm leaving in 4 months."

Looking almost sad Selena whines, "I don't want you to move away."

"I'll always come back to visit. I love Griffin way too much to stay away from *him*," I tease.

"I'm making dinner, come help?"

"Sure."

"Oh, and I cleared Wednesday morning with the bum," she adds to my growl. "He promises he won't be around all day, and I told him we'd be there by 7:30 to start packing and moving out your stuff. I basically had to threaten him, but he promised he and his skank wouldn't come back before 4 in the afternoon."

CHAPTER 15

"You owe me for this," Selena whines driving the U-Haul van we rented. "It's like 7:00 in the morning and I slept like shit. By the way, you mumble nonstop when you sleep," she turns to me with such a look of disgust I find myself grinning. "And the teeth grinding? You sounded like a sheep being sheared or something," she huffs which makes me burst out laughing.

"Sorry. Its stress," I admit which stops her growling at me. "I'm always way worse when I'm stressed out, at least according to Tyler."

"Well, if we ever sleep together again, I'm drugging your ass. Does *that* work?" Huh, I have no idea.

"If it helps, I slept like shit too, and now I feel almost hungover or something."

"That does help," she laughs like a bitch.

Pulling in front of my old apartment, I'm nervous Tyler or Kaitlyn will be there. I'm nervous about seeing my old home and my things like they're all tainted now. I don't know, but absolutely everything feels different here.

"Ha! Right out front," Selena smacks the steering wheel pulling into the empty spot by the front walkway.

Grabbing our coffee, I just jump down when Mike surprises me beside the truck. "Mornin'."

"Hey. Thanks for coming."

"No problem. Mornin' Selena," he grins knowing like I do Selena is NOT a morning person.

"Ugh... Don't be all chipper. Saige kept me up all night mumbling," she says as Mike laughs at me knowing about the mumbling too. "And my coffee hasn't kicked in yet," she grumps pulling out the bags of tape, markers, and garbage bags I bought for my clothes.

At the door to my old apartment, I knock before entering. I'm scared Kaitlyn is here and I'm not in the mood to open a door to a naked bitch sleeping in my bed, which of course is all I'm imagining.

When I open the door, thankfully my old apartment still looks the same. I don't know what I thought would be different exactly, other than red lighting, porn on the TV, and lingerie all over the place. But besides that, I really had no expectations.

Dumping the coffees, bag, and a bundle of boxes on the kitchen table I don't know where to start. "Would you look in the bedroom in case she's a heavy sleeper?" I laugh awkwardly as Selena walks past me.

"Nope. Coast is clear. Where do you want to start?"

"The living room I guess. Almost everything is mine, especially the bookcases and books. And the knickknacks are all mine." Looking around I don't know what I do first because I don't actually want some of this crap though it's mine.

"Okay we'll start here and work our way to the kitchen?" Nodding, Mike and I start making boxes while Selena empties the book cases.

"Everything but economics," I confirm as she nods.

After packing my books and crap from the wall unit, I stop to look at a picture of Tyler and me on vacation in Mexico 2 years ago. Holding the picture up it's from our first hour on the beach and I'm wearing a green bikini Tyler bought me. I'm not really a bikini kind of girl, but he insisted I wear it, and I'll admit I felt good in it when he looked at me.

"You look hot in a bikini," Mike says over my shoulder as I quickly hide the picture against my chest. Actually opening the back of the frame, I take out the picture so Tyler doesn't have it anymore before putting the empty frame back on the shelf.

Grabbing another picture of us at Christmas last year I pull it from the frame as well. Tossing the pictures in a box marked miscellaneous, I don't give into the memories, and I force myself to quickly move on.

Working our way to the kitchen, once again I realize almost everything is mine, or at least was *bought* by me.

Turning toward the living room I watch Malcolm suddenly walk in and simply freeze. Shaking hands with Mike, Malcolm looks at me with his cute smile as I smile back at him.

"I came to help," he says walking toward me.

"How did you know? Don't you have to work?"

"Selena told me last night on the phone. But don't be mad at her, she just thought you could use a little extra help moving the furniture so I took the day off. No big deal," he shrugs.

"I didn't mean for you to have to help."

"It's not a problem," he says as Selena rounds the kitchen wall. "Hey," he smiles at her.

"Hey yourself, big guy. So I need you to put all those big muscles to work. All the furniture's going," she says before I even have a say.

"No, it's not."

"Yes, it is. It's all yours."

"Selena, I'm not coming in here to gut the place."

"Why not? You paid for everything, so why should he get to keep it?"

"I agree," Malcolm adds and I can't stop the dirty look I give him which he only grins at.

"I'm not walking out of here leaving Tyler with nothing. I may have paid for everything but the kitchen set, but it looks really spiteful if I leave him nothing in the living room but a blanket to sit on."

Bursting out laughing, she grins, "It'll serve him right. And we'll leave him 2 chairs from the kitchenette and half the table," she says making me actually laugh at the thought of cutting the table in half.

"I'll take the couch, chair and my book cases, but I'm not taking any other furniture. Period."

"What about your bedroom set?" She asks and I'm saddened instantly.

I loved my bedroom set. It was my first real grown up purchase and it took me 6 months of tips to pay for. I loved the set, bought it, and once we moved it in I wanted to spend the first week we had it always in bed. Tyler and I had picnics in bed, and we made love constantly in our beautiful new bedroom.

Wiping a tear I feel falling down my cheek, I whisper, "The bedroom set stays. It doesn't matter anymore."

"But you loved it," she says softly.

"And I never will again," I counter until Selena stops.

"Okay, let's just get all your shit out of there while the men move your living room furniture out."

"Did Tyler pay for fucking anything?" Mike suddenly asks as I pause.

"Um, not really. I made more money because of tips," I shrug.

Feeling like an ass, I remember Selena's words from 2 nights ago and I'm embarrassed thinking maybe I was the caretaker. I was also clearly the only one to help financially in our little fake marriage.

Opening the bedroom door, Selena says angrily, "What a *bitch,*" before I know what she's talking about. "I guess those are your clothes," she points to the mound of my clothing on the floor beside my dresser.

Honestly, can this woman be any tackier? I can't believe she emptied my drawers and tossed everything on the floor. And I *really* can't believe Tyler let her. What a dick!

Ripping open the bag of garbage bags, both Selena and I are silently fuming. Handing one over, she heads for the closet and angrily rips hangers back and forth as she tugs my leftover clothing free. The noise is super loud and annoying, but I'm feeling pretty pissed myself as I slam shit around.

Scooping up all my clothes from the floor, I stuff my underwear, bras, pajamas and socks in a bag. Opening the second drawer, I grab all my t-shirts and sweat pants and also cram them in the bag. Under the dresser I grab my scrapbook box and toss it on the bed to pack in a box later.

Opening the top drawer I see all her sexy, lacy underwear and I want to scream until I see my own lingerie inside. Pulling out my green lace G-string panties and matching bra set I just lift them out when Selena says, "What a slut."

"Actually, they're mine," I laugh as she bug-eyes the 2 pieces.

"*Really?* I didn't think... huh. The green probably looks super-hot on you," she laughs at my blushing. "Was she keeping it?"

"I guess," I add looking at the rest of the stuff that is clearly hers.

"She was actually keeping your used underwear? As if it would fit her. What a dirty pig," she laughs again until I see Mike and Malcolm staring at the two of us grinning. Stuffing my underwear in the bag, I quickly take it back out again nearly gagging over the thought she might've actually worn them.

"Here," Selena takes them from me. "Trash bag," she grins stuffing all Kaitlyn's other lingerie in a new garbage bag as I watch silently. Leaving not even one pair of underwear, Selena hands it over to Mike and says, "Dumpster," as he laughs taking it with him.

"Do you want your wall unit?" Malcolm questions with crinkled eyes, almost laughing beside me at Selena's underwear theft.

"No, thanks. I hated it."

Once the men start moving out furniture again, I go through the side table drawers looking for anything I've forgotten.

"Keep that. You may need it," Selena deadpans looking over my shoulder at the vibrator Tyler bought me. Pausing for just one second, my chest explodes with embarrassed laughter. "Then again, she may have used that as well," she shudders like she's totally grossed out. "Better leave it," she laughs with me.

After searching my old room, pulling everything from under the bed, and in the closet, Selena and I are finally done. When she opens the hall closet, she starts cramming blankets, sheets and towels in a bag, choosing some and not others.

"I left Tyler the scratchy towels," she spits as I pass her. Man, I hope I never piss Selena off because she can be vicious.

Entering the bathroom, I see his and her tooth brushes- hers being *not* mine and for some reason this makes me want to cry.

It's such a stupid thing, so insignificant in the big scheme of things, but it really hurts. Seeing their toothbrushes together makes me realize they're actually together, and I still can't believe Tyler did this.

Fine he didn't want me, but to be with someone so soon when I'm still feeling like shit hurts me more than anything else. It feels so unfair to me that he still has a life, and I don't anymore.

*****

Joining Selena in the kitchen again, I drag my bags and grab a box for my bedroom and the bathroom. She's packing up bowls and pots and pans, and sadly leaving my favorite dish set I'll have to replace next week when I move into the bachelor apartment.

After filling the box, I look around one last time. It's only 12:15 and I think I'm pretty much done. I have all my knickknacks and the photo albums and everything else that was mine before, or collected during our time together.

I don't want any part of me left here for them, and besides the remaining furniture and under the sink it looks Saige-free all around. The living room looks a little funny with no furniture but the wall unit and coffee table, but that's not my problem anymore. Maybe Kaitlyn has a couch she can lend him, or maybe she'll just buy him a new one like I did.

Stopping beside the guys, Mike turns and asks, "What about the TV?"

"No, it's okay."

"I remember when you bought it like 2 months ago, Saige," he points to the awesome flat screen I bought for Tyler's birthday.

"It was a gift."

"Everything was a fucking gift for Tyler," Mike surprises me with his anger. "Did he buy *you* any gifts?"

"Of course..." I find myself defending Tyler again. Though usually of the lingerie or sex toy variety, he did buy me flowers and my favorite coffee once in a while.

Shit... I'm starting to see just how uneven our relationship really was the longer I look at it.

"If you don't take it, you're just going to have to buy yourself another one, and I doubt you have the money for that right now," Mike pushes embarrassing me a little when I watch Malcolm listening silently.

"I don't need a TV- I never have time to watch it. And the bachelor is small anyway until September, so I'll be fine, Mike. Please leave it alone- it was a birthday gift."

"Fine," he mumbles grabbing and stacking 2 boxes to leave the apartment again.

"I have an extra TV if you need it. It's just sitting in my spare room untouched," Malcolm offers.

"Really, I'm fine. But thank you."

"When are you moving into the bachelor?"

"Monday. We're taking my stuff to Selena's Mom's garage til then."

"You have to move again on Monday?" He asks grinning as I huff.

"Yeah... This move isn't the best. But I had to get my stuff out and away from Tyler. I should've done it weeks ago, but there was just so much other stuff going on."

"Saige! Look what I found in the drawer!" Selena yells running for me. Practically assaulting me with a piece paper she flips it around to show me my transcripts dated a few days earlier.

Grabbing it from her I just take in the number when I scream. Holy *shit!* Giggling and jumping on the spot I can't believe what I'm seeing. 97! Friggin' 97 percent!

"97 percent!" Selena screams grabbing me in a huge hug. "You're a fucking genius," she yells and honestly I feel like one right now.

"Holy *shit...*" I moan in shock. 97% in Handle's class is unheard of he's such a hardass.

"Read the red," Selena pushes already reading it out loud anyway.

'Well done, Miss Masters. I even deducted 1% for crying in the exam. ☺

It was an absolute pleasure teaching you, and I wish you all the best in your future. I look forward to seeing you again some day.

Professor Gregory D. Handle'

P.S. I hope one day you silence those ghosts in your past.

"What the hell? He even drew a smiley face. What an ass. And the ghosts comment? Ugh."

"I don't know," I quickly cut her off when Mike leans in for a hug.

"Wow, Saige. 97 percent. We're soooo getting you drunk tonight," Selena laughs hugging me again.

"At least my conditional acceptance will be lifted now," I mumble into her side.

"No kidding. To think you had 98%."

"Yeah, that's because I forgot the IIRIRA," I admit to silence as they all look at me. "You know, The Illegal Immigration Reform and Immigrant Responsibility Act," I laugh when the 3 of them are still just looking at me like I'm speaking a different language.

"Uh huh," Selena laughs with Malcolm. "Anyway, this is just so awesome, and so weird. You seem pretty normal for being such a freak of nature," Selena grins as I laugh at her. "Where should we go?"

"We all have to work tomorrow."

"You and I start at 1:00 so plenty of time to recover and Mike works the 11-11. Malcolm?" She asks and I don't know who feels more on the spot- me or him.

"I'm game. Congratulations, Saige," Malcolm says stepping toward me for what seems like a potential hug but stops at a touch on my arm. "That's pretty amazing as far as exam scores go. How do you feel?"

"Relieved. Everything else should flow smoothly now, once I get out of here," I look around my decimated former apartment.

"Let's hurry and finish," Selena claps her hand excited. "Saige has to buy us dinner for helping her move, then we have to buy her drinks for being freakishly smart!"

157

*****

Leaving my apartment a half hour later, I take one last, long look and close the door. I almost whisper 'Bye, Ty' like I had thousands of times in the last 3 years here, but he's not here anymore.

So instead I say goodbye to my past and close the door behind me for good.

CHAPTER 16

3 hours later after unloading the U-Haul at Mrs. Culver's house, returning home quickly to shower and change Selena and I cab it to D'Vecseys for dinner. Walking in to congratulations on my grade from Aileen and Hailey, Selena and I walk to the lounge to Mike and Malcolm already seated across from each other.

Joining in the conversation across from Malcolm and beside Mike everyone is complaining of various aches and pains from the move, but there's also a slight excitement in the air I haven't felt in weeks.

We all seem to get along really well, and Malcolm has fit right in with the three of us like he's been around more than just a few times. Selena even teases Malcolm just as much as she does me and Mike, and Malcolm is always quick with his funny replies.

He seems to be always relaxed with us, though there's still a funny kind of distance between the two of us like he's making sure to stay nonthreatening or something with me.

Finally, after our delicious dinner Malcolm suggests we leave for a pub his friend owns. He explains it's fun and not too crowded. So without much more prompting, I run and pay the bill to Malcolm's annoyance before we all pile into his SUV for the pub.

*****

Opening the wooden doors wide, Selena and I walk past Malcolm and stop. The pub is dark wood and burgundy bench seats everywhere. The feeling immediately welcomes you in and the music welcomes you home. Being assaulted by Mumford and Sons, there's definitely a Celtic feel all around and I'm in heaven.

Following behind Malcolm we grab a booth near the back pool tables and settle in before he walks to the bar for our first drinks order.

"He's amazing, Saige," Selena lifts her hand when I attempt to speak. "I know you're not ready, and I know too much has been going on these last few weeks. I'm just saying keep your options open. Settle into your new apartment on Monday, exhale finally, and just see what can happen with Malcolm."

"I don't think it's like that. Malcolm is almost big brotherly or something with me. Plus he's thirty one."

"So. I'm 29," Selena snaps.

"But we're not dating," I giggle when she accepts my excuse with a pout.

"I'll tell you this, if I didn't see him watching your every move I would've already made a play for him." A little shocked she would admit that, I definitely feel a little possessive of Malcolm suddenly as I stare at her. "Didn't like that, huh?" She smirks like she was playing *me* all along. "Good. Now get your scrawny ass drunk. You deserve a celebration, and a night without thinking or being afraid."

When she's finished her speech, Mike nods and takes my hand across the table. "She's right. Just have fun tonight. And Malcolm really is into you Saige, I can tell."

Blushing at the thought of Malcolm being into me, I just pull my hand away when Malcolm returns with our 4 drinks. Sitting in the booth, his face changes again to the attractive one when he smiles and tells me to drink up.

"She has NO tolerance for liquor, so watch her," Selena grins to my shut the hell up. "For being Scottish, she's a pathetic drinker."

"Sorry," I whine. "Not all Scottish people drink, ya know?" Waiting a fraction of a second, all three of them start laughing when I do. "Okay, almost all do," I concede.

After a few minutes of easy banter between the 4 of us Malcolm looks to the side of the room and asks me to play pool with him. Shaking my head no Malcolm asks me to come anyway with an adorable pout until I eventually give in.

Sliding out of the booth to the pool table I listen and watch and study his every move. I watch his arms and back and take in even the flick of his wrist when he shows me how to play.

Leaning into me Malcolm says so seriously I pause at his intensity, "There's no test after this, Saige," and then he smirks like a smartass.

"Damn. That's too bad, cuz I'm pretty good at tests," I grin.

"So I've heard. You're really amazing, Saige. And as Selena said really pretty awesome for being such a freak," he adds breaking and sinking 2 striped balls before I can respond.

"Show off," I grin trying to line up my first solid ball when it's my turn, but missing it totally. Trying again when Malcolm insists I take another shot I fail again, even hitting one of his balls into the pocket instead to his gracious nod.

After a few minutes of playing poorly a man I recognize stands beside us suddenly and I find myself actually moving closer to Malcolm. Unaware I was even moving, I'm very aware when I'm against Malcolm's side.

"Saige, this is Terry. You met him at the restaurant the night we all came in," Malcolm says softly then waits a moment as I stare at Terry.

"Hi, Saige. It's nice to see you again," he smiles extending his hand. Looking at Terry, I remember he was one of the four in the street, and he was the one who insisted with Malcolm that I take the tips. I remember him, and thankfully I don't seem to fear him.

After what seems like a very long pause with his hand still extended, I finally reach for it tentatively. Just touching, Terry is very gentle, not even squeezing my hand and then he quickly releases me.

Looking for anything to say, I whisper, "It's nice to officially meet you." With Malcolm standing right beside me, I feel safe and brave and *normal* actually, which suggests Terry wasn't the one who hurt me.

"I hear a celebration is in order, so all *your* drinks are on the house tonight," he winks at me before clapping his hand on Malcolm's shoulder. "Oh, and be careful of this one- he's a pool shark," he laughs with Malcolm before leaving us.

"You okay?" Malcolm asks leaning down to me as I watch Terry walk away.

Staring at Terry behind the bar I finally breathe a nearly silent, "Yes," before drinking the rest of my vodka and orange. "It wasn't him," I whisper to myself but I hear Malcolm say *good* beside me anyway.

Pulling me out of my head, Malcolm tells me it's my turn again. "Can I show you something? I'm going to lean against you but not touch you, okay?"

Nodding, I find myself nervous, but when he tells me to line up my shot, he does exactly as he said he would. He leans right against my side, and other than touching my hand and fingers while fake sliding the cue through them, his other hand doesn't touch me at all.

"There now," he says softly against my side. "Take the shot, Saige. Look at the solid green and use your arm, not your body to hit it with the white ball."

Slowing down everything, I imagine the ball and inhale the warmth of Malcolm before I hit it... and miss the green again. "I was wayyyy closer that time," I laugh as he straightens up from my side.

"Aye," he grins taking a sip of his beer.

Joining Selena and Mike back at the table, I'm already slightly buzzed. I finished 2 drinks while playing with Malcolm, and I see there's a shot and another drink waiting for me at my spot. Lifting my shot, Selena and Mike join me with their own as I gag it back.

"Why aren't you having any more?" Selena asks a laughing Malcolm watching my face contort after the shot.

"2 drink max. I never drink more than 2, especially when driving," he says as I look over.

I'm not sure if that was for my benefit, or if he was just being honest. Either way, I think of Alec instantly with a drunken sadness straight through my heart.

"I have to use the washroom then I want to play you," Selena head tilts to the pool table. "*She* may be a pool virgin, but I'm not."

"You're on," Malcolm says darkly, leaning toward Selena over the table. Actually growling, Selena holds his stare in challenge forever.

"Let's go, Kiddo," she pushes at me glaring at Malcolm as she rises. Standing, I watch the two of them until Malcolm eyes crinkle a smile.

Leaving the washroom, Selena is drunk and I'm pretty much. Turning to see who's at the pool table I walk smack into a man gabbing my arm and before I know what's happened, I freeze.

Feeling him against my front, his hand is on my ass and he's speaking in my ear, breathing all over me, but I hear nothing.

I'm frozen by his big body and my mind has totally blanked in fear. And then it's over.

So fast I scream, the man is on the floor with Malcolm's hand on his throat with his knee on the guy's chest. They're on the floor and I'm just stunned by the violence and speed by which it occurred.

Jolting out of my head I pull at Malcolm's arm and say all I can. "That was my fault. I walked into him."

"No, you didn't," he snaps at the man's face. "I watched this asshole jump up as soon as you two left the washrooms so he could bump into you. But he made a mistake, didn't you?" Malcolm says so menacingly, I don't know what else to say. "Apologize for touching her, jumping her, crowding her, and basically for being anywhere near her. *Now,*" he squeezes the man's throat harder until I yank at his arm again.

Waiting less than a second, the man looks over at me and Selena and croaks a pathetic 'I'm sorry' between gasps for breath. Between the knee on his chest and Malcolm's hand on his throat he's so red in the face I'm surprised he said even that much.

"Is that acceptable, Saige?" Malcolm asks not looking at me.

"Yes," I gasp loudly still pulling at his arm.

"You're lucky. If you ever jump another woman like that again and I see it, I'll break your fucking arms. Got it?" Malcolm says deadly calm in the guy's face as he tries to nod quickly.

And then it's over. Again.

Standing, Malcolm releases the man and turns to me. "Are you okay?" Looking up at him I find myself wordless. Malcolm seems so scary suddenly, and simply put, I'm scared shitless of his anger right now.

"Please don't look at me like that," he pushes leaning in a little closer to me before I accidentally step back a foot. "Saige, he did that on purpose. I watched him wait for you to be distracted and then he purposely smashed into you so he could grab your ass and hold you against him. I just stopped him, that's all." Nodding, I understand but I still feel uncomfortable. "Saige?"

"I'm fine. Thank you," I smile quickly before walking back to the table. Followed by Selena, I turn back to see the guy standing with help from someone else and then he's walking toward the front doors. Watching him leave slowly like he's hurt, Malcolm's reaction really bothers me.

I do actually understand what Malcolm did in reaction to what the guy did, but it was so quick and scary, and kind of deadly to watch. I can almost imagine Malcolm being able to snap that man's neck if he'd wanted to, and the calm way he held him, choking him while speaking to him made it even scarier.

Malcolm seemed way too comfortable doing what he did and that makes me *very* uncomfortable.

"Saige, please stop freaking out," Selena tugs at my sleeve. "Malcolm was protecting you, not hurting you," she leans closer to me like I needed the clarification.

"I understand that. It was just scary seeing him like that," I admit.

"It was *hot* seeing him like that," Selena giggles beside me. Looking at her, I'm stunned she thinks that caveman crap was hot. "It was. When was the last time a man took out another for you? *Tyler?* I doubt it. He probably would've stood behind you to let you outsmart the idiot."

Shocked she would say that about Tyler, the imaginary is pretty funny I'll give her that, and slowly that turns into a quick laugh picturing bigger Tyler cowering behind little me. Finally laughing with her, I exhale the fear I had seeing Malcolm so angry.

"Drink up. We have a pair's game of pool to win. Then we can go home if you want."

Feeling a little better, I take my drink with me to Mike and Malcolm at the pool table having their own game.

Watching Malcolm he's completely normal again, relaxed and joking with Mike every time he sinks a ball or Mike does in turn. He looks over at me frequently, smiles often, winks once when he lines up a shot to take out 2 balls, and basically seems just like himself again.

"Ready?" Malcolm asks as Mike sets up the balls again.

"Sure."

"I'm sorry if I scared you, but you looked so frightened when he was holding you, I had to stop him." Looking up at Malcolm I realize he's right. I forgot the first part to that scene. I forgot how I froze when that prick had me held against his chest with his hand on my ass. I forgot I couldn't move away or even scream because I'd frozen against him.

"It's okay. I appreciate you getting him off me."

"So, we're good?" He asks leaning down to look at me closely.

"We're good. But I'd be better if I could beat you at pool. I hate losing anything. Ever."

"Stubborn *and* competitive," he grins walking back to the pool table just as Selena yells she's breaking.

10 minutes later, Malcolm and Mike have cleared the table to us, well *Selena,* sinking only 4 balls. Laughing at our pouting, Malcolm walks to the bar to buy us each one more *losers* drink as he called it.

Watching him walk away, I keep smiling because I'm drunk, and watching because I'm intrigued. I think I really like Malcolm until I see a waitress all over him at the bar.

Laughing and touching his arm, Malcolm leans down to talk to her and with his arm wrapped around her back they seem really cozy together. Almost like Tyler and Kaitlyn did.

Feeling totally irrational, immature, neurotic and paranoid suddenly, I want to cry. I'm jealous and pissed off, and I'm mad at both of them. And at myself.

I'm being an ass but I can't really stop it. I feel like I'm acting like my mum did which is about all the reality check I need to stop the shit in my head and the feelings in my chest.

When I see Malcolm smile at me I turn my head away. I'm not doing this. I won't act like a jealous psycho because of him.

Malcolm owes me no loyalty, certainly not anything more than Tyler did, so he can do whatever he wants with whoever he wants.

"Here you go," Malcolm says sitting back down with our drinks.

"*Thanks*," I snap unintentionally.

Shit, I'm losing it. And my anger is directed at the wrong person, I know. Malcolm is *not* Tyler, I remind myself. God, he's not even my boyfriend so his fidelity doesn't even exist for me. And really, I don't want it to anyway.

"Saige," Selena pulls at my sleeve while I mentally chastise and berate myself for being an insecure idiot over a stranger I just met. *Shit.* Here I go on another round of internal pissed off.

"Saige?" Malcolm asks and as I turn to him I feel nothing but anger. He's been flirting with me for days and then flirting with another woman seconds later. Whatever. My mother was right. *You canna trust a man wee yer heart*. Not that he has my heart, but if I ever thought I might like him a little that just ended.

"Hello? What's going on with you," Selena demands and I feel such annoyance for Tyler *and* Malcolm I finally just spill.

"It's funny how a man can flirt and be kind to a woman when she's right in front of his face- then he can turn to another woman and flirt with her a second later, isn't it? I was just thinking about how men are and how they can never be trusted, don't you think Selena?" I ask her the question with a voice filled with so much hostility I've effectively silenced our whole table.

"If you're speaking about me I'd prefer you speak *to* me, Saige," Malcolm says angrily. "And if you're referring to the waitress at the bar, she's Terry's sister, Agnes, I've known her for 20 years, she's happily married, and I'm even godfather to her youngest son, Devon."

Feeling my face turn so red my ears burn, I lie quickly. "I wasn't referring to you, I was just speaking in general," I choke. "Um, even Mike said that, right?" Looking at Mike with my eyes begging him to jump in, he looks totally confused by what I'm asking. "Remember you said even when a man isn't looking, he still kind of is. *Remember*?" I beg desperately.

Leaning across the table to get my undivided attention, Malcolm says, "I'm going to politely disagree with Mike on that one," while still glaring at me.

"I wasn't talking about you," I lie again pathetically.

"Well, that's good. Because when I find what I want I don't keep looking, and I am NOT your ex-boyfriend. I don't cheat, I don't use woman, and I don't let women support and care for me emotionally *or* financially. I'm a man, Saige. Not a little boy."

"I didn't say you were," I choke. I don't know what else to say now. I'm blatantly caught being an insecure idiot, so I know I should just give up the fight. But I don't know how to when what I feel feels so real.

Exhaling and blushing again, I huff, "I'm sorry," to a silent nod from Malcolm.

"*Annnnd* we're done here," Selena says so comically I'm grateful for the reprieve from the tense situation I've caused. "Let's go," she tugs at me to rise after we both gulp the last of our drinks.

Walking out between Selena and Mike, I know Malcolm is following and I wish I knew how to stop feeling like a stupid kid with him. I'm embarrassed and even a little sad, especially when we walk up to his SUV and Malcolm unlocks the doors but still doesn't speak to me.

Thankfully in the SUV, Selena is loud, drunk, and funny. Mike is quiet but for his laughter at Selena, and Malcolm and I keep sneaking glances at each other in the rearview mirror before quickly looking away. Eventually though we see each other and Malcolm winks back at me which causes such a quick desperation-filled exhale, I know he heard me when he grins.

Parked out front, Mike stays put but Malcolm insists on walking us right up to Selena's apartment door. He rides the elevator with us silently, and walks to her door silently.

At our door, Malcolm says only, "See you tomorrow for coffee, Saige," as he walks away to me smiling my relief at his back.

"That is one fine man you got there," Selena moans stumbling to her bedroom. "Speaking of, I have a date Saturday night and was wondering if you'd watch Griffin for me?"

"Of course. Who are you going out with?" I ask excited for her.

"Dave," she giggles at her door to my open-mouthed shock. "Night, Kiddo," she smiles shutting me out.

(mis)TRUST

CHAPTER 17

At 5:45 I realize I've seen Malcolm every day this week. I saw him when I returned Sunday from my mum's, we had coffee Monday, and I saw him when he came to the restaurant with Dan Tuesday night before their basketball game for a quick bite. He helped me move yesterday and now I'm waiting to see him again. For not dating, I swear I see Malcolm more than I saw Tyler who I actually lived with.

"He's here," Aileen smiles brightly. "And he's so hot, Saige. Seriously." Turning to her, I'm a little uncomfortable talking about Malcolm to her, but it's fairly obvious something's going. "Go get ready. We can switch out easily, and I'll leave your tips with Mike after you leave."

"Thanks, but I still have 15 minutes."

"Who gives a shit? I was 20 minutes late on Tuesday and you covered for me. Go," she pushes me until I sneak to the back.

Changing into jeans, I wear a forest green turtleneck, and black knee high boots for some height. My hair is up in a bun and my makeup only needs to be slightly touched up. Running for the bathroom to pee and brush my teeth, I actually wonder why I'm brushing my teeth.

Pausing at the sink, I think about kissing. Kissing for me was almost better than sex- okay it wasn't *better,* it was just different because it was more emotional or something.

Sometimes when Tyler and I laid around on the couch we would just kiss each other for hours. Yes, sex usually followed, but not always. Sometimes it was just kissing and touching, and holding each other, and it was nice. It was just kissing between us, but I felt loved and secure in my relationship with him. I *enjoyed* my relationship with him.

Throwing my toothbrush back in its case in my purse, I powder my face and reapply my lipstick, inhale deeply, exhale slowly, and try to stop thinking about Tyler.

I may not be ready, or even want anything with Malcolm, but I sure as hell don't want to be thinking about Tyler anymore.

After Selena played me the pissed off messages she received from him about taking the couch I bought, my dislike for him was complete. He even gave us shit for throwing out Kaitlyn's underwear, calling it 'an invasion of her privacy' that we went through her drawers, as opposed to me who just had her clothing thrown on the floor. The asshole.

Anyway, Selena texted him to fuck off and never text her again, then she blocked his number from her phone. Thankfully, Tyler still doesn't have my new number so I'm safe from his anger for now.

✶✶✶✶✶

Walking around the bar I see Malcolm immediately. Talking with a smiling, blushing Aileen, Malcolm turns like he knew I was there. Smiling at me, Aileen fans herself dramatically behind his back as I try not to laugh.

"Good evening, Saige," he stands towering over me. "Ready for more coffee?"

"Yes. Um, where are we going?"

"Blenders again? Or my brother Tatum has a little pub not far from where we were last night?"

"Blenders," I reply immediately. "I'm comfortable there and it's only 5 minutes from here so it feels safer," I admit.

"You know it would take nothing shy of an RPG to get through me to you, don't you?" He asks so seriously I can't even reply. "Saige, you never have to be afraid of your physical safety when you're with me. I promise you."

Waiting for me to acknowledge him I think, I truly don't know what to say. I get that he's huge, but things happen, and bad people happen.

"I'm being super paranoid, I know," I sigh embarrassed as he leans closer to me. "It's just the police have no suspects and everything seemed so personal, and I don't know who would want to hurt me, or *why* they wanted to hurt me. Ah, and I still get scared all the time." Winding down my confession, Malcolm nods and exhales himself.

"I understand, or at least I'm trying to understand how that would feel for you. I've never had to worry about myself like that before, so I walk where I want and do what I want. I get that you're a woman, and a tiny one at that, but I beg you to try to relax when you're with me. As I said,

170

I can protect you, and I *will* protect you." When I gasp a little from his intensity, he continues, "I will, Saige. And even if I was somehow taken out, I guarantee I would give you enough time to get away. You will always be safe with me."

"Thank you," I nearly cry I'm so moved by his promise and intensity, and by just everything about him right now.

It's like I can put all the bad shit aside when I'm with him. I don't have to worry, and I don't have to be afraid for a while.

"Okay. Wherever you want to go. Blenders or your brother's place. Ah, I'll try to relax," I say a little stupidly but he smiles anyway.

"My brother Tatum's," he nods motioning for me to start for the doors.

Once seated in his SUV again, Malcolm asks, "Q&A now or inside the pub?"

"Inside," I smile looking out the window as we drive. Curious if he lives close by or not, I ask, "Where do you live?"

"Couldn't wait, huh? I own a house in Montgomery Park," he smiles when I ask *really?* "Yes, really. But don't get too excited- it might look nice now, but I bought it 6 years ago and I still haven't finished renovating. It was an absolute dump I bought at an estate sale."

"Still... I don't know much about this city, but everyone speaks so highly of Montgomery Park. It's like *the* place to live," I say totally impressed.

"It is," he grins. "But my house is the smallest in the neighborhood, I don't drive an Lexus, and I'm single. So basically I'm the black sheep of the neighborhood."

"What made you buy it? Was it overwhelming?"

"I was 25 and arrogant, and yes it was overwhelming. 2 months after I bought it Dan's guys plus 2 of my brothers had to help me replace the roof after a heavy rainstorm seeped through and destroyed all the walls upstairs. Then the electric was next, which I *can* do myself. But it was a huge job, and like I said it still isn't completed. It looks great from the outside, but there are still rooms upstairs that are incomplete. The kitchen is awesome though," he grins proud of himself.

"I'd love to see it," I think out loud before catching myself.

"Anytime. I can barbecue a mean steak, which doesn't require the kitchen at all, I know. But I love eating in my kitchen. So whenever you're craving a steak I'm your man," he says just pulling up to a storefront looking pub.

"Tatum's?"

"Very original, I know. My brother is an arrogant bastard that's for sure," he laughs opening his door as I do. "I should warn you, he's a big man," he adds as I look up at his huge body confused.

Walking inside past Malcolm's outstretched arm holding the door, I'm surrounded by him though still not being touched by him ever.

"Wait for it," he grins just as a huge man yells something unintelligible across the room. "He won't touch you," Malcolm adds when I brace myself and step back into Malcolm's chest watching him coming at me.

Holy *shit!* Whereas Malcolm is just big, brick shithouse large, his brother is like awkwardly tall. My entire body looks like I could fit in his pant leg, he is that HUGE.

"Wee Saige? I'm Tatum of Tatum's Pub," he says bending down low extending both his hands to clasp mine. "You failed to mention she was a little elf with witchy green eyes," he says so seriously to Malcolm I can't stop my shocked laughter.

"I hardly think my 5 foot 2 is the problem here," I shake his hands. "I'm leaning more towards the beast of a man in front of me. And these witchy green eyes? I know how to use them, so be careful," I scowl playfully until he barks a laugh so loud my ears ring.

"You look like a little Leprechaun for Christ's sake!" He howls making me laugh again. "I feel like I should put you on the bar in a soup pot so people can toss coins at you to make a wish!"

"*What?*" I gasp laughing.

"Okay, Tatum," Malcolm tries to interject but he's laughing too hard. "Stop teasing the wee elf," he says as I turn and smack his stomach. "The *vicious* wee elf," he quickly amends.

"Come on, let's get you a drink," Tatum turns back toward the bar.

Walking behind Tatum I'm embarrassed to admit I can't stop staring at his butt, and his huge pants, and his huge everything. In truth, he towers over even Malcolm's 6'4 frame.

Sitting on the high backed stools at the bar Malcolm nods at a few people but watches me closely. Once I'm up, he sits beside me and rests his arm against the back of my chair, kind of circling me in without actually touching me. And I feel protected and safe again with him.

"What are you having?"

"Um, do you have coffee?"

"Anything you like. Tatum's aims to please," Tatum grins and just like Malcolm his whole face transforms into handsome with his smile.

"She'd like a cafe mocha, no whip cream, with an extra shot of espresso?"

"Yes, please. But without the extra shot. It's getting kind of late."

"And for you?" Tatum leans over the bar closer to Malcolm. After Malcolm says a beer Tatum nods and turns for the end of the bar and an impressive looking Cappuccino machine.

"Okay, I have to know-"

"7'2. He and Andrew are only one year apart and Andy was growing tall too. It wasn't until Andy stopped at 6'5 that my parents thought to have Tate checked out. So when Tatum was 22 they discovered he had a tumor on his pituitary gland. Anyway, it was surgically removed and he stopped growing, but he was huge at that point as you can see."

"I see..." I look over again at Tatum bending down low to work the handles on the espresso machine. "Is he older?"

"Yeah, he's the oldest, then there's Andrew who lives in South Africa. Then Moira," he grins. "A good Scottish name for my sister. And after a 4 year hiatus after Moira, I was next followed by Alec, the runt of the litter at only 6 foot," he says smiling until his smile fades as my own darkens.

Alec? *Really?* I know it's a common Scottish name, but out of the thousands of names available, he actually shares a brother with the same name as my own.

"What's wrong?" Malcolm asks leaning closer to me.

"Nothing at all. I'm fine," I smile trying to stop the upset that's quickly squeezing my heart.

Looking at my face before I turn away, Malcolm pushes his stool back and tells me to come with him. Walking to a booth across the way around a few tables in the middle, he walks and waits for me to follow, which I do.

"I'm going to tell you a little about myself Saige, and I'd like you to really listen, okay?"

"Of course."

Feeling worried about whatever he has to say I tense right up until the silence becomes almost unbearable. Turning to Tatum walking toward us I realize Malcolm was just waiting for us to be served before he started telling me whatever he's going to say.

"Thank you," I smile up a Tatum.

"You're very welcome, Saige. Let me now if you need any food or another drink, okay?"

"I will. Thank you," I mumble again nervously waiting for Malcolm to speak.

"Thanks, Tate," he nods before Tatum leaves us alone.

Having a quick gulp of his beer, Malcolm looks at me and starts speaking when I raise the cappuccino cup to my mouth.

"Saige... I'm normal. *Mostly,*" he grins quickly. "I have 2 parents I love, 4 siblings I love, and *I* have loved," he says softly. "I don't lie, I don't cheat, and I don't abuse or use women. I may be large but you'll never see me fight without provocation, and certainly *never* with a woman." When he pauses, I realize he wanted me to really hear the last statement about fighting with women.

"I'm a working-class guy who hangs out with the nerd before the captain of the football team every time. I realize you don't know me or trust me, or maybe even like me as much as I like you, but that is *your* problem to deal with," he pauses for a moment until I nod.

"I will never lie to you or hurt you intentionally, which after last night I think you know, or at least have seen firsthand. If I am out with you even as just friends I would never flirt with another woman in front of you. And if we ever became more than friends I would never look for more when I'm with you. That's not who I am," he tacks on before breathing deeply.

Mesmerized by his speech he's so engrossing I can't speak. He's laid everything out in front of me, and it's for me to either believe or disbelieve like he pointed out. And I get it. I just have a hard time believing it, which is also my problem to deal with as he said.

"My parents are still in love, Saige. They battle like you wouldn't believe and my siblings and I always knew when they were fighting because the house was too quiet. But even fighting my dad is the first person to defend my mother to anyone. He would *go to the death for her* as he says every single day because he loves her." Pausing again, Malcolm eventually continues when I sit wordless waiting for more.

"Tatum is married to a wonderful little elf himself," Malcolm grins when I laugh. "Though to be fair, even if Melissa was an Amazon woman she'd still look like a little elf next to Tate," he smiles.

"Andy is married in South Africa to a beautiful woman named Gretcha he loves more than life itself. Moira is married to a friend of mine and very happy. And Alec is 29, single, but looking. I may even introduce him to Selena," he winks.

"I don't have bad role models for love, and I don't have a nasty history or past with women. I've been in love until it played out and I've been in long and short term relationships until they played out. But my relationships have *never* ended badly because of abuse or cheating or anything like that."

When he pauses again to take a drink I feel like I need to say something important. "Malcolm, I appreciate all you've said but-"

"I wasn't finished," he interrupts me until I apologize. "I'm not asking you for anything. I'm not telling you this so you'll start dating me at all. It's clear you're not ready for anything after this last month of hell for you, and I don't want to be a rebound for you anyway. I want to be your friend, Saige. I want you to talk to me when you need to, and I want you to listen to me when *I* need to talk. I want to get to know you, no strings or expectations attached. But you have to trust me to do that. That's why I told you all this."

After another quick pause, Malcolm leans over and actually takes my hand before I can pull away. "And I want you to understand something, and know it is the absolute truth. I will *never* touch you without you asking me to. I will never kiss you or touch you sexually ever without your express desire and permission. If we are ever with each other sexually it will be because *you* want to be. Just the thought of you scared of me or doing something you don't want to do not only repulses me but it makes me nearly violent. So again, I'm telling you, I am your friend. *Only.* I am the best weapon you could ever have beside you, and the best friend you'll ever need if you choose to accept my friendship." Squeezing my hand gently, he waits until I look back at him before speaking.

"That's all, Saige. I don't want you like this, and I wouldn't start anything with you when you have so much going on in your life right now anyway. Is all that clear enough for you? Can you finally just relax with me now?"

"Yes," I whisper instantly.

Without thought or hesitation, I said yes because I want to and because I need to. I want to be his friend so badly, and with all the relationship stuff out of the way I can finally relax and just enjoy his friendship.

"Good. Wanna go do it in the back room now?" He asks so seriously I almost spew the coffee I just drank. "No?" He laughs at me.

"Ah, no," I laugh wiping my chin. "But thanks for the offer."

Turning serious again, Malcolm says, "I also want you to know I'm trying to find out who hurt you, and I'm going to fix this for you."

"*How?* What do you mean?" I gasp.

"I've talked with the police and with Dan's brother Mario, so I know the details of what happened. I've spoken to my friends and I can say with 100% accuracy not one of them hurt you that night, with the exception of Keith saying he hung out with his sister for hours which still seems a little weird. But otherwise I have all the guys covered that night," he huffs as I cover my mouth scared.

"Listen to me, I'm not saying Keith did it, or even suggesting he may have. All I'm saying is he's the only person from that night that I'm not one hundred percent sure of. He was just too adamant and aggressive when Dan and I confronted him and I didn't like his reaction at all. But we told the police everything and just as you are, we have to wait for someone to try to hurt you again before we have any answers. And I know it's that fear that paralyzes you which is why I sent you the gifts you *don't* have on you and should," he seems to wait for me to agree which I do. "Good."

"Why do you care about this? I mean I just met you."

"Saige, when I met you a month ago, you handed Keith his ass, and stood up for yourself. For being a tiny little thing, you took care of yourself perfectly among us group of men. So I was attracted to you physically, absolutely," he grins when I blush. "And like a man who wants something, the next time we met you yelled at me when I asked you out, essentially told me to fuck off, and again, it was hot as hell," he laughs this time when I look down at the table.

"It *was*, Saige. But when I saw you next beaten up, freaked out, and scared out of your fucking mind, I was horrified. I couldn't believe what I was seeing less than 2 weeks after meeting you, and your almost animalistic reaction to defend yourself in the restaurant freaked me out and fucked me up. Even I was surprised by the intensity of my reaction to your fear."

Pushing himself back against the seat he seems to be struggling himself at the moment, and I appreciate the pause. My head is spinning again and that horrible night is so clear and so *here* right now, I feel kind of freaked out again.

"I *hated* seeing you like that in the restaurant," Malcolm exhales deeply. "I couldn't stand it, and seeing those bruises and cuts on your face mostly healed even now, I still can't stand the memory of seeing you hurt like that."

Looking up, he seems so sincere I kind of trust that he is. He already told me he doesn't want a relationship with me, so really there's no point to him saying all this if he did want more from me. Looking at the table, I find myself nodding at nothing and calming as he watches me.

"I'm sorry," I whisper though I don't know why. "I didn't mean to freak you out."

"What? See this is what I'm talking about. Why would you apologize for your reaction to me and Dan?"

"I don't know. I just feel insecure and nervous. I hate that you see me as weak, but I *feel* weak right now."

"Awww, Saige. You're not weak. You're just recovering from a shit time which *takes* time. I read up on sexual assault," he says as I flinch. "So I know it takes time to heal emotionally much longer than physically. Add in the fact that your boyfriend abandoned you 2 days before and of course you're struggling and nervous and insecure. But you have your friends and me now. Even Dan wants me to give you his number in case you ever need his help." Taking my hand again, Malcolm says gently, "I'm right here to be your friend, Saige."

"Thank you," I finally cry. Bursting into tears from the memories and his kindness and from everything around me, I can't hold it in any longer.

Covering my face with my hands I cry long and sometimes a little loudly. Using my coffee napkin I wipe up my face as needed and continue crying until Malcolm pulls my one hand away from my face.

"Don't. I'm hideous when I cry," I burst out laughing suddenly like a psycho.

"Are you okay?" I quickly look over at Tatum. On his knees on the floor beside me he's actually the same height as me sitting in the booth.

"I'm good," I grin wiping my nose. "The cafe mocha was delicious," I start laughing again when he looks both confused and unsure of what's happening. Looking at Tatum's confusion and Malcolm's grin I find it so humorous I laugh until I eventually calm again.

"Malcolm usually only makes women cry on the second date," Tatum adds so seriously I giggle again.

"This IS our second non-date date."

"Ah, then he's right on schedule," Tatum grins, slowly standing as I hear his knee crack. "Can I get you anything else?"

"Some more napkins?"

"Coming right up," he turns but not before glaring at Malcolm who shakes his head at him.

"Sorry for this. I was feeling a little stressed out."

"Don't be sorry, and of course you were. I don't mind crying, Saige. But if I can help you at all, please tell me how."

"You can't. You already have. Thank you for making me cry," I laugh at his confused expression. "No seriously. I don't cry often enough Selena says, so I kind of needed to. But now I'll be fine for a while."

"I'm glad I could help," he says sweetly. Thanking Tatum, I'm handed napkins before he walks away again. "Is there anything else I can do for you?"

"No. I really do feel better, but I would like to excuse myself for a minute," I say already sliding out of the booth with my purse.

Closing the stall to pee, I'm exhausted. That was the most amazing talk, and the best cry I've had since the last time I cried with Malcolm. God, he's so sweet and kind, and just amazing to me.

Looking at myself in the mirror when I wash my hands I laugh at how hideous I am. Being a redhead who used to have dark freckles as a kid that thankfully faded over time, my face still turns beet red and blotchy when I cry. My nose swells, my eyes get puffy, and even my lips get a little swollen. I'm not a pretty crier.

Washing and reapplying my make-up, I can't do anything about the puffiness, but I can at least cover up the red blotchiness and dark scars, while reapplying my mascara so my eyes don't look so gross.

Ignoring the other tables of people, I realize with Malcolm I never once felt scared, or really even noticed the people around us. I didn't see the men in the pub, and I didn't fear the men would touch me when I walked to the washroom. He really is my own little safe haven when he's around.

Walking up to him, I hug around his middle so suddenly I didn't even think about it. I just reacted to him standing against the booth waiting for me.

I hugged him because I wanted to and I hugged him because I want him to know I appreciate all the kindness he's shown me since we met.

"You're awesome, Malcolm," I whisper feeling his arms wrap around me very lightly when I snuggle in deeper to his chest. "Thank you for tonight."

"You're welcome, ya wee leprechaun," he says as I rub my forehead against his chest laughing. "Are you ready to go home?"

"Yes," I smile pulling away. "I'd like to say goodbye to Tatum first," I look around at the bar to Tatum watching and smiling at me as I approach. "Thank you for the delicious cafe mocha, and for the napkins," I grin as he barks a quick laugh.

"You're welcome, Saige. Come back anytime. And if you ever feel like making a little extra money, my bar and soup pots are always available to you," he grins as Malcolm laughs behind me.

"I'll keep that in mind," I shake the hand offered to me.

Walking back to Malcolm's truck, I feel the night around me but I also feel the safety of him beside me. And I'm okay right now.

"What do you have planned this weekend?" He asks starting the truck.

"I have a doctor's appointment tomorrow and work afterward. I'm babysitting Selena's son Saturday night, and I'm working Sunday. You?"

"I'm working tomorrow, have a game tomorrow night and I'm free this weekend. Would you like company babysitting?"

"Really?"

"I love kids. And they all love to climb me like a jungle gym," he smiles.

"I can see that," I laugh. "Um, I'll ask Selena if she minds. But be warned, Griffin loves Bubble Guppies."

"Oh, me too. Mr. Gruper is the best," he laughs at my scowl. "How are you getting home tomorrow night?"

"Mike. We close together so he insists on driving me home."

"Good," he nods effectively ending the conversation before we pull up in front of Selena's.

Walking me all the way to Selena's door, he waits for me to open it and then he smiles once before leaving me. "I'll call you tomorrow," he says turning back to the elevator.

*****

"Soooooo? How was it?" Selena begs the second I close the door.

"Good. Really good. He wants to only be my friend."

"You've been crying," she points at my face.

"Yeah, like a release cry, and he was really great about it. So that's it. He wants to be my friend only, and I want to be his friend. There's just something about him I like, like he's safe or something- I don't even panic when he touches my hand."

"That's good. But *friends?*" She asks skeptically.

"Yes. His words, not mine. Oh, and he wants to know if he can babysit with me Saturday night?"

"Sure," Selena says quietly. "*Friends,* Saige?"

"Yes, Selena. And it's a relief actually. I like him but I don't like him like him. So having him say he doesn't like me or want me that way was a huge relief."

"Okay," she nods not looking happy about it at all.

CHAPTER 18

After my doctor's appointment, I'm relieved to know I've healed properly though it was awful having a pelvic exam again to find out.

I hated being touched and inspected like that, but luckily my regular doctor is a female, which definitely helped. I was no longer sore after the first week I told her, and when I had my period 2 weeks after the attack I explained I was only a little uncomfortable with my tampons.

So other than all the mental shit I was feeling during my appointment, physically I'm fine now. My doctor was cool, talking a little about the attack but not pushing me when I didn't want to speak. She was sensitive but not overly so which didn't make me too uncomfortable.

Deciding to stay on the pill she refilled my prescription after she explained going off the pill now because I'm no longer with Tyler wouldn't be wise for my overall system. She suggested I keep things as they've been for the last 3 years since I started birth control.

And that was that. I have my 6 month prescription, I'm physically fine, and I can move on.

Eventually.

At home before work, Selena was sweet, asking questions without being pushy until I just explained where I'm at and how I feel. Afterward, she left for the day shift, and I sat around waiting for my evening shift to begin.

And I'm getting better.

I think of Tyler maybe only once every few hours now, and I think of Malcolm much more frequently, especially after his text this afternoon.

'I hope you're having a good day. Please call or text when you get in tonight safe and sound. Take care, Malcolm.'

*****

181

At work I'm good. The night is flying by, the tables are full, and no one is being an ass. I slept like shit last night and Griffin had me up early watching his cartoons, which I love with him but hate in general.

Truthfully, I can't wait to move into my little apartment on Monday. Yes, it's small and temporary but it'll be mine, and I've never had anything that was just mine before. I left my mum's house for the crowded dorms and then moved right in with Tyler when he asked after our first year of school.

I've never lived alone or decorated a place with just myself in mind. Not that I'll do much decorating only to leave in 4 months, but at least I can make it feel like my own space. Plus, with Selena and Griffin upstairs, I'll always either have company, or I'll go up and see them if I get lonely.

"Saige? Table 4 needs their drinks," Mike yells across the bar. Nodding, I grab my tray of drinks and continue to table 4.

"Is everything okay? You seem a little off tonight?" Mike asks.

Looking at Mike, the sudden sense of being a little emotionally better is so strong I pause before answering. "I'm fine actually. Just tired."

"Okay..." he smiles touching my hand briefly on the bar. "2 hours and we're outta here," he adds and suddenly 2 hours seems like a long time away to me.

This is my first Friday night since *that* night, and though I know nothing will happen, I feel the weight of that night suddenly baring down on me.

I know logically that I'll be walking out and leaving with Mike by my side. And I know I have Malcolm's pepper spray attached to my keychain and the alarm necklace around my neck, but the nervousness is there anyway. I wasn't able to bring the Taser which felt way too intimidating, but with the pepper spray close, I know I'll be fine.

I'd be safe anyway I have to keep reminding myself, but with the pepper spray I'll *feel* safe.

"Ready?" Mike asks after we've closed out everything, locked away the deposit and shut off all the family side lights. Standing with Kelsey, Hailey, Aileen, and Heather, I'm ready.

When Mike opens to let us all out, I feel almost a collective nervousness which though weird for the rest of them is comforting nonetheless. As Mike sets the alarm and locks the double doors and key locks behind him all of us just wait silently until we're off.

Walking to the parking lot, I hold my pepper spray as casually as I can waiting for Heather to start and lock her car, then Kelsey, then Hailey and Aileen who are driving together. As a group, we all seem to fear something that really isn't likely. For some reason though they seem to feel something as acutely as my memories sense them.

Finally Mike and I are locked in his car, breathing erratically, and safe. So safe that I actually huff a quick laugh like I just ran a marathon.

"You're fine," Mike pats my knee and I know I am.

"Jeez... Talk about drama, huh? Kelsey looked like she was ready to shit herself," I burst out laughing.

"I know!" He howls. "Fuck, she was hanging off me all night scared to leave with you in case *she* got hurt this time," he admits before catching himself. When he does though I see his embarrassed foot in the mouth face clearly. "I didn't mean it like that. Shit, I'm so sorry, Saige."

"It's okay," I mumble exhausted. "Can we just go?"

Closer to Selena's, Mike apologizes again, and though I feel like shit by what he said I know he didn't mean to be such an insensitive asshole. I know he didn't so I squeeze his own leg to let him know we're okay.

Eventually home I make a rash decision. I don't want to be chaperoned for the rest of my life, I have my pepper spray and keys ready, and truthfully, I'm sad by what Kelsey thought and by what Mike said.

"I'm going to run for it," I announce as we pull up.

"No fucking way," Mike counters.

"Yup. I need to do these things by myself. Ya know, like walking alone and stuff?" I smile, but he isn't budging. "I'll text the millisecond I'm in Selena's, and I'm literally going to run."

"Malcolm will kill me and Selena will cut off my balls. Let's just go," he opens his door.

"Mike! Stay in the car. I'm running now," I throw open my door and run like hell for the doors.

With shaking hands, I open the main door just to stop at the elevators that take for freakin' ever. And then I'm in. Alone. Safe. Almost home.

When the elevator doors open, I charge Selena's door practically throwing myself at it as I unlock and slam it behind me.

And then I laugh.

Resting my head against the back of Selena's door, I laugh and shake and exhale the adrenaline and stress I'm nearly choking on.

"You good?" She asks quietly making me jump anyway.

"Yes. I walked in alone and nothing happened, and I'm fine." Pulling out my phone I send a quick text to Mike telling him I'm in and safe.

'I'm sorry I upset you. I didn't mean to be such a prick.'

'Don't worry about it.' I text back.

"I need a drink before bed." Already walking to the kitchen to pour myself a drink, I think of Malcolm again. "Are you sure you don't mind if Malcolm comes over tomorrow night?"

"Of course not. He's more than welcome. But will you feel comfortable alone with him here?"

Turning to her with my wine glass I nod. "Absolutely. He doesn't scare me for whatever reason, and I enjoy his company. Oh, I have to text him I'm home."

Walking to the couch, I settle in, dump my jacket and kick off my shoes. Drinking quickly, I need the relief of a drink, and the calm of a buzz so I'll sleep tonight. I'm tired but I'm still adrenaline shaky and I know I'll never sleep like this.

"I'm going to bed," Selena walks past me. "See you in the morning. Come get me or crawl in my bed if Griffin tortures you too early, okay?"

"Never. He's too cute to torture me. Night, Selena."

"Night."

Pulling out my phone I decide to brush my teeth and get ready for bed before I text Malcolm and pass out.

'Hi. I'm home. Alarmed and secure. I hope you had a good night. Oh, Selena is fine with you coming over. So I'll see you tomorrow.'

'What took you so long? Did you crawl home or just wait to text me?'

'I had a drink first, got ready for bed, and I'm texting you now.'

'I was ready to send out a search party!!!'

'Dramatic much?' I text actually giggling as I type. Malcolm dramatic? *Please*. I think I have the market cornered on that one.

'You haven't seen me watch chick flicks. THAT'S dramatic.'

'What the hell does that mean???'

'I cry like a baby when the guy gets the girl at the end'. Smiling, I can't see it.

'I doubt it. But I bet like every other man on the planet you DID cry at the end of Marley and Me.'

'Like. A. Baby.'

'Typical. Anything else I should know?'

'I choke up when a woman sings the national anthem. The 1984 Whitney Houston Super Bowl National Anthem= Bawl my eyes out. And I like chocolate ice cream when I have PMS.'

'PMS??? Lol'

'Yup. I'm super moody, but chocolate ice cream seems to help. You?'

'PMS? Sweet and Salty. Like chocolate pretzels, or M&M's melted in buttered popcorn. Yum!'

'Sounds good. I'll bring the M&M's tomorrow, you supply the popcorn?'

'Deal. Good night Malcolm.'

'Night Saige.'

Pulling up my blankets I snuggle in but can't wipe the smile off my face. Feeling almost giddy and excited I realize I really like Malcolm.

*****

Spending the day with Griffin while Selena works, I'm exhausted. The little bugger had me up at 6:30 and considering for the second night in a row I've slept less than 4 hours I'm surprised I'm even functioning.

If I've learned anything from this last month here it's the fact that I was spoiled living with Tyler. We got up when we wanted to and slept as long as we wanted. I may have been studying like a mad woman for 2 months prior to my exam, but I always had enough sleep. This living arrangement? *Torture.*

Making dinner for the 2 of us Griffin talks nonstop and asks constantly when his mommy is coming home. He asks all the time, but usually my opened arms makes him crawl in and forget his mom for a half hour or so which makes me feel special. Smiling, I know Griffin really loves me, and I love having him love me.

20 minutes later after snuggling with Griffin and asking about his day, Selena is running around getting ready for her date with Dave.

"What changed between you two?" I ask in the bathroom doorway.

"I don't know. Dave was just so good about everything lately. Taking and watching Griffin, and helping me out a little. Then we were talking in the kitchen and he asked me out of the blue if he could take me out on a date. So I said yes without even really thinking about it."

"And how do you feel about it now?" Taking the curling iron from her I get the longer back pieces she can't reach.

"Excited, but not overly so. I know Dave. *Christ,* we were high school sweethearts, college break-ups, back togetherers, then married. So I don't actually expect much, or expect him to stay all grown up for me. But it'll be nice to just get out and get laid," she smirks when I pause with her hair in the air. "What? He's my ex-husband, Saige. So that's like freebie sex."

"Got it," I grin back curling more hair as she starts her makeup. "Shake it out," I wait as she does so I can find the uncurled hair while she applies mascara carefully. "Are you nervous?"

"Not really. I mean my expectations are fairly low," she laughs. "So I can't see Dave doing anything that would truly shock me anymore. He pretty much did that for the 2 years we were actually married, right?" Nodding, I know some of the shit he pulled, but I'm sure there's more. "Anyway, like I said, it's just a date with my ex, maybe a nice dinner, and maybe some sex."

"Will you be coming home?"

"I plan on it. But would you mind if I don't if I promise to come back super early?"

"Of course not. Go out and get some sex. It's been forever since the Kentucky guy, right?" I smirk remembering her hilarious story about *him* wanting to be tied up by her and Selena obliging, only to leave him tied up when he fell asleep.

"Ah, and Mike. *Once!*" She yells as I gasp. "Just once, the night you didn't come home."

"Last Friday?"

"Actually last Saturday," she blushes. "But it was just a stress fuck, and we both knew it and we've been fine ever since. He understands it was just once," she says almost pleading with me to understand.

"Oh my god... I don't know what I say. You usually tell me details and I reeeeally don't want any. Mike? *Really?*" I kind of laugh again I'm so shocked.

"Please don't tell him I told you," she begs until I glare at her. "I know you won't, but you just have to ask it, ya know? Anyway, like I said it was just once when we were stressed out and we talked about it Sunday morning and decided it wouldn't happen again."

"Was it good? Never mind. I don't want to know. Yes, I do. *Gah!* I feel like a pervert, but I'm so curious."

Grinning she admits, "It was good, Saige. Not Dave good, but pretty good for a 25 year old. *Fuck...* I'm like a cougar now," she says as we both start laughing.

"Ah, I think you have to be in your late thirties or early forties or something to be a cougar. So you're just the sexy older woman," I laugh again as she blows a kiss at me through the mirror. Wow, *Mike?*

"I've got to change," she pulls away from the curling iron in my hand. "Then I'll put Griffin down before I go."

"What are you wearing?"

"My slutty red dress with the slits up the sides."

"Well, you're certainly getting laid in that," I giggle when she shakes her ass for me to her bedroom.

(mis)TRUST

CHAPTER 19

Jumping on the couch with Griffin, he crawls on me immediately. Snuggling in between my side and arm, he talks and talks to my constant uh huhs and reallys while Selena finishes getting ready for her 8:00 date with her ex-friggin-husband, which I still find hilarious.

"Are you hungry for your bedtime toast now?"

"S'please," Griffin says not even blinking from another annoying show.

In the kitchen making Griffin his bedtime toast, I'm just finishing when Malcolm arrives. Opening the door with the toast still in my hand he asks, "Is that for me? Cuz mine is better," he grins lifting the biggest bag of M&M's I've ever seen in my life.

"Shit! Hide those," I groan hoping Griffin hasn't seen them.

"Hi," Griffin squeaks behind me as Malcolm actually tucks the M&M's in the back of his jeans under his jacket.

"Hi, you must be Griffin," Malcolm squats super low to shake his little hand. "Can I come in for a visit?"

"Yup. *MOMMY!* There's a boy comin' over!" Griffin yells already walking away with his toast to the couch.

"A *boy?* Usually I get giant or monster, or actually my godson calls me Gigantor, but I'm pretty sure Agnes put him up to that," Malcolm shakes his head walking in when I pull the door wide open.

"Gigantor? I guess he hasn't met your brother Tatum."

"Nope," he smiles looking as handsome as ever- when he smiles.

"Can you hide those in a cupboard," I motion to his back.

"The lower ones so you can reach?" He teases.

"Hi, Malcolm," Selena walks toward us looking absolutely beautiful in her hot red dress with her blonde curls bouncing over her shoulders.

"Wow. You look beautiful," Malcolm leans in to kiss her cheek as they hug. "I guess this is a special date?"

"Not really. It's with my ex-husband," she laughs. "So as I told Saige, my expectations are very low."

"Well, if it doesn't work out I have a dozen friends who would kill to go out with you."

"*Gerard* Butler, Malcolm. You're as smooth as Gerard Butler with the sexy growly handsome-faced thing, too," she shakes her head pained. "Why can't you be into a 29 year old, height and weight appropriate woman with a kid?" She grins bumping my hip.

"Who says I'm not?" He teases right back.

"Would you like a drink?" I interrupt their teasing a little annoyed. *Really?* Right in front of me?

Wow, I'm feeling jealous again, and I swear to god I was never jealous with Tyler. With this guy though, I'm constantly irritated when I have no business feeling anything at all. Plus, it's Selena, and she would never poach on my *not* man, I internally groan at myself.

Christ, I'm changing just like my mother did. I'm different now since Tyler cheated, and I hate it. I was never insecure or jealous before and I've never acted like this or even felt this way before.

"Saige?"

"*What*?" I bitch before catching myself.

Looking concerned, Malcolm asks what Selena usually does. "What are you thinking about?"

Leaning against the counter beside me his arms are crossed waiting. He probably thinks it has something to do with when I was hurt, and usually he'd be right. Not this time though. This time I'm completely irrational regarding him.

Turning to fake smile, I pretend, "Nothing at all. What can I get you?"

"A beer?" He says not buying the *I'm fine* story at all.

"Sure." Lifting the 2 brands Selena has in the fridge he takes the domestic and waits for me to pour a vodka and orange for myself before walking to the living room with me.

Sitting on the couch, Malcolm takes the chair beside me trying to make small talk with Griffin who can't look away from the TV long enough to answer Malcolm.

"It's bedtime, honey," Selena points to the clock. "Remember when your show started at the o'clock and ends at the thirty it's time for bed? Well, it's the thirty now, so bed time."

"Just one more show?" Griffin begs in the cutest voice imaginable and I don't know how the hell Selena always sticks to her guns. I swear Griffin could get a car out of me if he begged me with that voice.

"Not tonight, baby. Auntie Saige and her friend Malcolm are going to stay here while mommy goes to work. But I'll come in and kiss you goodnight when I come home, okay?"

Working up his proper pout, I almost interject that it's fine, but Selena glares at me quickly stopping my potential protest for him. God, she's so mean, I pout back at her.

"Let's go brush your teeth. Say goodnight to Auntie and Malcolm."

"Good night," he says with an actual quivering lip. Hiding my smile behind my hand I reach for his climb on Auntie Saige hug and kiss his hair and cheek.

Squeezing him tightly, I cave because of his pout. "Tomorrow I'll take you to MacDonald's Play Place, okay? But you can't tell mommy. So if you go to sleep now, it'll be tomorrow when you wake up, okay?" I whisper to Selena raising her eyebrow at me behind his back.

When Griffin pulls away, he fails like most 3 year olds do. "I won't tell mommy about MacNonalds," he says so seriously I fight my laughter.

"Good. It's our secret, okay?" I nod back as Selena rolls her eyes at me.

"Good night, Griffin. It was nice meeting you," Malcolm stays seated beside the couch but offers his hand as they pass.

"Good night," Griffin smiles much more cheerfully than when his mean mom told him to the first time.

"*Bribery,* Saige?" She shakes her head walking away with Griffin.

"When is she leaving?"

"Dave told her he'd be by at 8:00 after Griffin went to sleep. I guess they don't want to confuse him if he sees them together."

"Makes sense. How long have they been divorced?"

"Only a year, but they've been separated for 2 1/2, since Griffin was just turning a year old. He doesn't really know them together, so they're trying to keep things very separate for now."

"Okay. He's in. I told him there would be no *MacNonalds* if he got out of bed, so I think he'll stay down," she rolls her eyes at me again.

"What? I'll make him drink milk," I laugh. "Plus, I haven't had a date in years, and I love dating Griffin because he actually loves me back," I cringe immediately when I realize what I said.

"*Saige...*" Selena whispers. Shaking my head quickly so she'll stop, I see Malcolm turn to look at my face which is instantly flaming red.

"Go finish getting ready. Dave'll be here in 10 minutes," I shoo her away.

Sitting silently, the air around me is crackling with desperation and I wish I had shut my mouth. What a pathetic thing to say about a 3 year old, and in front of a man no less.

"You seem really tense right now. Is it bothering you having me here? I understand if it is," Malcolm says like he'll leave if I say yes.

Holding eye contact I confess. "It's not you. It's me, honestly. My thought patterns are a little screwy right now. I haven't read a text book or studied in a month so I think I'm suffering mental inertia."

"Mental *inertia?*" He laughs as I nod.

"It's a real affliction," I grin. "Think about it. For 8 months of the year I'm absolutely buried in texts, lectures, studying, and working. I'm constantly overwhelmed and mentally overloaded. My body becomes used to hard exhausted sleeps, then it's all suddenly over for a few months. So now I can relax if I want, but I don't know how to. And I can do nothing if I want, but that's boring. If I wasn't living out of 2 suitcases here, I'd be studying legal text books to keep in my mental reservoir for school next year."

"Why don't you do something else while you have the break?"

"Like what? I'm working, and I'll be moving on Monday. I've just been a little on hold this past month."

"So Monday night after you settle in you'll crack open a textbook for relaxation?" He asks without the sarcasm that sentence deserves.

"Yes. Pretty nerdy, huh?"

"No, not nerdy. It just seems a little lonely," he says softly. "You don't interact with anyone when you're studying, especially when you don't actually have to be studying. So why do you do it?"

"Because of her brother," Selena pipes up and I'm shocked and winded and so fucking pissed that she took that moment to interrupt us.

Glancing quickly at Malcolm he has his eyebrow raised at my no siblings lie. "Her brother?" He asks Selena who seems to understand she said something she shouldn't have.

"Ah... I've got to finish my makeup," she walks away seconds before Dave gently knocks on the door.

Jumping up, my words are lost and I feel like shit again with Malcolm. Christ, added to my list of personalities, the yeller, the psycho, the frozen one, now we get to add the liar, too.

"Is he asleep?" Dave asks as soon as I open the door.

"Yes. And you look mighty fine Mr. Heart," I hug Dave quickly. "Wait until you see her."

Watching Malcolm walk toward us, they take each other in and hands are extended. "Hi, I'm Malcolm, a friend of Saige's. You must be Dave."

"Yup. Selena's ex-husband and date tonight," he smirks. "Shit, Selena..." Dave quickly looks over at her grinning. "If you had looked like that every night I never would've let you divorce me."

"Ha ha," she drolls. "You look nice, too," she blatantly checks him out.

"And you look *gorgeous*, Mrs. Heart."

"*Mssss*. Heart," she amends smirking.

Looking between them, the air is filled with lust and love and whatever the hell these two had for each other for a decade before it all went to shit.

"Get going you two. Just make sure you text me if you, *you* know..." I grin to her bug-eyeing me. That was a little revenge on my part for the brother comment, but she can take it.

"Goodnight," they leave after Dave puts his hand on her lower back to escort her to the elevators.

Waiting, I don't want to turn around, and I don't want to talk. I wish Malcolm wasn't here suddenly so I didn't have to answer his questions or fill in the blanks.

"Saige?"

Turning to Malcolm I say the only thing I can think of. "Popcorn now or later?"

"Later." Dammit.

Inhaling deeply, I need to cut this off. "I don't want to talk about my brother, okay? I'm sorry I lied, but it was easier than admitting I had a brother in case you asked follow-up questions I can't answer."

"Saige, I-"

"*Please,* Malcolm?"

"Of course. I'm a patient man, Saige. Patient *and* stubborn, so you just bought yourself a little time. That's all," he grins again at my relief. "So what now? TV, a movie, a board game? Maybe a legal textbook to peruse for relaxation?"

"Smartass," I swat his arm. "I already told you I didn't have any here, but Monday night I'll hit you over the head with one if you'd like."

"I might like."

"Freak," I grin. "Um, we can watch a movie if you want. Selena has satellite."

"Okay. After Q&A. Popcorn now or with the movie?" Dreading tonight's Q&A I need to push it away somehow. "No brother questions, Saige. I promise," he says like he knew where I was headed again.

"Popcorn after. I'll just check on Griffin quickly while you think of new and interesting questions to torture me with."

"Deal," he squeezes my hand passing me.

Sitting on the other end of the couch, Malcolm looks huge again. When I tuck my legs up under me, I realize he absolutely dwarfs Selena's couch, which is normally more than enough room for normal-sized people, I suddenly laugh.

"Something funny?" He grins.

"No, just a nervous giggle."

"Nervous of me still?"

"No, not you exactly. I'm just weird and giggly tonight. I'm horribly sleep deprived," I admit fighting a yawn even as I speak.

"Would you like me to leave?"

"No, it's okay."

Turning on the couch to look directly at me, he says, "Good. And now it's Q&A time. What were you like as a teenager?"

"Awkward," I say and burst out laughing.

"*Awkward?*" He smiles.

"Very. I was super scrawny, and I couldn't gain weight to save my life. I was *that* girl, ya know?"

"No. Tell me," he prompts listening intently.

Shaking my head, I smile. "I was the girl you could easily make fun of. I was a redhead with freckles, who was super smart, and I looked like a stick figure. I didn't get an awesome hourglass body like my mum and cousins in Scotland. No big boobs or butt and tiny waist. I was just horribly skinny, shapeless, and awkward. I hated my red hair and my little girl body. And I hated how smart I was."

"Really?"

"Yup. I even went through a phase as a junior when I stopped studying to lower my grades, but when it came time for tests I knew all the answers anyway. Plus, the stubborn side of me couldn't help but answer properly." Grinning, I admit, "My average did drop down to the high eighties though, which was a major shock to see at report card time."

"The high eighties? I wish," he grins.

Nodding, I continue. "There was a lot going on for me personally though, so no one said anything about my grade drop, which for most students would still be awesome, I know. But I'll admit, I hated not having the highest grades and the best scores in school," I finally laugh. "Like I said, I was awkward. I hated being the ugly, scrawny Brainiac, but I hated not being the smartest student in school more."

"I doubt you were ugly," he whispers.

"I was, Malcolm. I may have filled out a little now, and I may have a small woman's body now, but-"

"You are *very* attractive now," he interrupts.

"Thank you," I blush immediately. "Anyway, I gained 20 pounds, my hair lost a little of the brassiness, and, really, I just stopped caring."

"About?"

"Social stuff. When I was 16 I made a decision to be the best, the smartest, and the most determined. I knew what I wanted to be in life, so I stopped caring about the little things in high school. And I've done alright."

"You've done very alright," he nods. "But did you have any friends?"

"Yeah, I mean I wasn't a recluse or anything. I had 2 girlfriends, one who was a nerd like me and one who was a borderline nerd who floated along the edge of the popular girls, which meant the 3 of us were sometimes invited to parties. People weren't mean to me, Malcolm, they just didn't gravitate towards me. Honestly, I wasn't bullied or ridiculed or anything bad like that. I just existed, as the super smart, super scrawny redheaded little sister of Alec," I exhale deeply. Taking a quick breath as Malcolm stares at me, I nod. "Yeah, small world- we both have a brother named Alec."

Not speaking, Malcolm seems to be holding his own breath as I battle my demons and decide what I do or don't say here. Opting for don't, I quickly change the topic.

"So I went away to University, met Tyler my very first week, and then he changed me," I smile. "He was good looking, and everyone liked him, and he really liked me. So we began dating, loving, living together, and that was it until last month."

"How did he change you?"

"I don't know, little things," I shrug. "He didn't mind my scrawny body, and he liked my red hair. He started suggesting things, like different clothes or colors and over time I eventually changed. I always wore baggy clothes when I was younger so I looked heavier, but he would tell me I looked hot in tight jeans, so I started wearing them. He said my eyes were gorgeous, so I started wearing more green clothing and changed my makeup to highlight my green eyes more. Um, blouses and tighter tops showed off my small chest which he liked," I admit a little embarrassed again.

"I don't know, just stuff like that. He made me feel good, and I grew confidence and a voice of my own. I embraced being the smart girl who was okay looking as well. I learned to stand up for myself, and eventually with him by my side, I was able to find my personality and grow into a confident woman I guess." Pausing for a moment, I smile thinking of my past. "It's all very classic ugly duckling stuff. But I do have Tyler to thank for most of it."

"Maybe you-"

"I think that's what made this break up so hard for me," I exhale as the sadness overwhelms me again. "I thought I was exactly what he wanted. But I wasn't good enough to love, I guess."

Looking at Selena's TV, I see the reflection of Malcolm's hand move toward me, then stop. I watch him watching my profile and I wish he would hold my hand, though I'm also glad he isn't. I'm trying so hard not to cry in front of him, but all I want to do is cry again for the entire future I thought I was going to have with Tyler and lost.

"I've never seen you in anything but big baggy clothes and jeans. Is that because you don't feel attractive anymore without him?"

Turning, I'm a little insulted he thinks I'm so pathetic. "No, Malcolm," I snap. "I wear bagging clothes so no one will rape me again. *Oh...*"

Watching him flinch as I cover my own mouth, I panic. I didn't think of what I was doing so clearly this last month with my clothes, but there it is. I'm dressing frumpy again so I won't get hurt.

"Sorry..." I moan watching him stare, apparently unable to speak.

Totally uncomfortable I stand quickly announcing I'm going to make popcorn as I bolt from the living room.

Holy *shit...* I sound like such an ass with this guy. If I'm not acting jealous For. No. Reason, I'm spewing my insecurities and paranoia all over him.

God, I need my textbooks. I want to study and chill out. I want a new bed and I want to sleep just once through the night without either waking up crying, or waking up panicked.

I would love to just feel normal again, whatever the hell that is for me now.

"Saige?" Malcolm says softly.

"I'm okay," I hold the counter behind me for a second. "I was all up in my head for a second there, but I'm fine now."

"I can imagine. Or actually I can't. But I'm trying to."

Looking at him, I take all of Malcolm in. Standing against the fridge, Malcolm is just so big and strong I bet he's never been afraid of anything his whole life.

"Do you ever feel scared?" I whisper as tears fill my eyes.

"Yes." When there's nothing but my disbelieving silence between us, Malcolm huffs a quick breath and continues. "I do, Saige. Maybe not because I feel physically threatened like you do, but I do get scared, and worried, and even panicked about things from time to time. Things can absolutely freak me out."

Staring at each other the silence is so thick I'm nearly choking on the questions and the answers all around us. I want to know and I know he wants to ask but neither of us can move out of our heavy silence.

"Can I tell you something?"

"*Anything*," I whisper wanting this frozen unknown to stop for us.

"I was truly scared, freaked-out and panicked the night I saw you in the restaurant after you were attacked." Oh God, my chest is pounding. "When I saw you jump backward to get away from me I was scared to death of your reaction *to* me. Then I was freaked-out watching you wrestle with what was real and what wasn't. But mostly I was panicked that for one moment you thought I could hurt you like that.

"I didn't know the extent of what happened at the time, but it didn't matter. I saw you absolutely terrified in that moment, and it wasn't until you realized I didn't hurt you that I felt true panic. I saw the black handprint bruise on your thigh, and I really saw the damage to your face under the makeup. I watched how you clung to Mike and I watched Selena try to talk you back to the present. I watched you with such panic my heart pounded in my chest."

Feeling tears slide down my face I can't look away and I can't breathe. I'm suspended in this moment with Malcolm, and I've never felt such intensity with someone else in my life.

"In that moment I almost grabbed you to me. I thought about picking you up and getting you out of there. I actually wanted to scoop you up in my arms and figure out how to make you not look like that on the floor. I couldn't stand the people watching, your friends crying, and you wide-eyed in shock because you saw me and Dan again. But thankfully, I found some sanity that made me not touch you when you were that emotionally vulnerable. But it was hard," he exhales a hard breath actually tugging at his dark hair.

"I didn't know."

"You didn't know anything in that moment except I wasn't the one that hurt you. And that's the only thing that kept me even remotely sane that night."

Thinking about everything he's saying, I don't know why he felt that way. I really don't get it because I was a stranger to him. "Why did what happened to me affect you so much?"

"*Saige...*" he exhales like I'm an idiot. "I have *never* seen a woman beat like that before, in real life anyway. Sure, in movies, or like the Rihanna thing that made me angry for her. But I don't know people who beat on women, and I can't think of a single time I've ever personally known, or rather *seen* the victim of an assault like that before. Not only that but I was looking forward to seeing you again, so when I actually saw you and you were like that I was gutted."

"You were?" I ask confused, I'm so mesmerized and overwhelmed by everything being said in this kitchen.

"After the night we met I saw you the following night and you shut me down, then we came back the next week and you weren't around. But the following week I finally spotted your gorgeous red hair and I wanted to get your number so I said your name- and you *lost* it."

"See, you were this sexy, Scottish, little spitfire to me. You were a tiny little thing who could put a grown man in his place without even raising your voice. You were intriguing and compelling and just the sweetest damn lass I'd ever seen," he grins quickly. "And then you were the girl on the floor with the bruises and busted lips and eyes, with sheer, unimaginable terror in her eyes. So I panicked alongside you. Obviously for different reasons- but it was still fear and sadness and horror that I felt finally seeing you again when you were like that."

Straightening up but not advancing on me, Malcolm finishes this for us. "Anyway, after I left I beat the hell out of my own dashboard, Dan made a call to his brother Mario while we waited for you to leave, and the following morning I found out everything that happened to you."

"*Everything*?" I gasp.

"Yes," he nods his head keeping eye contact. "But I didn't look at the pictures, Saige, I promise. And please don't report this or get Dan's brother in trouble. Yes, he broke procedure, but I begged him to tell me everything so I could help you in some way. Mario finally allowed me to read the report but he wouldn't have if I hadn't convinced him I wanted to help. *Please?*" He begs looking at me so sincerely I give in. A little.

"You didn't look at the pictures?"

"Absolutely not. They weren't shown to me in the file, and I wouldn't have been able to look at them anyway."

"Okay," I huff.

Shit, I don't know how I feel about the police releasing details like that to anyone, even if he was trying to help somehow. Actually, I think I'm really pissed. "What else?"

"That's it. I was allowed to read the report, off the record."

"That was an invasion of my privacy, Malcolm."

"I know, but I had to find out if someone I knew hurt you, but I'm sorry if I overstepped."

"You did overstep. *Grossly.* And I'm really uncomfortable with what you know. Those were horrifyingly intimate details that I only shared with Selena and the police, and I don't know how I feel about you knowing all those details. Actually, it feels humiliating, and like a major betrayal of trust."

"I'm very sorry about what I did, but I'm way more sorry about what happened to you. You can be mad that I looked into your assault, or you can understand what I did in the context I did it. I was trying to help, *not* invade your privacy. There was no other way to help because you were too much of a mess to talk to me or Dan that night. And I *needed* to do something."

Looking at me desperately, I actually do understand. But god, it's embarrassing knowing he knows about the physical and sexual damage to my body that night.

"I'm not hurt anymore," I whisper than blush so furiously I can't believe what I just said. Holy *shit!* I'm losing my mind.

Christ, I didn't want him to think about me sexually ever- now I'm worried he's thinking about me sexually damaged.

"Saige," he pauses reaching for my hand before I step away.

"We will never discuss what happened to my body ever, okay? I can't, Malcolm. I'm too embarrassed and uncomfortable. And I don't want you thinking of my body like that. But especially not damaged or messed up or anything. I can't do it."

"I won't. I don't think of you as anything less than the little Scottish spitfire who compelled me to her that first night," he finally grins a little.

"Okay," I exhale for the thousandth time in this kitchen. "*Christ*, I need another drink."

"So have one."

"I'll pass out I'm so tired."

"So pass out. I'll watch TV beside you and stay awake in case Griffin wakes up."

"I can't. But not because I don't trust you," I quickly acknowledge. "It just feels wrong to be drinking until passed out when babysitting- at least in this country," I laugh a little.

"Go sit. I'll make you a drink and some popcorn."

"Thank you."

"I'm very happy to know you, Saige," Malcolm says again with such intensity, the horror of that night vanishes again when I'm around him.

"Um, I'm glad you're here, Malcolm," I answer honestly.

"Me too," he agrees leaning towards me slowly so I don't panic until he gently kisses my forehead.

*****

Waking, I vaguely remember waking in the night to Malcolm moving me a little to get comfortable, telling me Selena would be home late, then telling me to go back to sleep. I also seem to recall using his leg for a pillow with the blankets wrapped around me through the night.

But that's all I recall from the best night's sleep I've ever had in my life.

CHAPTER 20

Running for my phone a text beeps through.

'How was your day?'

'Good. I took Griffin to MacNonalds ☺ Then Walmart afterward for some new apartment stuff. Thank you for staying last night, I finally had a good night's sleep.'

'You're welcome.'

'I bought myself a bed! And I'm excited to move in tomorrow. Finally.

'Coincidentally I have tomorrow off so I'll meet you at Selena's mom's house to help move you in.'

'Thank you, but we have it covered.'

'I'll meet you guys at 7:30. Don't be stubborn.'

'I'm not. I'm being considerate.'

'Stubborn.'

'Considerate. Grrrrr'

'Don't growl at me. It's hot ☺ See you tomorrow. Good night.'

'Thank you for all your help lately. Good night. Grrrrrrrrrrrrr 😲'

'Cheeky. Stubborn. Lass.'

*****

"When's your bed arriving?" Selena asks driving the U-Haul because like a smartass, she said she didn't think I can reach the pedals. Watching Malcolm following behind us from her mom's house, I know she and I couldn't have possibly loaded the truck so quickly without his help again, or even lifted my damn bookcases.

"The generic sometime between 12 and 6pm. It's okay. We're already halfway done and it's only 9:30, so as long as I pile my book boxes against the corners it should fit."

"You remember I have to work at 1:00, right? Do you think Malcolm will help you put your bed together?"

"Probably. He seems like the put furniture together type, doesn't he?"

Glancing over at me she smirks, "And the sexy type, the growly type, the handsome, sweet, delicious type. The you are *soooo* lucky type, and the I wish Dave was a little more attentive like Malcolm is type."

"The FRIEND type."

"Who would love you faithfully FOREVER type," she adds grabbing my hand when I look at her stunned.

"Selena... not to be dramatic or like my mum or anything, but I don't think any guy is faithful forever. And even if Malcolm could be we're just friends, and I need a friend right now more than I need a new complication while I get my shit together. Plus, I'm leaving in a few months, so there's no point starting anything with him. And honestly, I don't want Malcolm like that. I need a break from men."

"I know the timing sucks, but it can't be helped. He's here now, and he's really good, Saige."

"I know he's good."

"I don't know where he came from or why he hasn't already been snatched up, but he's here *now*. And if you just try to trust him a little, I really don't think he'll ever hurt you on purpose."

"Like Tyler wouldn't have?"

Glaring at me suddenly when we're at a red light, she snaps, "If you can even compare those two men in the same sentence, you're really fucked in the head. Tyler used you and-"

"*Loved* me!" I yell across the loud roar of the engine.

"Yes, he loved you. But only when it was convenient. And only until he found someone better- in *his* mind," she adds like that clarification will make this conversation hurt a little less suddenly.

"I hate you right now," I moan feeling heartbroken and confused, and just shitty.

"Well, I love you right now. And I want you to move on, with or without Malcolm. I just want you to be funny, snappy, independent, strong little Saige again. I miss her."

Exhaling, I admit, "Me too."

"But I do think Malcolm is amazing for you. *Annnnnnnd* he's really hot," she laughs as I do, effectively exhaling the tension between us.

*****

"Is that Dan?" I almost panic when we pull up front of our building.

"I think so... I guess Malcolm called in reinforcements." Malcolm *was* a little extra growly when Selena and I said we could carry my solid wood bookcases to the elevators together.

Stepping out of the truck, Dan walks towards us with a smile. Handing over a tray of coffee and donuts, I almost laugh at the typical moving breakfast of champions.

"I'm here," he shakes Selena's hand, "Because my best guy threatened to quit if I didn't show up to help."

"I didn't threaten to quit- I said *I quit* when you told me you were too busy to help," Malcolm adds taking a donut from my outstretched hand. "Don't panic, Saige. I quit once a year to keep Dan from becoming THAT boss," he laughs at my expression.

"He does. The prick," Dan shakes his head walking to the back of the truck. "Can we please get started so he'll come back to work for me?"

*****

"Everything hurts," I whine to Selena after we each dump a super heavy books box in the corner. Looking around, my new apartment is somewhat cute with an indented nook for my bed and a breakfast bar to at least separate the kitchen a little from the rest of the room. And for a bachelor apartment it's not closet tiny, but it'll certainly be cozy once my furniture is in place.

"We're almost done. And I have to go soon anyway," she looks over at the clock. "At least I got the kitchen, fridge and stove clean, and you did the bathroom, which was a little nasty before."

"I know. That tub was so gross. Um, will you come by with Griffin after work?"

"Of course. He's super excited to have you living downstairs. He thinks he has 2 apartments now in this building."

"Make sure he knows he does, okay? I'm going to miss him snuggling on me every morning. I won't miss his stupid shows, but I'm going to miss his quiet morning voice and his bedhead, and his little hands holding mine in the morning." Realizing how attached I've become to Griffin this past month, I'm sad to let him go. "Maybe you can send him down for morning cartoons sometimes?"

"We're only 4 floors from each other, Saige. Trust me, Griffin is going to bug the hell out of me to visit you all the time."

"Okay. Good," I feel a little relieved.

"The couch?" Dan yells hidden behind it in the doorway.

"Anywhere on this side of the room. I'll move it later."

Watching them, Dan and Malcolm just turn it a little and muscle it through the door fairly easily. Dan's not as strong or large as Malcolm, and you really notice it when they're carrying something together- Dan's side is always lower than Malcolm's.

"There's only 2 more groups of boxes, so you two can stay here if you want," Malcolm huffs dropping the couch.

"Um, I'd like to order pizza for you all for lunch. Do you have time?"

"I don't," Dan says. "This is my last time up."

"Okay. Another time?"

"I'd love to. We'll probably see you before Basketball tomorrow night anyway if you're working."

"I'm working, and I'll comp a dessert for you," I offer to him nodding. "Thank you very much for your help today. I promise to send him back to work tomorrow," I thumb over Malcolm's way.

"I'd appreciate that," Dan smiles before heading out.

"I don't have time either. I'll take a raincheck on the pizza but I'll be back tonight with Griffin," Selena wipes some dirt on her jeans and heads for the door. "I really have to get a shower before work. Are you okay?" She asks a little quieter beside me nodding over at Malcolm leaving the apartment again.

"I'm fine. Hopefully when you come back tonight I'll have this place looking like a place."

"K... See you later," Selena hugs me and bolts for the elevator through the opened door.

Calling in a pizza order I realize I have no plates or cutlery because I left it all with Tyler.

"One more round," Malcolm huffs unloading the boxes from the dolly. "When do you have to return the truck?"

"Any time before 7 tonight."

"Good," he says simply and heads back out the door.

After he brings up the last boxes, Malcolm collapses on the couch groaning. He looks absolutely exhausted and I feel bad that he came to help me move again today.

"I'm really sorry for-"

"All the text books? You should be," he glares. "I get that you're a book nerd, but seriously? There's over 20 boxes of damn books."

"I know. *Sorry,*" I squeak. "I can't throw any books out because I may need them later for case studies or research."

"I'm teasing, Saige. It's all good, and now I don't have to go to the gym this week," he says actually pumping his suddenly very impressive biceps. "I will have a hard time shooting from the three point line tomorrow at basketball though," he pouts.

"I have pizza coming. Does that help?"

"Definitely. Um, I have something for you, but don't fight me, okay? It's a house warming gift or something like that. Please, Saige? It's more for me than for you, okay?"

"Okay." What could possibly be more for him than me?

"I got it at cost from one of Dan's suppliers, so it's nothing." Rising from the couch, he actually cracks his back loudly, which sounds really gross, then walks the 30 feet max to my little kitchen for the backpack he carried in earlier. "Remember, No. Big. Deal. And it's mostly for me. Ah, where's your laptop and phone?"

"In the box on the stove." What the hell is it I wonder reaching for my phone.

Grabbing my laptop, Malcolm grins as he walks back to the poorly placed couch staring a few feet from a blank wall and hands me a box the size of a shoe box. Looking, it has only digits on it and a code of some kind. Shaking it gently, he motions to open it.

"What is it?"

"Look inside," he sits closer to pull out the rectangle shaped fire alarm I think. "It's an alarm for your apartment. You set it up online, then you can alarm, or shut off the alarm using an app on your phone."

"*Really*?" I ask excited.

"Yeah... We reno'd this guy's house last year and Dan and I found this alarm for him, bigger, and with more sensors and keypads, but I thought about it last week and bought one for you."

"How does it work?"

"Well, you set the alarm when you leave, or online, or by your phone itself. It's hooked up remotely via satellite so you don't need Wi-Fi access. I'll install the keypad beside the door, then you can activate it when you're here or leaving, or even online if you forget. And once you set the alarm, the app button lights up to let you know it's set. What's really cool is if you're at work and anyone comes in or trips the alarm the app starts flashing red, and after 1 minutes of flashing, a quiet alarms ring and a vibration starts which gets progressively louder until you either turn it off or acknowledge it."

Listening to Malcolm, I'm so excited and once again so overwhelmed by his kindness. Instead of crying though I hop up on my knees and hug him. Holding him as tightly as I can, I say everything without crying.

"Thank you so much. This is the most thoughtful gift anyone has ever given me."

"You're welcome, Saige. You didn't say anything, but I thought you might be a little nervous coming and going alone. Especially at night."

Pulling away with a smile, I admit, "I am nervous, but I didn't want to keep whining about all my stupid fears and insecurities all the time."

"I figured," he nods so close to my face I pull back a little and look at the keypad in his hand.

"This is so cool," I laugh like a kid with a new video game.

"Can I show you the site online?"

Handing over my laptop, we wait for Windows to load and google the alarm company. Waiting we go through the prompts for the initial setup and we enter the model code and number. When it's time to enter an email address I do then pause for only one second on the password. Seeing Malcolm turn away, I tell him it's okay to know my password. Actually, I may need him to help me if I screw it up some time, so I tell him my password and other than looking at me intensely for a second or two he nods with a smile.

Waiting for the app to load on my phone Malcolm continues explaining. "So you can set the main keypad up with 5 different passwords for 5 people, like Selena, and Mike, or-"

"No. Just Selena. I don't want anyone else having it. Not even Mike."

"Okay. But you'll be able to see who accesses your apartment if they enter anyway because of their individual code. I agree the fewer with a code the better though."

"Do you want a code?" I ask barely breathing.

When Malcolm replies no quickly I'm a little surprised until he explains. "Saige, if I have the code and something ever happened, you'd maybe wonder if I did it, had something to do with it, or put someone up to it. This way, you know I can't hurt you ever because I *don't* have access."

Squeezing his hand, I smile, "I know you wouldn't anyway, Malcolm."

"Maybe. But now you *know* I can't. And that matters to me," he breathes so heavily, we both stare and wait until we seem to nod our understanding at the same time.

"So pick a 4 digit code for yourself," he turns away again as I type.

"Done."

"Okay, then I'll set up the keypad by the door. It's doesn't require electricity, not that I couldn't tap into that," he grins. "But its battery operated with a battery life of 6 months, and it gives a warning if the batteries are getting low."

"This is really amazing. When I move can I take it with me?"

"Yup. There's a way to change the system activation to acknowledge the location change which corrects your phone as well. Come see," he stands pulling me up by my hand.

Walking to the door, he holds up the keypad moving a sensor in his fingers close to the door then tells me to turn it on like I'm going out. Looking away when I punch in my 4 digits, within 5 seconds with both of us watching, my phone lights up for a second, fades back down and the green little house icon on the corner is lit up on the screen.

"Now watch what happens when the sensor is moved," he says dropping it from his fingers into his other hand.

Waiting, I swear to god I'm not even breathing until I suddenly jump at my phone vibrating in my hand. Watching the house turn red it's flashing forever, or I guess for just one minute until I start to hear an alarm ringer sound. Just slightly louder than maybe low on my phone, it fades in and out getting louder and louder until Malcolm tells me to punch in my code on the keypad.

"What do I do if it goes off when I'm not home?"

"You call the police immediately. You tell them your apartment has been broken into, that its occurring that very second, then you wait for the police to instruct you as to what to do. Do NOT shut off the alarm on your phone until the Police tell you the coast is clear. See here," he turns my phone in my hand. "Use the normal volume control, so you can turn it down while you wait to find out what's happening."

"Does it do anything else?"

"Yeah, you can program others to get notifications as well if the alarm goes off."

"Like you and Selena?"

"Yup. And also see these 3 buttons?" He points them out when we click on the app. "Well, they're like speed-dials. If you hit one, whoever you choose gets a notification on their email you've contacted them."

"Like you and Selena," I say again feeling so much safer suddenly.

Leaning against the wall, I can't stop looking at my phone as Malcolm silences. This is BY FAR the best gift I've ever received and I'm so happy and relieved and just so overwhelmed I suddenly jump and scream when there's a knock on the door right beside me.

Yanked out of the way so fast by Malcolm I barely see the door open or the pizza guy's face before he screams like a girl.

Shocked we three stand there for seconds before I start laughing so hard, I look insane. Apologizing, I make my way to my purse on the stove and pay him with Malcolm beside me clearly trying not to laugh. Tipping him better than usual I just shut the door before Malcolm does actually laugh way harder and louder than any man I've ever heard before in my life.

"Did you see his face when I answered the door?" He asks still laughing.

"Did you hear his scream?" I barely ask before the giggles hit me again. "And that was *so* not his fault. I didn't see what you looked like, but I can imagine super intense, scary-faced, threatening Malcolm throwing the door open." Fake shuddering, "I know I'd scream like a girl too."

Grinning still Malcolm walks to the couch, tugs 2 boxes closer and hands out the pizza between us. Eating silently, I stare at my phone beside me on the couch like it'll somehow change or alert me again though it's not even activated. Looking at my phone constantly, I can't believe how relieved I feel.

"Did I mention how very, very cool this was?"

"Not really," he shrugs with a grin.

"Well, this is absolutely the coolest, most amazing, most thoughtful, most perfect house warming gift ever."

"I *was* gonna get you a plant. Good call, huh?" He deadpans which starts me laughing again.

*****

"Saige, I can't possibly organize these the way you want, so can I just unpack them and put them on the shelves for you to organize later?"

"Sure." From the kitchen I inwardly cringe at the placement of my textbooks, but at least it's a project for me later.

My kitchen is almost done, and I couldn't help laugh at some of the stuff Selena packed for me- like a turkey baster? *Really?* She did pack all my favorite red ceramic mugs though, which I think was a giant *screw you* to Tyler. He probably didn't even notice until he went to make his coffee the next morning, which he also couldn't do because she packed the coffee maker as well.

Grinning as I put my mugs away, Malcolm opens a box and pauses. Watching him not move, I'm too curious not to ask, "What did you find?"

Startled, Malcolm looks guilty as hell when he turns to me and raises my bikini picture in the air. "Sorry... Um, *wow*. You look-"

"Scrawny?" I add helpfully walking toward him to take the picture.

"Ah, no. Not scrawny," he says without finishing his sentence.

Taking the picture from him, I open the other half of Tyler then quickly bend it back again. "This was the only vacation we ever took together. And 5 minutes after this picture was taken, which was like 10 minutes after we arrived I had heatstroke and was horribly sunburned. I also had water poisoning from some ice cubes the very next day," I grin shaking my head to Malcolm just listening. "It was awful for me. And I spent the next 5 days so sick in bed I could only enjoy the last day we had there."

Thinking of that vacation from hell for me, I remember saving up for it, and being so excited when I booked it. I remember feeling like such an adult at 20 years old when we arrived together holding hands like a married couple on their honeymoon.

Jolting me from my memories, Malcolm asks, "Was he good to you when you were sick?"

"Yes," I whisper back until he nods, releasing me from our intense moment again.

"Well, you looked beautiful, Saige."

"Thank you. I didn't like wearing a bikini but Tyler bought it and insisted, so I couldn't say no. But I felt good, for 5 minutes anyway."

Taking the picture with me to the kitchen, I throw it in a drawer of miscellaneous crap and continue unpacking.

I don't know what to say, and I feel uncomfortable around Malcolm feeling sad about Tyler.

Saved by the downstairs buzzer minutes later, Malcolm lets the furniture movers in.

"Anywhere is fine," I look around at all the stuff everywhere. Really, I don't know where we have room to even put the bed frame together, but Malcolm quickly figures it out by just sliding my couch all the way into the kitchen with boxes on it.

After tipping the movers, I look at the 4 huge boxes and mattresses pushed against the wall regretting instantly not paying the extra fee for assembly. "I don't know where to start," I huff exhausted.

"Let me go get my toolbox from my truck. I'll have this done in less than half an hour, I promise."

"We'll see," I grin. "If it's anything like IKEA furniture- the relationship *destroyer*- we'll be fighting in no time and the bed frame will be assembled upside down."

"That actually happened to me once with a girlfriend I had in my early twenties. We lasted about 4 hours after she bought a desk from IKEA. And the rest is history," he laughs. "IKEA really should put a warning on their boxes, or offer couples counselling with each 'assembly required' purchase."

"I *know.* I helped Selena with a bookcase when she moved into her place 2 years ago and by the end, we weren't even speaking."

"So I'll get my tools, and you stay away from me while I assemble. We should be safe if we don't make any eye contact once I begin."

"Deal."

An hour later, I can't stop giggling hanging my clothes in the closet. Malcolm is swearing nonstop and he has the Scottish spin on swearing my mum has. I really don't know how it's possible for Nessie to do that, but the imagery of the Locke Ness Monster humping sheep is hysterical.

Watching Malcolm strong arm the first mattress over to the frame, I attempt to help until he says, "It's not safe yet," which naturally makes me start giggling again while attempting to hide it with weird coughing noises.

"Done," he barks sounding so pissed, I try to hide my smile but can't. "Stop laughing. They weren't even in English, and the stickers were alphabetical all the way to M, but F and J were missing, so it *should* hold," he shrugs looking pissy, and deadly, and violent, and actually kind of cute all pissed off.

"Thank you. Can I sit on it?"

"Oh, *Christ*. I hope so," he says so seriously I barely hold in my laughter as I sit down gently, holding myself still and nervous until the bed doesn't break or even creak under me.

"I think we're good," I lie back exhaling deeply every annoying ache and pain in my entire body. "Ummmph!" When Malcolm jumps on the bed beside me, I'm tossed up then right into his side with the dip of the mattresses.

Laughing my ass off next to him, I eventually hear him talking about the bed holding, build like a pro, and he was never worried. I hear him rambling, but I feel his warmth and just snuggle into the side of his arm for a minute peacefully.

"I'm falling asleep."

Shaking my arm, Malcolm reminds me, "You need to buy food and take the truck back. And Selena and Griffin will be here in an hour."

"I don't need food, and I'll take the truck back later," I snuggle closer.

"You NEED to get food. You have nothing but a few slices of pizza and a can of ginger-ale."

"The perfect breakfast," I whine as my eyes close.

"I'm going to dump your ass on the floor if you don't get up."

"*Please...?*" I beg again actually feeling myself being pushed to the edge of the bed.

"I'm warning you. Ass meets floor in 3 seconds if you don't get up yourself. Three-Two-One. Saige!"

"Fine. *Shit,* I'm up okay. I just wanted to try out my new bed." Hopping off the bed I'm super annoyed and tired and just crusty as hell. I'm probably even a little PMSy though I'm not telling Malcolm that.

"Let's drop the truck off now. It's after 6:30, so we have to go. Just drive behind me and we'll drive back together."

Punching in my 4 digits after Malcolm dramatically looks away, we both watch the little house light up green on my phone again.

"This really is cool. Thank you so much," I squeeze his hand quickly before I turn to lock the door.

*****

"Okay, your bed is made, your apartment is getting there, and YOU have to get to bed," Selena points to Griffin. "We'll see Auntie Saige tomorrow, okay?"

"K," Griffin pouts before giving me a huge hug.

"Okay, your bed is made, your apartment is getting there, and YOU have to get to bed," Malcolm points at me as Selena starts laughing.

"K," I pout before giving him a huge hug on tiptoes. Whispering in his ear I don't hold back. "Thank you so much for the alarm, for helping me move again, and for being the bestest friend a girl could ever have."

"You're welcome," he smiles. "Lock us out, and text me later."

"Will do. Thank you for my breakfast Griffin. I love Lucky Charms," I smile down at him holding the little baggie of cereal he insisted they bring me for breakfast.

"That's because you're a wee leprechaun," Malcolm adds like a smartass heading for my door cracking me up again.

"Good night, everyone."

Watching them leave for the elevators, Malcolm opts for the stairs so Selena and Griffin can go up, and after one last wave, Malcolm tells me to get in and lock up again.

Looking around my apartment, it's getting there. The corner of my kitchen holds a stack of empty boxes, and the makeshift living room looks like a living room with the exception of missing tables and lamps. But with my bookcases and books beside the couch it feels a little more like a home to me.

My new bedding doesn't match my couch at all, but it's all temporary I have to remind myself. Hopefully when I move to Cambridge I'll have an actual bedroom so I won't care about the all the crap everywhere.

Everything is temporary I have to remind myself almost hourly, especially when I see Malcolm talking to Griffin, teasing Selena, and being this constant huge, amazing presence around me.

This is *all* temporary.

Grabbing my phone after a quick shower I see a text from Malcolm.

'Good night, Saige. I hope you sleep well. Oh, and I think you owe me a comp'd dessert as well. 😊'

'Deal. xo'

CHAPTER 21

"I *never* get to see you anymore, Saige. I swear, if I hadn't invited myself to your birthday dinner with Malcolm, I wouldn't have even seen you last week," Selena pouts.

Laughing at her pout, I remember when Malcolm picked me up with beautiful flowers and a gift to Selena announcing she was 'chaperoning' us. Thank god Malcolm was humored and accommodating because her outrageousness could've been really awkward over dinner.

"Are you seeing Malcolm this weekend again for *coffee?*" She rolls her eyes as usual.

Selena still thinks all these nondates are funny. She keeps insisting Malcolm and I are actually dating, when in reality we actually are not at all. We may see each other almost daily but he's just my friend, and we never cross that line with each other. *Ever.*

"We're getting together Thursday afternoon when I'm done work to go to this recycle, refurbished place he knows where contractors drop stuff off to be reused. Hopefully, I'm finally getting a coffee table," I huff. "Do you have any idea how much you actually use a coffee table?"

"No," she grins.

"Well, you do. Like for everything, and after 3 weeks without one I'm going crazy."

"What else are you doing?"

"Ah, I was going to ask you if your mom could babysit Griffin on Saturday night so you could come to a party with us. Bring Dave if you want," I quickly add.

Nodding already, I know she's in. "What party?"

"Malcolm's freakily tall brother Tatum is throwing his own 40th Birthday party. And apparently it's a must go, and I was invited because Tatum thinks I'm a cute wee leprechaun," I laugh when Selena starts howling. "So, will you guys come? I think it'll be pretty wild, and their entire family will be there and I couldn't say no. But I know I'll feel a little out of place knowing only Malcolm and Tatum."

"I am soooo in. And I know Dave'll come because he's still in the honeymoon whatever YOU want, Selena, phase of our whatever."

"It'll probably be a very loud, drunk, Celtic nightmare."

"Then I'm TOTALLY in. Plus, I've got to meet the man who makes Malcolm look small and wimpy, which I still have to tell Malcolm you said about him," she teases again.

"Trust me, I'm sure he even thinks that next to Tatum. I asked Mike, too, but he can't get out of work. Oh, and Malcolm says he won't be drinking, so he's driving, and you guys can come with us if you want?"

"Perfect. I'll wear my sexy black dress," she muses with a dirty grin I'm sure is more for Dave than me.

"Which one? You look sexy as hell in all your dresses," I pout.

"Thanks, Kiddo. Oh! You have to wear that beautiful green wrap around dress you bought last year with me. Remember?" Nodding, I know exactly what dress she means. It was an 'I'll never wear this but I LOVE it, so I have to have it' dress. "Will you wear it?"

"Maybe."

*****

On Thursday in the middle of a giant warehouse I have to know if I'm officially crazy. "Malcolm, is it weird that I love a door?"

Laughing, Malcolm shakes his head no, but does find me funny regardless. "No, wee Saige... It's a fine look'in door," he brogues which still makes my heart melt.

Tilting my head to look at it again I admit, "I'm here for a coffee table, but I love a door. I'm thinking I've lost my mind this summer."

"Or you could buy the door, and together we can make it an amazing coffee table for you? I'll show you how to sand it down, repaint it, and even how to add the tempered glass in the panels to make it an even surface."

"*Really?*" Feeling excited I keep looking at the damn door, and I just want it. I can't explain it, and it makes no sense to me whatsoever, but there's just something about the age and shape of it that I love.

"You don't even need to paint it if you don't want to once the old paint is removed from all the moldings. You could just stain it natural dark wood again."

"You don't mind? Is it annoying or like time-consuming to do?"

"*Please...* It's what I do. Among thousands of other things," he grins to my growing excitement.

"Okay. I'm buying a door. But can you take it home with you?"

"Absolutely. We can start on Sunday if you want?"

"I want. God, this is exciting. I've never made, or sanded, or done anything like this before," I kind of bounce in the aisle.

Lifting the huge door to balance on his shoulder Malcolm starts walking through the aisles of unused, leftover, recycled stuff everywhere you look. Almost like an indoor junkyard, it has so much stuff everywhere, I don't even know where to look. And unbelievably only $65 dollars later we're leaving.

"How much is a new door?"

"Like this old one? Probably close to a thousand. But a newer generic door is only a couple hundred."

"But how do they make any money charging me only $65 dollars?"

"It's all dropped off and donated. Everything is as is, so the overhead is minimal. Just salaries I would guess. Plus the building is old, and there's no heating or air conditioning as you know."

"I know. I almost passed out in there. I was soooo not made for heat," I fan my still sweaty face in his air conditioned truck listening to some funky 70's music.

*****

"Um, how have you been with the nights? You don't really say anything anymore."

Looking over at Malcolm, he glances my way and quickly back to the road. Thinking, I realize it would be so easy just to say I'm fine because I should say that. But I like talking to Malcolm.

"I've been way better than I thought I'd be in my apartment. My alarm certainly helps," I say as he grins. "And I guess the fact that I'm walked directly to my car by either Mike or Hershal helps. Plus, *someone* makes me text him the second I start my car, then talk to him as I run from my car into the building, so it's a lot easier than I thought it would be," I whisper squeezing Malcolm's leg as he takes my hand. "I still have that weird feeling of being watched, or like something is going to happen to me, which I know is just paranoia but-"

Exhaling, I try to focus on reality again. "Um, the only time I get really

215

nervous now is running for my apartment, but with you just waiting silently on the phone, I feel much better- like you'll hear me get hurt and get to me quick or something. Which is stupid, I know. It's not like you live particularly close to me, but it just seems like you'd get to me quick, or get Selena, or the police, or something for me if anything happened again," I fade out when he squeezes my hand on his leg again.

"I would get to you quick. Or *something,* Saige. That's why I make you call until you get in your door and set the alarm- it eases me too. Especially since you won't keep the knife or Taser on you," he glares which makes me laugh.

"Il-leg-al, as I've told you a hundred times. I appreciate the thought behind them, but I can't. I have to stay a law-abiding citizen, Malcolm," I tease again after calling him a gangster one night last week when we argued over the Taser.

Looking out the window, it's still daylight even at 7:00. Its daylight and I feel like the last 7 weeks of my life have just flown by in terms of what little I've accomplished, but they've also crawled by because of all the fear and anxiety all the time.

"You know... This is the only summer in 4 years I've done nothing. Every year after school I was an intern at Dunsdun and Hallway Law Firm, and before that I either took extra credits or I volunteered my first year at the police precinct on Croft St."

"So why didn't you intern again? Because of what happened?"

"No. I actually chose to do nothing this summer but work. This was the last summer I had before Law School, so I wanted to spend it, um-"

"With Tyler," he exhales slowly.

Nodding, I barely find the words. "See, I'm going to be in school full time and interning every summer for at least the next 4 years. Then hopefully I'll intern in a placement with the ability to advance until I set up a case history that I can use to approach the City D.A.'s office. I need a portfolio and courtroom history to be hired as a Public Attorney.

"Anyway, this was it for me, for at least 6, maybe 7 years. I have the grades and the determination to get there, but like most occupations there's an element of nepotism. And I have no ins, except for my portfolio."

"So you wanted to spend time with him before you were too busy."

"Yes. And admittedly a little for myself as well. I needed just a little break to rejuvenate before I threw myself back into it for years. Anyway, when Tyler told me he wanted me to take the summer off to be with him, I agreed because I wanted a break myself. I would never admit this to anyone else, but sometimes it's hard keeping everything up all the time. My grades, my job, my studies even. Sometimes I get a little tired, but I'm not allowed to be so I force myself to continue. Even if I'd like to just relax and take a breather, or maybe just be a little more normal like other people my age are, I can't."

Well, that was the most honest I've ever been with anyone else my entire life. "But I'm not complaining or anything. I just wanted a little break, and then things changed so quickly for me between Tyler and what happened to me that now I feel like the awesome 4 1/2 months I was supposed to enjoy have been pretty shitty."

"I'm sorry you feel that way," Malcolm says pulling around the corner to my apartment.

"Do you want to come up for dinner or something?"

"No, thanks. I've got plans later, but I'll see you Saturday."

"Oh, okay." Feeling disappointed, I'm dying to know what his plans are and why he doesn't want to come up with me. Malcolm never turns down hanging out with me. "You're sure?"

"Yeah. I'll call you on Saturday before I pick you up. Text me the second you get in," he smiles quickly then just waits with the truck idling.

"Thank you for taking me today."

"You're welcome," he huffs a little before nodding toward the door.

Stepping out and down, I feel totally abandoned for some reason. Almost irrationally so. "Um, take care of my door table," I grin stupidly.

"I will. Go get inside Saige, and text me when you're in."

"Okay."

Running up the front steps, I have my key ready and my pepper spray handy. Waiting by the elevator, I know Malcolm can see me through the glass windows so I wave one more time though I can't see him at all through his tinted windows.

Waiting out the 3 floors, I run for my own door, check the green house on my phone and throw the door open to punch in my code quickly. Resetting it, I look around at nothing special, and exhale again before texting Malcolm.

'I'm safe and sound, alarmed, and locked in.'

   'Good. Have a good night.'

'I have leftover pizza???'

   'I'm good, but thanks. See you Saturday.'

'Okay.' Holding my phone I keep waiting for a leprechaun, or a stubborn, or a wee lass comment. I'm waiting for something from Malcolm, but nothing happens. So I eventually give up.

*****

Sitting on my couch, I'm bored almost immediately. I don't have a TV, or even a coffee table, and I'm not in the mood for anything right now. I could read but I'm not in the mood, and I should eat but I'm not in the mood.

Reaching for my cell I decide to call my mum strangely.

"Hello?"

"Hi, mum."

"Saige? How goes the batt'le?" She asks as she always does.

"Good. When are you getting your countertops? This weekend?"

"Ah, noooo... The bloody arseholes measured the sink wrong so now I have ta wait a week or two. Was ye no comin' to visit this week'end?"

"Do you still want me to anyway?"

"No, dunna bother. The kitchens no finished and I hae to go to a dance at the Rite on Satur'day anyway."

"Oh, okay." Pausing, I'm both relieved I don't have to go and a little disappointed she doesn't want to see me just because. "I won't keep you then. Enjoy your dance."

"Hae ye giv'in that scoundrel another chance, then?"

"No. Never."

"Well, tha's good. He dunna deserve it, and you'll no trust him again anyway."

"I know..." I exhale slowly. "Remember I told you about my Scottish friend?"

"Are ye seeing him, then?"

"No, we're just friends. Um, he's really great though. And his dad is from Edinburgh."

"Ah, so he's no half bad then," I can hear her smile.

"No, not half bad," I grin.

"I told ye be'fore, he'll be good in the sack, Saige. But tha's it. Just remem'ber tha and you and the wee bugger can enjoy yer *friendship,*" I can almost see her quoting with a dirty grin.

"He's not like that for me. He's just a friend, but he's very nice and he's not so wee. He's actually kind of a brick shithouse he's so big, though he's always very gentle and sweet when he's with me."

"Well then, throw him yer knickers and enjoy it while it lasts," she actually does laugh when I groan.

"Mum-"

"Wha? You think I dunna know what you and tha cheat'er were up to? I met your father at 19, love, and married him by 20. So I know aboot hormones, Saige."

"This just got really gross so I'm hanging up now," I cringe as she laughs again. "I'll call you next weekend to see about a visit, okay?"

"Sure. Bring the fella if ye want'ta."

"Ah, I'm not sure."

"Or don't. Just remem'ber-"

"Never give anyone my heart again, and I'll be fine. Right?" I ask a little irritated with her.

"Tha's right. And it's sound advice, Saige. Trust me."

"Okay. Anyway, enjoy your dance on Saturday."

"Oh, I plan on it. We'll be speakin' soon," she says before hanging up.

Holding my phone, I regret calling my mum instantly. She's never helpful and she's always jaded. She's the worst at advice on everything and yet I'm always drawn back to her because she's my formerly drunk, formerly crazy mum who I still love.

Plus she's the only family I have.

Sending a text before bed, I'm not sure why Malcolm ditched me other than he actually does have a life, unlike me.

But I like talking to him, and I miss him when he isn't around.

As a friend.

'Good night, Malcolm.' I text almost sadly.

(mis)TRUST

CHAPTER 22

Dropping off dirty plates in the kitchen I wave when I see Selena walking to the bar 5 minutes early.

"How was your night?" Selena asks

"I was soooooo bored," I whine.

"You didn't see Malcolm?"

"Um, no. He had plans," I almost sneer.

"Huh."

Looking across the dining room I pretend I'm not bothered in the least that Malcolm had plans to do something. Probably with some*one*.

"Okay, well you have something to celebrate tomorrow night, too," she says pulling out an envelope from her purse. "Here. Open it," she giggles excited when she flips it over so I see the Harvard insignia.

Gasping, I rip it open instantly. With Selena hovering over my shoulder I read as quickly as possible. "I'm in! I'm totally in. The conditional acceptance was lifted and I received the prestigious Beckett Award for scholastic excellence."

"What does that mean?"

"Ah, an entitlement of 25 thousand this year. And I can use up to 20% of it for personal living expenses which will definitely help. The other 80% has to go towards tuition though."

"Holy shit. What *is* the actual tuition cost this year?" She asks cringing before I even tell her.

"$56 thousand. Um, a year," I cringe myself as she gasps. "But I'll get the Federal Direct Stafford Loan, and I won a scholarship grant from my internship with Dunsdon and Hallaway of 15 thousand a year. So I'll only have to borrow about 30 thousand my first year for the tuition balance and for living expenses in federal loans. And if I keep up my grades, I can probably count on the scholarships to hold out year after year." Speaking fast, I hope she doesn't have a meltdown if I explain it all quickly.

"But you have to pay back the Stafford loan when you're finished school, right?"

"Yeah, but that'll only be about 30 thousand a year."

"Times 4 years?"

"That's nothing, Selena. God, I already owe 50 thousand from my pre-law degree."

"But that's so much debt. Over, what... 170 thousand?" She actually cries out a little like she's really worried about this.

Looking around, I hope to hell no one can hear us. "I know it seems like a lot, but it's really not that bad. *Honestly*," I add when she huffs like I'm full of shit. "It's really not. The average starting salary for a Harvard law graduate is over a hundred thousand annually, so if I live modestly, I can pay off everything in maybe 2-3 years tops."

"But-"

Exhaling, I cut her off before she gets really worked up. "Selena, this is my life. So it's like an investment. I have to do this now so I can have the future I want later. I don't have a choice."

"You have a choice. But you feel like you have to be a lawyer because of Alec. And that's not really a choice. Or a life, Saige."

Stunned she would say that or even think it, I'm a little hurt and overwhelmed by this conversation.

"Selena, I don't mean this badly, but what I do or *why* I do it is absolutely *none* of your business. I want to be a lawyer, and this is how you do it. So I'll deal with the debt afterward like every other goddamn lawyer does. I'll struggle, then I'll be free to make my mark."

"For Alec," she huffs totally pissed at me for some reason I can't understand.

"For *me*. And for him. And for everyone else who needs good council when they're in trouble."

"But-"

"Jesus *Christ,* Selena. Why are you acting like this? You've known since the day we met what I was doing- you even said 10 minutes ago I had a reason to celebrate. But now you're acting like this is all a news flash to you or something. Did you really think I could be the very best going to a local community college?"

"Like me?" She asks glaring at me.

"Did *you* want to be a lawyer before Griffin? Because otherwise, I'm not making that comparison at all. I'm merely saying I didn't bust my ass and potentially lose the love of my life just to half-ass it in a community college where I wouldn't get my damn degree anyway."

After a very tense silence between us, Selena finally nods. "I'm sorry. I just hate seeing you waste your life in school with huge debt for something I don't think you actually want anyway."

"First, I hardly think paying off a debt in 3 years- 4 years from now is wasting my life. Second, it *is* what I want. And I'm not sure why you suddenly think otherwise."

"Oh, I don't know... Maybe because if you weren't leaving you'd actually start a relationship with the best fucking guy I've ever met in my life."

"Wait, I-"

"Or because you still cry about Alec in your sleep but can't talk about him. Or because you say stupid fucking things like 'the love of your life'," she quotes obnoxiously, "when talking about that lying, using, cheating prick Tyler."

"Okay, we're done. I have to get to work, and I can't talk to you anymore," I snap turning my back to leave.

"*Run,* Saige," she laughs at me which makes me nearly violent.

Wanting to scream at her, I shake my head and walk away instead. I will not lose Selena over this, but it's getting pretty fucking close and I'm not sure why she's doing this to me.

Storming back into the family side of the restaurant, I put on my happy face and talk to my tables. I only have an hour left to get through, even though I feel that sad, draggy, I need to cry thing I used to get weeks ago suddenly weighing me down.

Entering my desserts slip for table 18, I think of Malcolm, then want to talk to Malcolm, and basically want to *see* Malcolm.

I'm not sure why he was a little distant to me last night or why he hasn't called or texted today, but I miss him. So deciding to go first, I send off a quick text.

'How's your day?' And then I carry on for a few minutes bussing my tables as Aileen settles in to trade off with me.

'Good. Yours?'

'It WAS good. Now, not so much. Want to have dinner with me?'

'Want to finally see my splendid manor in Montgomery Park? I'll barbecue us steaks?' Laughing I can almost hear the hoity pretend accent he used when he said Montgomery Park.

'Steak? I'm in. Medium Rare. I like it bloody.'

'You're a wee beast. 464 Orchid Ave. Need directions?'
'No. I'll find it. I have some good news.'
'Oh yeah?'
'Yes. Can I bring anything? Dessert?'
'2 slices of the cheesecake. And whatever you want. ☺'
'OK. See you in an hour.'
'Looking forward to it.'

*****

Walking out of the employee lounge after changing, Selena and I make eye contact and when she smiles, I can't help smile back. I mean she was way out of line, but I think she means well even if she gets a little too motherly with me sometimes.

Checking the MapQuest map again, I'm nearing Malcolm's house when all the beautiful homes, and beautiful landscaping, and beautiful everything starts. The roads are immaculate, and I swear even the people I see walking around are immaculate. God, it really is a whole other world when you enter Montgomery Park.
Seeing Malcolm's SUV first, I pull over out front and really look at his home. It's smaller than the surrounding homes, though not small at all. And it's absolutely beautiful.
From the black trim on the white stucco and siding, it fits perfectly in this neighborhood. He even has a burgundy door and mailbox, with matching landscaping which just makes the house that much lovelier to look at.
Grabbing the whole cheesecake I bought for him from D'Vecseys I just step out of my car when Malcolm and a woman step out hugging. Watching in another slow motion trance, you'd think I'd be used to this feeling... but here I am again.
Winded and shocked and just ill.
"Saige?" Malcolm calls out from his front steps. "You're early," he says as the woman steps back into his house like she's hiding from me.
What. The. *Fuck?*
I can't breathe as he approaches me and I want to jump back in my car but he advances on me quicker than my brain tells my legs to move.
"Is that for me?" He smiles at the cheesecake and I nearly throw up.

224

Staring up at his eyes, I wish I could even reach to punch him in the face. Instead I toss the box at him and rip my car door open. Almost in, Malcolm's arm suddenly blocks me and when I attempt to just jump in under his arm, he grabs my arm to stop me.

"What the hell was that for?"

"Fuck. *You*," I groan deeply, ripping the door right out of his hand.

"What the hell is wrong with you?" He asks as I turn to the woman stepping out of his house again with a goddamn baby in her arms.

With my rage barely in check, I stare at her dumbfounded until he turns back to her then back to my face understanding my anger.

"Are you fucking kidding me?" He seethes close to my face. "She's my sister Moira, and that's my little niece." Looking back at his eyes, I see behind him Moira standing in his driveway watching us.

"What did you think? I was screwing some woman in my home minutes before you were expected, and you just happened to catch us?" Unable to speak, I hold the door for support and try to find the words needed to make him not so angry with me. "Did you?!" He growls not looking so handsome anymore but more menacing as I lean back from his face. "Did you really think I was with a woman minutes before you were coming over for a goddamn barbecue?"

"Yes," I cry as the shakes hit me and the adrenaline quickly spikes. "I'm sorry. I just, um, Tyler was with a woman when I came home early."

"I. Am. Not. Tyler."

"I know, I just- it looked like when you hugged her you were happy, and I felt sad," I exhale as I feel the first tear fall.

"I *was* happy because she's my sister. Did you really think I would do that to you?" He asks barely above a whisper.

"Yes. I'm sor-" Before I even finish the word Malcolm leans in and hugs me. He doesn't wait for me to initiate the hug like usual, he just hugs me. Big, and warm, and so suddenly, I exhale my upset, and inhale his kindness into me.

"I'm sorry I thought that. I should've known better. I just didn't expect to see something like that again."

"You won't see that again. Not from me. Okay?" Pulling away Malcolm stares at my eyes until I agree. "Can I introduce you to Moira and Madeline now?"

"Okay... I really am sorry, Malcolm."

"We're going to talk about it later, Saige, cuz I'm kind of pissed at you."

When Malcolm bends to pick up the cheesecake box he also growls, "And if this is a whole cheesecake and you've ruined it our friendship is definitely over. Come on." Tugging my hand, I only have time for one quick cheek swipe of any tears before I'm standing in front of Moira.

"Saige, this is my sister Moira. Moira, this is Saige," he says still sounding a little pissed at me.

"Ah, the wee leprechaun," she grins. "I think you made quite an impression on Tatum."

"Well, if he keeps up with the leprechaun stuff, the fiery red-headed Scot in me will kick his ass," I grin back at her beautiful face. Tallish for a female, Moira has Malcolm's dark tanned skin and hair and his blue eyes as well.

"Will you kick his ass tomorrow night? Because we'd all pay to see that."

"I'll see how annoying he is and make sure Malcolm lets you know beforehand."

"Good enough. This little thing is Madeline," she leans forward with the baby in her arms. I've never really known a baby before so she might be 3 months, or maybe even 6, I really don't know.

"She's beautiful," I whisper gently touching her chubby little fingers. "How old is she?"

"4 months. We have to go but it was lovely meeting you. I'll see you tomorrow at the party."

"You too," I smile as she walks to her car in the driveway.

"I'll be back for you in a minute," Malcolm says very threateningly until I see a little smile as he turns.

Watching Malcolm walk Moira to her car I know there's nothing else I can say to take back my reaction 5 minutes ago. But I hate these quick bursts of irrational behavior, and I want to blame Tyler for this so badly I could scream.

Malcolm strapping in his niece is absolutely adorable. He's so huge all crunched into Moira's car doing whatever the hell he's doing that seems way more complicated then when I strap Griffin into his car seat.

Waiting, Malcolm finally steps out and says something to his sister who looks over at me and smiles again. "It was nice meeting you, Saige. I'll see you tomorrow."

"You too. I'll see you tomorrow," I wave as Malcolm steps back from her window to advance on me again.

Beside me, Malcolm blocks out most of the sun, and he looks really tanned today I suddenly notice.

"Ready to go inside, or would you like to throw something else at me?" He asks teasing but I flinch anyway.

"I'm so sorry for that. I was just shocked so I had a flashback to that day at my old apartment, and I freaked."

"Understood. But do you understand that I'm not your asshole ex?"

"I do. It's just hard sometimes not feeling- no, more like *waiting* for something like that again. Malcolm my dad cheated on my mom too, twice actually before he left her and me, and then when Tyler did what he did it just hurt so badly, I kind of lost faith in men, or faith in monogamy, or trust, or just about every other single thing you can think of. Ah, I have a few hang-ups," I roll my eyes as he laughs.

"You don't say?" Throwing his arm over my shoulder Malcolm reaffirms, "I would never invite you over just to have a woman walk out of my home like we were together. It's not my style, Saige, or even *a* style. Please ask me questions before assuming the worst- I may surprise you."

"You do," I respond immediately. "You always surprise me, Malcolm."

"Good. Want to see my house now?" He asks sounding excited.

"I *really* want to see your house now. And by the way, it's the most perfect house on the street."

"Outside. Trust me there's still much to do inside. But yes, the outside is nice," he says with such pride, I wrap my arm around his waist and squeeze him.

Opening the front door I gasp amazed. "Oh, it's beautiful!"

Between the dark tiles that turn into hardwood floors surrounded by white walls, everything you first see walking in is white and dark and beautiful. Even the stairs are dark wood with plush beige carpeting on the middle of each step.

"This is just the entrance. Trust me, it doesn't stay like this everywhere." Turning for the first room to the left I kick off my shoes and walk into his gorgeous library/den combo with browns and beiges everywhere. Photos line the mantle on a real wood fireplace, and all the photos on the walls are brown wood frames on crisp white walls in geometric patterns across the walls.

God, there's so much to look at, and yet it's simple and classy and it almost has a cottage feel, which I imagine would be amazing in the winter with the fireplace lit.

Touching the brown suede feel of one of the slouchy chairs, I have to know. "Did you design this yourself?"

"Would you be really impressed if I said I did?"

"Yes."

"Damn," he grins looking around the room himself. "Did I ever mention Dan's wife Karen is an interior decorator?"

"No."

"Then I designed it myself," he smirks as I laugh.

Pulling me forward by the hand, we walk through white French doors into a dining room with the same colors and feel. It has a huge wooden table with beige placemats and a lovely chandelier overhead. The walls are still white and the geometrically placed photos continue in this room like the pattern from the library/den.

Walking through another set of French doors we enter the biggest, most beautiful kitchen I've ever seen in my life. Like the pages of a magazine it's breathtaking. The entire back of the house is the kitchen with the entrance hallway leading right to it from the middle, and the whole back wall is glass looking out onto a deck with long beige drapes to give privacy. Pausing to take it all in, it's so beautiful it's almost overwhelming.

"This is amazing," I whisper looking at the white wooden cabinets, and all the little touches of color everywhere.

Even the island with hanging pots and pans overhead is white and brown. And the tall breakfast bar of marble around the side of the kitchen actually sits 5 comfortably.

Glancing to the right of the next set of French doors, there's a long rectangular table with an actual bench seat against the wall, and 5 chairs on the opposite side with 2 chairs at each end.

Shaking my head, I whisper, "I can't believe you did this."

"I'll show you the before and after pictures. Then you'll know why it's taken me 6 years and lots of help from Dan and his crew. We had to gut the entire place. It was actually a tiny almost galley kitchen in this back corner with another closed room right here," he motions to the space holding the long table. "Anyway, we turned it from 2 rooms into this one. And it looks pretty good," he says quietly like he doesn't want to brag even though he absolutely should.

"It doesn't look pretty good, Malcolm- it's the most beautiful kitchen I've ever seen in my life. I never thought I'd like so much white before, but it looks so natural and lovely and just amazing. Against the dark wood floors and throw rugs, this kitchen is a dream for most people. Do you always have parties with so much space?" I ask looking around at everything until I see almost nothing specifically.

"Not often, but I do like to have the Thanksgiving party with my friends and family here. It's quite loud and eventful with so many people and liquor and crazy shouting to be heard."

"And you *love* it."

"*Once* a year," he grins. "Last room?" He turns toward another opened set of French doors beside the long table into a huge living room.

Realizing it's the space of the whole den and half the dining room, I understand where they took the room from for the huge kitchen.

It's much longer than it is wide, but it's positioned in such a way that the television is against the wall going up the stairs. The couch rests against the opposite wall, and 2 big club chairs rest on each end pointing towards the TV as well. There's a pool table exiting the kitchen and even an armoire under the gigantic TV which I'm sure houses all the man stuff so nothing looks cluttered or takes away from the simplicity and comfort of the room.

"Malcolm... this is unbelievable. You must be so proud of yourself for this? I mean, I know it's your job but you've done something so special with this house, I just can't believe it. I'm at a loss for words," I fade out looking out the big picture window at the front of his house to the street beyond. "If I ever had a dream house in mind, *this* would be it."

"You didn't ever have a dream house?"

"No. I only ever imagined getting to where I need to be. But this is always going to be the model I dream of now for my future house. Maybe one day you can build me one?" I grin still a little shocked by what I'm seeing.

"I can do that," he nods smiling. "Now, just so you don't think everything is perfect, the upstairs has 3 bedrooms and only mine and the 2 bathrooms are finished. The basement? Damp, dirty and gross. But that'll be the last project once the upstairs is finished. Can I show you upstairs?"

"Yes, please," I say already exiting the French doors beside the stairs and front hallway.

Walking up the stairs, I think of my ass and hope to hell he's not looking at it. But when I turn to him, he's smirking like he's looking right at my ass which actually makes me laugh at him. "Perv..."

When the stairs end, the banister wraps back along the hallway halfway to end at a door. In front of the stairs are 2 closed doors, and one door in the middle of the hallway itself.

"The 2 unfinished bedrooms," he grimaces which naturally makes me want to look.

"Holy. *Shit*..." I mutter opening the first door. "Wow, that's a lot of wallpaper," I laugh looking at the pink wall on one side and the 3 other walls of vivid blue kind of wrap around multi-colored flowery *what the hell* wallpaper? "Um, the floors are nice," I add trying to stop giggling.

"Did I mention I bought the house at an estate's sale when the little old lady who previously lived here was put in a nursing home?"

"Ah, no. But that explains this 60's looking nightmare. Is she still alive?" Looking at me like my question was weird, I explain. "I just thought it would be cool if she could see what you've done to her house. Then again, she might go into culture shock at all the plain white downstairs," I muse.

"I'm not sure, but I doubt it. My neighbor told me when they moved her out she was 92 and that was 6 years ago." Nodding, I get it.

"What's the other room like?"

"The same but pink with green flowers," he laughs. "Plus it's filled with tons of crap right now. So if someone stays here, this is their only option. And I've got to tell you a drunk buddy crashing here once in a while is pretty funny. There's the extra TV I offered you," he points to a hideous blue dresser with a TV on top.

"No, but thank you."

"Okay, the bathroom is finished," he says pulling the door closed behind us to walk down the hall.

"Wow." Looking at the bathroom it's actually pretty big with double sinks and a huge claw-foot tub beside an enclosed glass shower. "Is this your bathroom?" If it is, he's a total neat freak I didn't realize before.

"No, I have my own in my room. Come see," he's grinning excited again by my reaction I think. "I took the 2 original bedrooms at the end of this hall and made them one master bedroom. This hallway actually extended further for 2 doors, but I closed it off to make one large room."

Opening the door for me, I'm just astounded. His room is big with white and brown and beiges like in the library/den. It's totally masculine, but it feels so soothing and comforting I don't think of it as strictly a man's bedroom. Even the dark hardwood floors have a huge area rug in swirling designs of all the neutral colors that softens up the masculinity.

"Is that another wood fireplace?"

"Yes, it was already here, but I fixed up the mantle to make it-"

"Beautiful," I exhale. "Malcolm, I'm speechless. I'm just like stunned I think. I can't believe you did this."

Looking at his huge king size bed, it's facing the door in between the 2 large windows I assume were each in the original 2 bedrooms. It faces the door and there's at least 20 feet between the end of it and the door to enter. On the side, there's a long sliding door closet with a tall bureau beside it, and on the door wall there's another door, and also a huge flat screen TV mounted on the wall.

"That's my bathroom," he motions to the door beside the TV.

Finding myself finally moving, I plop down into the huge slouchy chair the same as the ones in the den and I'm so impressed I'm almost weirded-out or something.

The chair is beside the fireplace, and I can't even imagine what his room looks like in the winter with a fire lit. It would be so beautiful and relaxing, and just amazing I think.

"What are you thinking," he smiles leaning against the wall.

"I don't know. This is the most beautiful house I've ever seen, besides that bedroom monstrosity I walked into," I laugh quickly. "And for some reason it seems overwhelming, or intimidating, or something."

"Why?"

"I don't know. We're just so different. You're an adult living an adult life, and I'm just starting out, starting another 4 years in school. I feel like a little kid beside you, and I've never felt like a kid even when I was one." I also feel sad for some reason I can't understand.

"Saige, this took me *years* to do. Day after day I worked at it and it sure as hell didn't start out like this. If I didn't have friends who were in contracting there's no way I could've done this on my own, or even *afforded* to do it. Plus, I've been working since I graduated college 8 years ago."

"I know, but I feel embarrassed that I'm so much younger than you, I think." Is that it?

Shaking my head, I think it's more that this isn't somewhere I ever thought I'd be. I *never* pictured anything so adult and welcoming and just so beautiful in my future with Tyler. My expectations were actually fairly low with Tyler I suddenly realize.

"What is it?" He asks walking slowly toward me before sitting on the other comfy fireplace chair.

"I don't know. I just feel sad," I exhale desperately trying not to cry.

Leaning forward, Malcolm looks so beautiful to me in this moment, in his room, surrounded by his scent and his life all around us.

"Why?"

"I don't know."

"Come here," he extends his hand.

Looking between us, the silence is so thick and my emotions are so high I move without thinking right into his arms. Pushing back into the chair, Malcolm positions me against his chest and I don't even try to fight it anymore. My sadness is real and the feelings are insane so I let go against him and cry.

Not loudly, or hysterically- more like a sad exhale I cry against his chest. And Malcolm doesn't speak, or console, or try anything at all.

He sits with one arm wrapped over my shoulder and his other hand on the arm of the chair. He sits silently still as I cry against him everything I'm not, everything I've lost, and everything I'll never have again.

"Are ye alright, wee Saige?" He asks in his delicious accent after I've finally stopped crying minutes later.

"I'm hungry," I say instead of answering. Feeling his laugh against my cheek, I pull away to apologize. "I'm very sorry for this. I'm not sure what happened but I swear I love your home," I grin.

"Well, that's good to know. I've never had a woman cry because of my home, or even *in* my home before. At least not that I'm aware of," he grins. "Come on, let's get dinner on."

Rising from his lap, I see my tear wetness on his shirt and I'm embarrassed again until he looks down at it and shrugs. "It doesn't bother me," he says placing his hand on the wet mark on his chest.

CHAPTER 23

On the back deck off his kitchen, I realize this is the first perfect night I've had in forever. It's still light out though it's nearly 8, and everything is just so calm and soothing in his beautifully landscaped yard.

Actually, I wish there was a pool, but otherwise, I could happily spend the rest of my life out here with Malcolm.

"Bloody enough for you?" He grins at my plate as I eat.

"Perfect. And you didn't ruin a perfectly delicious steak with anything other than a baked potato. Thank you, this is amazing."

"You're welcome. But can you actually eat that whole steak?"

"Watch me," I wink spearing another piece of steak with my fork.

Muttering *bloodthirsty* as I chew, Malcolm asks, "So how was your day?"

"Awful, then great, then awful again, and now great again," I laugh like a moron.

"Awful how?" He asks digging into his second baked potato.

Trying to control my anger, I let him know about last night and this morning. "Somehow Tyler found out my new cell number and he kept calling and texting he wants to see me all night. Though I ignored him, and only answered one text in a way that could *not* be misinterpreted, he kept sending texts anyway."

Looking at me with a spoonful of sour cream in the air, he asks the obvious question I wish I could answer. "How did he get your number?"

"No idea," I shrug. "I mean I gave it out to a few people at work if they wanted me to take their shifts, but I didn't think it was to anyone who would either know Tyler or be stupid enough to give it to him. Mike and Selena have had it since I changed numbers and Tyler didn't get it from them. So I assume it was someone from work."

"Did you block his number?"

"This morning, when the fiftieth text came through since last night."

"Good. But if he keeps bothering you, you'll let me know," he says in a tone that doesn't allow for argument until I agree.

"Okay, so how was your day good?"

"I received my letter with the conditional acceptance lifted from Harvard," I smile.

"*Harvard?*" He nearly jumps. "You're going to Harvard in the fall?"

Looking at Malcolm, I'm a little surprised by his reaction. "Yes. Didn't you know that? I thought I told you."

"No, you didn't mention Harvard. I knew you were starting school again, but I didn't know it was at Harvard. So, *wow*... Harvard," he says looking either impressed or I don't know what. When he suddenly looks out at his quiet backyard, I don't understand what the problem is.

"What's wrong? I kind of thought this was cause for celebration. Or at least it is for me."

Turning back to me, Malcolm smiles but shakes his head at the same time. "It's amazing, Saige. And you must be so proud. Actually, I'm proud for you, I just didn't realize you'd be moving away to Cambridge."

"But you knew I was only living here temporarily."

"Actually, I thought you were only living in *that* apartment temporarily. I didn't know it was because you were moving away."

Reaching to squeeze his hand quickly, he seems like he'll miss me or something which is kind of sweet. "I'll still visit when I can. I'll need to see you guys sometimes, and I'll really need my Griffin fix."

Watching Malcolm he smiles again and squeezes my hand back but doesn't speak for a few minutes. Swatting a random fly away, we both eat somewhat comfortably under his soft white deck lights, until I finally concede I can't finish my steak.

"I can't do it, dammit. I ruined myself with the potato." Sipping my glass of water, I wait for Malcolm to say something other than his grinning *I knew it,* but he doesn't acknowledge me other than little looks and smiles as he continues eating.

"What's wrong?" I finally lean back in my deck chair, grateful I'm wearing a loose sundress so I don't have anything tight on my stomach.

"Nothing at all. So, that was your good thing, what was your next awful?"

"Um, Selena and I had a fight and some tension after I read my letter."

"Why? She doesn't want you to leave either?" *Either?* I almost jolt when I hear Malcolm say the word either.

"Um, no. She's freaked about the loans and debt. And basically she doesn't understand that this is normal and something I'll deal with afterward."

"It's pretty bad, huh? I had a friend that went to Yale for a year, and he's still paying it off."

"Yale for a year? Why would he leave? That's insane."

"He couldn't handle the course load. So he dropped out and went to a community college here. He's actually quite successful now."

"Yeah, but he could've been much more successful if he had stuck it out at Yale."

"He did alright for himself, Saige. And not everyone is cut out for the Ivy League," he says like I'm a snob or something, which I'm not at all.

"I didn't mean that badly, Malcolm. It's just if you have the grades to get into Harvard or Yale, which most people would kill for, it's kind of sad to let that opportunity go to waste."

Looking at me Malcolm breathes, "Yeah, but not everyone needs to be the best, or needs to have the best of everything. Some people are happier just living their lives, and that doesn't make them any less valuable than the Ivy Leaguer who strives for the best of everything."

"That isn't what I'm doing, Malcolm."

"Isn't it?" He asks stunning me.

"No, it isn't. And I'm surprised you'd think that of me. Do I seem like I'm shallow or need to have the best of everything?"

"No, I didn't mean-"

"What? Because I want to excel at Harvard means I'm a snob?"

Huffing, he says, "No." But there's something I'm not understanding.

"So why would you say that to me? I've never acted better than anyone else, and I don't have to be better than anyone else. I just want to be the best so I can help people. That's why I'm doing this," I yell a little.

Reining in my infamous red-headed temper, I calm before speaking. "You don't know me, and clearly you don't understand me at all. *Christ,* after today I realize no one understands what I'm doing this for. But it's none of your business any more than its Selena's. So if you think I'm such a shallow snob or whatever, maybe I should just leave."

"Don't leave," he says quietly. "Just explain it. Why are you fighting so hard for something you don't even look like you give a shit about?" He questions almost angrily which surprises me again.

"*Excuse* me? I *do* give a shit!"

"*Bullshit.* You read because you're bored, and you study because you

235

have to fill your days and nights. Don't tell me it's because you actually want to. Tell me why you do it!"

Shocked he's yelling at me, I snap. Actually standing over him, I've had enough of people today. "Well, I don't do it so I'll be rich one day driving a Lexus, living in a fancy house in Montgomery Park. Because I'll tell you working as a Public Defender for most major cities pays about half what I could make in a private practice. So screw you and your judgements. I didn't ask you or anyone else for help, so between Selena lecturing me about all the debt I'll incur which is none of her business, and you thinking you know me so well and don't, you both can piss off as far as I'm concerned."

"Why do you do it?!"

"None of your *fucking* business!" I scream at him and silence instantly.

Catching my breath I see my hands on the table and my posture leaning toward his face. I'm seething but he's just calmly watching me. He isn't reacting or fighting back, and I don't know what to do with all this shit around us.

"Thank you for dinner, but I'm leaving," I push my chair back turning for the kitchen sliding glass doors.

"Don't run, Saige. Talk to me," he says which pisses me off even more.

Glaring at him, I need to shut this down. "Ya know, that's the second time I've heard this *running* bullshit today and it needs to stop. I have run from nothing my whole life. If anything, I've run *to* the answers and the requirements needed to make a difference. I have never run from anyone or any*thing* my entire life."

"Yes, you do. You're doing it right now."

"I'm not running, Malcolm. I'm *leaving* because I can't talk to you right now I'm so pissed off."

"Tell me about your brother," he suddenly says making me flinch.

"Not. A. Chance."

"Tell me about him. He's the kid who was sentenced for a DUI, right?"

"I'm leaving," I move past him for the house.

Practically ripping the door off the track I storm through his kitchen and almost laugh when I realize I was still polite enough to take my plate with me to the sink.

"*This* is running," he yells behind me.

"No, it isn't. *This* is a woman pissed off. Too bad you're too stupid to know the difference," I scoff walking down the hallway for his front door. Grabbing my purse off the long table against the wall, I just bend to put on my shoes when he stops behind me. "Piss off, Malcolm. I'm leaving."

"You can leave. Just tell me he was your brother."

"Why?"

"Because I want to know. Because you matter too, Saige. I want to know if all this is just because your brother had a bad sentence when he was a kid. I want to know what drives you."

Actually squeezing my arm hard enough to get my attention but not hard enough to hurt or threaten me, he whispers, "Talk to me," in a voice I can't fight anymore.

"Yes, my brother was the one who was sentenced at 18."

"So he's out of jail now?"

Smiling, I know this is horrible but I want him to feel as badly as I do right now. "Nope. He's *dead* now." Watching Malcolm flinch and release my arm I laugh sarcastically. "Glad you brought him up? No? Well, neither am I!"

"Oh *fuck...* Saige. I didn't know. I assumed-"

"*What?* I didn't talk to him anymore because he's an ex-con and I wouldn't possibly be associated with a criminal? Or maybe I'm such a snob I think I'm better than him so that's why I say I have no siblings?"

"No, I-"

"*What,* Malcolm? What did you think?"

"I don't know. I assumed he was out of jail, trying to get by and maybe you wanted to help him, or thought you could help other people because he wasn't helped. I don't know..."

"Well, you're half right anyway. I'm doing this for other people's brothers or sisters, or for whoever can't afford good counsel because they don't have the money for it. I don't want to see someone else who may have had a chance, lose their *only* chance... to live," I whisper without crying.

God, this conversation plays out so often in my head I never cry anymore over it. I'm simply numb to my sad reality, and frozen by my dark past. And I still miss Alec every single day.

"Come here," Malcolm motions to the stairs beside us. "Tell me what happened to him."

"I don't want to talk about it."

"You already are talking about it. So finish this, Saige. Tell me about Alec," Malcolm says so gently, I feel the pain of Alec's name tear through my heart again. "How did he die?"

Waiting in silence, Malcolm sits on the stairs and moves over to give me room. He doesn't ask again, he just waits for me to decide on my own without forcing me to do anything.

Looking at his beautiful blue eye begging me to speak, I feel like I should give him something. I feel like I owe him something for all the patience he's given me this last month we've really gotten to know each other, and for the few weeks even before that.

Taking a big breath, I sit down beside him and admit Alec's horrible truth. "He intentionally overdosed in jail."

"What?" He asks shocked. Nodding at him, Malcolm doesn't move or speak after his initial gasp, and once again his silence gives me a kind of strength I wouldn't normally have discussing Alec.

"Yeah... Um, he didn't even last 4 months in jail. Only 4 months out of 6 years, which probably would have been reduced to 2 1/2 years with good behavior."

"4 months?"

"He was in jail for only 4 months which wasn't enough time for me and my mum to fix anything. We tried though. I contacted high priced lawyers and begged them to take on his case pro bono. I begged the city, and even the Mayor of New Haven to look into his case. I went to the paper and we wrote an article they published, and it was slowly working. People were taking an interest and people were curious about the hefty sentence Alec received for essentially being sober but for .001 over the acceptable limit on his 18th birthday."

Turning to look at Malcolm again for a second I confess, "Thinking back to that time, I'm amazed at what I started to accomplish for him. You can actually google Alec Masters and read all about him and what happened afterward," I stop before Malcolm can ask what I mean about Alec's afterward.

"Anyway, I didn't know anything about the law at that point. And before everything with Alec happened I was actually planning on being a Linguistics Professor like my father was, but then I jumped in to try to help and I didn't stop even after Alec stopped."

"Where were your parents? What were they doing?"

"Truthfully, my father wouldn't get involved. He was a very terse man, and basically an unfeeling asshole. He would just shrug and say Alec got what he deserved, which wasn't true at all. But he wouldn't bend no matter how much I asked for his financial help. We needed a good lawyer fast, but my mum and I had no money and that's when the worst Public Defender on the planet was issued to Alec by the courts. And that was pretty much the end for him."

"And your mom?"

"She did what she could. She sent him letters in jail every day and tried to support him as best as she could. See, Alec was her favorite, but not in a bad way, like where I would be jealous- just in that mother/son way that made their bond special. She loved Alec so much, and after my father left her my mum used Alec as the male stand-in. He became the person she asked for advice and the person she spent her time with when he was around. So it was extra hard for her losing Alec only a year or so after my father left her. But she tried."

"You said he intentionally overdosed?" Malcolm asks holding my left hand on his thigh.

"There was a suicide note, and he didn't ever do drugs before that night. Plus, the drugs he took weren't beginner drugs, so the quantity he paid whoever for in jail was obviously meant to kill him. No one takes that much morphine for the first time without wanting to die. So he died," I shrug.

Waiting an eternity against Malcolm's side, his body is warm and his hand is so huge holding mine I can't stop looking at it.

"Did he say why?" Malcolm asks looking really sad beside me. "I understand he was probably afraid at 18 facing 6 years in jail, but-"

"It's bad, Malcolm," I cut him off.

Looking at my eyes so sadly my eyes fill with tears, Malcolm squeezes my hand and whispers, "It's okay. Tell me."

Trying to speak without sobbing, I finally tell Malcolm the horrible end of my sweet Alec.

"Um, we found out afterward during the State's Inquest into his overdose that Alec was brutalized by his 43 year old cell mate." Choking back the bile in my mouth, I barely say the words I hate. "He was raped so violently he was actually hemorrhaging from the internal damage he had suffered hours before he overdosed from a weapon of some kind."

"Oh, *Saige*..." Malcolm chokes up beside me which just breaks my heart all over again.

"If he hadn't overdosed, the medical examiner stated he may have died through the night anyway, the internal damage was so severe."

"I remember this story now," Malcolm says quietly. "I remember hearing about him in the news."

"Yeah, probably. It was pretty big news when it happened for about 2 weeks," I huff. "Then the public lost interest. Anyway, residual semen found on Alec's clothing proved his cellmate was the man who raped him," I gag thinking of how he hurt Alec. "Ah, he was later convicted of aggravated sexual assault with a few years added to his sentence. But what did it really matter at that point? Alec was already dead because he just couldn't hold on no matter how many times I told him I was going to fix this for him."

"You didn't do this."

"I know I didn't do it!" I snap angrily. "I'm not delusional, Malcolm. I just regret not helping him sooner, or raising the red flags, or just doing *something* sooner. I *knew* something was wrong with him the Sunday before he died when I visited, but I didn't think to ask and I don't think Alec could've told me anyway. Probably because that would've been embarrassing for him as a man I'm sure, but also because I was his little sister who absolutely adored him."

Choking back a giant sob from my chest, I tell the truth. "And I did, Malcolm. I loved Alec so much, he was just everything to me. He was my older brother by just under 2 years, but he was my best friend and my favorite person in the world. He egged my mum on and drove her crazy but he was so good to her. And he was very popular, and good looking, and funny, so everyone loved him, too. But I was *special* to him- he actually told me that," I smile sadly. "So *no one* messed with Alec's geeky, super scrawny, red-headed, little sister because he would've gone after them."

"Saige..." Malcolm squeezes my hand a little.

"But he didn't love me enough to tell me what was happening. And he didn't love me enough to keep living."

"Saige, that wasn't it. He probably just couldn't handle what happened to him. So right or wrong he found the only escape he could. That would've been atrocious for a young kid to suddenly be going through, so he probably just tried to get out of it the only way he thought there was."

"You don't know that, Malcolm. Would *you* have killed yourself? Or would you have told someone and fought back trying to get help?"

"I can't answer that."

"It doesn't matter anyway. He's gone now, and I was left to pick my drunken mother off the floor when she couldn't stand the pain of what he did to us."

"Saige, there's more to it than that. From a male perspective, being raped would be-"

"*What?* Worse than a *female* being raped?" I yell.

Flinching, I know Malcolm sees my point and wishes he had the right answer. I can see him trying to think of the way out of this but there really isn't one.

"Hundreds of thousands of women are raped annually, Malcolm. Sometimes so violently, it causes real internal damage and life-long physical and emotional scars. They are *brutalized,* but do you know what the suicide rate is for them? Next to nothing. You know why? I'll tell you why- Because women are stronger and tougher than we're given credit for."

Squeezing my hand, Malcolm moans, "Yes..."

"So why the hell didn't Alec tell me or someone else? Why did he choose to leave me alone instead of trusting me to help him?"

"I don't know."

"Because he didn't love me enough to live. That's the truth of it."

Quite adamantly, Malcolm argues, "I disagree." But I don't care.

"It doesn't really matter that you think or if you agree with me or not. That's the way I see it and that's what I've felt for almost 7 years now. He could be free right now, but he didn't hold on for me, and he's been dead a long time. So that's it for me."

"What does that mean?" Malcolm asks turning right on the step to look at my face.

"It means what it means. I won't go through that kind of pain again, no matter what."

"*Meaning?*"

"Meaning, I just don't have it in me anymore to give myself like that again. I can't."

"Can't what? *Live? Love?* What can't you do?" Malcolm asks sounding almost agitated.

"All of it. Everything. I'm just done now. So the only thing I can do is help people when I pass the bar."

"Saige, you have to-"

"Malcolm can I please go home now? *Please?* I'm exhausted and I want to go home and sleep. I'm not running, so don't you dare say that to me after all I've shared with you tonight. I'm just really tired now and want to go."

Sounding a little desperate Malcolm says, "I understand. But do you want some dessert? Or a drink, or something?"

"No, but thank you. I'll see you tomorrow for the party though."

"I'd like to follow you home to make sure you get in okay."

"I'll be fine."

"For *Christ's* sake, Saige, could you not be stubborn for once? I'll just follow you and leave, alright?" He stands over me suddenly.

"Fine," I bitch standing for the door.

"Let me get my keys," he huffs moving down the hall toward the kitchen as I push open his front door to darkness. Catching my breath I run for my car, unlock it and hop in before Malcolm's even locked his front door.

Peeling away I feel pissed and exhausted and kind of mental, actually. I feel so unhappy that when I see Malcolm behind me in my rearview I gun my pathetic old lady engine a little to try to lose him which makes me start laughing instead of crying.

Rounding corners a little quicker than usual, at one red light he actually turns on his interior light behind me so I can see him pointing and laughing at me which cracks me right up.

I know I'll never lose him in my jalopy as Selena calls it, but the thought of hitting the quick expressway across town and really trying to lose him excites the hell out of me as I peel away again through the green light.

Twenties five minutes later I'm pulling up to the side of my building in my designated spot as Malcolm parks right beside me.

"*Really?*" Is all he grins when I hop out laughing.

"It was fun though. Thanks for following me home."

"Let me walk you to your door," he insists already moving. Bending down low, he says almost as an aside, "You really should have Selena teach you a thing or two about driving if you want any hope in hell of ever losing me."

"I will," I grin entering the elevators.

At my door, I turn to Malcolm and hug him. Tightly and fairly unexpectedly, I hug the hell out of him until he gently hugs me back.

"Thank you for dinner, and the conversation, and for just being so understanding about everything all the time. You really are amazing, Malcolm," I exhale again against the chest I'm beginning to absolutely love.

"You're welcome. Again. Now get inside and go to sleep. You're gonna need all your energy tomorrow for the party."

"Is Tatum going to call me a wee Leprechaun all night?"

Smiling down at me he says what I expected. "Most likely. But I'll stop him before he sets you in a soup pot on the counter. Unless you want the extra cash?" He grins as I swat him.

Turning to open my door, I mumble *smartass*. "Good night, sweet Saige," Malcolm whispers making my heart pound when he kisses the back of my head before I push my door open.

Alone and locked in, I reset my alarm and say through the door, "You can go now," to him laughing and knocking once against it before walking away.

(mis)TRUST

CHAPTER 24

"You look *gorgeous!*" Selena squeals entering my apartment.

"Really? I'm nervous I'm showing too much cleavage," I panic pulling the wrap around dress tighter again.

"Nope. Just the perfect amount. I knew that dress would look amazing on you. Look, Dave. Doesn't she look beautiful?"

Kissing Selena's head Dave actually says, "Second most beautiful, only to you," as both Selena and I burst out laughing.

"*Wow,*" we say together laughing all over again at his cheesiness.

"Okay fine. She looks fuckin' hot. Better?"

"Yes," she grins kissing his lips. "Go make us a drink while I finish the back of her hair." Already pulling me to my tiny bathroom, Selena grabs the curling iron and starts tearing into my scalp. "Hair up or down?"

"Ponytail?" I ask knowing the answer.

"Nope. He always sees you in a ponytail. You're either wearing it all up, or all down. Pick quickly. He'll be here in 15 minutes."

"Down?" I question again to her ripping out the back of my hair with the goddamn curling iron. "*Ow!* I'm attached to that hair, Selena," I moan as my head is yanked backward again.

"I know," she huffs. "Your makeup is perfect too. Dramatic eyes and pouty pink lips. I love it and with this green dress your eyes are gorgeous. There, I've got the back curled. Let me see," she turns me around quickly. Flouncing my hair on my shoulders, she pushes one side forward, then both sides back, then both sides forward again.

"I want to pin one side around to the back so just your right side has hair falling forward. Trust me," she glares when I groan.

Pushing me against the sink, she bobby pins one after another and a few minutes later she smiles. "I think it looks hot."

Turning back to the mirror, sadly I agree. Dammit, I hate when she's right. My hair is twisted from the left to wrap around the back of my head until all my hair pours over my right shoulder and it looks awesome.

"Good?"

"Yes."

"Okay. Let's go. I'm so excited to get drunk and have fun tonight."

"Me too," I agree.

Joining Dave on my couch, he complains about needing a coffee table which makes me want to hit him. "I'm making one," I admit to Selena looking at me like I've lost my mind. "For real. I bought something I'm going to use and Malcolm's going to help me make a table. Starting tomorrow actually."

"I *love* that man," she moans making Dave glare at her. "I wish *you* were more like Malcolm," she actually says to my shock and Dave's complete insult. "No offense," she tacks on like that'll make a difference.

Saved by my buzzer I jump up just as they start fighting in hushed voices. Not that I can't hear them in my apartment which is about the size of Malcolm's whole bedroom, but I appreciate the effort.

Opening my door to Malcolm stepping off the elevator, we both stop moving. Taking him in, I find myself staring, while Malcolm seems quite happy to stare. Blushing furiously, Malcolm grins and finally walks to me.

Taking my hand, he kisses my knuckles before kissing my cheek. "Do I have t'tell ye wha a Bonnie wee lass ye are?" He rolls his r again as I unexpectedly shiver.

"Yes..." I whisper. "*Oh.* I mean no. Thank you," I giggle.

"Saige, you look absolutely stunning," Malcolm says all breathy. Shivering again, I actually flush as well.

"Um, thank you. You look very handsome and *tall* Malcolm. I think it's all the dark. It makes you seem even bigger or something," I ramble moving back a step to really take him in. "You wore green."

"I couldn't stop thinking of your beautiful eyes today so I wore green. And now look at us, we're color-coordinated which will cause endless teasing all night from Tatum," he grins. "Think you can handle it?"

"Absolutely. We're just finishing one drink before we go. Would you like to have one?"

"No, I'll save my 2 drink max for the pub. Something tells me I'm going to need it tonight."

Walking in, Malcolm places his hand on my back and before I can even enter fully Selena's already yelling, "You look so cute together! Oh my god, you *match*!"
"Were you drinking before you got here?" I ask.
"Maybe," she replies as Dave says, "Definitely."
"Hey Dave," Malcolm and Dave shake, and even against Dave, Malcolm is striking. Between his size and demeanor, his black suit-jacket and dark jeans he looks growly, gruff, and sexy as hell tonight.
"Are you ready?" He leans in close enough for me to catch his warm scent.
"As ready as I'll ever be. Ah, is there anything I should know?"
Leaning against the door, Malcolm confesses, "Andy flew in from South Africa with his wife Gretcha as a surprise, and my parents will be there as well. You've already met Moira, so other than my younger brother and the spouses everyone else should be mostly friends. But be warned," Malcolm looks at all 3 of us seriously. "Tonight will probably turn into a kind of mayhem I'm not sure you're used to."
"Perfect!" Selena claps.

*****

Pulling up just past Tatum's we already see it's very crowded out front, it's covered in balloons, and the doors have a flag across them.
Turning as we pass, I ask, "Was that the Lion Rampant?"
"Of course," Malcolm nods.

Walking toward the pub, people are smoking outside calling immediately for Malcolm. Chanting and even cheering, he's called Mallie and Malcolm m'boy before we even enter.
"*Mallie?*" I laugh at his grimace.
"I hate it. Only my dad and family members who dare, call me Mallie."
Leaning close to him, I'm a little nervous of all the noise and chaos, though beside me Malcolm calms me as usual.
Taking my hand, Malcolm looks down at me with intense eyes. "You'll be safe tonight, Saige. And I won't leave you for a second."
"I know," I squeeze his hand tighter leaning into his everything amazing.

As we enter, the cheers and shutouts start all over again. Everywhere I look there are people coming for us, clapping hands and shoulders and even kissing Malcolm. We're surrounded, and even though I have heels on I'm fairly overwhelmed quickly though no one actually touches me and Malcolm never let's go of my hand like he promised.

Yelling over the music, Malcolm nods toward the only empty tables in the front center of the pub so I assume they're designated for Tatum's family.

Walking up to an older couple standing nearby talking to people passing, Malcolm smiles down at me frequently as we make our way through the crowd.

"This place is packed!" Dave yells over my head to Malcolm.

"That's what happens when the owner of the pub turns 40. Everyone who's ever been here shows up for the party."

"Mallie," an older man says grabbing Malcolm in a huge hug that pulls me with them against Malcolm's side. "Ah, well if this isna the wee lass. Saige, isnit?"

"Hi, yes. It's a pleasure to meet you," I offer my left hand because Malcolm is still holding my right one tightly.

"An what the bloody hell kinda name is Saige, any'way?"

"Um, my mum's Scottish. And weird," I grin as Malcolm senior bursts out laughing.

"Carrie!" Mr. MacNeil calls loudly to a heavier set woman with a beautiful face.

Smiling at me Mrs. MacNeil greets me with an actual hug before speaking. "Saige, it's wonderful to meet you."

"Lok at those witchy greens," Mr. MacNeil says. "Now thas the Bonnie lok I miss."

"The Bonnie look you left behind in the old country, Malcolm. And don't you forget it," Mrs. MacNeil gently slaps his cheek in teasing.

"There's no one like ye Carrie in the old or new count'ry. So you dunna worry aboot it none."

"Aye," she grins back at him before they actually kiss on the lips.

"Mom and Dad, these are Saige's friends Selena and Dave. Carrie and Malcolm MacNeil," Malcolm introduces over the loud music.

"Are ye Scottish, dear?" Malcolm Senior asks Selena.

"Sadly, no," she grins.

"Aw well, you canna be perfect, can ye? Did ye meet me oldest?"

248

"Not yet, sir. We were just settling in," Dave replies.

Shaking Dave's hand, Malcolm Senior growls, "Well, you canna miss the wee bastard. He's the bugger hittin' his noggin off the bloody ceilin'."

Laughing at the way Scottish people look angry every time they speak, I remember my aunts from Scotland. Whenever we'd visit they'd tell the most boring stories but with such inflection and drama you'd think they murdered a person, instead of the pastry they ate for breakfast. Actually, my mum is quite the same.

"Want to go meet Tatum and grab a drink?"

"Sure," I agree with Selena and Dave already walking towards the bar.

"It was lovely meeting you, Mrs. MacNeil."

"*Carrie,* dear. And the pleasure was all ours. This is our reserved table, so seat yourselves as you wish."

"Thank you," I smile again as she squeezes my arm.

"Your parents' are-"

"A trip?" Malcolm laughs down low so I can hear him.

"Lovely. I can't believe they still kiss each other. It's very sweet."

"Why wouldn't they kiss each other? Kissing isn't the problem, it's finding them groping each other in the kitchen that's gross," he winces making me laugh.

"They don't."

"Oh, they do. Ask Moira what she walked in on once as a teenager. She says she still gets night terrors remembering it 20 years later."

"There she is!" Tatum yells behind me and before I know it I'm actually lifted from behind in a bear hug until Malcolm yells at him and everyone freezes around us. Yanked out of Tatum's arms by Malcolm, I'm dropped to the ground so quickly I actually twist my ankle on Malcolm's boot.

Gasping at both the sudden movement and the pain, there's no time for me to freak out because Malcolm is covering me totally hunched over my body right in my face. "Are you okay? I'm so sorry, baby. Are you scared?"

"No. No, I'm fine. Actually I hurt my ankle on your gigantic boot, but I'm okay," I exhale across his face.

"I'm sorry, Saige. I didn't tell anyone anything so he didn't know not to grab you like that."

"It's okay. I heard his voice first so I wasn't scared. I'm embarrassed though. Is everyone looking at us?"

"No, just Melissa and Tatum. Selena's on her way over though."

"Okay. I'm fine. Let's just be normal," I whisper as Malcolm kisses my forehead.

Turning to a very concerned looking Tatum, I fake scowl and threaten him to ease the tension. "Remember I told you I know how to use these witchy greens? Well, it's not a good idea to scare the shit out of me, Tatum. OR to pick me up," I growl as he grins.

"Understood. I was just looking to help you make some cash on the bar tonight," he adds as a woman elbows him in the side.

"I'm Mel, this idiot's wife. It's nice to meet you," she also yells over the music. Shaking hands, Melissa is actually fairly tall for a woman, though next to Tatum she looks freakishly short of course.

"Martin! Yo! *Marty!* These 2- on the house," Tatum yells pointing at me and Malcolm as the bartender nods. "I'm sorry if I frightened you, Saige. I'm a wee bit tipsy."

"He's drunk off his ass he means," Mel adds as Tatum roars with laughter. "Enjoy yourselves. We have to make the rounds again," she pulls at Tatum.

Leaning against the bar with Malcolm crowding my back, he asks again if I'm okay. He actually looks so worried, I lean over and quickly kiss his cheek to let him know I'm fine. Dancing against the bar to Of Monsters and Men's 'Little Talks', we wait for Selena and Dave to order.

"A vodka and orange, vodka and cranberry," he motions for Dave, "and a rum and coke. And these 2 are on the house as well," Malcolm adds pointing to Selena and Dave.

"I *love* you, Malcolm," Selena teases. "Have I mentioned that before?"

Grinning at Dave, Malcolm plays along. "Yes, you have. Though not in front of your *husband* before."

"**EX** husband," both Selena and Dave say at the same time before kissing each other again.

"She's drunk," I mouth.

"No shit," Malcolm counters.

Waiting for our drinks, the music changes to 'Ho Hey' by the Lumineers and the entire pub instantly transforms into a Males Only karaoke bar.

Laughing, Malcolm and Dave sing along with every other man in the whole pub with heads back, yell-singing as all the woman watch laughing and clapping, myself included.

Leaning against each other, belting out the song, the men singing is so entertaining I need a picture. Watching Malcolm sing, 'You're my sweet-*heart*' to me is making me all warm and fuzzy inside and I haven't even had my drink yet.

Digging in my purse, I pull out my phone before hearing a high pitched noise that shocks me. What the hell is that? Still laughing at Malcolm singing I look at my phone lit up vibrating and ringing loudly. Pulling it from my purse, Malcolm glances down and freezes in shock like I am.

Tearing it out of my shaking hand, Malcolm looks at my phone and grabs me right off the barstool. Tugging me, we pass his friend Dan and a brunette against his side. Stopped for only a second Malcolm says something to Dan and before I know what's happening Dan is turning back toward the bar while Malcolm and I are pushing through people to the back of the pub to an employee's only door.

Holy *shit!*

"Saige, call the police. Now," Malcolm demands pointing to the office phone as he shuts out most of the noise of the pub. "Tell the police someone's broken into your place and they need to send someone over immediately."

"What the hell's happening?" Selena yells as she rushes into the room with Dave followed by Dan and the woman.

"Someone's in her apartment," Malcolm yells lifting my phone into the air even though he turned the sound down as soon as we entered the room. With the noise still heard from outside the doors, the muffled siren is muted by there's no hiding the flashing light or Selena's bug-eyed reaction to it.

"What do we do?" She panics.

"Make the call, Saige. Now." Dialing, Malcolm turns to his own phone while I wait 2 rings for the 911 operator.

"Um, Police. Someone's in my apartment."

"A break and enter," Malcolm tells me.

"They broke in and the alarm is going off. No, no I'm not there. I was alerted to the alarm. Yes, I'll stay on the line. 226 Hesler Ave, Apartment 3-E. What?" I ask Malcolm talking to Dave and Dan.

Turning to me, Malcolm barks, "The alarm company notified you over 5 minutes ago!"

"I didn't hear it over the music," I flinch.

"I know. Sorry," he adds just as quickly. "Look, I need you to stay here with Dave and Selena. I'm going to run over to your place with Dan and talk to the police."

"*What?* No, you're not! Are you *crazy?*"

Walking to the door, Malcolm barely acknowledges me. "I'll be fine, Saige. I just want to see if they catch him."

"Malcolm, please..." I actually reach to grab his sleeve. "I'm nervous and scared and I really want you to stay here with me. Please?"

"Saige-"

"*Please?* Yes, I'm here. Okay, how long? Yes, I'll stay connected." Placing my phone against my chest, I try to keep him here. "Malcolm the police are pulling up to our building in 3 minutes. Please stay here? I can't have you hurt or doing anything stupid. *Please?*" I beg desperately knowing everyone is watching our exchange.

Malcolm doesn't look happy, but he does eventually nod. Giving Dan a weird look even Selena catches I can't ask before the operator speaks to me again to tell me they've arrived and are going in the building.

"Hi, I'm Saige," I extend my hand to Dan's wife I assume.

"Karen," she smiles. "I've heard a lot about you."

"Yeah, I can imagine," I huff as we laugh a little. "You are the most amazing Interior Designer I've ever seen. Malcolm's house is stunning."

"Thank you," she beams leaning into Dan's side.

Waiting out the silence, I see Selena lift her drink to her lips so I motion to hand it over which she does. Gulping back her gross vodka cranberry I just swallow when the operator requests my presence at the scene.

"Right now? Um, is he still there?" God, I'm scared suddenly. "Okay. Malcolm, can you turn the alarm off now?" I ask watching him mess with my phone after the operator asks me to shut it off. When she tells me my apartment is empty but for the 2 responding officers, I'm told they want me back home to make a report.

"It's off," Malcolm growls.

"Um, do I hang up now? Okay. Thank you," I end the call. "I have to go home to make a report, and no one's there anymore."

"Okay, let's go," Malcolm starts for the door immediately. "Dan'll drive you guys home if you want to stay," he offers Selena and Dave who instantly say no. "Dan, just tell my parents Saige was feeling sick or something, okay? And you look gorgeous, Karen," Malcolm smiles sweetly kissing her on the cheek as we pass.

"Get going, Malcolm," she swats at him. "I'm sure we'll meet again soon, Saige."

"I hope so," I just speak before Malcolm is tugging me through the door again by my hand with Selena and Dave following closely behind.

Pushing through the crowd, Malcolm gets us to Tatum in the far corner near the doors. Whispering something to him, I wait nervously until Tatum smiles down at me. "Thanks for you coming, Saige," he slurs pretty noticeably. "Welcome back any time. Sorry you don't feel well cuz this is just getting started."

"Happy Birthday, Tatum." Reaching up to him, he lowers enough to hug me and once again lifts me right up off the floor. Hearing Malcolm swear behind me I giggle for a second as Tatum says something about a wee leprechaun before I'm placed back on the floor against Malcolm.

"Have fun big guy. Do everyone a favor though- lie down when you feel like you might pass out. Or at the very least yell tim-berrrr, okay?"

"Will do, Mallie," Tatum hugs Malcolm before we're moving again.

Outside the pub, walking past the crowd of smokers and endless people trying to talk to him, Malcolm is polite but quick to get us out of here. Still holding my hand tightly, he walks us to his truck and once inside starts driving before we even have seat belts on.

"I'm really sorry for all this. I know you were excited about the party, and about seeing your brother and his wife from South Africa."

"I'll see them all tomorrow at my parents' house for dinner. And don't be sorry, honey, you didn't do this."

Looking behind us, Selena is snuggled up against Dave. "It's okay, Saige. We'll fix this," she whispers choking me up a little.

Turning back around, I look at Malcolm's profile as he drives. He looks so strong and determined, but very attractive in his growly, intense way.

Glancing at me, Malcolm's blue eyes soften when we look at each other though his jaw is set like he's still ready to fight.

"I really wanted to dance with you once," I whisper sadly hoping Selena and Dave can't hear me.

"We'll dance together, Saige. Whenever you want, I promise." Gently squeezing my knee, I hold Malcolm's hand in both of mine, and silence my growing sadness.

*****

With the 3 of them in tow, I feel almost brave when the elevators open until I see a cop leaning against the outside wall of my apartment.

Immediately going into panic mode, I start rambling in the hallway. "I live here. I'm Saige Masters. Ah, this is my apartment and I called the police when I realized my alarm was going off."

"Good evening. I'm Officer Hendricks and my partner is inside taking photographs. You can step inside but please don't touch anything yet."

"Saige was viciously attacked almost 2 months ago and no one has been apprehended yet. Can you call Detective Mathers? He has all the details and would probably like to know about this," Selena speaks for me once again.

Absently, or maybe because I'm scared shitless I think quite randomly I had better start raising my voice and speaking quicker and more effectively than I have been lately if I plan on ever becoming a successful friggin' lawyer.

"Saige?" Malcolm says softly like I'm losing it, which I am on the inside, though I thought I looked okay on the outside considering.

Wow, I'm stressed out.

"You're going to have to look around without touching anything and try to catalogue your belongings and what's missing for the final report. I will warn you your apartment has been ransacked, Miss Masters."

"Okay."

Ransacked sounds pretty bad, but stepping over the threshold as I gasp a quick breath, I realize it's much worse than I thought ransacked meant. My place hasn't been ransacked, it's been *slaughtered.*

"Oh my *god...*" Selena cries exactly what I'm thinking.

"Mother *fucker,*" Dave adds making me burst out laughing I'm so shocked.

Shaking my head to clear it, I'm simply winded. There's nowhere to look that isn't messed up. From the kitchen cupboards to my closet, absolutely everything is either upended or broken. My clothes are everywhere, and even my dishes have been smashed on the floor. My absolutely everything has been damaged and I can't even comprehend what I'm looking at.

"Saige!" Malcolm yells in my face. "Come on, honey, I need you to snap out of this." Out of what? I'm right here I want to yell back but my mouth won't move. "Come on, Saige. Snap out of this," he pushes again squeezing my hands a little tighter against my chest. "Saige, *please*..." Malcolm begs effectively waking me from my whatever the hell I'm suffering this time.

"There's nothing left," I choke out.

"Sit on this chair," Malcolm forces me down.

Actually kneeling beside me, he talks to the police for me. "The alarm company only alerted her 5 minutes before she called you, and you guys were here quickly. So that's like 10 minutes or so. How is it possible to cause this much damage in only 10- *maybe* 15 minutes tops?"

Suddenly feeling almost claustrophobic with this many people in my tiny apartment, I need to get out. "Um, I have to go. I can't breathe with you all in here and I don't want to look at this anymore."

"Do you see anything missing?"

Suddenly laughing again, I ask the next obvious question, "How the hell can I tell? I don't even have a floor anymore."

"Her jewelry box is missing. And her mementos box and her photo albums. Look," Selena points to the area where all my textbooks are on the floor. "The photo albums should be with those books and they're not, and her jewelry box was on top of that book case," she points.

"Can I please come back in the morning to make a report? *Please?* I can't even think straight right now."

"Okay. This is an active crime scene anyway and Detective Mathers is on his way, so give me your contact information and you can leave. I'd like you back here by 9am tomorrow if it's possible though?"

"Sure. Here," I start rambling my name and phone number and basically anything else I can think of I'm so desperate to get out of here.

"Feel like a roommate tonight?" I ask Malcolm without thinking.

"Absolutely. Feel like sleeping among blue vines and pink walls," he grins to soothe me I think.

"Absolutely."

Standing, I practically run from my apartment. I can't look back, and I don't want to see that place again. It was just my temporary apartment anyway. Not quite *this* temporary, but temporary nonetheless.

"You can stay with me," Selena offers but I'm shaking my head before she even finishes.

"Not a chance am I bringing this shit to your door. Oh god, I'm sorry, Malcolm. Do you mind? I didn't even think about the position I was putting you in."

"It's fine, Saige. Let's go. I think you're a little in shock right now."

"Ya think?" I giggle stupidly before crying a little sadly. "Why does this keep happening to me?"

"I don't know. We'll be back at 9:00," Malcolm speaks to the police.

"Please be careful, Selena," I cry when she hugs me. "Please... I can't-"

"I'll be careful," she whispers in my ear. "Plus I still have your Taser and knife at my house, okay? Oh, and I have Dave here," she pulls away smiling. "Go to Malcolm's and sleep. I'll meet you guys in the morning before I pick up Griffin."

"Okay. Have a good night you two," I try to tease with a wink but it falls so flat I start laughing again a little hysterically.

"Saige," Malcolm pulls my hand to the opening elevator. Waving bye to Selena, the elevator doors close on everything.

The silence around me is suddenly so heavy my hands start shaking again, and my heart is pounding so loudly in my ears, I actually cover them with my hands.

Driving, Malcolm speaks to me sometimes but I'm wordless. I either grunt or nod, but otherwise I have very little to say.

"Saige? We're home now. Let's go in, okay?" He asks pulling my hands away from the seatbelt I was squeezing tightly to my chest.

Standing beside my opened door, Malcolm looks so concerned, I exhale and jump out of his truck too quickly to steady myself on anything but his chest.

Moaning, I walk numbly when he leads me to enter his home.

*****

Standing in Malcolm's living room I don't know what to do. I wasn't exactly prepared for this, and I wasn't allowed to take or touch anything anyway.

Bursting into tears finally, I cry, "I have nothing to wear," which sounds so stupid under the circumstances, but that seems to be the catalyst right now for this round of hysteria.

"Come with me," Malcolm insists.

Walking me to the kitchen he pours me a huge glass of vodka with a little orange juice more for coloring than anything. Lifting the glass to my mouth we both hold it as I drink half down before I gag a little and swallow compulsively.

With my hand held, I'm walked up the stairs to his room as I watch him pull a t-shirt and a pair of Nike shorts from his bureau.

"Go change in my bathroom, Saige. You can use my toothbrush if you want to and I'll wait for you out here. Look at me," he waits for me to look up. "I promise absolutely no one will get to you here."

On autopilot, I open his bathroom door and cry some more as I change. The drawstrings on his shorts aren't tight enough to hold them up but the shirt hangs to my knees so I toss the shorts aside before using the washroom and brushing my teeth with his electric toothbrush like he offered.

Washing my face, I realize how pale I look and I wish things were so different tonight. Remembering Malcolm singing and laughing to the Lumineers, I realize I really wanted to dance with him tonight.

"Saige? Are you okay?" Opening the door, Malcolm is in pajama bottoms and a t-shirt as well.

"I'm okay. Just tired and a little freaked out."

"Come here for a second. Stand here," he says walking to the bureau beside his closet. "If you ever tell anyone this, I'll never forgive you. And yes, I like this one," he grins at my confusion until I gasp when Martin Gore's voice fills his bedroom surrounding us in calm and peace.

Walking back toward me Malcolm says, "You wanted to dance, so I'm all yours," in the sweetest voice I've ever heard in my life.

"This is my favorite from this album. You like 'Somebody'?"

"Yes," he says before taking me in his arms to dance with me slowly in his room.

Breaking my heart, Malcolm is the most amazing person I've ever met in my life. He is everything in this moment and I can't thank him enough for all his constant kindness towards me.

Leaning my head against his chest, I wrap my arms around his body as he moves us slowly, shrouded in Martin's magic voice begging to be loved and understood by *somebody.*

When the song ends, Malcolm looks at me for something, but I don't know what to give him back for this special moment I'll never have again.

"Can I sleep with you? To sleep?"

"Of course you can. Come lie down, Saige."

Eventually curled up on my side, Malcolm uses the bathroom then shuts off the lights but keeps the bathroom light on and the door slightly open.

Watching him walk toward me for his bed, I turn on my other side to face him when he settles in. "Thank you for the dance. That was the sweetest thing anyone has ever done for me."

"You're welcome," he leans forward and kisses my head before pulling away. "Good night, wee Saige."

"Good night, Malcolm."

Closing my eyes I feel the fear fade and the sadness calm. I hear Martin begging for somebody to love, and I feel Malcolm and his warmth all around me.

Exhaling my present dark reality, I actually feel peace in this quiet moment with Malcolm.

CHAPTER 25

After making the official reports, cataloging missing things and speaking with a very kind and sympathetic Detective Mathers, I was eventually allowed to grab some personal belongings and clothing before leaving, locking, and setting the alarm on my apartment.

And somehow I'm officially living with Malcolm now. *Temporarily.*

He was adamant I stay with him so I felt safe, and really I was just too upset and kind of numb in my apartment to protest. But it is weird to think I met this amazing man nearly 2 months ago and suddenly he's essentially my best friend and I'm a guest living in his house.

Changing out of my green wrap around dress I had to wear again this morning, I sink down low in Malcolm's awesome huge tub. Calming, I realize I'm no longer sad but more angry that my apartment was destroyed. Feeling pissed that I was just getting things settled until this happened, I'm less frightened than I am irritated that things won't calm down for me.

Exhaling this morning among the bath salts Malcolm had, I'm looking forward to my afternoon with him. We're starting my door table, and afterward I'm going to his parents' house for dinner because he insists, I really don't want to be alone in his house, and because I've been invited by his mom as of this morning.

Malcolm is acting like he usually does, attentive and sweet, and I'm acting the way I usually do, which is freaked out and somewhat quiet.

Hailey is working my shift tonight and because I'm taking hers Tuesday evening I'm scheduled every day or night this coming week.

I'm working my ass off this week and I need to. Between my dwindling savings and all the shifts I keep missing, I need to make as much money as I can, and I need to stay focused on school. It's the 2nd week of June and I have just over 2 1/2 months to get my head, and my shit together before I start my future at Harvard.

＊＊＊＊＊

Entering the kitchen Malcolm has his back to me fixing a sandwich on the counter. "I'm making some lunch, you hungry?"

"Starving, but you don't have to feed me Malcolm. I already feel like I'm putting you out with all the drama all the time."

"I'm making a peanut butter sandwich. With jam," he grins. "So relax about putting me out. Want one?"

"Sure, but without the jam."

Sitting at his breakfast bar, Malcolm looks so relaxed and carefree in his kitchen. Actually, he looks so at home I have to know, "Do you cook often?"

"What do you think?" He laughs patting his stomach. "Of course I cook. Not well, mind you, but well enough to feed myself. You?"

"Always. Tyler wouldn't," I stop quickly. I really have to stop with the Tyler shit all the time. "Anyway, I don't cook very well either. I can bake my way out of prison though," I laugh when he turns to me surprised.

"Really? Do you know how much I love baking?" He again pats his stomach.

"I can guess," I grin back at him. "What time are we leaving for your parents'?"

"4. Dinner is at 5:30, so that'll only give you an hour dealing with the mayhem before supper. Then we'll split as soon as we boys tidy up the kitchen."

"The boys clean up?"

Turning to me again Malcolm hands me my peanut butter sandwich on a plate. "Every meal. My dad started it when we were little because my mom was exhausted after cooking for the bunch of us. Actually, I was very young, but I remember quite clearly the huge fight they had."

"They fought?"

"Yeah. My mom went a little postal on my dad when he placed his dirty plate on the clean counter beside her and turned to walk away after eating one night. Me and Moira could see from our angle at the table my mom picking up his plate and actually throwing it at him. Right down his back," Malcolm laughs shaking his head.

"Ah, then she started screaming about raising 5 kids, cooking, cleaning, doing laundry, etcetera. As I said she went postal, and then the last thing she yelled was something like he was a lazy ass who couldn't even clean the damn kitchen after everything she did for everyone else."

"What happened?" I ask laughing at the lazy ass comment.

"My dad just turned to her all calmly and said, 'Well, why didya no ask me to wash up afta'?' And that was it. My mom punched his arm once and my dad gave her a hug. Then they kissed which was gross for us to watch, and after that my dad always did the dishes after supper. He would even joke that he didn't want to have gravy pouring down his back again if he didn't hop to it quickly enough when he was finished eating. And once we were around 8 years old we had to start cleaning after dinner as well. Almost like an assembly line we washed and dried while my mom had her tea and dessert alone, in the somewhat quiet dining room," he smiles again so sweetly, I can actually picture Mrs. MacNeil having a cookie and tea after dinner to exhale her day away.

"Your parents seem pretty great, Malcolm."

"They are. They're fun certainly. And hot tempered often. And even a little too affectionate for us kids," he mock cringes. "But they always loved each other which was nice growing up."

Picking up his sandwich, Malcolm passes a bag of chips over and asks, "And yours? I know you said your dad cheated, but what were they like before that?"

"Not like your parents. Ever, I don't think." Musing as I chew I try to remember any affection between them and I come up empty. "My mum hugged and kissed me and Alec always, and my dad even hugged us a little as kids. But I don't remember ever seeing them kiss or hug each other."

"Maybe they were just more private?"

"*Maybe*. But I really don't think so. My mum loved him way more than he loved her, I know that much. I mean she followed him here after spending only one day together at Stonehenge, so I think maybe she surprised him by moving here to be with him. That was always the impression I got anyway. Or maybe it was the things he said when they fought. I don't know."

"Were they ever loving?"

"Not really. They spent time with us, and my dad always spent Saturdays with me and Alec. But I kind of have the feeling that my mum was always a little desperate or something for him to love her, or acknowledge her, or to just be a husband to her. So then he cheated the first time and my mum went kind of crazy."

"How old were you?"

"12. But they stayed together, kind of. He still lived at the house but my mum was a mess after that. She cried all the time, and got unnaturally skinny, and she did this awful thing with her hair to look younger, but it backfired sadly and she lost her mind even more. She actually looked worse and *she* was just worse, ya know?"

"What did she do to her hair that was so bad?" Malcolm asks confused. He's a guy, so he probably doesn't understand women and their hair.

"Well, she's a natural blonde. Almost an ash blonde, but I guess she thought he might like a brunette better, or maybe the woman he had an affair with was brunette. Again, I don't know why she did it, but she came home without her signature blunt cut *and* it was dark brown which looked just horrible on her. She ended up dying it back to as normal as they could match 2 days later when my dad told her he hated her hair."

"He told her that?"

"Yeah, but I'm sure she made him. Like I said she wasn't all that mentally well at that point," I kind of smirk, but not in a funny way.

"What happened after that?"

"She was super paranoid about every single thing he said or did. Like if he was late he was with another woman. Or if god forbid, he went away on a conference she would freak right out. Basically, after the affair she went off the rails- crying and yelling and begging to go to his conferences or begging to go with him every time he left the house. She called him constantly, called his coworkers, and even called the University to check up on him. She eventually went on medication when he threatened to leave her if she didn't stop with all the crazy."

Shaking his head, Malcolm asks, "And then he cheated again?"

"Yes. 2 years later. God, I remember that day so well. My mother lost her friggin' mind because it was actually the woman who showed up at our house."

"No..." Malcolm breathes shocked.

"Yup. Classy, wasn't she? Anyway, Alec and I were home from school, it was almost dinner, and this woman shows up and says simply, 'I'm Helen. Collin and I have been together for months now. So don't expect him back this evening. Or ever again.'"

Flinching, Malcolm asks. "What did you do?"

"I remember the shock of her standing in our doorway, and my mum's shocked cry as she covered her mouth. I even remember Alec yelling, 'Get the fuck out of here' before he actually closed the door in Helen's face. But I couldn't move. I just stood there kind of devastated."

"Oh, Saige..." Malcolm takes my hand.

"I never understood why Helen did that to my mum, or really, why my father allowed it. To this day I don't know why that went down the way it did. Not that my father should've lied, but *Christ*... He could've left my mum better than that."

"Then what happened?"

"Nothing. Everything. I remember that night specifically thinking my mum was going to kill herself. Actually, I was sure of it and so was Alec. So we both slept in her bed right beside her while she cried her eyes out and drank until she eventually passed out. Um, Alec even stayed home from school the next day in case she did something crazy when we weren't around."

Choking on the memories of my zombie mother, I admit, "I remember being so afraid back then that Alec and I would be left all alone if she killed herself. I was so scared, thinking like a 14 year old that we would have to pay the bills and try to buy food and stuff because my dad was gone. I wasn't thinking about child or spousal support at the time, I was just thinking about my dead mother and where Alec and I would go if we couldn't stay in that house together."

"And your father?"

"Did nothing," I cut off Malcolm as his eyes widen. "Really, he left us all that night. I can honestly say my own father walked out on not just my mum but on me and my brother as well. He rarely called us and he never set up visitation or anything. He just left to be with Helen and that was it for the 3 of us. Even all these years later Tyler only met him twice and it was me who set it up. I wanted to see my father those times for whatever reason," I shrug like it doesn't matter.

"Saige, he's still your dad. Even if he's a total prick," Malcolm squeezes my hand when I nod.

"I know, but it still surprises me that he just left us. I was his *daughter,* and I was going to follow in his footsteps. And he always bought me Chicken McNuggets on Saturdays," I choke a little laugh.

"McNuggets?"

"Yup. And I still love them when I'm stressed," I grin. "Anyway, that's that. Oh, and Helen and my dad were still together when he died so I guess it was worth it to him to leave my mum, and me and Alec. It certainly makes me feel better."

Kind of grimacing again as he stands with his plate Malcolm leans closer to me across the breakfast bar looking almost confused. "Your father died? How does that make you feel better?"

"Yeah, in a car accident. But I don't feel better that he's dead, just happy because then it wasn't all for nothing. My mum was a mess, like really bad, and now she's much better. And Collin and Helen were still together until his car accident 2 years ago. So at least everything Alec and I went through with my mum wasn't for some quick affair that didn't mean anything to him. My father may not have loved us, but at least he loved the woman he ended up with. He even died still loving her." Shrugging that's all I can say.

When Malcolm blows out a big breath, I almost brace for what's coming and he doesn't disappoint. "Your father sounds like he was the biggest douche on the planet, Saige. Between the cheating and messing with your mom's head, that's bad enough. But leaving you and Alec behind? He sounds like the most selfish prick I've ever heard of. You were his goddamn *kids*," he huffs.

"It's fine, Malcolm," I smile to settle him a little.

"I don't think it's fine, Saige. And I can't even imagine how that made you feel. But I won't push it right now with everything else going on around you." Turning away from me he offers another glass of water I decline and shakes his head frequently while wiping down his counters. "What a *dick*," I hear him mumble.

Watching him, it's almost humorous to me how a single guy without any kids can be outraged by another husband and father's choices.

It's funny, because it really is what it is. I can't change the past, and I could never change my father. So I gave up wanting him to love me as his daughter years ago- until he died still not loving me at all.

"Are you ready to get to work?" Malcolm asks in a normal voice like he scaled back his annoyance with my father.

"God, yes," I jump off the high stool excited.

*****

"*Pleeeeeease* tell me it's time to quit?" I beg.

"Do you need to shower before we go?"

"Yes!" *Christ,* even if I didn't, which I really, really do, I'd agree just to get the hell out of here. My body is throbbing and my arms are all jelly-like after using the vibrating sander for so long. "Thanks for this, but I need to shower. So, bye."

"You're such a girl!" Malcolm laughs at me as I run for his deck and kitchen doors.

I'm such a girl? Good. I can't believe how hard it is sanding a hundred year old door. Though it was cool to see it get down to the original wood, I have a huge blister on the palm of my hand and my shoulder hurts so badly I can barely turn my head without it aching. And that was only finishing one side totally and half the other side in 2 damn hours.

Wiping down the foggy mirror after a long, soothing shower, Malcolm suddenly bangs on the bathroom door startling me to say, "45 minutes? Such. A. Girl," and nothing else as I laugh.

After drying my hair and tying it up in a bun, I put on a cute little dark blue sundress and apply only a little makeup. I'm going to be surrounded by Malcolm's family, and I definitely don't want to look like a tart, as my mum would say.

So with only the ring I was wearing last night and the necklace from my mum for my 18th birthday, I'm ready. I have no other jewelry left since it was all stolen last night, and these 2 items were my favorite anyway. Though admittedly, it still pisses me off that whoever broke in stole some of my personal belongings as well as trashing my place.

Opening the door to the hallway I just step out and see Malcolm in his room. Shirtless with jeans on, I can't believe how tanned, and big, and gorgeous he looks. He may have a huge chest with many muscles in the front, but from behind his back looks like he's all muscle and strength, and just... *wow.*

Staring, Malcolm walks out of my line of sight so I move against the opposite wall and banister for a better look. Suddenly standing in his doorway holding a shirt in his hands, I'm busted.

Blushing furiously at getting caught looking, I say the only thing that comes to mind. "You're big. Um, I'll wait downstairs."

Spinning on my feet I sprint down the stairs quickly hearing him laugh at me. Ugh... *You're big?* What a stupid thing to say. The man's a beast for Christ's sake.

Waiting on the couch in the living room, I hope to hell he doesn't say anything or mock me for my stupid comment.

"Ready?" Malcolm asks grinning at me.

"Yes." Hopping up casually to grab my purse I head for the door.

Waiting after I slip my sandals on, he sets his own alarm, and leans down to murmur, "You're small. Let's go." Speaking with the stupidest grin ever, I blush and growl at him. "Careful, Saige. I already told you that growl was hot," he laughs again as I stomp toward his truck.

*****

"You all lived here?" I ask after the half hour drive to his parents'. Looking at the size of their home I can't even imagine it.

"Yup. And my mom still cried when each of us left home."

"It's very nice, it just doesn't look big enough for a family of 7. God, my mum's house is bigger and I swear I couldn't get away from her sometimes."

"My dad built 2 bedrooms in the basement for Tatum and Andy, Moira had her own room, and Alec and I shared a room upstairs. So it wasn't too bad. There's even a washroom in the basement that Andy and Tatum used which saved us from killing each other in the mornings. It was a little chaotic with the 5 of us upstairs in the 3 rooms though. And once Moira turned into a teenager it was hell. Alec once dented the bathroom door he was so pissed waiting for her to do whatever the hell she did as a teenager to get ready for school," he grins. "We used to tease her about falling in the toilet, or drowning in the shower, or just disappearing altogether for hours until she magically returned and opened the door."

"Did you tease her?"

"Of course. I was her little brother," Malcolm flashes a cheeky grin. "Don't worry though, if the teasing got to be too much for her she pulled out the daddy card, and my father would come after all us *wee bastards*, as we were affectionately known when he was pissed."

Laughing suddenly, I can picture it totally. "My mum always called Alec a wee bastard, too. Whenever he would tease the shit out of her for her accent, or Scottish words and phrases that made no sense, he'd rile her up until she'd chase him with her wooden spoon screaming at him."

"Did she ever catch him," Malcolm turns in his the seat to look at me.

Laughing suddenly I shake my head. "Nope. He would throw me at her and run like hell to his room, lock the door, and wait her out."

"He *threw* you at her?" He asks laughing himself. Nodding, I remember that time so well, I miss Alec so much suddenly my chest hurts.

"He did. And it was funny, and just fun. I loved watching those 2 go at it because otherwise our house was always quiet and kind of lonely or something." Thinking about Alec, I keep smiling at nothing and shaking my head clear of everything. "God, I miss him so much some days, I can't believe it's been 6 1/2 years since he left me."

Squeezing my hand and leaning closer to me, Malcolm only whispers my name as I push back the sadness and loss and the never ending regret that is Alec.

"I'm okay. But we better go in before the tears start," I grin up at him when he kisses my forehead gently.

"If anything, I guarantee the next 3 hours are going to distract you from sadness."

"Perfect."

*****

Watching the loud chaos that is the MacNeils' house I'm out of place, but not awkwardly so. I just don't have a loud enough voice to carry on or participate in most conversations. But everyone is great, and welcoming, and entertaining as hell.

Luckily, Malcolm's brother Alec looks nothing like my Alec, so after introductions were made I wasn't sad again or even nostalgic for my own brother. Alec is actually just a slightly smaller version of Malcolm's dark, tanned, blue-eyed growliness, and I have a feeling Selena *would* like him if Malcolm ever introduced them.

"Mallie tells us yer to be a lawyer, no?" Malcolm Senior asks in between bites of his dinner.

"Yes, sir."

"At Harvard no less. Ye must be a smart lass fer tha."

"I am," I reply quickly then laugh at myself. "I'm quite the book nerd."

"Ah well... there's no shame in bein' smart. Where ye be livin' fer now?"

"Off Taylor, near the university," Malcolm replies quickly cutting me off. Almost like he's ashamed or embarrassed to tell them the truth, I have a quick stomach drop of sadness after he speaks. I know I'm not *actually* living with Malcolm, rather just staying with him in the short term, but his quick reply was pretty telling for me.

Looking at Malcolm's profile he doesn't acknowledge me before he starts talking about Manchester United making Mr. MacNeil and the other people at our table change the subject quickly and effectively as they get heated about English football.

Listening to them everything seems so normal and friendly around me I'm surprised by how sad and kind of out of place I suddenly feel beside Malcolm.

Finished eating, I leave the table to Malcolm calling my name softly which I ignore. Walking away from him I make my way past the second table to Tatum laughing so loud in a quick burst he silences the whole house for a second before the conversations start up again around him. Laughing at him, I keep going until I'm stopped by Mrs. MacNeil reaching around her chair to ask me if I've had enough to eat.

"I'm stuffed, and everything was delicious. Thank you very much for inviting me," I smile at her when she pats my hand.

Actually squeezing my hand, she pulls me toward her and says for me only, "Don't let these fools intimidate you, Saige. They're all harmless and you'll get used to the noise quickly enough." Smiling at me, she actually tugs me a little closer and whispers, "Welcome to the family, dear. You're always welcome at my table."

Both warmed and saddened by her kindness I feel my eyes fill when I smile back at her. "Thank you for saying that Mrs. MacNeil."

"Let's go get the desserts," she stands with her plate for the kitchen.

*****

After listening to stories about a young Malcolm while the men cleared and cleaned the tables and kitchen, I'm ready to leave.

The desserts were to die for, and I couldn't stop myself from a second little piece of traditional money cake but now I'm overfed and exhausted. Malcolm and I slept for about 5 hours the night before and after being outside for 2 hours in the sun and eating more today than I have in 2 weeks, all I want to do is lay down.

Not necessarily at Malcolm's house anymore because that sharp feeling of being someone he hides from his family is still simmering just under the surface of my skin.

I'm angry and hurt and if we weren't with his family, I definitely would've told him off and left right after he insulted me. I would've told him he was an asshole at the time, but I'm much calmer now and I feel too tired to yell at him anymore.

Making the rounds 20 minutes later I find myself staying away from Malcolm as much as I can without being obvious about it. I speak with everyone and I'm invited to the following Sunday dinner. Mr. and Mrs. MacNeil both hug me goodbye and Andy's wife Gretcha from South Africa hugs me as well. Complaining about being an outsider too, she tells me we'll need to stick together among the crazy MacNeils, and I like her immediately.

Moira and her husband are nice, and Tatum is Tatum. Threatening to pick me up to carry me back to the end of the rainbow, I quickly remind him that. I. Am. Scottish, and if my mum ever hears him referring to me as Irish she'll kick his ass *for* me, which he loves.

Walking out the front door, Malcolm tries to hold my hand as he normally would have before dinner but I just can't do it.

Pulling away from him, I think it's funny how his family all like me, even inviting me back for dinner but Malcolm doesn't want to be seen with me. He didn't hold my hand once or squeeze my leg like he normally does until we've left their house so his family won't see.

Because he's an asshole.

As far as friends go who cares if I'm TEMPORARILY staying at his house? I doubt anyone would have cared, except Malcolm apparently.

So pulling away from him, I climb into his SUV, clip my seatbelt and turn my head to the window to ignore him.

Actually, I decide pretty quickly as my anger returns that once we get back to his place I'm calling Selena to crash at her apartment again. She did offer last night and this morning, and I miss Griffin anyway. So I'm leaving Malcolm's as soon as we return.

(mis)TRUST

CHAPTER 26

"Saige, you're killing me here. What's wrong?" Malcolm asks for the 10th time since we left his parents' house.

Almost groaning I'm so frustrated, I've told him nothing is wrong. I've told him I'm tired, and I've even told him I didn't feel well. But he keeps asking anyway.

"Did someone say something to upset you?"

"No. Everyone was very nice to me. They even invited me back next Sunday for dinner, *not* that I'll go," I slam his truck door in the driveway.

With him right on my heels following I have to wait to get inside as he unlocks the door and shuts off the alarm. "Why wouldn't you go?"

"No reason, Malcolm. Just forget it," I huff feeling super irritated again.

Finally inside I kick off my sandals and jog up the stairs for the spare room. Collecting my things, I remember I left my other purse from last night in Malcolm's room, so walking toward Malcolm leaning in the hallway I smile politely and excuse myself as I try to pass him.

"Saige? You have to give me a clue here," he begs blocking my way.

"There's nothing, Malcolm. But I'm going to ask Selena to come get me since my car is still at my apartment. I'll just crash there again."

"What? *Why?*" He jolts in front of me. "Would you just talk to me? What the hell happened? You seemed fine after our talk in my kitchen, then you were fine at my parents' I *thought*. But now you're doing your distant quiet Saige thing again, and I have no idea why."

"Malcolm," I huff. "I'm fine. I just want to go back to Selena's."

"Why?"

"Because I do," I glare at him feeling my anger start to boil.

"Why do you want to go back to her place?"

"Because I don't want to stay here anymore. Last night was enough for both of us, I think."

Leaning down to me as I continue glaring at him, he asks, "Why was it enough for both of us?"

271

"Because," I answer like a friggin' child.

"Because *why*, Miss. Lawyer?" He actually mocks me.

Storming past when he's no longer blocking my way, I grab my purse from the fireplace chair and stop again when he's blocking his bedroom door this time.

"Move, Malcolm."

"Not until you talk to me."

Ready to shove him I'm so pissed, I bark, "Get the hell out of my way!"

"No. I deserve an explanation for this bullshit one-eighty you're doing. So let's hear it!" He yells.

Staring at him, I hate him yelling at me. It's the first time and I really don't like it at all. Not that I think he'd physically hurt me or anything like that but it's a little hard staring up at a beast of a man yelling down at me without being overwhelmed.

Feeling a little nervous of him I calm myself down so I can get out of here quickly. Taking a step back, I know Malcolm noticed when he exhales and looks back at me angrily.

"*Really*, Saige? After all this time *now* you think I'm going to hurt you?"

"No, I don't. But I want to leave, Malcolm, and you're not letting me." Reining in the last of my temper I say calmly, "I really want to go now. You've been an amazing friend to me this summer and I'd like to leave now before our friendship is ruined. That's all."

"Why would it be ruined?"

"Because you hurt my feelings tonight and embarrassed me," I admit embarrassed again when he looks totally stunned.

Leaning forward again, Malcolm looks much calmer suddenly when he asks, "How did I hurt your feelings? Tell me."

"When you said I lived off Taylor."

"So?" He asks like an idiot which pisses me off again.

"So, I know you didn't want your family to know I was staying here because you were too embarrassed to admit it!" I yell mortified and sad and just fed up with everyone. "What the hell is so wrong with me?"

Shaking his head angrily he yells again, "Are you kidding me right now? *Please* tell me this is a joke."

"No, I'm not kidding. Tell me, Malcolm. I'm smart and attractive and I'm a good person and there's nothing really wrong with me, so why didn't you tell them I'm staying here?!" Finished screaming, I'm nearly angry-crying, but thankfully I just hold in the tears as he advances on me again.

"I did that for *you*. Did you really want all the grinning and teasing, and my mother and everyone assuming we were a couple if I said you were staying with me? Did you want everyone torturing you all night about us because we're 'living' together?" He quotes. "*Did* you?" He yells when I can't speak.

"Saige, you have feelings for me- I *know* you do. But for whatever reason you won't admit it, or feel it, or whatever the fuck. But you do. And I didn't think tonight at my parents' house surrounded by my whole goddamn family was the best time to discuss it."

"As a friend," I exhale trying to understand what he's saying about his parents' house. It makes sense I guess. "I didn't think you wanted them to know because I'm me," I admit again like a pathetic ass.

"Look at me," Malcolm demands when I look at the door to my freedom. "Fucking *look* at me!" He yells again as I jump. "I'm not embarrassed about *anything* with you."

"I thought you didn't like me because-"

"I'm in love with you, Saige," he suddenly whispers as I flinch.

Gasping, I cry out, "No, you're not."

Actually laughing in a quick sarcastic burst, Malcolm growls, "For being so goddamn smart, you're being really fucking stupid right now. No offense," he smirks with an eye roll, and I almost laugh. But then I don't laugh when the reality of what he's saying hits me hard in my stomach.

"I am so in love with you I feel like a jackass kid in high school who gets his feelings hurt 3 days ago when you said this has been the worst summer ever, when for me it's been the best summer of my life. Seeing you nearly every day, speaking to you every day, being just... *Fuck*," he huffs.

"I wait to see you, and I wait to hear from you. I want to know how you slept, and what you ate. I want to know that you're okay, and that you *feel* okay. There is nothing I don't think and feel about you every goddamn day and it's making me crazy."

"Malcolm-"

"Don't tell me what I feel, and don't tell me I'm wrong. I'm a grown man and I'm in love with you, Saige. Fuck, I even listen to your shit-awful music when we're not together because I imagine making love with you to goddamn Depeche Mode," he laughs sarcastically.

"I want you to fall in love me as much as I've fallen in love with you.

But it's hard feeling what I feel because I don't know what to do with you. I'm scared I'll freak you out, or scare you, or just make you run. I'm afraid you're not emotionally ready to love again, and I'm scared to death you're not physically ready for anything with me after what happened to you."

"Malcolm, I-"

"But I was prepared to wait for you to get there on your own. I'm a patient man, Saige. So I wanted you to see what everyone else sees we already have and *could* have together. Selena, and Mike, and even my friend Dan all see what's between us. God, I see it, and know it, and *feel* it. But you're so fucking stubborn and hurt and scared, and just not ready to love again, so I was going to wait for you to come to me when you were ready."

Stepping only a foot from me, Malcolm stares at my eyes as I try to find the right words for him.

Shaking my head, I know he's wrong. "I have no love to give you," I whisper so sadly I feel like I'm breaking up with my best friend suddenly. "Tyler was my last try after loving Alec and my father."

"Tyler cheated on you, Saige. He didn't love you enough to stay faithful to you, and your brother left you because he couldn't see a future that still included you because he was scared and hurt."

"Malcolm," I raise my hands in front of me to keep him away. My chest is getting so tight I can't breathe properly. And the longer he speaks the less okay I feel.

"Saige, They. Left. You. You didn't do the leaving, so you can't take the blame or punish yourself anymore."

"I'm not punishing myself."

"Your dad left because he was a selfish prick, and Tyler cheated because he was an immature asshole looking for something more than you. Which *trust me,* doesn't actually exist."

"Malcom, please."

"And your brother *loved* you, Saige. But he was a just a kid who was hurt badly and he didn't know what else to do. He made a horrible mistake when he killed himself, but he didn't do it to hurt you."

"Malcolm, I'm getting really messed up right now, so I think you should maybe stop speaking," I cry a little as the shaking takes over my whole body.

"Saige, you could love again."

Shaking my head, I need him to understand the hollow that is my heart. "Malcolm, I have no love to give you. It was used up and thrown away, and it would never work between us."

Shaking his head he cuts me off again. "You haven't even tried."

"I *did* try. I tried so hard. I gave *everything,* and now I have nothing again."

About to touch my face, I pull away quickly. "You haven't tried with me. And you have me to love," Malcolm moans so sadly, I actually feel his sadness.

"I'm so sorry, but I don't want to love you."

"Yes, you do," he pushes.

"I really don't, Malcolm," I say desperately. "Why is that so hard for you to understand? Why can't you see that? There is nothing left inside me and no love left to give you. All I have now is the sad determination needed to move past my life so I can help other people instead. Plus, I'm leaving in 2 months."

"So? You don't think I'd wait 4 years for you? You don't think I would give up anything for you?"

"It doesn't matter. It won't work out."

Bending down low so he's level with my eyes, Malcolm says only, "You're so wrong."

Shaking my head I plead desperately. "I'm not wrong about this, I *know* it."

"Who do you call or text first thing in the morning? Who do you call or text before you go to bed at night? Who do you look forward to seeing, and who do you spend all your free time with? Who do you hug when you need to be comforted, Saige?"

"You. But as *friends,* Malcolm."

Looking exhausted and frustrated and maybe even sad, Malcolm whispers, "Kiss me, Saige." Wanting to cry because his blue eyes are begging me to kiss him, I just can't do it. "Kiss me!" He yells in my face jolting me from my sadness.

"No." Trying to turn away before I make another mistake I won't survive, Malcolm actually pulls me back to him by my arm and waist.

Suddenly leaning his forehead against my own he moans desperately, "*Look* at me," until I freeze against him in panic and shock.

Begging me, Malcolm breathes across my face all his desperation. "You know I would *never* hurt you, so stop using that as an excuse to never move on. Stop looking for me to disappoint you like they did. Look. At. *Me*," he growls when I try to look away.

"Kiss me, Saige. Kiss me like you want to and watch me take nothing more than you can give me. Watch me follow you as far as you can go. And watch me love you until you love me back. Kiss me..." He moans so sadly my heart actually breaks for him.

Breathing against each other, his hand moves from my waist to hold my face in his hands. He doesn't move his body closer, and I can't move at all.

My mind is spinning and I'm so scared and desperate to get out of this, I don't know what to say anymore.

"This will ruin everything," I cry, pleading with him to understand.

"Kiss me..." he moans again as I cry out against him. "Just kiss me, Saige," he chants softly. "Kiss me like you want and I'll take only what you can give me. Please kiss me, Saige," he begs so sweetly, my heart starts pounding against him.

"Malcolm, I can't."

"Kiss me, Saige, and you'll know only the love I have to give you. You won't find the father who left you or the brother who hurt you or the boyfriend who betrayed you. Kiss me, and you'll only find *me* wanting to love you."

"I don't know how to give you what you want."

"Stop thinking, and just kiss me, Saige," he actually chokes up against me and I can't take it anymore.

Raising my head, I stare at his beautiful eyes one last time as they are in this moment, and with dread in my heart for the heartbreak I'm promising myself, I give in to him and kiss his lips.

Softly, I touch his lips with my own until I feel his whole body shudder. Opening my eyes, he whispers, "Just kiss me, Saige," as I rise back up to his mouth.

Kissing him, my hands hold his sides and my head turns for a deeper kiss. Kissing, Malcolm sighs against my mouth but he doesn't move and he doesn't take more from me than I can give.

Kissing softly, he finally opens his mouth for me to taste him, and like the darkness lifting I inhale his breath into me as we both moan.

And he still doesn't move.

Looking up at him, I see him crouched over me unmoving, looking so afraid I'll stop, I feel his heavy sadness and fear. Crying, I feel everything he has to offer me as he waits.

"Come here," I turn taking his hand to lead him to the slouchy chair by the fireplace.

Watching him sit slowly, I wait.

Watching him questioning me without words, I finally move.

Crawling right in his lap with my legs on either side of his thighs, my dress rises but I don't care. I need to kiss Malcolm suddenly with an intensity that is both exciting and frightening at the same time. I suddenly find myself *wanting* to kiss the man sitting so still, grasping the arms of the chair waiting for me.

So wrapping my arms around his neck I lean in and kiss him like I want to. I kiss him and I finally experience Malcolm.

Softly, I explore him until hungrily I devour him.

Rising on my knees, my body towers over his as I kiss him as hard as I want to. I don't ask permission, and I don't offer more. Malcolm offered himself to me and I'm taking him.

Tugging on his shaggy dark hair I lean and move and kiss him until we both make noises of desperation.

Moving against him, I find my body heating up and my mind clearing. From dread to desire I kiss him harder, moving against his chest with a growing need I never thought I could ever feel again.

Pulling away, Malcolm looks almost pained below me. His face is tight and harsh looking, and his eyes are wide and intense. He's breathing deeply in quick hard pants, and his body seems so tense with the control he's exerting I need to do something to ease him.

"Kiss me back," I offer as he moves under me.

Slowly, I see his hands unclench from the chair arms to take my head in his hands again. Giving me time to react, Malcolm is slow and gentle and I just adore him for his patience.

"I'm okay."

"Okay," he grins before pulling me to his mouth for a stunningly deep, breathless kiss.

After forever, I find myself shifting and moving against him again. I kneel up or slide down his chest but he never moves with me and he never releases me from his grasp as we kiss.

He is constant, like he always is for me, and I suddenly feel his constant all around me.

Kissing him deeply again I'm surprised by his amazing mouth. "You're so soft," I sigh against his lips between kisses.

"Not everywhere," he replies.

Understanding what he means in my kissing haze I burst out laughing when he grins at me like he always does. Kissing the laughter from my mouth, all the intensity and the fear is suddenly gone from my chest.

Looking at his eyes watching me as I giggle away the tension, everything returns back to just Saige and Malcolm in his room.

When I wrap my arms around him and bury my face in his neck, I hear myself sigh away all the stress and fear of this night between us.

"I'm not ready for *that*, Malcolm. Not yet," I acknowledge as he pulls back to look at me.

"I know. And I'm not asking for that," he grins again as I smile at him.

"What do you want, Malcolm?"

"Just kiss me when you can and I'll wait for you to be ready for more. That's all I want from you, Saige. I promise." Kissing me again sweetly, he actually seals his promise to me. "But I need you to understand that every single word I said to you was true. I *am* in love with you, and I do want to show you. But I'll wait for you to get there with me."

"Malcolm..." I have no words and I feel too much suddenly.

"Will you sleep with me? To sleep?"

"Yes." Crawling off Malcolm I notice when he moves uncomfortably in his jeans. Blushing furiously I look down and back to him smiling at me.

"It can't be helped. Not when you're climbing my chest writhing against me." Almost laughing again, I attempt to apologize until he stops me. "Don't be sorry. I can't even tell you how many times and in how many ways I've dreamed of you crawling up my chest to kiss me. And incidentally," he whispers leaning closer to me, "You were so much better in reality."

Nearly crying from his words, I smile instead. Pulling away from his intensity I walk backward with a stupid grin on my face until bumping into the wall I giggle stupidly and turn quickly for the bag of my clothes in his spare room.

Changing quickly into 2 piece pajamas, I wash my face and brush my teeth in the main bathroom. I'm nervous and excited but I'm so ready to climb into Malcolm's huge bed to sleep beside him. I'm ready for that, and I hope I'm ready for more soon because I have a feeling Malcolm will be amazing to me.

"Come here," Malcolm extends his hand when I pause in his doorway. "Just to sleep, Saige. I will never touch you unless you ask me to- and if you *beg* me to, even better," he smirks as I laugh at him.

"I'll *never* beg," I cross my arms over my chest.

"There's my stubborn wee lass. And I soooo love a challenge," he walks toward me with a swagger I've never seen before. Stopping in front of me, he bends to kiss me in the doorway before taking my hand. "Crawl in, Saige. I really want to hold you tonight," he sighs pulling me until I crawl into his opened arms in his bed.

Settling in against his side, I smell his scent and his warmth when I inhale him into my skin and settle against his heart.

"Good night, Mallie," I tease with a huge smile just for myself.

"Good night, ye wee Leprechaun," he counters as I squeeze his side tightly.

(mis)TRUST

CHAPTER 27

Waking to too much sunshine, I barely open my eyes before Malcolm speaks. "I have to go to work, Saige."

"Good morning, Malcolm," I croak looking over a him.

Smiling at me as he leans forward in the chair, I'm told, "There's coffee made in the pot, and I'll take my lunch break at 12:00 so I can drive you to work."

"I can take a cab. And I have to get my car anyway." Sitting up against the headboard I really look at him this morning. Dressed in cargo pants and a t-shirt, he looks huge and growly, and even a little sexy gruff.

"What are you looking at?" He grins.

"You."

"Oh yeah?"

"Yes. Um, would you like me to make you some breakfast?"

"No. I've been up for an hour," he says as I look at the bedside clock. "I've already had breakfast, and I don't need you to make me breakfast anyway. I'm a big boy," he smirks.

"I know you are. I just thought I should do something for you. To make this even or something. Until I leave," I say a little softer.

"When were you planning on leaving?" He asks rising from the chair to sit beside me on his bed. Leaning in he looks like he's going to kiss me but pulls away when I do quickly.

"Morning breath," I cringe covering my mouth.

Tilting his head a little, Malcolm exhales slowly and stands back up. "There's no rush to leave, but I'll take you back whenever you want. You work til close tonight, right?" When I agree he continues. "So today isn't a good day and tomorrow you also work 1-12?"

"Yes. Wednesday, I'm just the morning until 1:00 though."

"Okay, so we'll go back to your place Wednesday afternoon and see how you feel there."

"But you have to work," I protest immediately. "I can just drive home with Selena."

"Saige, let me take you home. I'll feel better, and I think you'll feel better with me being there, right?"

"Yes," I admit a little embarrassed that I feel nervous still.

"Okay, so you'll stay here until Wednesday to see how you feel in your apartment. There's no rush, and I like having you here," he finally smiles leaning against the TV wall near the door.

"Okay. Thank you. I guess I'll see you around 12:30 then."

"Have a good morning, and help yourself to anything. I'll set the alarm when I leave. Bye, Saige," he grins again.

"Bye, Malcolm," I grin back stupidly.

After a shower and dressing for work, I walk around Malcolm's house and snoop just a little. There isn't much stuff anywhere, and other than opening cupboards and drawers which are all tidy and organized, I can't find one single thing to make me question him or his motives.

There are no hidden pictures of wives or children, and there are no guns or knives hidden in strange corners like he's a paranoid freak. By all accounts, Malcolm seems totally, ridiculously normal, which is kind of annoying actually.

Not that I need any drama, but *god,* this guy is way too organized. Even I have a junk drawer of just miscellaneous crap I can't figure out what to do with or don't want to throw out for whatever reason. Huffing, I can't even find a junk drawer in his house, it's that organized.

Unless that's his problem? Maybe he's like the Sleeping With The Enemy husband and all the soup cans have to be positioned labels out and organized in his cupboards properly.

Argh... running back to his kitchen I throw open the cupboards and *nope-* all the food is normal looking with some stacked, and some side by side with no label harmony whatsoever.

Deciding I'm losing my mind, I send Malcolm a text.

'Are you a serial neat freak who kills people who don't line up labels properly on the shelves?' Waiting, I think I may have actually lost my mind.

'Yes.' He replies making me laugh.

'Why don't you have crap anywhere? Not that I'm snooping, but not even a junk drawer? Are you psychotic?'

'Yes.'

'I'm seriously asking you. Are you a freak, or secretly married, or recently released from prison after butchering kids at a secluded summer camp in the woods?' Holy *shit*. Even for me that one went a little too far, I burst out laughing.

'Yes. To all of the above.'

'Arse.' I type grinning.

'Karen won't let me have a messy house. She'd kick my ass and tell on me to Dan who would threaten to kick my ass. So I learned to keep it tidy.'

'Not even one junk drawer?'

'Beside the stove, bottom drawer. Are you snooping, Saige?'

'Just a little. Sorry. I didn't get to the stove before I panicked. 😬'

'Spare room as well. A whole mess of shit in there I don't know what to do with or where to put. So don't worry, I'm not a married neat-freak summer camp murdering psycho.'

'Whew... '

'See you at 12:20ish.'

'Thank you. See you then. Sorry I seem like a paranoid, snooping psycho.'

'No worries. Just don't look in the basement if you don't want to find the dead bodies. ☺'

*****

When the alarm shuts off and Malcolm walks in I realize I missed him all morning. After my snooping/text escapade I was bored with nothing to do so I made him dinner to heat up later.

Turning to me, Malcolm asks, "Did you find the bodies in the basement?"

"No," I laugh. "I didn't make it to the basement yet. But I did make you dinner after my freak out."

"Really? What did you make?" He actually sniffs the air.

"Chicken cacciatore. You just have to heat it up later."

"Thank you. But I told you I didn't need you to cook for me, though I'm sure it'll be delicious."

Feeling totally awkward suddenly, I have to explain something so Malcolm understands. "I'm not a freeloader, Malcolm." Watching him visibly cringe at my words, I continue. "If I'm staying here I have to either pay you or work for it. So please just accept the dinner I made because I don't want to be obligated to you."

"Of course you don't," he says a little coldly. "Understood. Are you ready for work?"

"Yes." Looking at him NOT looking at me, I try again. "I didn't mean anything badly by that and I wasn't trying to offend you or anything."

"I know you didn't, Saige," he exhales hard. "Let's just go. I have to get back to the site," he waits back by the door as I slip on my shoes.

Leaving his house, there's definitely tension that wasn't there before, and I don't know how to fix it. I know I didn't say anything wrong- I was actually explaining something right so he understood me. I don't use people, and I don't want him to ever think of me like that.

"Q&A?" I ask trying again in his SUV.

"Maybe later," he smiles briefly before rounding Montgomery Park for the expressway.

Parking out front D'Vecseys with his hazards on, Malcolm finally speaks. "So I'll be waiting for you right here at 11:45. Just text when you're ready to leave, okay?"

"Okay. Thank you." Turning in my seat, Malcolm's watching me and I'm watching him and everything feels so tense between us.

"What did I do wrong, Malcolm? I don't like all this tension."

"You didn't do anything wrong. I'll see you when you're done," he repeats again effectively stopping the conversation.

"Okay. Have a good day and evening."

"You too. Thanks again for dinner."

"You're welcome." Opening the truck door, I feel awkward again. Do I lean over and kiss him? Is that what's missing? God, I don't know what to do. So I do nothing.

"Bye."

"See ya," he smiles driving away immediately.

Opening the big wooden doors to the restaurant I feel awful inside. I can admit I love spending my time with Malcolm hanging out, and I know this summer would've been so different for me without him in my life. I know I wouldn't have felt half as strong and secure, or even half as ready to move past everything Tyler did had I not met Malcolm.

I know I wouldn't have moved past the depression and the fear half as fast, and I wouldn't have been distracted from when I was hurt if

Malcolm hadn't been such a huge, awesome presence around me.

I love so much about my time with Malcolm this summer but I'm not in love with him- I know I'm not. I know he told me how he feels last night, and it *was* amazing to hear. But the bottom line is, I don't feel the same.

I like him a lot, and I love being around him, but I'm really not in love with him, and I don't know how to make that okay between us now that he's told me how he feels about me.

By 6:30 I'm exhausted. I have only 4 1/2 hours of service to go before the cleanup but I feel so drained and sore and just exhausted from everything again. Maybe between my emotionally exhausting weekend with the break-in at my apartment, or the physical exertion from working on the door yesterday, I don't know. But my arms are killing me, my shoulders hurt, and I'm feeling a little sadder today than I have in a while.

"I'm leaving," Selena interrupts my internal whining. "How are you?"

"You've asked me that question every single hour today, and the answer won't change. I'm fine," I smile at her.

"Yeah, okay. Anyway, I know I asked, but how was last night with Malcolm?"

"I already told you it was fine."

"You did tell me it was fine. Over and over again. But you look like shit and somehow I doubt it's because everything was fine. So spill."

Looking at Selena, I actually do need advice. I need to know how to make this friendship/kissing thing with Malcolm work, and I need to know what to do about all the other stuff.

"He told me he's in love with me," I whisper to her huge smile and gasp. Repeating every single word he said, Selena giggles, swoons, tears up and smiles the more I speak. Actually holding my hand by the end, I'm crying and she's smiling shaking her head.

"I don't know what to do," I beg desperately.

"You do whatever you want. If you feel like kissing him, you kiss him. If you just want a hug you snuggle in deep. And if you really don't love him you tell him now so this thing between you doesn't become bigger than either of you can handle."

"I like him so much, and I love being around him, but I'm not in love with him. And I don't want to lose his friendship because of it."

Shrugging, that pretty much says it all. "I'm scared if he can't have me like he wants, he won't have me at all."

Hugging me, Selena says, "I doubt he would stop being your friend even if you told him you weren't in love with him. But if he did that's his problem to deal with, not yours." Looking at Hershal I have to get back to work, but I really need Selena to tell me what to do.

"Stop thinking so much, and just enjoy him, Saige. Malcolm is the kind of man most women wish their men were like, and he's the kind of person you want to keep in your life always."

"I know. Shit, I have to go. Hershal's tapping his watch," I grin when she looks over at him and waves. "Please don't discuss this with anyone."

"Never. Call me later if you need to talk."

"I may be moving back home on Wednesday."

"Well, that's awesome for me and Griffin, not so awesome for you and Malcolm," she pats my hand. "Don't make any decisions yet, Saige. Just chill out until you *know* what to do."

"Thank you." Hugging Selena again, I'm no closer to an answer with Malcolm, but the sadness isn't as heavy as it was before talking to her.

By 10:00 I'm done. Cleaning and tidying before the official close I'm obsessed with thinking of Malcolm, and I'm totally obsessed with what I should do when I see him. Between jumping him in his SUV with a kiss to make him happy, or crying and telling him I'm *un*happy, I can't figure out what to do.

Checking my phone I see a message from a few hours ago from Malcolm.

'Dinner was delicious. Thank you. I'd like to talk tonight if you're not too tired when you're done. Have a good night. I missed you today.'

Well, talk is good, certainly better than not talking. And I'm glad he missed me today, because I missed him, too.

*****

Walking out the front doors, Mike nods at Malcolm as he walks to me. Leaning down low, he hugs me before I can even speak.

"Hi," he smiles letting me go.

"Hi back," I reply like we always do.

"Ready?" He turns opening the passenger side door for me so I can climb in. "You look tired," he says before closing the door on me.

"I was just on my feet for 11 hours, so yeah, I'm a little tired," I huff not really at him but more at this weirdness between us. "Can we just go?" I reach for the door handle to close him out.

Waiting only seconds for him to get in on his side, I decide to speak first. I can't stand this shit between us, and I won't deal with it if he's going to always be frosty when he doesn't like something I do or say.

"Malcolm, I don't kiss with morning breath, and I don't kiss just because you want me to. I kiss because *I* want to."

"I know. I-"

"Just listen to me," I interrupt until he quiets with the truck Idling. "I remember every single word you said to me last night. I remember it and it was probably the most amazing night of my life. But I also remember the rest of what you said. You said you would be patient and you would wait for me. You said you were afraid to push me too hard and too fast. You said you're in love with me, but that you'd wait for me to get there with you. You said that," I push.

"I know I did."

"Okay, so here's where *I'm* at- I like you and I care about you. I'm even attracted to you, and really, I just think you're amazing to me and maybe even *for* me. But I'm not where you are, and even though I kind of wish I was, I'm not. So if I don't act the way you want or reciprocate the way you want you can't be mad or frosty with me."

"I know."

"You can't be frosty with me for not feeling what you feel because *you* told me you'd wait for me to get there. But the very first morning after the most beautiful confession anyone has ever said to me, when I didn't kiss you because I think it's gross to kiss with morning breath *not* because of you, you were weird with me. Then hours later because I cooked you friggin' dinner because I wanted to, because it made *me* feel better about this temporary living arrangement you got frosty with me again. And that's not fair, and I hated it. And you made me sad today."

"I'm sorry," he leans over to take my hand when I let him.

"So this is it, Malcolm- take it or leave it. I DO like you. Actually I *really* like you and how I feel when I'm with you. I love the teasing and the funny and all the comfort I experience when I'm with you, but I'm not in love with you. So if you can't handle me being independent, trying somehow to make things a little more even so I don't feel like I'm using you, then that's *your* problem. Just like it's my problem if you say things to me I have a hard time believing. But I'm not going to change, and I'm not going to pretend with you. I won't stick around if I feel pressured to be or do something you want when I don't feel it yet."

Winding down my speech, Malcolm doesn't interrupt so I can finish this between us. "I enjoyed kissing you last night, and I really enjoyed sleeping beside you. But I'll walk away before I let you make me feel badly for not feeling what you feel. I will, Malcolm, because I don't need any more stress right now, not from a friend and not from a *more* than a friend. Okay?"

"Absolutely," he replies turning right in his seat to look at me again. "I get it, and I'll stop getting *frosty,* as you put it. I was more nervous than anything this morning that you would change your mind or regret the kissing so when you pulled away from the kiss it made me feel like you were pulling away from me. But I understand- no morning breath kissing," he smiles a little.

"And about dinner, that too was just an over-reaction to you using the word *obligation*, though I also get where you're coming from. I don't use people either and I would hate to be seen like that. So yes, I would probably do the same thing under the circumstances to 'make things more even,'" he quotes. "I just don't feel that way about you, Saige. I like you in my home and I love you around me, so obligation for me doesn't apply. But I get it."

"And the other stuff?"

"Much harder. I *did* say I would be patient, and I actually meant it. But it's hard to be patient because I want you and I want you to want me and I know I have to wait for you to get there. But I'm there, so it's really hard to want something kind of in my reach that I just can't have."

"Yet," I whisper sensing his sadness.

"Yet," he nods. "I can wait for you. I've been waiting for you for 31 years, so," he sighs, "I can wait a while more. But I need you to understand something too- I'm telling you the truth of my feelings and that won't stop whether you walk away or not. I'll wait for you, because I have to. Okay?"

"Yes."

Looking at Malcolm I go for the spontaneous. With the SUV still idling and Malcolm looking both relieved and growly handsome watching me,

I flick off my seatbelt quickly and jump him.

Kissing him he actually startles beneath me and moans when we touch. He doesn't move though until I beg, "Kiss me," and finally he takes my head in his hands, pulls me right over him and kisses me back.

Almost desperately we kiss hard and fast and heavier than the night before. We kiss until I'm breathless and we kiss until my ass suddenly hits the horn and we both jump against each other.

Bursting out laughing, Malcolm exhales across my face and grins in his way that lights up his whole face. "Horny?" He laughs at his stupid teenage joke making me laugh again.

Pushing myself back over his lap and seat I slump into mine and blush again as he watches me. "When I kiss you, Malcolm, I *always* want you to kiss me back."

"Okay," he squeezes my hand. Leaning toward me again, Malcolm kisses my cheek and breathes in my ear, "And when you hand me my ass, it's hot as hell, Saige."

"Good," I kiss his lips quickly before he pulls away to start driving. "Then I'll do it often," I grin as he laughs.

"Q&A?" I ask a few minutes before we enter the expressway.

"Hit me."

"Why aren't you married?"

"I didn't meet the right woman before you," he grins over at me.

"Good answer," I giggle before getting serious again. "But why not? You're pretty awesome, Malcolm. So I doubt it was because you didn't have women who wanted to marry you."

"Do you get jealous?" He asks instead of answering.

Thinking about me and Tyler I know I wasn't. But then I remember what I was like with Malcolm and that woman Agnes, and even sometimes when Selena flirts and teases and I suddenly realize I can be.

"I never was before. But Tyler was my only boyfriend, and I trusted him," I scoff a little. "But, I've been jealous around you, so," internally groaning I admit, "I guess I can be."

Looking over at me Malcolm grins quickly then smiles when I glare at him. "Good answer," he smiles wider. "I like that."

"Pfft, you would. Men are such idiots," I whine. "Do *you* ever get jealous?"

"Yup. I have and I will again. And with you I could be jealous of everything if I let myself be."

"Why?"

"Because I'm in love with you, Saige," he says so simply the air in the truck thickens as my heart starts pounding. He doesn't look at me but he does smile at the road like he knows he shocked me.

Shaking my head, I try to focus on my original question. "So women... Have you ever *been* married?"

"No. Marriage is for life, Saige. To me, anyway."

"Okay, but you must have been close or had a longtime girlfriend or something. I mean you *are* pretty old," I tease as he laughs.

"What do you want here? Numbers? Their names? I'll tell you anything, but I don't want to suffer because of it. I've been in this position before Saige, and once answered some women hate the answers and can't move past them."

"Ugh, that many?" I ask cringing.

"How about relationships instead of numbers?" He looks over as I huff. I really want to know how many women he's slept with, but I also think he's right- I'll *hate* knowing how many. "Saige?" He squeezes my hand again.

"I've only ever slept with Tyler," I suddenly admit feeling really uncomfortable. "So I don't have any experience other than what he taught me and I'm probably not as good as you in bed." God, I feel so embarrassed I HAVE TO stop speaking. But I think I'm going to have nothing to offer Malcolm when -if- we ever sleep together.

"Are you insecure about that?" Blushing deeper I can't even speak. "Oh, Saige, I can't even tell you what I feel for you or what I imagine sex will be like with you. I don't care that you've had only one partner. If anything, the possessive animal in me likes that."

"Yeah, but what if I'm not good at sex? You'll go somewhere else," I nearly gasp when I realize how pathetic I sound again. Pathetic and hideously insecure. "Sorry. Ah, Tyler screwed with my self-confidence when he cheated I guess."

"I'm not Tyler, Saige."

"I know."

"No, I'm NOT Tyler, Saige. I don't cheat and I will never make you feel insecure or self-conscious when you're with me. That's not what I do with women, and it's not what I'll ever do to you if we're together."

"Um, can I tell you all my bad things now?"

"No."

Speaking over him, I go for it anyway. "My boobs are tiny, like almost nonexistent without a really good bra. And I have an ugly brown birthmark on the top of my right butt cheek. Um, my hip bones stick out kind of harshly if I'm on my back and it's really gross. And I'm nervous to be with you like that in case I'm not as good as the other women you've had," I exhale finally. "I've also never felt this pathetic or vulnerable in my life, Malcolm. I'm usually pretty strong and secure. But right now I feel like an insecure ass and it's pissing my off."

"So stop being an insecure ass with me," he says with a grin as I laugh and swat his arm. "I don't need large breasts, and I look forward to finding your birthmark," he winks at me.

"I kind of want to have sex when we get back to your house to get it over with," I flinch at my own statement when he turns his head to glare at me.

"Yeah... that's never going to happen, Saige. I'm not banging you to *get it over with,* and I'm not having sex with you because you're all up in your head. Never mind the fact that you were hurt 2 months ago so you don't even know how you feel about sexual touching, let alone sex itself. But I sure as hell am not having our first time being about 'getting it over with'," he quotes a little angrily. "Wrong guy, Saige."

"Sorry. I didn't mean to say it like that. I'm just strung out I guess over-thinking and insecure."

Looking over at me he reminds me, "We just kissed last night, Saige. Last. Night. So relax about anything else, okay? We will or we won't, and we'll know when we're ready. I can have sex anytime, Saige," he says which makes that jealous bitch in me sit up straighter. "But that isn't what I want since I met you. You are *all* I want since I met you."

Uncontrollably, I smile at him because of his words, squeeze *his* hand because of his sweetness, and turn my face to the window as we enter Montgomery Park because I feel happy inside.

Opening the front door and shutting off the alarm, Malcolm asks if I'm hungry, which I am a little. "Come on," he tugs me to the kitchen. "Meal, or snack?"

"Snack."

"Sandwich, crackers or chips, or something?"

"Peanut butter sandwich?" I decide as he moves for the cupboard of peanut butter and opens the fridge for bread.

"Sit," he smiles but I don't want to. Walking toward him, he turns against the counter and closes the knife drawer as I advance. "What's up?" He grins when I press against his chest tip-toeing for a kiss.

Lifting me right off the floor, Malcolm sits me on the breakfast bar, takes my head in his hands again and kisses me.

Long and deep, he kisses me until one of us eventually pulls away for air. Snuggling in deep, I wrap my arms around his neck and rest my head on his shoulder as he gently runs his hands up my back softly. Gently like I remember, I almost cry when I picture Tyler suddenly.

"Don't rub my back like that. Tyler always did that," I croak sadly and he stops immediately. Pulling away to look at my face I turn my head just as he kisses my lips quickly before stepping away from me.

"Let me make you a sandwich," he says and I could actually bludgeon myself. Feeling the air around us change again, I feel like I should apologize, but I'm not sure what I'm sorry for. The memories I can't seem to help, just like I can't help disappointing Malcolm when I'm nostalgic for Tyler.

God, this is hard.

Talking about nothing important while I eat, I learn about the house he's demo-ing and about the profit he's going to make on the side job Dan gave him. He tells me it'll take 2 weeks to finish and then he's starting a new project with Dan's contractors.

"What time are you getting up for work?" I ask putting my plate in the dishwasher.

"7."

"Can you wake me up then? I'd like to have breakfast with you in the mornings."

"I can do that," he smiles kissing me quickly before taking my hand for the hallway to the stairs. "My room, or spare room?" He asks sounding unsure of where I'm at, which is understandable since I've been hot and cold since the moment he picked me up.

"Your room."

CHAPTER 28

After another night snuggled in Malcolm's warmth, we've had breakfast together both mornings and I'm enjoying myself. I feel welcomed, and at home, and I haven't even snooped once since the first day I was alone. I don't know where the bodies are hidden, but I really don't care anymore. I love being here and I love being around Malcolm.

Picking me up at 1:00, we're going back to my apartment to see how I feel about it. And though Malcolm hasn't asked me to stay, I can tell he hopes I want to go back to his house afterward. He even took the afternoon off to spend the rest of the day with me wherever I end up.

Actually he gave some smartass excuse about Wednesdays being hump day, so when he winked at me I laughed of course. We're really no closer to *humping* but I'm also not dreading it if it should happen one day like I did before our talk Monday night.

"Want me to come with you guys? I'm off now, too," Selena offers.

"No, I'm good. We're going to tidy up a bit and see what I feel like at home, I guess."

"And how do you feel about maybe leaving Malcolm's?"

"Truthfully? A little unhappy," I admit as she nods. "I like him, Selena. And though I'm only staying with him by default, I actually *like* staying with him. We snuggle in at night and have breakfast together in the mornings. And it's nice."

"Sounds nice. Have you, ah...?" She doesn't finish but does wiggle her eyebrows which makes me laugh at her.

"No."

"Anything beyond kissing?"

"Nope, but-"

"What?" She asks actually leaning in closer almost giggling.

"Well, I don't feel afraid of him." I know she knows what I mean without me having to say what that means for me emotionally.

"Aw, Saige. I know you're scared and have lots to be afraid of, but I really don't think Malcolm would be too fast or too hard with you. He knows what happened, right? So he's probably going to do the exact opposite of just sex with you," she says and I know what she means. Malcolm seems like he'll be extra careful with me mentally and physically if we ever get to that place together.

"Hi," Malcolm says behind me as I gasp and spin. "Sorry. Shit," he reaches for my arm. "I swear I don't mean to scare you," he pleads.

"I know. I'm just jumpy as usual." Looking between Selena and Malcolm, I feel like such an ass again when they look at each other like I'm all frail or something. "I'll be ready in 15 minutes," I smile touching his arm before heading to the family side to switch off with Hailey.

Looking back, I see Malcolm and Selena talking closely and it instantly bothers me. I know logically they're just friends, and I know Selena is with Dave again. I even know Malcolm says he's in love with me, but I'm irritated, almost irrationally so whenever I see them speaking.

I'm not sure if it's jealous or possessive or what, and I hate feeling like this. But I hate them speaking alone together more, which is ridiculous.

"Ready?!" I snap with a snarky tone aimed at Aileen now. Seeing Malcolm and Aileen talking together at the bar, I'm getting mental and I know it.

"Ah, yes," Malcolm looks surprised at me and Aileen looks a little hurt.

"Sorry," I look at Aileen. "I'm just tired. Ready to go?" I ask Malcolm again in a much calmer sounding tone. Standing from the bar stool Malcolm hands her a business card and I almost lose my shit.

"Just call me and I'll quote the damage," he says to her totally ignoring me though I'm practically ripping his arm off to get us moving. Smiling at Aileen, he takes my hand to start leading us through the restaurant.

Outside alone with Malcolm, I freak on the sidewalk before he can. "I'm sorry. Shit, I feel like such an ass. I don't know why I was like that, and I've never been like that before, and I don't know what's wrong with me. I'm not usually psychotic, Malcolm. I swear."

"Come here," he tugs me into his arms. "Calm down and breathe." Actually leaning against the restaurant wall, Malcolm hugs me until I calm down again.

"I. Am. Not. Tyler, Saige," he says for the hundredth time since we met and I almost cry I'm so embarrassed. "I'm in love with *you*, Saige. No one else, and I'm not looking, thinking, or even fantasizing about anyone else. *You* are what I want. Only."

"You say that, but-"

"I *mean* that. And there's no but. Look at me," he says gently until I raise my eyes. Actually kissing my forehead scar, Malcolm exhales, "I don't screw around, Saige. I'm telling you, you could find me naked in bed with a woman and there would be a good goddamn explanation that didn't include cheating on you," he laughs when I glare at him.

"If I ever catch you in bed naked with another woman or *man*," I add making him crack up, "I will actually trash my entire future and kill you both where you stand- or lie down as the case would be."

"Understood," he nods still laughing at me. "But you need to trust me."

Nodding back, I whine, "I'm trying."

"You need to try harder," he says no longer laughing. "That was cute back there, seeing you jealous. But I don't think it'll be cute long term, Saige. Actually, I'm fairly sure your distrust will hurt me eventually until I don't think it's so cute anymore."

"I'm not trying to hurt you. I've just been hurt, Malcolm."

"I know, but it wasn't by me. Try to remember that, okay?"

Choking up I lean back against his chest when he pulls me into him and mumble, "I'll try."

Illogical. Irrational. Immature. Fucking Psycho. That's the new Saige apparently, and like my mum I hate it but I don't know how to stop everything from affecting me so strongly. Malcolm isn't even the asshole who cheated on me or made me this way, which I know is totally unfair of me to put on him as well.

"I'm really sorry, Malcolm."

Leaning down low again, Malcolm smiles and I feel instantly better. "Yer a wee red-headed lass. I'd expect nothin' less than a fiery temper wee ye," he says in his sexy Scottish brogue before kissing my lips quickly. "Let's get going."

*****

After opening the door to my apartment and looking around I know I'll never live here again. Even days after it was trashed the feeling inside is one of complete violation and destruction. Besides all my books all over the floor and couch, there is nothing of mine that hasn't been disturbed or broken. And it's just so awful to see and feel.

Plopping down on my couch I scream bloody murder just as my ass hits the cushion. Screaming and jumping up as Malcolm grabs for me I'm stunned by pain and shocked by him yelling *Saige* so loudly my ears ring. Flipping me in his arms to look at my body I try to figure out what the hell just happened, but I can't even breathe.

"What the *fuck?!*" He yells moving me around like a rag doll until I'm placed on my stomach on my bed quickly. "Jesus *fucking* Christ!" He yells again. "Um, you have a knife sticking out of your thigh, Saige."

Gasping as I try to look, I'm winded by both the sudden sharp pain and by the look on Malcolm's face. "What do I do?" I cry out.

"Let me look, baby," he touches my thigh as I gasp again. "Okay, it's not that bad. Um, do you have band aids or antibiotics or anything? Does Selena?" He asks sounding like he's panicking a little but trying to hide it.

"She does because of Griffin," I cry as he nods.

Not only does this hurt, but it's just so weird lying half on Malcolm with my ass in the air in my work skirt no less. The shakes are starting quickly and another freak out is close I can tell.

Reaching into his back pocket, he dials Selena while looking at my eyes. Gently rubbing the back of my lower thigh by my knee, he's not being inappropriate though he's staring, and I can tell he's freaked out by his extra growly face.

"Selena are you home? Yes, can you get down here fast? I need any medical shit you have. No, um, there was a knife in between the cushions on her couch and she was- Yes. *Relax,* okay? Hurry."

Watching Malcolm, I finally notice his hands shaking. His whole body is tense and he's not blinking much, and he's kind of freaky like this.

Wiping my tears, I whisper, "I'm okay," so he calms down a little.

"That was on purpose," he speaks slowly like he can't believe it. "And that could have stabbed you anywhere else in your body if you had sat differently or moved differently."

"It's okay," I try to soothe him though my own brain is going to explode thinking about where I may have been stabbed by the knife too.

Imagining my vagina, or higher right in my ass or just, yeah... I don't want to really think about it or why someone would even do it to me.

"Should I go to the hospital or something?"

"No, it's not too deep," he stops speaking again. "Just stay still for a second," he inches out slowly beneath me as I groan from the pain.

Walking to my couch I watch him look between the other 2 cushions and unbelievably he pulls out another steak knife, barely seen between the cushions but quite obvious when the cushion is pushed lower by his hand.

"I'm going to fucking *kill* whoever is doing this to you," Malcolm spits so angrily I actually believe him. In one split second I see what murder looks like and I'm scared to death for whoever did this to me.

"Malcolm, please come here. I have to call Detective Mathers about this," I flinch when I move a little sideways to take a better look.

"Wait for Selena and we'll call. I can't stand this. I'm sorry, I'm just..." Walking to my bathroom shaking his head, Malcolm returns with a towel a minute later just as Selena bursts through the door.

"She was- Holy *shit*. You've been stabbed?" She yells jumping on the bed beside me which makes me move and reach for the knife as I cry out again.

"Sorry! *Shit*. Stay still," she says lifting my skirt higher until I flinch. "Um, let me cut around your skirt- ah, the knife is right through it. Is it deep Malcolm?" She panics walking to the kitchen to find scissors I think based on the metal on cutlery sounding noises.

"I don't think so. Look at how much blade is still showing," he holds up the other knife.

Looking myself, I see around an inch or more missing inside my leg. When Selena sits back down gently, she lifts my blood soaked skirt and cuts up to the blade then around it a little.

Looking as shaken as he did that day I lost it on him at the restaurant Malcolm breathes deeply, "I think we can pull it out but it'll hurt because of the serrated edge. Do you want us to do it or would you prefer going to the hospital?" Trying to decide, I think a hospital will feel better, but I can't even figure out how I'll get there like this. "I can carry you if you're worried about sitting?"

"No, just pull it out quickly." Holding my breath, I motion to Selena who looks like she's going to throw up.

"I can't," she shakes beside me. "I'm so sorry, but I can't hurt you, I-"

"Move," Malcolm says a little angrily though I'm sure it's not really directed at her. "Okay, you call the police and I'll take it out."

When Selena nods and starts looking through her phone for Detective Mathers' number Malcolm sits back down beside me looking like he's going to hit something, or someone, or I don't know.

"Don't worry, I'll go to the hospital so you don't have to do this."

"No, I'm okay. I can do this. Um, can you look away though? I can't stare at your witchy greens while pulling a knife out of your leg," he tries to joke. "I'm so sorry, Saige," he whispers leaning towards my face to kiss my forehead softly.

"*Ahhhhh!*" I scream actually kicking my legs like a child having a temper tantrum.

Gasping for breath I hear Malcolm saying, "It's out and you're okay. I'm so sorry, I'm so sorry, Saige..." over and over again against the back of my head until I settle down after the initial shock of pain.

Letting out a huge breath with some residual tears, I turn to my side to see Malcolm holding a towel against my leg rubbing his teary eyes quickly on his shoulders.

Looking at the wound when he lifts the towel away it's actually not that big, it's just pouring blood and hurts like a bitch. Christ, even wiggling my toes hurts my leg right now.

"I need to get drunk," Malcolm moans and I can't help laughing at his face.

"Mathers said he'll be here in an hour or so. And he's pissed we both touched the knife, though he seems more pissed that the responding officers didn't check the couch or closets for weapons. Apparently, falling knives from closet doors, and knives in between cushions is common practice for Psychos."

"The closet was fine because we grabbed clothes Sunday morning."

"Yeah..." She exhales looking like *she* needs a drink, too. "Here," she hands Malcolm a sowing box filled with creams and antibiotic ointments and bandages in bright colors with super heroes on them. "I'd like to put Wonder Woman on your ass," she laughs again as Malcolm looks through her makeshift first aid kit for Griffin. "Use that glue stuff after you clean it- it's like stitches," she points out to Malcolm who is way too quiet suddenly.

"Malcolm?" Looking up at me he smiles his lovely blue-eyed smile, but the humor isn't there. There are so many jokes he could making about this but instead he seems horribly lifeless beside me. "Please make a joke about touching my ass, or my pink underwear, or something? I really need you to be normal right now because this is really scary and kind of awful for me."

"I'm sorry," he tries to smile. "I'm going to spray it with this but it'll sting, okay?"

"Yes." Waiting it does sting like hell but I force myself not to react hiding my face in my bed so he doesn't feel worse.

"God, I'm so sorry for this," Malcolm whispers like he's somehow to blame for this craziness.

"Don't be sorry. You're awesome at yanking knives from people." I try to make him laugh, but other than a quick grin, he fades away again.

After a few minutes with both Selena and him touching and cleaning and bandaging my upper thigh, he finally sits up and away from me walking to the kitchen sink to wash his hands.

Selena also stands but she goes to wash her bloody hands in the bathroom. On the floor by my closet she grabs a pair of my loose sweat pants and a t-shirt to help me change into once I slowly stand holding in a flinch and moan when my skin pulls tightly.

"I'm good," I offer them both as I limp my way to the bathroom holding the back of my skirt closed.

Closing the door I force myself not to cry again. I'm tired of crying and tired of all this shit all the time. For 2 months I've been dealing with too much of this shit and I don't want to anymore. So I'll make another goddamn police report, listen to whatever Mathers has to say, then I'm getting drunk. Period.

Once Mathers arrives and the 2 knives are placed in a sealed plastic bag he begins having heated words with a yelling Malcolm who starts in on him the second Selena opens the door.

"What the fuck are the police actually doing?!" Malcolm yells again with Selena standing beside him. Watching, I lean against the far wall away from the drama.

"Have you spoken to anyone from that first night to see where they were Saturday night?" Selena asks Mathers what I was thinking.

"Of course. With the exception of Keith Forrester, I've personally spoken with all suspects or persons of interest."

Nearly jolting from the wall, Selena reacts quicker than me as usual.

"Why not Keith?"

"I haven't tracked him down yet. He appears to have taken a last minute trip over the weekend according to his co-workers."

"What?" I squeak shaking. "Aren't you his co-worker?" I ask a suddenly silent Malcolm.

"No. He did some work with us a few times but he actually works for a different company."

"Did you know he went away?" I ask nearly breathless.

Shaking his head, Malcolm exhales, "No. I've spoken to him twice since the night you were hurt and both times he pissed me off so I stopped talking to him. I was never his friend to begin with, we just hung out sometimes, and now we don't."

Looking at Mathers, Malcolm asks, "Will you let us know when he returns? I'd like to speak with him myself." Looking totally pissed Malcolm shuts up and doesn't make eye contact with me again while Mathers moves on to asking me questions I still can't answer.

After another 15 minutes talking, I'm ready to leave. Selena and I tidied up a little before Mathers arrived and I grabbed some textbooks and packed more clothes for myself. It went without saying I wasn't staying in my apartment ever again, and somehow without discussing it I'm on my way back to Malcolm's.

The pictures of my thigh were taken by Mathers, and he said I should've had stitches. Looking at my wound he figures the adhesive spray bandage Malcolm used is good enough for now.

At best it looks like it'll heal, at worst I'll have a one inch scar on the back of my upper thigh which is fine considering it could've been so much worse for me had I sat down differently.

God, just thinking about where I could have been stabbed in my body makes me shiver again uncontrollably beside Malcolm.

"I'm so sorry you were hurt again, Saige. I can't stand this, and I'm losing to mind right now imagining-"

Cutting him off as he starts to freak out totally I tell him my immediate plans. "I'm getting drunk when we get back to your place, Malcolm. Like hammered until I pass out, okay?"

"Whatever you need to do, Saige," he squeezes my hand resting between us in his SUV.

*****

"It's time for bed, baby. There's a bowl beside you on the night table if you feel sick, and I'm right here for you, okay?"

Giggling, he looks so cute in his jammies until groaning I push my foot back on the floor in front of me. My thigh is *killing* me, and I'm not sure but I actually might throw up soon.

"I have the spins," I laugh and moan at the same time. Jesus, I did get drunk. "Um, how much did I drink?"

"An even five very strong vodka and oranges. I tried to stop you at 3 but you got mad and yelled at me," he grins.

"Sorry."

"No worries. Can you lie down now?" He asks pulling down the sheets.

"I'm not that drunk, ya know? But I really should sleep now I think."

"Just lie back slowly and I think you'll pass out quickly."

"Okay," I giggle again leaning back until my leg throbs. "I can't believe I got knifed today," I burst out laughing. "I'm like a gangster chick now," I laugh so hard Malcolm lifts me up into bed to pull the covers over me.

"Yup. A badass gangster chick. Just think, you'll be a lawyer in a few years and you can get yourself off."

Wow, I think he meant that innocently, but my mind goes dirty instantly. "I don't really get myself off cuz it's kind of boring and pointless when you could do it- *Oh!*" Giggling as I blush beet red, I catch myself from saying too much.

"Saige... *Please* don't be a drunk tease," Malcolm growls so sexily I kiss him quickly before he pulls away from me. "*Never* drunk like this," he grins. "It's time for you to pass out now."

"Okay. Thanks for taking care of me tonight again. Like with my leg, and stuff."

"You're welcome," he smiles down on me.

"Malcolm?"

"Yes, Saige?"

"Um, why do you like me? And I'm not being insecure and pathetic. Well, I *am*, but not really. I just want to know because you say such nice things to me and you do so many good things for me, and I reeeeeally like you, too. So I just want to know why you like me."

Sitting back down beside me as I sit up against his headboard, Malcolm asks, "Are you going to remember this tomorrow?"

"Yup. I'm drunk, but not *drunk* drunk, so I'll remember everything you say."

"Okay, well, what's not to like?"

"Oh." Pouting, that isn't what I wanted to hear. "I don't really know." Shrugging again, I kind of let him know without saying what I think is wrong with me.

"Okay, forget it. You want to know what I like about you?" Nodding at him he smiles and actually says, "How could I not like you? You're everything I could have ever wanted in my life, Saige."

"Really?"

"Yes, really."

"Like how?" I almost giggle.

"*Fishing*?" He grins.

"Nope. I need to know, but I'm not looking for compliments or anything. I just want to know what you think you like about me so I understand." Huffing, I admit, "Because I don't really understand anymore why *you* would like me when you're you, ya know?"

When Malcolm sits higher on his bed and leans against the headboard beside me he actually lifts me over his legs in between them against his chest. Flinching at the quick pain, he slows his movements and apologizes for my leg being hurt when he moved me.

"You break my heart, Saige."

"I'm sorry."

"Don't be. And I don't mean it like that. I hate seeing you in pain, and I *hate* what's happened to you this summer. That's what breaks my heart."

"Is that why you like me then? Because I've been hurt a lot and I'm kind of weak?"

Shaking me a little, Malcolm breathes a heavy, "*God*, no. That isn't it at all. That's just something I hate. And I honestly don't think you're weak at all. Yes, physically," he adds when I attempt to argue. "Yeah, you're tiny and physically weak, but I mean emotionally. You're not as weak as I think *you* think you are right now. You've been through a lot these last few months, but you still go to work, still argue with me, still fight each day to keep going, and you're still moving forward. That isn't weak to me."

"Malcolm?" Whispering his name, I feel so sad suddenly. "I'm leaving in just under 2 months. On the 6th of September I'll be moving away."

"Do you know how far Harvard is from here?"

"Really far," I exhale.

"It's a 3 1/2 hour drive, Saige. That's it. It's the kind of drive I make mid-afternoon Friday to see you by dinner, and the kind of drive I make late Sunday evening after we've spend 2 whole days together. It's nothing I wouldn't drive to see you," he says actually raising his legs to shelter me within the warmth of his body. "It's nothing, Saige," he whispers again.

"You're going to visit me?"

"Every weekend. And you'll come home to me on your breaks and over Christmas and during reading week, and every other break you get. So you leaving doesn't have to mean anything for us." Holding me tighter, Malcolm kisses my head and says softly, "Distance means nothing for us."

"Oh..." Suddenly seeing a future that can still include Malcolm changes the way I *see* Malcolm. He doesn't have to be someone I can't have. "You aren't someone I have to leave then."

"No, you don't have to leave me. And I'm not going to be someone who leaves *you*, Saige. I'm not them," he says against my hair squeezing me tighter to his chest.

He's not them.

Feeling a huge weight lifted off my chest, I feel peace settle in its place. I feel tears coming, but finally they're not sad ones.

I'm not sad, and I'm not scared because he's not them and he says he's not going to leave me. And I don't think I want to be left by Malcolm ever.

"You're not going to leave me..." I moan into our silence.

Against me Malcolm breathes, "Never," as a shiver works its way down my spine. "I'm not leaving you, Saige. I'm just going to love you."

"*Why?*" I whisper desperately.

"Because you're my fiery, red-headed lass. You're smart and strong, and you hand me my ass and do it with style. You are someone I want to come home to and someone I want to love. I think you're beautiful, Saige. Physically, you're just this gorgeous little sprite I want to hold, but you're so smart you're also a woman I want to love with. You make me want to be like my parents."

"*Really?*"

"Yes, really. Always loving, sometimes fighting, and always fu-"

303

"Oh!" Gasping I cover my face with my hands giggling.

"Fun. I was going to say *fun*," he bursts out laughing, which makes me turn redder. "*Jesus* woman, get your mind out of the gutter," he laughs again as I giggle against his chest. "Loving, and *fun*, and fiery, and real. I want to love you, Saige. That's all."

Not looking at Malcolm, I ask, "And the other f-word?"

"I want that, too. *Obviously*. But again, I'll wait until you're ready, and I'll wait until you trust me to stay."

"I think I do trust you."

"No, I think you *dis*trust me less than others. But I don't think you truly trust me yet with your body and mind, or especially with your heart. And I get why you wouldn't- I know the shit you've been through and the losses you've had. I actually understand why you can't trust me, it just sucks for me because I'm real and I'm right here."

"I know that, Malcolm. And I think I actually feel it now."

Shaking me slightly, Malcolm whispers, "Saige, it's *that* voice, so unsure and so sad that breaks my heart. When you *know* you feel it, I'll still be right here waiting for you, okay?"

"Okay," I choke up a little when he hugs me tighter. "I *really* like you, Malcolm. I want you to know that."

"I know you do," he kisses my head again. Slowly lowering us in the bed I'm still wrapped in his arms lying down with him.

Leaning over me to turn the light off, Malcolm actually spoons me for the first time and I feel so warm, and sad, and happy, I kiss the arm resting across my chest.

"Good night, ye wee leprechaun," he whispers as I grin.

"Good night sweet, sweet, Mallie," I croon squeezing his arm against me tighter.

THE FUTURE

(mis)TRUST

CHAPTER 29

"I'll see you at 12:20," Malcolm kisses me quickly practically running for the door.

"You know I have a car, right?"

"Yes, but I like spending my lunch-hour with you," Malcolm says so sweetly, I lean in to hug him. "And we'll go straight to Dan and Karen's when I pick you up at 6."

"Okay. Have a good morning," I walk him to the door. "We'll grab the wine on our way?"

"No, I'll get it after work. Oh, don't forget the cheesecake though. Dan said we can't come without it."

"Yeah, Karen mentioned that in her text," I grin. "See you later," I lean in for a last kiss before he runs out the door late.

"See you soon," he kisses me back against the wall. A little heavier than usual as I wrap my arms around his neck and tip-toe for more. Kissing, Malcolm finally pulls away only to lean against my forehead moaning, "*Killing* me..." Which naturally makes me laugh.

"Sorry," I squeeze him tight. Going for it, I say the unimaginable at the worst possible time as he's running out the door. "Um, I don't think I'll be *killing* you for much longer." Blushing furiously, Malcolm's eyes widen and his sexy growly smile makes me nearly jump him on the spot.

"See you at 12:20," he beams turning for the door. "Set the alarm," he says walking to his SUV backward so he can keep looking at me blush. "Text me your thoughts, Saige."

"I will," I smile at him before closing the door and setting the alarm.

Diving on his couch, I think about the last 3 weeks here and I know I'm ready. Malcolm has been as sweet as ever, and I actually feel ready now. The spooning at night has been so amazing he warms me inside and outside but he never does anything or tries anything because I haven't said I'm ready yet- just like he promised me he wouldn't.

A few days after I unofficially moved in I even started my period and though we didn't discuss it, I knew he knew by my bedtime track pants and t-shirts, and yet he was exactly the same with me, if not sweeter.

One night he brought out a bowl of popcorn with melty M&M's mixed inside and just held me in his arms while we watched a show about super-hot firemen. He brought me my favorite snack, though not for PMS, but it didn't matter. He remembered what I liked and brought it to me without discussing anything I was uncomfortable discussing with him yet, like having my period.

Then there's just all the normal things we do. We have breakfast together no matter what, and we have dinner together whenever I'm not working. Malcolm even goes to the gym when I'm working so our free time is spent together. We cook together, tidy together, and even clean the house on Saturday mornings together.

We've had a water fight in the yard which I won, and we finished my awesome coffee table, which I love. We've cuddled up in the backyard at night with a bottle of wine just talking, and we've kissed each other breathless under the stars.

It's been so normal and nice, I look forward to all my time with Malcolm.

And yes, I want him. Plain and simple. I want to have sex with him, maybe even tonight after dinner.

'Don't reply okay?'

'OK.' He replies making me laugh.

'Smartass.'

''

'Okay. I think I'm ready for touching now. I'm not sure if I'm ready for actual sex, but I do want to touch you and I really want you to touch me. I'm nervous though because I haven't had anyone touch me since that night. Obviously. And sometimes I still feel his fingers inside me, hurting me, and I hate it. I don't think I could handle you behind me yet, but I don't think of you bad at all so I doubt I would confuse my feelings with you with what happened to me that night. But I AM nervous I might. Don't reply.'

'OK.' He replies and I almost cry for the lightness he always gives me when I'm stressed out.

'I'm falling in love with you finally. Or maybe always. I don't know. But you were right, there IS something special between us and I love it. I've been in your home for 3 weeks, and every day just gets better. I love our breakfasts together and I love sleeping beside you. I even like cooking dinner for you when I'm home because you don't expect it or need it like Tyler did. I just do it because it makes me happy to feed you, which is way too domestic I know. ☺. Don't reply.'

'OK.'

'So after dinner, if this feeling is still here, which I think it will be, I'd like you to touch me a little when we get home. I love your huge paws Malcolm, and I kinda want to be pawed now.' Grinning, I know he just laughed at that.

'Lol' I *knew* it.

'So tonight after dinner I'm going to say touch me when I'm ready and I hope you're ready to touch me too?' Waiting for his reply, it comes back quickly.

'I'm ready, Saige. But YOU have to be sure. I don't want to scare you, and I don't want to hurt you ever. I'm nervous to touch you because I don't want to be the man who freaks you out.'

'You're not. You're the man who DOESN'T freak me out.'

'That was the sweetest thing you've ever said to me. And I'm grinning like an idiot on the side of the road right now. I'm glad my crew can't see me.'

'You're going to be late.'

'Don't care. I care about you, Saige.'

'I know. Now go to work. I'll see you soon. xo'

'I'm very happy Saige.'

'Me too. When you pick me up please don't talk to me about this, okay? I need to just feel this without discussing it again until later. Can you try to be normal when you drive me to work?'

'I'll try. But I can't promise I won't be grinning, or smiling, or whistling, or dancing, or even singing when I see you.'

'Yikes! I'm driving myself to work then. 😴'

'Not. A. Chance. Fine, I won't sing.'

'Thank god.'

'Smartass.' Malcolm texts the last word as usual.

*****

When the alarm signals Malcolm at 12:20, I'm nervous we'll be tense or somewhat awkward.

"Hi, Saige."

"Hi back," I smile when Malcolm approaches me.

Ducking down low, Malcolm kisses me long and deep until lifting me right off the ground I'm gently pushed against the wall with my legs wrapped around his waist.

Kissing me breathless, Malcolm finally pulls away to ask, "Is this okay?"

"Yes," I moan feeling myself move my body a little against his stomach unconsciously. "It's very okay."

"Good. Now let's go," he smirks letting me slide down his body to the floor. Almost irritated that he stopped, I mutter *who's the tease* as I make my way to his SUV.

Once in the truck, Malcolm is smiling nonstop, and it's infectious. Every single time I glance over at him he's smiling, and I'm smiling, and we seem like total idiots, which eventually makes me laugh as well. But we still don't talk about anything like I asked him not to.

"I'll see you at 6:00," he smiles again leaning over the front seat to quickly kiss my lips.

"With cheesecake, I know."

*****

By 6:00 I'm officially delirious.

I keep thinking about tonight wishing I hadn't said anything so I could have just sprung it on Malcolm. But then I'm also glad I told him so we're on the same page tonight if I'm still ready.

"How's my wee Leprechaun?" Malcolm asks behind me and my whole body shivers as I lean into him. With my back against his chest, Malcolm kisses the side of my neck and whispers, "I missed you today."

"Me too," I nod.

"There are *no* expectations tonight, Saige. We're just having dinner with the Ciccone's and then we're going home together. Everything can move when you're ready, or stop if you're not. I promise."

Pulling away from his arms I turn to look at his stern, I'm making a promise to you face. He's so serious and such a man of his word, I realize I love his honesty and patience with me always.

310

"You're so special, Malcolm," I choke up when his face softens in front of me. "Let me go get changed."

"Saige, I feel like you're saying goodbye or something right now. There's something you're not saying, and I feel nervous suddenly."

Breathing deeply, I say the exact opposite. "I'm not saying goodbye at all. I hope I'm finally able to show you why I'm here with you, and where I want to be with you."

Looking at me closely, Malcolm looks almost sad, but not quite. There's some unknown emotion on his face I can't read, but I don't want it there. I don't want him to feel anything but happiness with me tonight and always.

"Are you happy with me?"

"Very," he nods.

"Me too. So let me go change and grab the cheesecake."

Walking away from Malcolm, I'm amazed that we're still in the restaurant surrounded by watching eyes. I know Mike watched our whole exchange, yet I felt so absent from everyone and everything I didn't notice anyone but Malcolm.

As often happens, Malcolm makes everything else fade away until I only see and feel him in front of me. Nothing else exists for me anymore but Malcolm, I suddenly see clearly.

And tonight I'm going to love him back.

*****

Laughing my ass off at Malcolm and Dan going at each other, I'm relaxed and happy. Though older than me, Karen and Dan welcomed me into their gorgeous home and after a brief introduction to their 2 daughters before they were picked up by Dan's sister for a sleepover, everything has been very fun, relaxed, and amazing all evening.

Malcolm and I are side by side across from Dan and Karen and dinner was delicious.

"Time for dessert?" Karen asks with Dan and Malcolm both nodding yes. "I guess this cheesecake is the shit. Dan didn't even want me to make dessert tonight," she pouts as we walk to the kitchen together.

"Yeah, it seems to be everyone's favorite. I prefer the bread pudding, but I'm Scottish so that's kind of our thing," I grin. "Your home is stunning, Karen," I look around at her kitchen which closely resembles

311

Malcolm's.

"Thank you. Interior Designer wife plus Contractor husband equals a beautiful home. Or an epic fail," she laughs.

"Beautiful, definitely."

Watching Karen brew the coffee and take the cheesecake from the fridge I have the feeling were going to have a heavy conversation soon. Like the typical warning 'don't hurt Malcolm', or the 'I don't think you're good enough for him' speech. Maybe even the 'I think you're too young for him' observation- *something* is coming, and I'm almost sad that it's going to happen after such a good night.

"I love Malcolm to death, Saige," she turns to me smiling. Here we go, I cross my arms against my chest bracing for it. "We always joke I picked the wrong man the night I met him and Dan together, and though obviously we don't mean it, there's a part of me that loves Malcolm just a little bit more than brotherly, you know?"

"No, I don't," I just catch myself from snapping at her as I breathe deeply.

"Oh, not like that," she reaches for me. "More like, he's the only person I would give my kids to if something happened to me and Dan. He's just *that* guy, Saige. And Dan feels the same way about him. Malcolm is our best friend and our brother, and he's just so good, I want him to find something special with someone."

"I-"

"And you're it for him. Yes, you're younger, but he doesn't care. You should hear him talk about you- it's so friggin cute. Not that he acts cute, or like gushy or anything. It's just the way he says things like, 'I have to go get Saige so she's not alone', or 'I want to get back to Saige so she's not afraid.' Um, he wants you to be happy and secure I think, and I know that matters to him which is what's so cute about all this for me."

Everything Karen's saying makes me feel like Malcolm thinks I'm weak and pathetic. "Does he think I'm incapable of dealing with anything myself? Does he just want to take care of me because I'm weak?"

"Not at all," she squeezes my arm again. "He's totally, completely, ridiculously in love with you. I just know your physical safety is important to him and he wants you to feel better than you did when you first met. I know what happened to you," Karen says gently but I flinch anyway. "Dan told me the night they saw you at the restaurant, and Malcolm asked me about it from a woman's perspective," she adds quickly.

"I'm not talking about that with you. And I'm a little embarrassed that Malcolm would have."

"He was afraid to freak you out, that's why he talked to me about it. And you know what I said?" She asks cutting off my irritation until I shake my head no. "I told him to be patient and to just wait for you to be ready. I told him he'll never understand as a man, but also as a huge, confident man what it feels like to be afraid of being hurt by others. I told him to be patient and to be there for you however he could be until you finally saw how amazing he is."

"I know how amazing Malcolm is," I sigh. "I've always known, but it's hard to just move on sometimes. There was other stuff going on as well, and I'm leaving for Harvard in September so I didn't think it would work, or that I could even make it work."

"*Didn't* think," she grins. "But now you think it might?"

Nodding, I say everything. "I want it to work out now."

"Good. Because Malcolm is dying to love his *wee leprechaun*," she actually tries but *butchers* the Scottish accent so badly I burst out laughing. "Not good?" She laughs.

"Horrible. You sounded almost Middle Eastern or something," I laugh again. "Thank you for the talk. I can see why Malcolm loves you so much."

"Because she's hot?" Dan suddenly asks from the doorway.

"That too. Thank you for having me over for dinner. I've really enjoyed myself," I turn back to Karen who hands me the cheesecake. "And this is to be split evenly between you and Malcolm, understood?" I glare at Dan.

"Of course," he agrees. "But Karen's piece comes from Malcolm's side," he laughs exiting the kitchen ahead of us.

*****

"Did you have fun?" Malcolm asks in his truck.

When we were leaving Karen hugged me and actually said, 'Rumor has it from Malcolm's ex-girlfriends that he's an amazing lover, Saige. So trust him to be amazing with you, and *enjoy* him.' Then she laughed when I pulled away shocked.

"What's wrong?" Malcolm asks holding my hand.

"Nothing at all. I'm just thinking about something Karen told me about you," I laugh uncomfortably.

"Oh yeah... And what was that?" He asks looking between me and the road.

"Apparently she's heard," I almost groan, "You're an amazing lover."

"I am," he says so deadpan I burst out laughing again when he grins at me.

Minutes later when there's nothing but silence between us, I realize I feel happy beside Malcolm. All the nervousness has faded, and I'm excited about our time together.

I don't fear Malcolm, and I suddenly trust him with my body and with my emotions like I didn't think I could ever trust anyone again.

Feeling so light beside him, I know I need to be with him now. I want Malcolm to be the man who loves me back normal, and I want Malcolm to be the man who makes me stronger.

I want Malcolm to be the man who heals my heart finally.

"I want to be with you tonight," I whisper sounding almost sad.

It's not sadness in this SUV between us though, it's the past finally leaving me that I feel.

I don't want Tyler anymore, and I'll never regret not having my father's love again. They chose someone else, and I'm choosing Malcolm.

Crying softly, I realize even my beautiful brother Alec would've loved Malcolm- I *know* he would have.

Feeling an unbearable weight finally lifted from my chest, I think it's going to be okay for me now.

"Saige?" Malcolm questions softly in his driveway when I don't move or speak. "What's wrong, baby?"

Looking over at Malcolm's unsmiling, unhappy face I tell him the truth. "Absolutely nothing is wrong anymore. I've just finally said goodbye to them all. And it's time for me to go inside with you, Malcolm."

CHAPTER 30

Standing in the steamy bathroom, I'm finally ready for Malcolm. I've showered and shaved quickly, my teeth are brushed, and I actually have my hair down which is pretty rare for me.

I'm also dressed unlike myself as well. No 2 piece pajamas tonight, or sweats and t-shirt for comfort. I'm wearing a beautiful dark green knee high negligee with lace around the bodice and spaghetti straps.

I actually bought it over a year ago, not necessarily with Tyler in mind, but just because it was beautiful and I wanted to have it. And luckily, I never once wore it with Tyler, so now it can be all about Malcolm.

Walking down the little hallway to Malcolm's room I pause until he notices me. Watching him move across his room, he looks thinner than I thought but more muscular than I remember. He's also so tanned this summer, I can't believe he has any Celtic in him whatsoever. With no shirt on in just plaid pajama bottoms he looks huge and sexy as hell.

"Saige... You look so beautiful," he smiles and I'm instantly less nervous.

"You look way more muscular," I mumble like an idiot in the doorway. "Um, did you lose some weight?"

Looking at his body I realize Malcolm is all large muscle now, tapering to his v waist. And I'm staring at him unsure of what to do next.

"Did you think only women lose weight at the start of a new relationship?" Malcolm asks in a voice I can't tell if it's teasing or not. "I'm kidding. I always lose my soups and stews winter gut in the summer when I'm working outdoors more."

Actually sliding his hand across his huge chest down his tapered stomach I'm hypnotized when he stops at the waistband of his pajama bottoms. Waiting, part of me hopes he continues down the path he started but looking at his eyes quickly, I realize he's teasing me with his suggestive show.

"Come here," he beckons with his hand as he sits on the end of his bed. Watching me patiently, he waits until I finally walk towards him.

"To the gallows?" He grins.

Exhaling a nervous laugh, I admit, "No. Not to the gallows anymore."

"Well, that's good," he nods pulling me closer until I'm standing between his spread legs facing him. Feeling slightly overwhelmed as I overthink Malcolm only holds my hands waiting for me to settle.

"Stay here," he rises again as I step back.

Walking to the bureau, Malcolm starts The Black Celebration CD and I'm instantly dying inside. Excited and nervous, my whole body feels the start of the album with the start of our tonight.

Lowering the bedroom light dimmer we're bathed in the soft light and comfort of Malcolm's room with Depeche Mode all around us.

"Pretty smooth, huh?" He asks with cheesy wink.

"*Very* smooth. I bet you've done this once or twice before," I growl playfully.

"Not like this. And *never* with you," he replies with an intensity that makes me warm inside.

Moving behind me, Malcolm lowers to kiss my shoulder while his hands slowly rub up and down my arms. "Did I mention how beautiful you look tonight?"

"I don't believe so," I tease, turning my head sideways so he can kiss the side of my neck.

"You are *stunning*, Saige," he whispers before kissing my ear. Biting my earlobe softly, Malcolm whispers, "Just touch," as I shiver against him.

Feeling his hands move from the top of my arms to slide across the top of my chest, I lean closer to him. Feeling his hands touch the top of my breasts I push them toward him. Feeling his hands slide slowly under the bodice of my nightgown to gently cup my breasts I moan for him.

Oh *god...* His hands are so gentle and so big against me, I feel my breasts engulfed in his hands as he lightly pinches my nipples. Breathing heavily in my ear, his shaggy hair tickles my neck and his hands make me crave more.

Turning to face me, Malcolm sits back on the end of his bed staring at my eyes. Watching me he raises his hands slowly to my spaghetti straps and slides them down my arms to fall at my elbows. My gown actually stays on but my breasts are free for his touch.

"They're very small," I choke embarrassed when he focuses on my chest.

Quickly looking up at me, Malcolm says, "They're soft and fill my hands, and I've never seen such sweet pink nipples before. They make me want to kiss them," he groans leaning forward.

Taking my breasts in his hands again, he kisses and sucks my nipples in deeply until I move closer to hold his hair in my hands.

Breathless, I feel his tongue and his hands lifting my breasts to suckle me deeper. Moaning with him, I pull his hair tighter to my chest as my body moves closer between his legs.

Back and forth he moves between my breasts until his right hand moves behind me to pull me closer to him as my back aches for more.

"Please..." I whimper unsure of what I want.

"Shhhhh..." he whispers as he moves my hands so my gown slips from my elbows to pool on the floor.

Gasping, I almost cover myself but can't before Malcolm is holding my hands in his kissing across my chest to my ribs.

Looking up at my eyes, Malcolm pulls back slightly and as he looks at my body quickly everything changes. Instantly, he's dark and growly intense, and I feel very attractive when his breathing becomes as erratic as mine is.

Releasing my hands, Malcolm holds my rib cage in his hands circling my body as his thumbs continue to tease my nipples.

"You're as soft and as beautiful as I thought you'd be, Saige," he whispers again looking up at my wide eyes before his hands sweep down my ribs to hold my small waist.

"Let me look at you," he begs.

Watching my eyes, I exhale a nervous smile as he pulls back a little to really look at my whole body. From my face down and back again, Malcolm looks at all of me as his left hand leaves my waist to move slowly across my stomach.

Watching him touch me, the contrast between his large dark hand and my small pale stomach is amazing. His hand nearly covers my entire stomach and when his thumb spreads to graze across the top of my public bone, we both watch in silence.

"Your red hair against your white skin is beautiful. I now know why all those innocent sailors fell for the red-headed sirens of the sea," he smiles looking at my eyes. "I love that you have a little hair here."

Blushing furiously Malcolm says, "Kiss me," as his hand continues to hold my stomach grazing along my pubic line until kissing I feel his hand moving a little lower.

Ignoring what he's going to do, I kiss him harder. Pretending he isn't going to touch me I kiss him with such strength he moans in my mouth. Feeling nothing, but hoping this passes soon, I kiss him until I can't breathe.

"Saige, stop," Malcolm pulls away from my mouth as I gasp for breath. "I'm not touching you," he whispers sitting still though I'm not sure why he stopped when I didn't stop him.

"What's wrong?" I ask as I feel the shakes wracking my whole body.

Held tightly, my body is strained and stressed hard. Oh, *god...* even my legs are tightly closed and shaking as I try to keep him away.

"Sorry, I- I'm okay," I promise as my body shakes again.

"Saige, look at me," he says softly until I do. Staring back at his eyes, Malcolm nods when I inhale deeply and exhale slowly with him.

"I want you to open your legs for me. Just open them but look at me. Don't ever look away from me, okay?"

"Uh huh," my head nods erratically.

"Open your legs, Saige," Malcolm says again softly never looking away and never looking down.

Moving my legs apart, Malcolm croons, "That's it. Just a little more. No, look at me," he says again as my eyes focus back on his. "Let me see those witchy greens," he smiles as I huff a quick breath. "Put your hands on my shoulders and relax. But look at me," Malcolm says again in such a soothing tone, my body obeys and reacts immediately.

Leaning toward him a little my hands settle on his shoulders and my legs stay apart for him.

"Just touch, Saige," he breathes again and my body relaxes further. Staring at his eyes, he never looks away, though he does nod at me when I settle. "Just touch," he croons again.

Feeling his hand dip lower to graze me lightly I jump but don't move away. My legs are apart, and Malcolm is holding me still with his eyes.

Waiting an eternity, my mind blanks until all I hear is my favorite song around us. Unbelievably Martin sings *it's a question of trust* in my soul just when I feel Malcolm's finger gently move against me.

With just one finger he's slow and gentle, and all I hear is the sentence, "It's a question of trust" playing in my head and heart as Malcolm eases me back to my present.

Staring at Malcolm's eyes I don't feel any pain and I'm not afraid anymore. There is no past here, and no agony to be found in this room.

Staring at Malcolm's blue eyes watching me so closely, I feel a tear slide slowly down my cheek. Listening, I hear Martin Gore reminding me to trust Malcolm because, "It's a question of trust," I sing softly filled with such understanding in this moment I can't stop myself from singing that one sentence for Malcolm.

"You know me, and you want to keep me anyway," I cry to Malcolm nodding as he tears up himself. "Thank you," I gasp leaning forward to kiss him.

With my arms wrapped around his neck, still standing, still able to run if I have to, Malcolm knew to give me room to run and room to breathe. He knew to stay sitting, and he knew not to tower over me or press me into a mattress.

He knew what I needed, and I need this with him.

Moving a little against his finger, I feel the craving for more and the desire for everything Malcolm.

Wanting more, I feel Malcolm's thumb circle my clit as I move against the finger slowly moving inside me. Rising a little and moving back and forth against his gentle intrusion I take what I want, and give what I can.

And it suddenly feels good.

"That's it... ride my hand like you need," Malcolm says so darkly against my lips, I feel my arousal dampen me further.

"Please more," I beg with a hoarse voice until I feel more.

Sliding another finger inside me I moan at the slow penetration and lower my head until my hair curtains us together when I move against him. Rising and lowering, my hips sway and my body rocks on Malcolm's hand as he increases the speed of his enter/retreat for me.

"I need..." Suddenly climbing on his bed I straddle Malcolm's waist as he adjusts his hand between us.

Pulling his head back to me I kiss him with the growing urgency inside me as I continue to move against his hand. Kissing him, I rise and move on my knees while his fingers and thumb continue to torture me.

"I want more. I want you," I groan as the pressure slowly builds inside me.

"What do you want?" Malcolm begs moaning himself. "Tell me what you need- *exactly* what you need."

"You. Everything. I want you and I'm so ready, I promise," I moan continuing to move on his hand and fingers.

"Let me pleasure you," Malcolm begs.

"*Yes*," I move for his mouth again until I'm gently turned onto the bed.

Releasing his shoulders, Malcolm drops right to the floor on his knees, and before I can acknowledge our change of position, my thighs are pushed up and open as he pleasures me with his mouth.

Rubbing my thighs softly he keeps me here with him as his tongue penetrates my body. Groaning the quick pleasure, my hands reach for his hair to pull him to me when I feel him tease me with his tongue.

"Just touch," he breathes against me as I beg for more.

When I feel a finger slide back inside me Malcolm actually pauses until I move myself on his hand again. Arching my hips I push down until he takes back over when he understands I'm okay with what he's doing to me.

God, he feels so good, and his mouth is so sweet against me, I feel the desperation climbing with the tempo of the music. No longer the songs of love and trust, these songs cry of desperation and need wrapped all around me as I writhe and beg Malcolm for more.

Shaking against him, my legs are moving and my hands are pulling him in deeper. My stomach is shaking and my hips are moving so much he places his hand flat on my stomach to weigh me down.

And it feels so good.

"I'm near, so *soon*..." I hear my own voice broken and desperate around us. "Please just a little more," I cry as my body thrusts against his mouth.

Crying incoherently, my pleading and praying and moaning drowns out all the other sounds and memories from my mind. Time continues as the music changes song after song and still I feel only pleasure.

Crying, I'm on the precipice and I know I'll never come back from this moment untouched. This is forever right here in this room between us and I don't want to waste another moment I could spend with Malcolm.

Pleading as the orgasm builds to unbearable, I release on a strangled cry turning my face into his bed as the orgasm rips my body apart.

Unable to breathe I gasp my release to Malcolm talking me back down. Wrapped in his arms, I feel his hand still between my legs as I writhe my last spasms against him.

I don't know when he moved, and I can't remember feeling him stop. I just know he's holding me tightly, whispering words I can't understand in a voice I'll *never* forget.

When I'm finally coherent enough to understand, I hear Malcolm ask me repeatedly if I'm okay. Nearly moaning the words, he's getting more and more agitated each time he asks until I finally speak.

"I am so, *so* okay. You were amazing, and you felt so good, and I didn't get confused or forget I was with you."

"But were you scared? Did I touch you too hard or too much?"

"Malcolm... I just had an orgasm begging you for more. And I guarantee if I wasn't with you in my head that never would've happened. I'm right here with you and I'm very happy."

Exhaling a hard breath across my face, Malcolm still looks unsure.

"Listen to me. Better yet, *look* at me. I'm in an orgasm coma over here and I'm so happy I could cry. Good tears," I add quickly. "Thank you so much."

"You're welcome," he kind of half grins like he's relieved himself.

Looking at Malcolm I ask, "Can we keep going? I'd really like to be with you. I'm not finished yet, and I want to touch you, too."

"Tomorrow," he replies surprising me. "I'm so overwhelmed by you tonight. The way you looked and the way you felt. The way you *tasted,* which was so much better than I ever imagined," he says all sexy growly. "So before you're overwhelmed by anything I want with you, I'd like to just sleep next to you before we try more. Okay?"

"Okay," I shrug feeling not quite rejected but a little surprised he wants to stop when I don't.

Squeezing me tighter to his side, Malcolm kisses my ear and groans, "Saige, I'm going to come in about a minute and a half if I touch you again. And I really want to keep my amazing lover status- especially with you."

Lifting to face him, his arm slides over my hip as I rest against his chest. "I don't think you need to worry about your title- it's pretty much cemented after tonight. For me anyway," I smile kissing his chest. "I'm going to use the washroom. But don't look," I giggle embarrassed.

"I believe I've seen your gorgeous little body tonight, Saige."

"You haven't seen my ass or my birthmark. So close your eyes, Malcolm," I lean up to glare at him.

"Okay," he laughs rolling onto his back covering his face with his forearm as I hop off the bed. Grabbing my negligee off the ground, I run for the main washroom before he decides to peek.

Once inside, after cleaning my body with a quick rinse off shower, I again brush my teeth. I also hear the water running in his bathroom, and I look forward to crawling into his fresh Malcolm scent and warmth.

And I'm happy.

I never once felt the other hands on me, and I never once felt fingers pushing into me that I didn't want.

I felt Malcolm everywhere inside me and around me tonight, and I couldn't be happier in this post-orgasmic haze than I am with him right now.

Walking back to his room, Malcolm's in the covers in the middle of the bed watching me closely. I can see his intense face, and I know he's wondering and waiting and probably a little nervous I'll eventually lose it.

So hopping on the bed like a little kid, I tackle his chest as he huffs a quick laugh and straddle his stomach to kiss the hell out of him.

"I'm really good. And happy," I say between kisses.

"I noticed," he replies against my lips. "Ready for-"

"More?" I ask rubbing my body suggestively against his stomach.

"Sleep?" He laughs pulling me into his arms until I settle spooned against him when he tugs the blankets around us.

"I'm ready for many things with you, Malcolm," I sigh happily.

"Tomorrow," he whispers his promise with a light kiss on the back of my head.

CHAPTER 31

Rubbing against Malcolm with my ass, I whisper his name. I think I maybe dozed off, but I suddenly feel very awake and *very* aroused. Trying to wake him, I want my more now. "Malcolm?"

"What's wrong?" He croaks sounding much more asleep than I was.

"It's tomorrow now," I sigh moving my hips against him again. Flipping myself over, I look at Malcolm's eyes looking at my own. "It's tomorrow now," I whisper moving my hand down his naked chest to his pajama bottoms.

"Ah, Saige?" He stops speaking when I quickly peel down his pajama bottoms to look at him. Definitely sized-appropriate to the rest of his huge body, I'm a little stunned looking at him only half erect I think.

Lowering the waist band of his pants Malcolm lifts up when I pull them down to his knees so his entire area is exposed. "Wow... *Okay*," I laugh a little looking at Malcolm watching me closely.

Trying not to babble, I look back up at Malcolm watching me with a grin and crinkled eyes. Touching my cheek with his warm palm Malcolm smiles, "You're very cute when you're flustered," he grins again as I look back down at him lengthening the longer I stare. "I'm a man, Saige, with a man-sized cock."

"I see that," I whisper.

Hearing Malcolm say cock sounds almost dirty and not as gentle as he usually speaks to me, and I really like the difference. Almost like maybe he doesn't think I'm as fragile as I thought he did.

"What are you thinking?" He asks leaning forward to kiss my lips.

"I'm not fragile, Malcolm."

"I know you're not," he quickly agrees.

"Do you?" I ask hypothetically hoping he doesn't answer me.

Deciding not to hesitate or speak anymore, I wrap my left hand around him and start a slow slide as he rolls to his back again.

Kissing down his chest, I open my mouth to suck on the tip sliding my hand up to meet my lips. I think I can take in half his length without gagging so crawling over his legs I try.

With my hair falling forward, Malcolm reaches to sweep it all over my right shoulder as he watches me. Lifting right up on his forearms, Malcolm moans softly and watches as I take him as deep as I can while my hand works him as well.

Looking back up, his eyes are wide and his lips are slightly parted. He looks so intense like this, I suck a little harder hoping to watch him come undone. I want to see him release and I want to watch him give me everything I can take.

When he groans my name I smile around him and increase my speed. Tyler loved this and said I was amazing at it, and watching Malcolm I'm pretty sure Tyler was right. Suddenly shaking my head, I force thoughts of Tyler from my mind to focus on Malcolm panting in front of me.

"Saige, I-" Malcolm stops speaking as his head snaps back when I suck harder on him.

Moving my tongue along the underside I feel a thick vein and work it as fast as I can. Slipping my left hand under him to his tight sack his legs spread wider and his hands actually grasp the sheets beside my head. Watching him react to me, I feel good, and strong, and secure with Malcolm like this.

I love watching him pant, and I like feeling equal to him this way. He isn't this huge presence around me suddenly, he's the presence suffering in pleasure under me.

And I'm very aroused being in control of him this way.

Feeling my hair lightly pulled Malcolm begs, "Stop, Saige. I don't want to finish like this. *Stop*," he moans when I shake my head and keep going.

Squeezing him a little tighter in my hand, I lift higher on my knees and take as much as I can in one deep suck. Swallowing around him, I know when he felt the pressure on his head because there's a louder groan and a movement under me nearly toppling me forward.

"Stop, Saige," he begs so low in his throat I smile again before rising from him slowly to pop him out of my mouth with a cheeky grin.

With one last lick across the head, I look back at Malcolm staring at me with eyes wide and his chest pumping hard and fast. Watching him I realize I've never seen anyone look as hungry as he looks right now and I love it.

"Why did you make me stop?" I whisper flicking my tongue across the tip once again.

"Jesus *Christ,* Saige," Malcolm actually huffs as I smile.

"*Yes?*" I tease again when he grunts and actually pulls his own hair.

"I need to be inside you so badly, I can't even think straight. I need to feel you, Saige."

"So have me," I whisper crawling on my knees up his body to kiss his lips.

Just making contact, I cry out when Malcolm bruises my mouth against his. Kissing me hard and deep, I gasp in his mouth around his tongue. There is nothing gentle in his kiss and nothing left of my sweet Malcolm. He is all feeling, and all male under me suddenly.

Sliding a hand down my front as we kiss, his hand lowers to my negligee to pull it out of the way as he reaches to touch me again. Stilling slightly, his hand is slow but his mouth is desperate against me. Malcolm actually seems conflicted by his need- but I'm not.

"Touch me," I beg in his mouth as his fingers quickly impale me. Arching my back, I lift for him and cry in his mouth when he pushes down on my clit. He isn't gentle anymore, and I love it.

"You're so wet," he groans again.

"*Yes,*" I arch for his hand between us.

Moved again, Malcolm has me on my back, ripping my negligee overhead before he dips down my body so quickly I have no time to cry out before his tongue thrusts inside me. Instantly thrown into a maelstrom of sensation, Malcolm moans in my body and laps up my arousal.

Crying out, I'm surrounded and engulfed and so ready for him, I don't want to lose this feeling ever.

"Now, Malcolm. I need you now," I cry as my stomach and hips jump with my climbing arousal.

"Are you-"

"I'm sure, Malcolm. Oh, *god...* I want to feel you inside me," I pant and cry when I feel the last swipe of his tongue against me flicking my clit.

Crawling back up my body, Malcolm reaches for the bedside table and pulls out a condom so quickly my arousal doesn't lessen any while I writhe against his thigh between my legs.

Rubbing my arousal against him, I need him and want him, and I feel so desperate I nearly tell him to forget the condom. I know I'm on the pill, but I don't know who Malcolm's been with, or even if Tyler was lying to me about using condoms himself.

Watching Malcolm lean back down toward me he bends one leg beneath mine so my leg rests over his hip and his other leg stays between us angled.

Brushing my hair away from my face, he holds my head in his hands and leans down to kiss me. Taking my lips, he's changed the speed again as I rock against him nearly begging him to enter me.

"Saige, I-"

"Please don't," I smile before kissing him harder. "I'm so good right now I'm dying to feel you inside me."

Kissing me again, I feel Malcolm's slight movements and his slower penetration. Back and forth he moves as my hips follow.

Wanting him inside me my hands reach for his hips and try to pull him in quicker. Frustrated with his slow, I arch my hips again and try to force him in me deeply.

"Baby, slow down," he breathes in my mouth. "I want to feel this with you," he almost begs and again the air around us changes from desperate to loving in a second.

Everything slows down and everything seems so real and beautiful between us, I slow my desperation to match his need.

Feeling his size enter me and the pressure of Malcolm stretching me, I pull away from his mouth to watch him. With gritted teeth and a strained neck, Malcolm looks so harsh like this the contrast between his soft eyes for me and his sexual intensity is amazing.

He looks like he could fuck me until I scream, but he moves like he's making love to me. And it's then when he stares at my own eyes that I realize he *is* making love to me.

"Give me everything, Malcolm. I want you to have all of me while you want me like this," I whisper surprising even myself with that sad confession.

"I'm going nowhere, Saige. I'm never leaving you," he chokes up a little as he moves slowly inside me.

Deeply he pushes inside me until I arch from the depth and pressure. Stopping all movement, Malcolm again takes my face in his hands and kisses me deeply as I adjust to his size. Waiting, our breath is transferred between us as we feel.

And then he moves.

Slowly Malcolm enters and retreats kissing my lips softly. He moves slow as a dream and fills me completely. I feel him deep inside me and I actually see him with me in this, and that's when I beg for more.

"*Please*... I need more and harder," I plead as he nods darkly.

Bracing himself on his bend leg, Malcolm lifts my hips to move a little faster. Using his ass muscles to grind against me with his thigh for strength, I counter thrust against him. Lowering his head he sucks my nipples into his mouth hard as I cry out and arch below him. Raising my hips, Malcolm gets more depth until I feel almost too full of him.

Rising on his arms, his leg still powers him into me as his own back arches. "You look like a fucking goddess," Malcolm says low in his throat as I smile quickly before moaning again.

Licking his fingers he goes back to my body and as his hand suddenly touches my clit I gasp the pleasure lighting up inside me. Reaching for Malcolm's ass, I pull him into me as he moves. Harder and a little deeper, Malcolm continues to work my clit bringing me back up again.

After forever with him moving deep inside me I know my internal clenching, and I know the hip movement I can't control. I know when I'm close and Malcolm knows it as well.

"*Please...*" I whine turning my face into his raised forearm.

Grunting suddenly, I moan an *oh god* as I feel my muscles tighten up around him. Inside and outside, everything is tight and stressed and when I feel his fingers suddenly pinch my clit my hips jump on the bed.

Gasping his name, I mutter incoherently until he bends back down to my mouth. Ripping his hair out to hold his lips to mine, I just cry when he pinches me again and everything explodes around us.

Screaming my sudden release in his mouth he never lets me go. Stabbing into me a few more quick hard thrusts, Malcolm releases in my mouth a guttural sound unlike anything I've ever heard before as I spasm around him inside me.

Bruising our mouths, I hold him so tightly my body actually lifts as he does. Turning us, I'm dropped on his chest as our mouths part. Hearing Malcolm groan once more when I bare down on him still inside me, I exhale deeply on his sweaty chest. Feeling his hands on my ass grinding me slightly against him, his thrusts continue slowly until he can't seem to take anymore.

And then everything stops but our panting and gasping.

Rubbing my hair against his chest to get it out of my face, I bite the nipple near my mouth as his hips rise once more pushing his softening cock inside me with a low groan.

"I've died," he finally breathes as I smile against his chest. "And it was the sweetest death I'll ever know," he adds leaning his chin down to kiss my head. Combing all my hair to the side of my head, Malcolm looks at me as I raise my own eyes to his.

"I love you, Saige," he says so sweetly, my eyes fill immediately. Nodding against his chest looking at his beautiful eyes telling me everything between us, I believe him.

"Are you okay?" He asks gently stroking my head and hair.

"I'm very okay," I wiggle feeling him slip out of my body completely. "But I would like to shower before I pass out."

"As you wish," he says playfully. "Any regrets or anything you need?"

"Nothing, Malcolm. You were amazing and I feel so good, I can't wait to be with you again."

"Give me 10 minutes," he laughs.

"In the *morning*," I giggle against him. "Can you push me out of bed though- I don't think I can stand up on my own."

Moving his legs quickly, Malcolm actually hops out of bed like he's still full of energy while I feel nearly comatose. "Here," he says sliding me to the edge and picking me right up in his arms.

Like a child, he carries me, and even though I laugh at being carried I snuggle into his chest as he walks us from his room.

Placing me on the counter of the main bath, he starts the shower and with the cutest grin ever says, "Well, I finally see your birthmark," looking at the reflection of my ass in the mirror as I swat him away. "And it's not ugly, Saige. It just looks a little like South America," he says so seriously studying it through the mirror I burst out laughing again when he hugs me tightly to his chest.

Pushing myself off the counter still laughing, I tell him to leave me and my birthmark alone. "Want some help?" He asks grinning.

"No. I think you've done enough tonight," I fake growl at him.

"Being with you tonight will never be enough," he breathes deeply as my chest constricts. "Have your shower and hurry back to bed," he smiles one last time before kissing me softly.

*****

328

Walking back to bed in my negligee again, I'm all smiles and giggles. I'm warm and clean and I'm dying to get back to Malcolm. It's just after 3:30 in the morning, and I feel exhausted but kind of wired.

Waiting for me, Malcolm only beckons with his hand before I'm moving across his room hopping on his bed to snuggle in his arms.

And I'm still happy.

"How do you feel?" He whispers against my wet hair.

"Happy," I whisper back with tears in my eyes.

"I love you, Saige," he confesses without thought or expectation.

Kissing the arm across my chest I mumble, "Good night, Mallie," to Malcolm holding me tighter to him.

(mis)TRUST

CHAPTER 32

Waking slowly, I open my eyes to Malcolm drinking coffee watching me from the slouchy fireplace chair. "Finally awake?"

"Good morning," I croak in the deepest morning voice ever. "What time is it?"

"10:00."

Stretching my arms out I wince when my thighs ache. "Ugh... everything hurts," I cover my face with a pillow to block out the sunlight.

"Bad hurt or good hurt?" He asks way too seriously.

"Very good hurt," I smile pulling the pillow away. "I don't want to go to work today," I whine finally sitting up with the sheets pulled to my chest.

"No? What would you rather be doing?" He asks taking another sip of his coffee.

"Anything with you," I answer so honestly I know I surprised him.

Leaning forward, Malcolm hands me his coffee to drink and says simply, "That was an awesome answer. I'll pick you up at 6:00 and we'll figure out what we'll do for the rest of the night."

Grinning, I sip on his coffee which we happen to like the same, and I imagine our night together. When I heat up immediately I wish I had the day off to spend with him.

"I'm supposed to go see my mum tomorrow," I shrug.

"I'll take you if you want?"

Treading lightly I don't want to hurt his feelings with this but there's NO way I'm introducing him to my mum. "Ah, my mum is intense, and not someone I really want you to meet yet. But it's not you, I promise. She doesn't think highly of men in general and she can be very rude and inappropriate at times with her opinions."

"Saige-"

"Honesty Malcolm, it's not you. I'm not hiding you or anything like that. But she's instilled in my brain that no man will ever love me, I should give no man my heart, and all men cheat. Period." Shrugging again, I don't know what else to say.

Replying so heavily, I feel his conviction all around me wrapping me up tight, Malcolm replies, "She hasn't met *me* yet."

"I don't want her to meet you yet so she won't try to ruin anything between us. Because she'll try to, Malcolm- for whatever reason. Please understand?" I beg finally so he doesn't feel hurt.

"Okay," he relents sitting back in the chair.

Still looking at me, I don't know what to say to make him understand. "*Please,* Malcolm? This isn't about you or even us. I swear, it's just about her. I'm not ready to defend us to her when there's no history I can defend us with yet. Does that make sense?"

"Yes," he finally smiles. "But you better get up and get ready for work now," he stands to take his mug from my hand with a kiss on my forehead. "I want to have breakfast with you before we leave."

"Okay..." Watching him leave his room I feel like shit, but I can't help it. I won't cave with this one. Until Malcolm and I are cemented as whatever we are, I'm not allowing my mum to destroy us, or manipulate me into distrusting Malcolm because of her own issues with trust.

Joining Malcolm in the kitchen, he smiles and leans over the breakfast bar to kiss me. "How are you?" He asks again like he's still unsure.

"I'm really good, Malcolm. I loved being with you and I look forward to being with you again," I blush immediately but don't care. I need him to understand where I'm at. "I feel *really* good today."

"You can tell me anything, even if it's about my technique," he winks. "I can handle it and I'd rather talk than not know if you need something from me."

"Malcolm," I interrupt grabbing his forearm. "You were amazing. I felt nothing bad with you last night and I still don't. I'm very happy with you and what we did last night. Like, *really* happy," I nearly groan as a memory of him washes over me.

"What are you thinking?" He asks with such a dirty voice, I feel my arousal climb immediately.

"The way you looked when you were inside me."

"Yeah?" Walking around the breakfast bar, Malcolm spins my chair and lifts me right onto the counter. "Wanna know what I'm thinking about?"

"*Yes...*"

"Lie back, Saige," he says in a way that makes me shake with arousal.

Leaning back on my forearms, Malcolm steps between my legs watching my eyes as he slowly runs his hands up my thighs under my skirt. Never looking down or away from my eyes Malcolm touches the crotch of my panties and runs a finger along my center as I moan a little.

"Put your feet on the counter," he whispers. Totally mesmerized by his eyes darkening for me, I spread my knees wide and wait for whatever he wants to do next. "I need to see you?" He asks staring at me as my head nods. Unable to speak I'm watching Malcolm watching me feeling my body growing wetter for him.

When he moves my panties to the side, Malcolm finally looks down at my body. Mumbling something that sounds like *pretty pussy* I actually dampen further from his words. I'm still, and unable to think as I feel a finger lightly graze over my body.

"So wet," he moans ducking his head quickly to taste me.

"Oh, *god...*" I cry loudly in the kitchen when I feel his tongue enter me. Panting, my foot slips off the counter until he grabs my foot and holds it on his shoulder. "*Malcolm,*" I cry out as my head snaps back from the sudden pleasure.

Shaking my head, I look toward the windows as my eyes close and *No!* Snapping my legs closed around Malcolm's head with a scream, he stops. Gasping, I scream again as Malcolm jumps up shocked.

"What's wrong!?"

"There's someone *watching* us! Oh god, a man was watching us," I cry shaking so hard, Malcolm grabs me into his arms. "I saw him on the deck," I point. Shaking violently, Malcolm attempts to move, but I hold him to me. Ripping at his t-shirt, I hold Malcolm. "Stay here. *Please,*" I cry again.

"Saige, honey, there's no way. They'd have to climb the back neighbor's fence to get in. He couldn't-"

"There was someone *HERE!*" I scream so he knows I'm serious. "I know what I saw Malcolm."

Sitting up fully, I jump off the counter fixing my skirt with shaking hands and a pounding chest. I *know* I saw someone. "I'm not fucking crazy," I cry for both me and Malcolm.

"What did he look like?"

"I just saw dark, like his clothes maybe before he jumped away from the doors."

"Okay. I'm going outside-"

"No!"

"*Listen* to me. I'm going outside and I want you to wait right here. Grab a knife. Here," ripping his phone out of his pocket and quickly grabbing a knife from the butcher's block, he pushes them into my hands. "Stay right here, Saige," he yells at me until I unconsciously nod. "Do NOT come outside."

"*Wait!*" I scream but he's already gone.

Throwing open the sliding doors, Malcolm points right at the handle as I jump forward to flick it locked, and then he's gone.

Running around the side of his house where the end of the garage and side gate is, I hold my breath. Watching him run past the deck to the far corner of his yard where all the trees and bushes are, I watch with my hand on the glass. Watching him run back and throw himself belly first under the deck I hold my breath until he eventually comes out the other side looking around slowly at all the corners of his property.

Running back up the deck stairs Malcolm stops at the glass and just as he goes to raise his hand to my own I scream pointing.

I see the reflection of a hand against Malcolm's dark, dirty t-shirt in front of me. Larger than my own but smaller than his, I know it wasn't there before. I know it wasn't because Malcolm did yard work and I cleaned the deck and windows Thursday night after a bad summer storm.

Shaking his head slowly, Malcolm seems frozen, unsure and unaware of what I'm pointing at. "*Me?*" He asks desperately through the glass until I realize what he thinks I'm accusing him of.

Ripping open the door, I grab him to me as he lifts me for a hard hug. "Not *you*. Look at the glass. There's a man's handprint where you were standing," I cry shaking so hard my teeth are chattering when Malcolm closes the door quickly to look.

"What *is* that?" Squatting down while lifting his hand, almost touching the handprint from the inside, Malcolm's hand is clearly bigger but it's the slimy looking smear across the glass above the hand that confuses me.

"He *licked* it?!" He yells as I gasp again. "Holy *fuck!* That looks like a tongue print," he says so angrily I'm shocked he's still able to hold me against his side.

"Malcolm..." I shake harder looking all around his backyard.

Standing, Malcolm holds my side and lifts me right back onto the tall stool in the kitchen. Leaning close, he exhales his breath across my face and soothes, "You're okay, Saige. No one will touch you or ever hurt you again. *Trust* me."

Unable to speak I realize I'm so scared I don't know what to do.

Malcolm's house was always safe for me, and now it's not. Malcolm's house was the place I could get better. I could relax here and prepare for my life to start again in September. But that's gone now because whatever the hell is happening to me has come here too.

"Your house isn't safe anymore," I moan so sadly, Malcolm pulls me into his arms for a hard, warm, Malcolm hug, and it's almost enough. His arms are nearly enough to keep me calm, but they're not enough to protect either of us from whoever wants to hurt me.

"I should go," I whisper shocked by what's happened and scared to death of what *could* happen here now.

Pulling away, Malcolm actually looks at me so angrily, I lean away from him. "That's not happening. My home *is* safe and it'll be safer soon."

"Malcolm whoever this is has been *here* now. He can hurt *you* now. And I don't want you to get hurt. I'll die if something happens to you."

Smiling, Malcolm shakes his head before speaking. "That was pretty much a confession of love, Saige. And I'll take it," he grins again when I look at him like he's mental. "We'll discuss that one later. But for now you're calling the police and I'll call Mike to let him know you won't be in."

"I have to go in. I need to work when I'm scared."

"Then I'll tell him you'll be late. Good?" He asks as I nod. "Call the police, Saige."

"I need my purse for Mathers' number." Nodding Malcolm almost walks away but I grab at him instead to turn back. Feeling overwhelmed and scared shitless, I hate the thought of Malcolm walking away from me or worse yet getting hurt. "The alarm isn't on, and maybe-"

"Saige, look at me," he begs when I start shaking again. "I'll set the alarm and I'll be right back. Give me 2 seconds," he waits for me to agree. "Stay right here," he says again before jogging through the living room to the stairs.

Waiting alone, I last 2 whole seconds.

Running for him, I just make it to the stairs when Malcolm rounds the banister at the top with my purse. Shaking as we look at each other, Malcolm walks back down to me calmly.

"I told you I'd be fast," he grins. "I may be huge, but I'm fast too. And I told you to sit."

"I was scared."

"I know, but you don't have to be with me, okay? Let's call the police."

*****

After 2 hours with Detective Mathers asking questions I can't answer, taking pictures and taking a saliva sample from the glass, I'm exhausted.

Mathers said he finally spoke with Keith about the night my apartment was trashed and he was out of town with a solid alibi. Mathers also interviewed a few other 'persons of interest' but wouldn't tell us who they were.

"I'm gonna fix this, Saige," Malcolm says for the hundredth time since we left his house for the restaurant. Nodding silently for the hundredth time, he squeezes my hand again in reassurance.

Walking into work through the front doors, Malcolm holds my hand and it isn't until I pull away at the bar and employee hallway that he finally lets me go.

"I'll see you in 4 hours."

"Okay," I try to smile but I know it falls flat from the sympathetic look he gives me.

"Just 4 hours, and I promise I'll distract you *all* night from this," he gives a dirty growly look that actually excites me for a second.

I might be scared shitless and I may even feel like bawling my eyes out, but I do love his attempts to ease me. "Bye, Mallie," I tiptoe for a quick kiss before leaving him at the bar with Mike.

*****

Finished my shift with next to no drama other than Kelsey asking what's going on repeatedly, I make my way to the employees lounge to change.

Grabbing my bag I open the door to Mike looking really angry at me.

336

"Saige, Tyler's here again," Mike says totally pissed off. "He's waiting by the front doors causing a scene, and Hershal's getting pissed again. So I suggest you make this stop before Hershal starts getting pissed at you. This is getting fucking retarded, and I'm sick of all the calls all the time from him."

"But what can I do?" I whine exhausted by Tyler and everything else around me.

"I don't know. Go talk to him and tell him to fuck off or something. *Fuck*, sick Malcolm on him- that'll scare the shit out of him," he laughs a little like that's the best idea he's ever had.

"I've tried everything. I've never answered or returned his calls, I changed my number, and Selena did the same. It's been months, and I don't know what to do anymore. Shit, I don't want to piss off Hershal with this, but I don't know what else to do."

"I know that, believe me. But Tyler isn't walking away like he should've so you have to shut him down now before Hershal kicks you both out."

"Okay. I'll deal with him."

(mis)TRUST

CHAPTER 33

Bracing myself for seeing Tyler, I walk out from the end of the bar to Malcolm standing as I approach. Looking as big as ever but sexy in jeans and a tight t-shirt, he smiles so brightly when we look at each other, I instantly smile back. God, his whole face changes from stern, almost mean looking to gorgeous when he smiles at me.

Walking toward him, I see Tyler suddenly step into the lounge watching me. Making eye contact with Tyler, I look back over nervously at Malcolm to him looking back and forth between me and Tyler as well.

"Hi."

"Saige," he says softly and I actually feel calmer when he smiles down on me. "Are you ready to go?"

"Yes. But would you mind giving me a minute? That's Tyler, and I have to talk to him quickly before we leave. I need to tell him to stop coming here." Looking back over at Tyler who's watching me and Malcolm with a shocked look on his face, I turn back to Malcolm. "Is that okay?"

"Of course. Go talk to him," he says without anger. "I'll wait at the bar for you."

Touching his forearm briefly before walking toward Tyler, I smile, "Thank you. I'll be right back."

Calming myself as best as I can, I know Mike and Malcolm are watching out for me and somehow that gives me the support I need to finish this once and for all. I don't want to talk to Tyler, and I really don't want to see him ever again. I need Tyler to go away forever like he wanted to when he chose to be with someone else.

"Saige, I-"

"What do you want Tyler?"

"To talk to you- to see if you're okay. To know what the hell happened and why you've been shutting me out of your life," he spews so suddenly before pulling me in for a hug I quickly shoulder myself out of.

"Don't touch me. *Ever,* Tyler!" I snap when I'm free of his arms.

"Sorry, I wasn't trying to- I just wanted to hug you. I didn't mean to scare you or anything," he sighs as I watch him closely. "Will you sit down with me for a minute?"

"No."

"Please? I just want to see you. I've been asking everyone how you are but no one will talk to me. Can't you give me 5 minutes?"

Leaning against the hostess' podium, I find myself looking over at Malcolm who's talking to Mike but watching me closely. Wondering if Mikes telling him about all the times Tyler still calls my friends and comes here looking for me, I'm a little nervous. This is *my* past in front of me and my past to deal with.

"Saige? Who's the guy?" Tyler asks sounding totally jealous which is hilarious considering what *I* walked in on months ago in my own home.

"None of your business," I turn back to Tyler after Malcolm acknowledges me with a nod. "You can't come back here again. You're going to get me fired, and I need this job, Tyler. Especially now. Hershal doesn't want you here anymore, so please stay away."

"I wouldn't have to come here if you'd just call me back."

"Tyler," I exhale totally irritated. "I don't want to call you. How many people and in how many ways do you have to hear that to finally get it? We're done, so please don't try to contact me again."

Leaning closer to me, Tyler looks like he's actually going to touch my face until I back up a step. Pausing with his hand in mid-air, he whispers, "Was it really bad? What happened to you, Lovey?"

Flinching at that annoying name, I look at Tyler closely and I want to cry again for our past. I want to cry because his loving concern and his gentle voice doesn't affect me anymore. I want to cry for him and to him because I'm so over him I feel sad seeing our end so clearly.

Honestly, I want to cry because a tiny part of me still wants Tyler to make the last few months go away, and I want to cry because I *don't* want him to hold me in his arms like I used to.

Staring at him in a trance of nostalgia and sadness I realize how much I actually loved him when I had him. But with absolutely perfect timing- timing so good I could almost kiss them- a couple walks in and Tyler and I have to move to the side of the podium to allow them through.

Breaking the spell between us, I greet the couple before looking around the restaurant to see Kelsey walking toward us all.

Keeping my voice lowered, I finally have my chance to say everything needed to end us forever. "Tyler, we're done. You cheated on me and broke my heart, so it's over between us. Don't call my friends looking for me and don't come back here looking for me. This is done, and has been done for months now."

"What happened doesn't mean I don't still love you- that I don't still care what happens to you," he pushes stepping closer to me again as Kelsey and the couple walk to a table.

Looking at Tyler I see clearly everything I loved about him. From his sweetness to his humor, to even his appearance and his heart. I see it all but I don't see it the same way I used to. "You're not the same for me anymore," I whisper so sadly we both tear up a little. "You're *not*, Tyler. The man I loved isn't standing here anymore and I want you to go away now. I didn't break us, so please leave me alone to move on."

"You still love me."

"Even if that was true, it really doesn't matter."

"It *does* matter, Saige. We still love each other, even though everything is messed up right now."

Feeling like I'm looking at a fucking idiot all of a sudden, I lash out at him. "Things aren't 'messed up'," I quote. "Things are *over*. You cheated and that's all there is now, and you really need to understand that. We. Are. Done. Whether we love each other or not doesn't matter and it doesn't change anything. We're totally done, so leave me alone."

Stepping closer to me Tyler says almost angrily, "I don't think we are."

"*Done?* Then you're fucking delusional," I seethe as quietly as I can.

"Don't swear at me, Saige. And *don't* blow me off. You might be mad right now, but I know we can work this out."

Absolutely stunned once again, I remind him of the obvious. "Are you still with Kaitlyn?" Unwilling, or maybe unable to answer, a long moment passes between us but his eyes stay on mine always as he struggles to answer.

Looking like he's weighing his options I almost walk away but then he finally speaks. "Not really. It's complicated," he exhales deeply.

"Not to me it isn't. You screwed her, so keep her or don't. Just know I will NEVER take you back and I don't give a shit what you do anymore. I've met someone else, a really *good* man, so I need you to leave me alone," I yell turning away only to be hauled back against him by my arm.

Panicking for one second, I look at his eyes and feel real fear for the first time with Tyler. "Let me go. *Now*," I snap wrenching my arm free.

Leaning in close to him, I notice Mike and Malcolm feet from me in my peripheral so the fear vanishes as quickly as it came. "Do NOT come back here, and don't look for me. We are *so* done, I actually can't stand you anymore. Leave me alone, Tyler!"

"Or what?" He actually laughs at me causing my rage to spike so suddenly I just hold back from hitting him he looks like such a smug asshole. "You still love me or you wouldn't be this angry that I cheated on you, Lovey," he smirks like a dick.

"I did love you but I don't anymore. Too much has happened and too much was done for me to ever love you again."

"*Saige...*" Tyler growls as some kind of a warning I don't understand.

"Good bye, Tyler. For the last time, do NOT try to contact me or come near me again or I'll get a restraining order to stop you."

Spinning away, Tyler doesn't grab for me again probably because Mike and Malcolm are like 3 feet away from us, but I don't care why. If he had grabbed me again, I know I would've got physical to get away. One, because he should never touch me like that, and two, because I really did feel threatened like I did the night I was hurt. Shaking, I really didn't like the feeling of physical insecurity that washed over me when Tyler was in my face.

"I'll see you soon," Tyler says to my back and everything changes instantly. From complete disgust to utter horror, *everything* changes.

Gasping a quick breath I spin back toward him and when I see his face I know the truth of everything.

"It was you," I moan as we stare at each other. "It was YOU!" I scream.

Completely out of my mind, I dive for Tyler. Just barely making contact with his face his shocked look hits me just as an arm wraps around my stomach to yank me back against a hard chest.

Ripping at the arms holding me while kicking at their legs, I'm insane with the knowledge staring back at me.

"It was *YOU!*" I scream again as the adrenaline rips through my body.

Watching Tyler pushed against the wall by Malcolm's forearm I'm stunned silent staring at Tyler's wide eyes as he stares back at my horror.

Remembering that night, I feel the punch on the back of my head, and I hear the gravel move and scrub against my face. Gasping, I feel my body huff a quick exhale as I'm knocked to the ground.

I feel the hands pull my arms backward in a tight grasp, and I feel my legs being pulled apart.

I feel the agony of having my pussy and ass torn apart, and I feel the horror of my inability to stop everything he did to me.

I hear the grunts, and I know the pain.

Jolting against the body holding me still, I know.

I see it without seeing it at all. And I remember.

"*Why?*" I croak as the madness settles in deep.

Waiting for anything, my body starts shaking so uncontrollably, I actually feel myself die a little. I feel the death of reason, and I know a betrayal I'll never recover from.

I remember it all, and I know that voice.

"Why did you hurt me?" I cry out as the pain swallows my past into a darkness so deep I'll never climb out of it.

Waiting for something, *anything* to make sense, Tyler stands still staring at me with wide eyes. He isn't blinking and he hasn't moved. Malcolm is still holding him pressed against the wall saying something right in his face, but Tyler isn't even trying to fight.

With the darkest eyes I've ever seen, Tyler is telling me something I can't understand.

He is telling me, and like a slow funnel pouring knowledge into my brain I wait for something to make sense.

I'm waiting for anything to make sense in this moment between us as everything else fades away but our Tyler/Saige eyes holding us entranced.

"*Why?*" I whisper once more.

But Tyler still won't speak.

Feeling myself pulled away, I reach out to Tyler when he tries to reach for me past Malcolm's huge body holding him away from me. With my hands extended and my eyes pleading I need him to tell me so I understand. I need him to make sense of this for me because I don't understand anything anymore.

"Tell me *why*!" I cry out as I'm carried backward behind the wall into the lounge. Watching Tyler's face fade away, the darkness takes me so fully, I'm unable to even feel my own body anymore.

"Why did you hurt me?" I ask no one but a blank wall.

"Saige?" Kelsey speaks softly. "Let me take you to the employees lounge. Come on, come with me," she whispers helping me stand from the first bench seat in the bar.

Moving with Kelsey I let her walk me because I don't know what I'm doing, and I let her soothe me because I don't know what I'm feeling.

I think I've truly lost my mind over this and I don't think I'll ever get it back.

This makes no sense to me.

Tyler wanted us to break up. Tyler chose Kaitlyn. Tyler let me walk out and walk away. Tyler did this, so...

"...Why would he do this to me?" I cry suddenly.

"I don't know," Kelsey whispers wiping a tear from her cheek.

Looking past her body to the bathroom mirror I see the pale ghost of Tyler's Saige. I see my haunted eyes, and my broken heart. I see my confusion, and I see the pale death of sanity leaving me.

*****

"Good evening, Saige," Detective Mathers says as I raise my blurry eyes to him. "We have Mr. Jackson in custody, but I would like a statement from you if you're able?" Waiting in the silence, Malcolm is shaking angrily against the wall, Mike is beside me on the couch, and Mathers pulls up the spare chair to face me.

Sitting comfortably, he seems to wait for me to start and when I can't he finally starts for me. "Tell me what happened after I saw you earlier today."

"Tyler said 'I'll see you soon'." Nodding, Mathers starts writing then pauses for me to continue I think. Looking at me calmly, he doesn't speak but I think he's waiting for more.

"Um, that's all. I just had the feeling it was him when he grabbed my arm because I didn't want to talk to him. And then he said 'I'll see you soon' angrily and I just knew. He didn't admit it or anything. But he didn't deny it either," I add as he nods. "But I just *know*. And Tyler knows I know. But I don't understand why he hurt me," I shake my

344

head confused. "He could have had me always," I moan between breaths. "I always had sex with him- I was his girlfriend, and he loved me. So why would he want to r-rape me when we broke up?" I cry my final question to Mathers' silence crushing my chest.

Sobbing, the confusion and pressure is so great, I don't know how to release the pain. I don't know what will make this heartache go away, and I don't know what will make this confusion make sense in my head.

"Was anything else said?"

"No. But I just know it was him," I nearly gag as the memories of that night hit me again.

"Saige, I have to tell you what's happening so you're fully aware. Mr. Jackson has denied all involvement and he had an alibi that night."

"But-"

"We're going to hold him overnight, and I promise you I'll be looking into his alibi again. However, I want you to understand he will most likely be released tomorrow because unless he confesses we have nothing I can charge him with."

"But she says it was him!" Malcolm finally speaks. "For fuck's sake, *do* something," Malcolm yells pointedly at Detective Mathers. "She said it was him!"

"No, she said she *feels* like it was him." Turning back to me Mathers sounds exhausted. "You can't remember him specifically as your attacker, and there's no confession of guilt. So at this point I have nothing concrete to charge him with. As a stretch, I could maybe charge him with domestic battery because he grabbed your arm in front of many witnesses. But other than that I don't actually have a confineable offense unless a DNA match can be made against your glass door to prove stalking. Then maybe I have something solid against him," he looks at Malcolm quickly. "But he'll be released regardless while we wait."

"It was him," I state for the first time with absolute conviction.

"And I believe you. But without proof, or an eyewitness account, or even a clear visual account or memory by you there's very little I can do tonight. But as I said, I'll be looking into his whereabouts that night and speaking with his alibi again."

"It was him," I moan again because that's all I know right now.

"I understand," he nods. "But I want you to be aware that he'll be out at the latest tomorrow afternoon. *However*," he adds quickly when

Malcolm begins to interrupt. "We'll make sure he understands he is to stay far away from you, with absolutely no contact in person or by phone. And if he does contact you in any way, you are to call the police immediately and reference this case number," he adds handing me his business card again with his cell and a case number on the back.

"What does she do?" Mike asks to my relief because I can't even think straight anymore. "She's moved out of her apartment, and we've all told him to leave her alone, but he keeps coming around and he won't stop bothering her."

"He'll be locked up for at least a 24 hour hold. Then I suggest you speak with the county courthouse on Monday morning to start proceedings for a restraining order. Use my name as responding Officer and this case number and it should go through fairly quickly."

"And then what? He attacks her again? Or rather he *tries* to? What the hell are the police actually doing for her?" Malcolm yells again clearly losing his shit.

"We're investigating, Mr. MacNeil," Mathers says like he's saying something without saying it to Malcolm. I'm so goddamn confused and broken right now though I can't figure anything out.

"What does she do?" Mike asks again looking between Mathers and Malcolm.

"Do what you normally do, and try to not let this turn your life upside down. Go to work, be with your friends, and go home. Just be extra careful, and watch where you go and with whom."

"She'll be with me," Malcolm snaps at Mathers again who ignores him.

"And if I was talking to my own daughter I might tell her to carry a weapon of some kind with her at all times. But I'm not speaking to my daughter so I would never say something illegal like that," he stares unmoving at me and Mike. Waiting for us to clue in I think, both Mike and I nod to his sharp nod as he stands. "Okay, if there's nothing else, I'll let you go now. But again, feel free to contact me if you think of anything that can help the investigation."

"Thank you," I mumble because I'm supposed to.

"I'll call your cell tomorrow the very second he's released to let you know."

"Okay." Leaning over me, Mathers offers his hand once again before leaving us in the quiet of our employee lounge.

"You can't keep going through this," Malcolm says angrily after Mathers leaves.

"And you can't keep *doing* this, Malcolm. I'm going to move my stuff out first thing in the morning when Tyler's still in jail so I can leave your house safely. I don't want you around this, and I don't want you to keep dealing with all my shit because you're babysitting me."

"I'm not *babysitting* you, and you're going nowhere."

"Malcolm, *please*... You work to support yourself, and because of me and driving me around and picking me up all the time you keep missing work and hours and I know that must hurt you financially. I'm so sorry for all of this," I burst into tears again. "I have to leave your house. God, what if he comes back?" I choke back the agony ripping me apart at the memory of what Tyler did to me.

"He won't. He may know where I live but he won't be that stupid."

"You don't know that."

"We have an alarm at the house."

"But you have to-"

"Be here for you right now, Saige. We're together now, and I love you. And I'm going to fix this for you," Malcolm says practically begging me to understand as he kneels down in front of me.

"You keep saying that, but you can't fix this," I moan sadly actually seeing our relationship ending before my eyes. "You can't help me, Malcolm."

Taking my hands, Malcolm exhales slowly, "I absolutely can, and I will. I'm going to figure all this shit out for you."

"Saige, honey, you have to go home with Malcolm right now. Just go home and relax and be safe for tonight. Okay?" Mike begs himself as I stare at Malcolm's stubborn face waiting for me to agree.

"Thank you," I cry overwhelmed by Malcolm's kindness once again.

Hugging me to his side Mike kisses my head before rising from the couch. "I'm going back out there, but take as long as you need."

"Thanks, Mike," Malcolm nods never looking away from my eyes.

Still freaking out, I look down at my shaking hands in my lap and I just can't believe what's happened.

Jolting aware of my surroundings when Malcolm sits on the couch I realize I'm lost. I'm overwhelmed and confused and when he takes my hand I look at Malcolm with more confusion. Honestly, he must think

I'm a psycho after all the drama he's seen with me so far.

"Malcolm," I sigh in our silence. "You've never seen me normal yet."

"I *have* seen you normal," he leans against me squeezing my hand. "I've seen you laugh normally, and cry, and fight, and even sleep with me. You're normal, Saige- you're just in *abnormal* circumstances right now."

"Oh, *god*... I totally lost it out there," I burst out laughing as I cover my face.

"Saige... I promise you I'm not thinking about that or judging your reaction. No one is. That was so awful and scary and just unbearable to watch for *all* of us. You having to face that fucking asshole who hurt you is the only thing we're going to remember about today."

"It was bad, huh?"

Nodding, Malcolm looks wordless until he says nearly silently, "I'll never forget how you looked. The fear and shock and pain on your face was something I'll never forget as long as I live."

Sitting in silence again, I try to put Tyler out of my mind. I try, but obviously everything we've ever said or done together is playing out. I remember everything amazing between us one moment, and then I remember the feeling of his fingers tearing inside me thrusting hard as I heard his belt buckle jangle.

Thinking of the quick painful entry in my broken body I cringe and moan, "I know it was him. And I don't understand why or how he could do that to me. It makes no sense, Malcolm."

Pulling me tighter in his arms, Malcolm huffs before speaking like he's looking for the right words. "I don't know how or why, baby. But you need to stop thinking about him tonight. Just stop for now until the shock fades and then hopefully you can remember something from that night that'll help the police."

"I can't stop thinking about him."

"Try to make yourself stop for now," Malcolm hugs me warm as we silence.

*****

Leaving for his home 15 minutes later, Malcolm leans me against his truck. "Are you okay?" He reaches for my face then stops before touching me.

Looking at Malcolm, he stands still and quiet waiting for me to make the first move so he doesn't frighten me, I think. Loving his sweetness, I hug him tightly and soak in his warmth for a long moment before he opens my door for me.

Sitting silently in his SUV, I don't even realize we're driving until I see Malcolm turn to look at me once we pull out of the alley.

Closing my eyes as I lean my head back, Malcolm squeezes the hand on my leg once in a while. But besides that little gesture of his, the radio is off, he's not speaking, and my mind spins and swirls around Tyler's face staring at me the second I knew what he did to me.

Thinking back to the look on his face, he was both scared and angry and I'm not sure why. When he hurt me he was clearly angry, so why be angry now? And when he hurt me he wasn't scared at all, so why be afraid now?

Tyler's expression, almost imploring me to say something between us was the strangest moment of confusion I've ever felt in my life.

And I wish he had told me *why.*

After exiting the expressway we quickly drive through McDonalds eating in the truck right in the parking lot. I couldn't wait, and as the tears slide down my face slowly, Malcolm doesn't acknowledge my upset.

"How did you know?" I whisper holding a McNugget in my hand.

"I know you, Saige. And I'm right here for you," Malcolm says so sadly, my tears fall harder.

"I need to shower... and can I sleep in your bed tonight?" I ask pitifully.

"Of course you can. Just crawl in when we get home if you want." Weeping as the shakes start again Malcolm rubs my hand still trying to comfort me. "Just relax, Saige. I'm going to fix this, I promise."

Turning to him as he tosses away his uneaten food I admit absolutely everything left in my head. "This just doesn't make any sense to me, Malcolm. Tyler never hurt me even once when we were together. He never hurt me with sex, or forced me, or anything like that. He never hurt me until the end. And I just don't understand what happened, or what's happening anymore."

*****

349

Entering Malcolm's home he once again asks what he can do to help me. With a desperation that's both sweet and sad, he begs me to let him help me until I finally give in and ask if I can have a bath when sleep doesn't immediately appeal to me.

Taking my hand, Malcolm leads me upstairs to the main bath and places me once again on the counter like he did the night before. Just like last night he easily lifts me, but unlike last night there's no teasing or laughter for us. Tonight there is only an intense determination on his face to make me well.

Watching him prepare the tub with bubbles, Malcolm finally turns to me slowly and raises his hands to lift me back down. Keeping constant eye contact, I actually allow Malcolm to undress me like a child.

Being undressed is when I recognize I'm truly fucked up. I'm childlike and kind of frozen in my head, but I can't get out of my head enough to protest, or really to even care right now how fucked up I am.

Eventually stepping in the tub, I curl my legs up and inhale the soothing scent in my head and the sudden warmth in my skin.

"Would you like your hair washed?" Malcolm breathes sitting beside me against the tub.

"Yes, please..."

Waiting, I see in my peripheral Malcolm move to the end of the soaker tub before he reaches right in and pulls me closer to the end. Using the hand-held, Malcolm begins wetting my hair which soothes everything dark inside me.

He's so gentle, and his hands are so careful as he massages my scalp, I find my tears pouring again. Not with sadness or confusion though, but from this simple act of kindness between us.

I've never had my hair washed by anyone, and it's such a lovely feeling of being cared for, such a beautiful moment for me, I take and hold Malcolm's hand against my lips as I cry.

"Thank you..." I sob when he leans closer to rest his own head against the back of mine. Speaking not a word Malcolm leans against me for a lifetime as I cry over my past.

When I'm nearly asleep sitting up, I finally stand with his help before I'm wrapped in a thick towel. Walking away, Malcolm returns quickly with my favorite sweats and t-shirt to help me dress.

Watching me, he extends his hand and begs, "What do you need?"

Asking in his desperate voice I wish I could tell him one thing I need, or just one thing he could do so he felt better about my sadness, but I have nothing.

I can't think anymore and I can barely function at this point. Between the hour long crying jag I had in the bath and the shakes that have given me stomach cramps I'm so messed in the head I'm almost convinced I must've done something to provoke my sweet Tyler to hurt me somehow. I'm struggling to understand what I did, and I'm nervous suddenly I'll make Malcolm mad at me too one day.

In the bath beside Malcolm I realized quite quickly Tyler isn't who I thought he was at all, and then I cried harder because I trusted Tyler with my life.

"How does a man who says he loves you beat the hell out of you, nearly crush your spine with his knee and your skull with his fists? How does a man rape someone he loves?"

Staring at Malcolm his eyes sadden when he seems to be holding in something dark between us. Bracing myself I wait until he finally speaks slowly so I understand. "A man doesn't, Saige. An animal does."

Nodding, I walk down the hall for his bed and collapse on the side. Pulling my legs in tight my swollen eyes are itchy and my head is pounding.

"Can I hold you, Saige? Can I keep you warm?"

"Yes, please." Feeling the tears begin again I wish I had narcotics or a tranquilizer or just something to make me sleep without thinking. I wish there was some way to erase Tyler from my memory and the last 4+ years from my life. I wish so many things, but all I can do is cry my shock and sadness in Malcolm's bed.

"*Baby*..." Malcolm moans and I wish I could help him. I wish I had some way of not letting this affect him. I wish there was something I could do to help him, but there's nothing left of me.

I don't have the strength left to suck this up or to ever move past it. Crying harder I realize this is a reality I can't see myself ever surviving.

"I'm sorry," I gag between sobs.

Feeling Malcolm hold me tighter, my exhaustion eventually takes me from Malcolm's arms, and his room, and his love.

(mis)TRUST

CHAPTER 34

Waking alone, I open my eyes to Malcolm watching me again from the fireplace chair. Watching him watching me I don't know what to say. I have no words, and I can't feel anything at all.

"Good morning," he says softly leaning forward a little.

"Good morning," I mumble.

"What would you like to do today? Are you still going to your Mom's?"

"No. She cancelled yesterday before everything happened." Feeling like weeks have passed I can't believe it was only yesterday that Malcolm lifted me onto the breakfast bar after our amazing night together.

Looking at Malcolm's concerned eyes unsure of what to say, I feel nothing, and I have nothing to give him. I'm empty and hollow.

"I need to call Selena so she knows what's happening."

Uncrossing his leg he responds softly, "I did already. Last night when you were sleeping."

"You got out of bed?"

Nodding, Malcolm doesn't speak for seconds but finally sighs, "You were crying for Tyler all night, but you didn't sound like you were hurting, Saige. You sounded more like you missed him and wanted him back or something. I had to wake you a few times and you were always confused when you'd look at me." Never looking away from me, Malcolm seems almost hurt which really isn't fair.

"I'm confused in general, Malcolm. This is pretty hard for me to understand. Plus I was sleeping." When he nods I continue. "Um, this isn't about my feelings for you though, okay? I'm just messed up thinking about what Tyler did because it doesn't make sense to me."

"I know you keep saying that, but I have a hard time-"

"Malcolm, this *isn't* about you. So I can't really talk about what Tyler did or said to me because that was my life before you- *he* was my life before you." Stopping myself from speaking any more that might hurt him, I can't really explain myself, and I don't know what else to say.

Nodding again, Malcolm exhales slowly before speaking. "I know he was your life, Saige. But I'm worried you're going to forget the life you've been building without him."

"I haven't forgotten. I just need some time."

"Away from me?" Malcolm asks sadly.

"I don't know," I whisper with tears again. "This isn't about you, so I'm not pulling away from you or anything. But I'd be lying if I said Tyler wasn't kind of my focus right now. I need to understand this before it eats me alive. He *loved* me, Malcolm."

"I love you, Saige," he leans forward again, looking at me desperately until I nod.

Smiling slightly I whisper, "I know you do." And I do know, I just can't feel for Malcolm right now when my heart hurts so badly thinking of Tyler. "I just need a little time to process this."

Sitting on the side of his bed suddenly, Malcolm takes my hand and kisses my forehead. Waiting, we stare at each other forever before he finally speaks. "I understand you need time, but I'm nervous you're saying goodbye to me because of your feelings for him."

"I'm not saying good bye to you."

"But you might if you can't handle this. I just finally got you in my arms, and I'm nervous that fucking asshole is going to tear us apart."

Choking up a little, I beg him. "Please, Malcolm? I just need-"

"Time. I know," he exhales heavily the tension around us. "Just please don't distrust me because you trusted him." Looking pointedly at me Malcolm says everything, "Because I've *earned* your trust, Saige."

"I know you have," I finally cry.

Flipping to my side, I hold Malcolm's hand against my chest and cry for Tyler, and Malcolm, and for my past, and for that horrible night. Crying, I try to reason what's happening and I try to forget what's happened. I try but my brain is too filled with confusion and misery to understand anything.

"I've invited Selena over tonight for you. She said she's bringing Griffin, and I'll give you some privacy so you can just do your thing with them, okay?"

"Thank you," I choke between tears. "I'm so sorry for all this Malcolm. I really wish I could let it go, but it's too big right now."

"I know it is. Just do what you have to and know I'll be here to help you in any way I can if you'll let me. I'm here if you need me for anything, okay?"

Looking up at Malcolm sounding almost pained, I feel bad for him though still worse for myself. I can't stop feeling as horrible as I feel but I feel horrible making Malcolm feel like shit with me.

"Thank you for everything. I, um..." God, of all the times to drop the love bomb this doesn't feel like it- especially when I'm fucked out of my head right now thinking about Tyler and our past and everything I thought was true of him. "Thank you," I whisper instead before he kisses my forehead and leaves his room.

"I'm going to make you something to eat."

"No. I'm okay."

"Saige. I'm going to make you something to eat," he huffs. "I'm not going to watch you struggle and starve because you don't know what the hell to do with all this shit in your head. So I'm making you something to eat."

"Okay."

*****

"Saige? Can you wake up for me?" Malcolm asks softly. Feeling his arms around me, I'm warm and not sad for one moment. But then it fades quickly and the upset slams back into my heart with my memories of Tyler. "Saige? I have to talk to you and you've been sleeping all day. Can you please get up? Selena's going to be here in half an hour."

Pulling his arm tighter around me I try to hold off the tears again. "I'm awake. What time is it?"

"4:30."

"Oh..." I have nothing. I'm empty still and so tired I can't move. "Can I sleep for just a little more? I'm really tired, Malcolm."

Shaking me a little, Malcolm moans, "Please? I really need you to get up now. I'd like you to eat something before Selena arrives."

"I'm really not hungry," I beg him just as the tears start again.

Holy shit, I feel like I'm actually losing my mind. This has got to be depression, because I'm empty but sad, and heartbroken but numb at the same time. And I still don't know what to do.

"Saige? Let me bring you something to eat, okay?" Malcolm asks not even waiting for a reply. Walking from his room, he leaves quickly but stops at the top of the stairs to look at me through the doorway.

Making eye contact, I'm frozen and unable to look away. And from his desperate looking expression, I think Malcolm feels the same way I do.

Pausing, he smiles just a little and steps down the stairs releasing me from his upset before I fall back asleep.

*****

When Selena arrives alone I'm sad but relieved. I miss Griffin but I didn't know how I was going to pretend to be happy Auntie Saige when I feel like heartbroken, dying Saige.

Crawling in Malcolm's bed beside me, Selena doesn't even pretend I'm okay. "I always wanted in Malcolm's bed- not like this, but..." she shrugs with a grin making me suddenly laugh.

Scooping me right up in her arms she stays silent as another round of *what the fucks* hit me hard. When my shaking takes over and the tears pour from my face, Selena does nothing but hold me tight.

"I can't believe it," I moan when I finally find my voice again.

"Neither can I," she whispers.

Pulling away slightly, I flip to my side and really look at her. "No, Selena, I mean I *really* can't believe it. Tyler wasn't abusive to me ever."

"I know, but maybe he snapped or something when you left him. You did say he kept trying to still be your friend. Maybe he didn't think you would actually cut him off completely and that made him angry." Slouching down the bed, Selena leans on her side to look at me.

Shaking my head, I try to explain us. "Tyler was always careful with me during sex. He may have got a little wild, or like really into the sex sometimes, but he *always* took my small size into consideration. Like, he never put all his weight on me, or, oh, once he bruised my hip slightly and he totally freaked out. He didn't realize he was holding me so tightly, and even though I thought it was nothing, Tyler didn't. He was really upset about just one little sex bruise on my hip. So how could he possibly do what was done to me that night?"

Shaking her head again, she continues trying to reason me out of my confusion. "This was different though. You left him and wouldn't speak to him. And remember you sent him that fuck off text? Maybe he was really mad at you? Anything could have made him snap."

"I don't think so. Even angry, he never hurt me ever. And he's the one who cheated, so that doesn't make any sense. You don't cheat on your girlfriend, then get mad at her for leaving, right?"

"I don't know," she huffs, but I think she's coming around a little. "You were so sure it was him yesterday. Mike told me how badly you reacted in the restaurant, and Malcolm told me you were just destroyed, so maybe-"

"I *was* destroyed because it doesn't make any sense."

Watching me, I can see Selena thinking. I actually know when her eyes dart to that right and back to my face she's thinking of something to say.

"I don't know what to say here, kiddo. *You* were the one who accused Tyler at D'Vecseys."

"I know I was," I agree confused myself.

"So maybe you *are* sure, but like psychologically you're trying to make him not the one who hurt you because it hurts too much to accept."

Stilling, I actually hear Selena. I know what she's saying, and I even believe it's possible. But I just don't think so.

"Why didn't he say you were wrong when Malcolm was holding him? Why didn't he defend himself when Mike was holding you back?"

"I don't know," I huff. I've thought of that a million times since last night myself. "He just kept staring at me for some reason I couldn't understand at the time."

"Maybe because he didn't think you'd figure it out after all this time?" She asks calmly, which I've also thought about.

"I don't know."

"Well, until you do know, let the police check into his alibi and let him freak out for a while. If you're wrong, no harm no foul. But if you're right Tyler can burn in hell," she says so angrily, I actually smile. "What?"

"I just love you," I whisper not choking up for once.

Huffing her own smile, Selena leans closer and wraps her arm over my hip again. "You better, cuz you're pretty high maintenance, Saige," she smirks teasing me.

"I know," I grin. "Is Malcolm still home?"

"No, he left when I came up. What do you want to do tonight? Drink?" She asks with eyebrows raised and a huge smile.

"Not yet. I need to shower, but help yourself. I'll meet you downstairs in like 15 minutes. Thank you for helping me with this."

"Of course," she adds standing. "Let's get *really* drunk, okay?" She shimmies backward out of Malcolm's bedroom to my humor.

*****

Hopping in the shower, I can't stop obsessing about Tyler. Obviously. But its more- there's *something* more. After speaking with Selena I know there's more because Tyler isn't a rapist, nor is he abusive. He may be an asshole for what he did to me with his whore, but even when I slapped him that last day together he never raised a hand to me.

Shit!

Before I even know what I'm doing, the shower is running and I'm dialing Tyler standing as far from the water and door as possible. Nearly throwing up, my stomach is so tightly knotted as his cell rings I barely hold in my nausea.

"Hello?" Oh *god...* unable to speak, I'm almost hyperventilating.

"Hello?" Tyler asks again in the weariest voice I've ever heard. "Fuck y-"

"Tyler," I manage to choke before he hangs up.

"*Saige?!* Oh, fuck, Lovey. Is that you?" He begs crying.

"Yes..." Suddenly gagging, I hold the phone tightly against my chest as I breathe deeply through my nausea.

"-did this. What's happening?" I hear lifting the phone back to my ear. "Talk to me, Lovey. Please tell me what's going on?"

Shaking my head to clear my confusion, I beg, "What do you mean?"

"Why are you doing this to me?"

"*Me?* I'm not doing anything to you, Tyler."

"Yes, you are. Why did you tell the police I attacked you?" he pleads. Listening, I can hear his dark voice, and I hate how upset he sounds. "Why are you doing this to me? I'm so sorry I cheated on you, but-"

"Did you hurt me that night?" I ask over his rambling.

"*God*, no. Come on, Saige. You *know* me."

"I thought I knew you."

"You *do* know me, and I've never hurt you before. Never once did I touch you angrily or sexually, or anything like that. You know I didn't."

Nodding my head, I know he didn't. I always knew he wasn't like that. If anything Tyler was almost gentle because of how small I am even though he didn't have to be. I do remember that about him.

"Saige? Please listen to me. I didn't hurt you that night. I didn't. I was with-"

"Don't." Flinching, I try to stop him before he says he was with her.

"I was with Kaitlyn that night," Tyler keeps explaining past my interruption. "I *was*, Saige."

"So Kaitlyn is your alibi?"

"Yes."

"But I don't trust either of you."

"I don't trust Kaitlyn either."

"Why?" I choke.

"I have to talk to you, Lovely-"

"*Tyler*," I growl.

"Sorry. Shit. Please meet me. There's so much going on, and I swear it wasn't me who hurt you," he actually sobs this time. "I would NEVER hurt you like that. Come on, you know I wouldn't."

Trying to clear my head again, I'm silent. I hear his voice, and I remember the way he was with me. I remember the Tyler I loved for years, and he's right- this doesn't make sense like I felt it did yesterday.

"Why didn't you defend yourself to me, Tyler? Why didn't you argue or try to convince me yesterday in the restaurant that I was wrong? Why did you just stand there looking guilty as hell when I accused you?"

"Saige? Who are you talking to?" Selena asks banging on the door.

Gasping, I lie on the fly. "Ah, Malcolm. He's just checking up on me."

"With the water on?" Jesus *Christ!* What's with all the questions? Reaching over, I quickly stop the shower and close the glass doors.

"I'll be right out. Can you pour me a Vodka and orange? I'll be right out," I babble again as my anxiety spikes.

"K..." she says as her voice fades away.

"Saige? *Saige?!*" I hear Tyler calling me louder and more desperately.

"Tyler," I whisper in the echoey bathroom, "I can't talk right now."

"Then meet me!"

"I can't."

"*Please?* Just 5 minutes? I'll meet you anywhere." When I can't speak Tyler gets more agitated begging. "Please, Lovey? I have to tell you what I think's going on."

Weighing my options, I know I shouldn't. I KNOW I should stay put. But there's something about his desperation that tells me I can trust him. The more I think, the more I believe he didn't hurt me. I'm just not sure why I think he did- or *thought* he did yesterday.

"Please, Saige? I'll meet you anywhere." Listening to Tyler, my mind calms and my memory of my good Tyler surfaces again. "I swear I didn't hurt you, and I swear I *won't* hurt you."

"Okay..." **Fuck!** "Um, where?"

"You choose. But please hurry. I don't want to get in trouble for

359

talking to you."

Thinking as my desperation climbs, I blurt out the only place I can think of. "Blenders? On Market Street?"

"Fine! I'll be there in 15 minutes waiting out front. Please show up. *Please?* I have to tell you something."

"Tyler, I'm going to be about 45 minutes or so, I can't-"

"Just hurry. *Please?*"

"Okay," I agree hanging up to rush out of the bathroom.

Standing at the top of the stairs, I need to convince Selena nothing's going on so she'll leave me alone until I leave. I need to see Tyler once and for all so I can either let this go, or tell the police I know he's guilty.

Wrapped in a towel I yell, "I just have to dry my hair! I'll be down in 10 minutes," to buy myself some time.

"No prob. I'm just starting my second drink," Selena yells up from the kitchen I think.

Running for the spare room I dress quickly and throw my hair in a sloppy bun. Entering the bathroom, I have the presence of mind to start the hair dryer and rest it on the sink. Looking in the mirror, I see my face is super pale and my eyes look way too big for my little face. My eyes look somewhat crazed and way too dark against my skin.

Grabbing my purse and keys I walk gently down the stairs against the wall. Suffering only one little creak I hold my breath until I stop at the silent bottom.

Poking my head around the corner I see Selena at the breakfast bar with a magazine completely unaware of me. Opening the front door quietly to my freedom I run for my car. Locked in within seconds I pull out of Malcolm's driveway as quickly as I can.

What the *fuck* am I doing?

Suddenly overcome with nausea, I just get my door open at the first stop sign to barf up the nothing I've eaten in 2 days. Gagging and wrenching, the bile, and really, my entire stomach lining splatters on the pristine streets of Montgomery Park.

Laughing under the pressure, I gag one last time before I finally pull it together enough to drive through the goddamn stop sign.

CHAPTER 35

Barely on the expressway, my phone starts ringing. Rounding our street, my phone blasts continuously until I shut off the ringer. Seconds before I pull up to Selena's and my building, the first and second texts come through from Selena. Before I've even made it to the elevators, the first 3 texts from Malcolm beep through. Once I open Selena's door, the 4th and 5th texts from Selena jolt in my hand, and as I reach for the shoebox in her closet, the 8th text vibrates from Malcolm.

Dumping the shoebox Selena and I decided was safely away from Griffin I grab the Taser and knife and run for her front door again.

Laughing at my manic shaking, I may be a fucking idiot for meeting Tyler, but I'm not a *total* fucking idiot.

Running back to my car safely locked in, I decide I need to tell them something. Quickly drafting my joint text to Selena and Malcolm I type all I can.

'I have to meet someone, but I'm safe. I can't talk now, but I'll tell you everything soon. I'm sorry if I've worried you but I have to do this.'

'WHAT THE FUCK ARE YOU DOING?' Almost laughing I KNOW that text was from Selena because Malcolm doesn't talk to me like that.

'WHERE THE FUCK ARE YOU?!' Huh. I guess he does talk to me like that, I burst out laughing after reading Malcolm's text. Feeling almost hysterical, or mental, or just out of my goddamn mind, I reply once more to try to calm them a little.

'I'll text you both soon. I'm shutting off my phone now. But I'm safe, I promise.'

Nearly throwing up again, I toss my cell and start my car for Blenders.

Driving a little erratically I'm nervous Tyler isn't still waiting. I'm nervous he left, but I'm nervous he's stayed. Basically, I want to see him to finish this, and I don't want to see him because we're finished.

Fuck me... I don't know what the fuck I want anymore.

Driving down Market Street I see Tyler in the distance. Leaning against the wall, he steps forward and back as each Sunday night slow moving car passes. Leaning and shaking his head it isn't until I pull over across the street to watch him that he finally jolts from the wall when he recognizes my car.

Running toward me, I quickly slap the lock button again as my heart races. Shaking all over, I watch him dash the hundred yards to me and stop just short in the road. With his hands raised out front of his body, Tyler looks desperate, and I *feel* desperate.

God, there are so many things, and so much history, and so much life unfinished before us. There are goodbyes to have and forgiveness to be sought. There's an entire life I have to say goodbye to with Tyler.

Walking the last few feet, Tyler begs me with his eyes but says nothing. Waiting for me to either acknowledge him or not Tyler knows not to push me or try to force something I don't want to do. He knows me, and as I stare at his red eyes I realize I know him too.

And Tyler didn't hurt me.

Suddenly exhaling a hard cry straight from my heart I break our eye contact to try to get my shit together.

My entire world has just shifted again and I'm nauseous from these constant changes within and around me.

Tyler didn't hurt me.

Holy. *Shit.* I was wrong.

Lying across my steering wheel I'm sobbing with both relief and confusion still. God, I was so sure. I was SO sure it was Tyler who hurt me when he spoke yesterday. I heard his voice and I felt the abuse and I remembered... but now I know I remembered nothing accurate.

Turning my head, Tyler is hunched down with his forearms on my window ledge and door sobbing. He's watching me crying, crying himself, and I don't know what to do.

"I didn't hurt you, Saige," I hear his sad voice through the closed window. "I *couldn't* do that to you," he cries harder until I finally nod my belief in him.

Unsure of what we do now, I take in Tyler and wish I could just hug him. I wish he was my old Tyler and I wish I was my old Saige. I wish we were who we were so we could comfort each other. But I know we're not those people anymore. The old Tyler left me, and this is the new Saige I've become.

"We're not us anymore, and we can never go back," I mumble through the window to him crying again in a quick burst of pain. "I'll tell Mathers I was wrong, Tyler," I acknowledge before lowering my window just enough so he can hear me clearly. "I'll tell Mathers I made a mistake," I sigh.

"Can I sit in your car for a minute? I won't touch you. I swear, Saige. I just don't feel safe in the street like this," Tyler begs actually looking left and right on the street.

"Why?"

"Can I please talk to you?" Waiting, Tyler doesn't move, and I can't decide. Waiting, he knows me and I know him. So nodding, I exhale hard as he walks slowly around my car to the passenger side door.

Slowly, and with his hands still kind of out front of his body, Tyler doesn't even go for the door handle but just waits for me to let him in.

Grabbing the Taser from the center console, I keep it against the door in my left hand and finally unlock for Tyler as he opens the door and slowly sits inside almost gently.

"Thank you," he chokes not looking at me at all. "God, I miss you," he moans unexpectedly making me cringe in my seat.

"That isn't why I let you in, Tyler."

"I know," he turns to me finally. "But I had to say it. Cheating on you was the biggest mistake of my life. And I miss you every single day. I love you so much, Saige."

Leaning over quickly, Tyler kisses me before I know how to react. With his lips against mine, I fall into old Saige. I feel his mouth against me and I know his breath within me. This is my old Tyler, but I'm *not* my old Saige.

Pulling away abruptly, I actually hit the door as he moans staring at my face. Sitting away from me, Tyler whispers, "I love you."

Not acknowledging his words, I pull my shit together. "What do you need to tell me? Just spit it out or get out. I've pissed off a lot of people to come see you, so please speak."

"Okay... Um, I'm pretty sure Kyle and Kaitlyn set this up on purpose."

"So?" I almost gag hearing her name.

"So, I think they purposely did this so they could each have us."

"So? I don't like or want Kyle. I never did. So his plan didn't work-*hers* did though. *Didn't* it?" I bitch a little angrily thinking of them together while thinking of Tyler just kissing me with growing disgust.

"But they wanted-"

Cutting off Tyler's excuses I speak over him. "Whether they intentionally tried to break us up or not doesn't matter. You fell for it and slept with her and we broke up. And that's the end of everything between us as far as I'm concerned."

"I know I did but-"

"There's no but, Tyler. No matter what they wanted you fell for whatever they were doing, and you broke my heart and broke us up. So what does it matter if they set it up? It doesn't matter what they tried to do, it only matters what *you* did. And you chose to fall for her."

"Saige, would you just listen to me for a fucking minute," Tyler suddenly growls turning so quickly in his seat I jump. "Kaitlyn and I aren't together anymore, and-"

"I don't give a shit if you're together or not."

"I know," he shakes his own head. Looking back at the road, Tyler looks absolutely exhausted, which I guess he would be after spending a night in jail. But I think there's more, so I stay silent until he can tell me the more.

"Kaitlyn's pregnant," he whispers loud as a scream in my head and heart. "It was an accident and I don't even know if it's mine, but she won't take a paternity test until after it's born because she doesn't want to endanger the baby. But- what do I do, Saige? Tell me what I do."

"You get out of my car, Tyler," I manage to say before covering my mouth so he can't hear the misery in my voice. Nearly screaming inside, I'm so hurt by this I'm pissed at Tyler for telling me, and pissed at myself for still caring enough that this even hurts me. "Get out of my car, Tyler."

Reaching for my hand, I rip it away and actually lift the Taser toward him making him smash back quickly against the door in shock. "What the fuck, Saige?"

Laughing at his horrified face, I smirk, "Yes, what the fuck? Cool, huh? And I swear to fucking god if you don't get out of my car I'll use it on you. I fucking *hate* you, Tyler. So much, I can't believe I ever thought there was more to you than what I see now. You're such a loser. And the greatest thing you ever did for me was cheat on me and free me from what I thought was a good relationship."

"We *did* have a good relationship!" He yells leaning close to me.

"Ty!" I scream against his mouth when he's suddenly pulling the back of my head and my body toward him again. "NO!" I scream against his mouth fighting hard until he quickly releases me. "Get the fuck out NOW!" I scream again lifting the Taser right up to his face as he snaps back against the door and struggles with the handle to open it.

Quickly shouldering the door, Tyler lands half on the door and half outside trying to get away from my fury. "Saige! *Wait!*" He tries again.

"If you *ever* kiss me again I'll have Malcolm beat the fucking shit out of you!"

"Malcolm? *Really?* The guy who has cops threaten to kill me if I talk to you again? The guy who pinned me against the wall yesterday and threatened to kill me as soon as I got out of jail today if I said even one fucking word to you in the restaurant? THAT fucking guy?" Tyler yells back leaning in my car by the door.

"Yup! *That* guy," I snap sarcastically.

"I love you, Saige, and I made a huge fucking mistake. That's all. I didn't hurt you and I never meant for this to end us. I just thought-"

"You could fuck someone and I'd stick around?" I ask laughing again.

"Please don't hate me, Saige. I can't stand the thought of you hating me. I'm sorry I kissed you, Lovey. I'm sorry-"

"Fuck off, Tyler. *This* is our final goodbye. I'm going home to Malcolm now. I'll tell Mathers I made a mistake, but that's it for us. I *never* want to see you again. Fuck off and die," I laugh at his shocked face before actually putting my car in drive with an *I dare you* smile as he still holds my door leaning half inside.

"I love you, Saige," Tyler says dramatically before slowly closing the door and actually pressing his palm against the glass. Like some cheesy chick-flick he stares at my eyes and keeps his hand in place against the glass probably hoping I reciprocate and place my hand against his. But it's not gonna happen.

Gunning my old lady engine, I drive away from Tyler for the very last time. Leaving him as he walks a step in the street, I peel further away from his reflection in my rearview mirror. Reaching his hand out to me in the street he looks like the pathetic loser Selena always said he was.

Laughing and crying, I reach for my phone, plug in my USB and search for an old favorite of mine. Laughing again when Pearl Jam surrounds me, I find the song I want and scream sing along with Eddie Vedder. I've never seen things so much clearer than watching Tyler in the street from my rearview mirror.

'Rearview Mirror' by Pearl Jam is the very last memory of Tyler I ever want to remember. Seeing him standing in the street he looks like some lovelorn hopeless romantic desperately begging me to love him, begging me to forgive him. Scream singing in my car, "I gather speed from you fuckin' with me," I laugh-cry louder just aching for Malcolm.

I know there is nothing to forgive and nothing to love anymore with Tyler. The memories I have of Tyler are tainted by his excuses and his choices. And we're done.

Smiling, I realize I have a whole life waiting for me with Malcolm, and I want to finally live it.

Pulling up to my old apartment again, I just need one moment to myself. I need to settle before I take on Selena and Malcolm's anger. I need to get my story straight, and I need to call Mathers before I go to Selena and Malcolm sanely.

Walking inside my abandoned apartment, still somewhat messy and destroyed, I'm surprised by how little I feel here. Though surrounded by my own things, I feel like it all belongs to someone else. I feel like this was a lifetime ago, and a life ago.

Looking around, I realize I don't care about anything anymore but Malcolm. Without any further doubt I know I love him totally.

I want to live with Malcolm by my side now. I want to love him and live with him and grow with him together. I want to know his warmth, and I want to love his life wrapped around me always.

I want Malcolm forever.

Turning on my phone quickly, the endless texts beep through like a manic orchestra of desperation. Opening up the texts I see many from Malcolm, and I know everything loving, sad, hurt, and scared he's feeling for me without even reading them.

Texting, I say all I can.

'I love you, Malcolm. I'm so sorry if I worried you, but I needed to be sure, and now I'm sure. I want you to know I trust you totally, and I'll be home soon. xo'

Scrolling through my limited contacts list I dial Mathers' cell ignoring a text that beeps through as I tell Mathers everything. With few interruptions, I let him know I made a mistake accusing Tyler.

Apologizing for the drama, Mathers tells me to go home because he's still actively looking for my assailant. Mathers explains because I saw someone outside Malcolm's home yesterday just a few hours before I finally had my showdown with Tyler, it's almost logical my brain confused Tyler as my attacker when I was so emotionally vulnerable.

Mathers even offers me a kindness by saying it's common for victims of abuse to mistake others as their abusers under stress, and not to worry about accusing Tyler for now.

And then I'm done.

Grabbing a few textbooks from the floor, straightening my couch and throwing leftover clothes in the bottom of the closet, I turn to look at my temporary life for the last time before closing and locking the door for my new life with Malcolm.

(mis)TRUST

CHAPTER 36

Ignoring my ringing phone, I shut it down and drive in silence back to Malcolm and Montgomery Park. I don't want to talk on the phone and I don't want to miss Malcolm's anger. I deserve all he wants to give me, and hopefully after I explain why I snuck out he'll forgive me.

No matter what though, I had to know about Tyler, and now I do. He wasn't my attacker and I suddenly feel sane and at peace with that knowledge. Knowing the truth of the man I loved for years is worth the anger of the man I *want* to love for years.

Smiling as peace finally settles deep in my heart, I prepare for all his anger and his love as I drive home to Malcolm.

*****

Pulling out front, I make a mad dash for Malcolm, until stepping out from the side of the garage and walkway Kyle scares the shit out of me. "Saige?" Kyle says as I gasp.

Grabbing my pounding chest, I startle from the shock of finally seeing him again. "What are you doing here? Don't tell me... They called you to start looking for me again?" I laugh a huff from my scare.

"Yup," Kyle smiles. "You're always disappearing, Saige," he kind of smirks walking closer to me.

Nodding, I try to explain. "I had to talk to Tyler, and I know now he didn't hurt me," I exhale the relief of that knowledge again.

Exhaling deeply, Kyle seems relieved as well. "I know he didn't."

"I was so sure, but then I talked to him..." Looking at Kyle, he has such a smirky look on his face, I'm instantly weirded out. Thinking quick, I wonder how he knows Tyler didn't hurt me. Maybe he talked to Tyler or maybe Selena told him what I was doing? Maybe-

Grabbing my arm hard, Kyle spins me away from the front walkway. "Do NOT speak. And don't scream or fight, Saige. I have to tell you what's going on, and I can't do it here." Trying to tug my arm I just open my mouth to scream when Kyle squeezes me so hard, I'm stunned

369

silent. Crying out, my face is immediately covered by his hand as I kick his shin and start wailing on him as best as I can.

This is soooo not happening. NOT Kyle. Oh, *fuck...* I hear my own shocked moans under his hand.

Lifting me by his arm around my waist, Kyle keeps my mouth covered and fights me fighting him right out of Malcolm's driveway. Screaming and kicking, my hands desperately try to rip his arm off my ribs when he squeezes even tighter until there's no air left in my lungs at all.

Thrashing in his arms, I eventually make contact with his face. When I feel the explosion of impact on the back of my head with his chin, he too almost falls forward from the pain.

Growling in my ear, Kyle says the only thing that will make me listen. "If you fight me before I can talk to you Malcolm is dead. So calm the fuck down until I can explain. Keys," he says finally as I hand them over.

Carried by my waist to my car, my feet still can't reach the ground, and with no purchase I'm at his mercy for now. Opening my door quickly as he drops me to the street Kyle actually shoves me over the passenger seat as he pushes in behind me punching my ass so hard my eyes sting.

"Drive the fucking car away from here or he's dead," Kyle adds with such hatred my shaking hands take my keys from his hand and start my car immediately.

"What's happening?" I choke as the shakes hit my whole body. Leaving the curb I drive knowing this is bad, but I'm unsure which is worse- fighting to help Malcolm, or leaving with Kyle to help Malcolm? I don't know what I'm supposed to do.

"Saige, you are in *so* much trouble."

"What? *Why?*"

"He wants you so badly, and he's never gonna stop. I tried to help you though- I told him you were nobody he needed. I told him you were alone, and didn't love anyone. But he-"

"*Who*?!" I scream trying to get Kyle to focus.

"I tried to help you but... do you love that guy Malcolm?" Kyle asks so suddenly in a weird kind of dreamy voice, I don't know what answer is the right one. Looking over and back at the road, I don't know what to say. "It's better if you do," he exhales slowly and I'm so confused I'm wordless. "Saige?"

"Yes..." I whisper kind of holding my body tight in case that was the wrong answer.

Turning in the seat to look at me, Kyle leans forward and suddenly hits the side my face with an opened hand as I cry out hitting the window with my shoulder.

"Drive straight!" He roars as my mind fractures.

"What are you doing, Kyle?" Begging, I try anything. "I helped you. I was the cutie redhead who helped you, remember?"

Laughing in a quick hard snap, Kyle raises his hand again as I flinch away afraid. "I know you did. And I waited for fucking ever for Tyler to be out of the picture. For. Fucking. *Ever.* And then that asshole swoops in and takes you away from me. I was totally ignored after being your Knight in shining armor. Remember *that*? But fuck it. You're a fucking whore anyway!" When I flinch again at his yelling, Kyle starts laughing. "Like your pussy eaten, Saige?" *WHAT?!* "Really? On a fucking kitchen counter? I didn't realize you were such a slut or I would've made my move sooner," he laughs obnoxiously again.

"That was you yesterday?" Speaking my outrage I try to picture the outline of the man outside yesterday.

"Nope. It wasn't me, but I saw a picture," he laughs again as I cry out shocked and humiliated and so fucking afraid of Kyle suddenly, my mind is fighting just to drive straight like he demanded.

Finally gasping back to the present in my car, I beg, "Who took a picture of us?"

"You'll see, and I'm really sorry about all this, but you're important to him. I only wanted to check up on you last night like I always do. But guess what I had to see? A picture of your fucking pussy on a kitchen counter like a cheap whore. Tell me, Saige, did Malcolm pay you for your services, or were you just working off room and board?" Laughing his ass off at his joke, I really don't know what to do.

I'm driving as slowly away from Montgomery Park as I can trying to understand what's happening and what'll happen. Who took the picture of us if it wasn't Kyle? Who the *hell* am I important to?

"Turn THERE!" Kyle screams when we drive near a kid's park. Named Mulberry Park, it's too sweet and cute, and just totally fucked up under my current circumstances.

Turning, I have a quick thought of accelerating and smashing into a tree like I've seen in the movies. I didn't get my seatbelt on when I was forced inside though, so unlike the movies, I'll probably end up just as hurt as Kyle does.

WHAT. THE. *FUCK*. DO. I. DO?

"Stop there," he points to the end of the parking lot. With only 2 other cars I drive past, we're basically alone next to trees on one end and empty spaces beside us.

Shaking so hard my teeth start chattering, I fight this crazy to try to calm Kyle. I can freak the fuck out later, but right now I need answers and I need Kyle to remember who I am to him.

"Kyle..." I whisper as he stares at me. "You were a good friend at school, and I need your help. Please tell me what's happening? Why are you so mad at me?" I beg in a whisper keeping eye contact which Kyle holds.

Suddenly choking up, Kyle groans and looks outside. "I was a good friend?" He asks not looking back at me.

"Yes... I loved studying with you." Fighting the shakes and my fear, I continue trying to soothe him. "I helped you study and you helped me when I didn't know what to do with myself that night. Um, you are-"

"Nothing to you," Kyle says so sadly I almost *feel* his sadness.

"No, you *are* a friend to me. You, and Mike, and Selena are the only friends I have." Purposely leaving Malcolm out of this conversation, I hope I'm convincing enough. I hope he believes me, and I hope I can get out of this.

Turning to look at me, Kyle's eyes are shining with tears. "Well, I guess then you *mis*trusted me, huh? Is that what you think now?"

"No, never. I think something's going on and you're trying to tell me about it. What is it, Kyle? I need you to help me like you did when I needed your help a few months ago."

Actually placing my hand on his, I barely hold in my repulsion at my fake tenderness. I actually want to punch him in the face, but instead I soothe him. And nearly laugh at my sudden reality.

Holy *shit!* Kyle has kidnapped me, knows who hurt me, hit my face, and called me a whore. Yet here I am telling him we're friends still and I need his help again.

Screaming when Kyle suddenly tackles me in my seat, he's all over me tearing at me, trying to kiss me as I struggle under him. Ripping my shirt, he grabs my chest hard and bites my lips until I cry out. Forcing a hand down my jeans as I fight him with everything I have, Kyle pushes me harder into the seat with his weight.

When I hear the quick bumping sound of my seat crashing backward,

Kyle digs his knee right into my thigh as he tries to climb over me under the steering wheel as I fight him.

Thrashing my head back and forth, my hands are punching and pushing and pulling at his clothing. I'm kneeing him with one leg and punching his chest with my fists.

Screaming as loud as I can, I suddenly have one horrifying moment of clarity. With a shock of sadness deep in my soul I know this end and I know I can live with my choice. I know I have to stop this this time if I ever want to save what's left of my mind.

Reaching quickly in my door well, I feel and turn it in my hand. Moving quickly I Tase the shit out of Kyle's chest watching him snap back in such a strange back-breaking arch, he's on the passenger seat a moment later. Fighting still, I follow his body and keep Tasing with tears pouring down my face until Kyle stops moving completely but for weird involuntary jerks of his torso.

Pausing for one moment in shock, I actually reach past him, scared shitless he'll come to and grab me like in every horror movie I've ever seen. Nothing happens though as I unlock and push his door open.

Leaning, I use whatever strength I have left and shove Kyle out of my car. Falling head first, his torso slumps on the ground and honestly I'm scared his neck is going to be hurt but then I push his legs out of the car as well with a loud grunt until his legs rest sideways away from the door.

Holy. *Shit.*

I've lost what was left of my fucking mind this weekend. And I still have NO answers.

Slamming the door, I peel out of the park laughing hysterically, crying crazily, shaking uncontrollably.

Dialing quickly, I say all I can once the operator turns me over to a police officer who immediately asks my emergency.

"My name is Saige Masters and I've Tased a man named Kyle Murphy unconscious in Mulberry Park in Montgomery Park. He kidnapped me and just tried to rape me in my car. But I saved myself and got him out and now I'm driving to Malcolm MacNeil's house at 464 Orchard Ave."

When he starts asking questions, I cut him off quickly. "Detective Mathers knows me, so please call him. I'm on my way to Malcolm's in case something's wrong. And Kyle knows who raped me in April. He was going to tell me, but then he attacked me and I had to stop him."

Again with the interruption. *Fuck!*

"*Listen* to me! I was attacked and Mathers knows all about me! Call him and come get Kyle from the fucking park! I'm not the bad person here, and I'm trying to get *home!*"

Screaming the word home kind of clears out my head. Hanging up on the police feels good. Exhaling as I peel through the calm Sunday night streets of Montgomery Park is relaxing... in a psychotic sort of way.

I'm suddenly so calm I know exactly what I have to do.

I'm going home to Malcolm and I'm going to let him be mad at me for being careless and foolish and for letting myself get a little hurt again tonight. I'll let Malcolm be mad at me at first and then I'll beg him to forgive me until he does.

Malcolm loves me, I smile for the first time in forever.

Looking in the mirror, I wipe my mouth of the little trail of blood I didn't notice, and I fix my clothes as best as I can. My shirt was torn at my shoulder, and there's a noticeable mark around my neck I don't remember getting. But other than my crazed looking eyes, and super pasty skin I think I can downplay this a little so Malcolm doesn't go off the rails because I allowed myself to get hurt again.

Sending another quick text I tell Malcolm I'm almost home. I know I'm breaking the law texting and driving, but what the hell? I've Tased someone tonight, so texting while speeding seems like a minor infraction at this point.

Bursting out laughing again, I can't believe this is my life.

*****

Spotting the police lights down Malcolm's road, the fear is immediate. My hands are instantly shaking and my heart is thumping so painfully in my chest, I don't know how I continue driving. I can't breathe and I can't see anything beyond the chaos of lights and sound.

What the hell is happening? Am I being arrested?

Pulling up 4 houses down, the police have blocked access to the road. Opening my door, I pause for one shocked moment before my legs start running for Malcolm's house.

Screaming, I run as fast as I can until I'm nearly tackled by a police officer holding me at the end of Malcolm's driveway.

"I LIVE here! What *HAPPENED?!*" I scream in a broken voice as my mind shatters. "Oh *god...*" I feel myself collapse in unknown arms as I watch more police enter and paramedics exit in a slow motion nightmare before me.

Pausing as the world spins around me, I watch the large body on the gurney wheeled by 2 paramedics to the waiting ambulance. Watching, I hear no sounds, and I see nothing except the man straddling Malcolm's huge chest.

Totally numb, I hear no one speaking to me as I watch Malcolm die in his driveway.

"What happened?" I whisper to the person holding me back.

Sitting crossed legged, my mind fractures as I watch Malcolm's body jump on the gurney from paddles as they all step away quickly. Watching him jolt, I see nothing but his hand fall off the gurney to rest awkwardly off the side.

I actually see Malcolm's hand reaching for me so I crawl to him immediately.

Ignoring the voices and words in the background of my mind, I crawl to Malcolm's hand. Screaming at the hands holding me back, eventually I'm left alone to kneel at his side. Taking his huge hand into my own I gasp a cry so heavy, I know neither of us will survive the night.

Wiping away the blood, I kiss and squeeze the hand that has given me nothing but love and kindness since the day I met him. I kiss Malcolm's cold hand and feel my world end with his.

"I love you," I finally tell Malcolm as he's ripped from my hand by the moving gurney.

Watching him lifted and carried away from me I don't move. There's nowhere to go and nothing left for me anyway.

Realizing the end of everything between us, I rest on my knees in Malcolm's driveway and hope for a quick release from this life of constant loss.

I know I'll never live through another one, so all I can hope is death takes me soon.

(mis)TRUST

CHAPTER 37

"Saige?" I hear her voice and though I feel one quick moment of relief, it's just as quickly washed away with Malcolm being driven from me very fast down the street. "Saige? Can you hear me?" She asks again louder than the remaining sounds, and the fading lights and sirens of Malcolm's end.

When there is no more Malcolm to see, I turn and raise my eyes to a haunted looking Selena. Crouching down low with her hand's on her knees she's covered in blood.

"Is that Malcolm's?" I ask absently.

"What?" She questions.

"The blood. Is that Malcolm's blood all over you?" Nearly laughing for some absurd reason, I look back at Malcolm's front door to all the police still around. "Why are you alive, Selena?"

"What?" She asks again in a voice that sounds horribly distorted in my head.

"Oh, I'm glad you are," I acknowledge quickly before inhaling deeply all the pain in my chest. "But I love you."

"What do you mean, Saige?" Selena asks touching my shoulder until I shrug her away.

Exhaling slowly, I see everything in front of me. Blood trails, and noise, and people everywhere disturbing Malcolm's beautiful house. Like a red wine stain on a white carpet, his home is forever stained by his death.

"Well, I love you, so I'm surprised you're still alive, Selena," I burst out laughing. Feeling my mind completely break, I laugh until I fall forward on my face then fall to my side to curl up into a ball of madness. "You're gonna be next," I laugh crazily until it slowly changes to those fucked up laugh/tears everyone knows when their heart is broken and their mind is shattered.

"I'm alive because Malcolm stood in front of me, took bullets for me, and screamed for me to get to safety. I'm alive because Malcolm wanted me to live- because he wanted *you* to live."

"He *went to the death*," I whisper in Malcolm's Scottish brogue remembering him describe his father's love for his wife. "He went to the death for me," I whisper again numb with my heartache.

"Saige? You have to snap out of this now. Malcolm is still alive and we have to get to the hospital. The police are waiting to get my statement at the hospital and they're waiting to take us to him."

"You go."

"We're both going," she pushes trying to lift my dead weight.

"I'm not going just to watch him officially die, Selena. I saw him. I felt his cold hand and I told him I loved him, but he didn't squeeze my hand back like he always does. Malcolm is gone," I moan shaking my head to ease the pain in my chest.

"He's not gone yet. And you need to pull your shit together until he is. You *owe* him that."

Nodding, I know I do, but I just can't. I didn't see Alec before he died, or my father's broken remains in his car. I don't want to see this- I *can't* see Malcolm actually die.

"I can't. I can't watch this happen to another man because of me."

Growling down low in my face, Selena pulls my head up by my hair shocking me out of my numb despair. "Get your fucking scrawny ass up and come to the hospital with me- right fucking now. Malcolm might not live much longer and you're going to see him before he's dead whether you like it or not. *Your* name was the last thing he said to me before he faded away in my arms so I'm not allowing you to close down now. Get the fuck UP!"

"*Selena...*" I cry desperately.

"Saige, if he dies, you can have a complete nervous breakdown. I'll even watch out for you and care for you after that. But until he's officially dead you're getting the fuck up and getting to the hospital now. Let's go," she wrenches my arm so hard, I cry out but eventually try to move.

Standing, my head is so sloppy I list into her but continue moving. Walking with her arm wrapped around my waist tightly, I don't speak or acknowledge anyone around us even when an officer opens his cruiser door for us. I don't feel my seatbelt clipped and I don't know anything but a roaring ache deep in my chest.

"What happened?" I finally have enough sense to ask as we're driven quickly to the hospital.

"Someone knocked on the door and we thought it was you because you just sent Malcolm a text saying you were coming back. Ah, but when he ran for the door and threw it open a man stood there, handed Malcolm a photo album of yours and then just shot Malcolm," Selena moans quickly before shaking her head. Not looking over, I feel my hands shake in my lap and my breath huff against the cool glass.

"Um, Malcolm pushed me into the den and started fighting the guy as I got away. And he kept yelling for me to get away safely. He just yelled for me to be safe and to make sure you were safe," she finally bursts into tears. "He wanted me safe, and he fought so hard, but I kept hearing the gunshots going off when I ran through his house looking for somewhere to hide so I could call the police."

Finally thinking beyond my own agony, I look at Selena covered in Malcolm's blood, grey and shaken and I realize I never once thought of her. I didn't think to ask if she was okay, or if she was as fucked in the head as I am right now. I saw her, but I couldn't feel beyond my own nightmare to ask my friend if she's okay after going through what she has.

"Are you okay?" I whisper to her nearly silent *no.*

After a moment of silence, Selena attempts to take my hand but I pull away. There's a sick part of me that honestly believes she's next to die so I don't want to love her anymore.

"Where's Griffin?"

"With Dave."

"You need to have the police check on them to make sure Griffin is okay, because I love him, too."

"Griffin is going to be fine, this-"

Turning my head to her finally, I scream uncontrollably. "He's NOT going to be fine. You're going to be dead soon and so is Griffin!"

Feeling the car stopped suddenly, the 2 officers turn right around to face us through the cage.

"Call somebody to check on Griffin! Please? Call it in. Selena, tell them Dave's address! *Please?!*" I scream psychotically.

"Saige! Griffin isn't going to die! What the fuck?" She yells grabbing me up in her arms again.

"Yes, he is," I moan broken. Thinking of his sweet little face, and his morning bedhead, and all his stupid shows, I know he's going to die. "I love him so he's going to die. I know it," I sob uncontrollably against Selena's chest. "You're both going to die because I love you," I scream and cry feeling the car start moving again.

"I'm not going to die, Saige. I promise," Selena cries against my head.

"Just like Malcolm promised?" I moan the final words until we silence because we both know I'm right.

Lead by police escorts into the hospital, I'm ushered into an adjoining room beside the ER as Selena starts talking to 3 officers. Not even listening, I sit slowly in a chair wondering why I'm even here. I can't see Malcolm die from here and I can't say goodbye to him from this room.

I'm trapped in a room alone waiting for the inevitable.

"Saige?" Detective Mathers squats down in front of me. "How are you?" He asks so sadly, I burst into tears and actually reach for him desperately. A total stranger and a man who though always kind to me is nothing to me, I find myself holding him tightly like he'll somehow stop all this shit for me.

"Please fix this? *Please?*" I beg as he pats my back awkwardly.

Pulling away from me Mathers huffs, "I'm working on it, Saige."

Nodding, I feel totally defeated. "Did Selena see who did it? Does she know who it was? I forgot to ask her that at Malcolm's because there was so much blood and his hand was cold," I cry harder when he takes my hands in his. "Does she know who killed Malcolm?" I whisper a last breath before my lungs close completely.

"She didn't recognize him before Malcolm pushed her out of the way," he admits as I feel my sad frustration build. "But we're combing the area, and it looks like the perpetrator was bleeding by the time he left based on the blood droplets on Malcolm's driveway."

"Good. I want him dead," I gasp unsure if it's illegal or not to say that but vaguely remembering it's not. Like if my brain still functioned, I'd know that, I think.

"Kyle knows who it is. He was going to tell me but then he attacked me in my car. Ah, I hurt him to get away. Did you get the call?"

"Yes, and Kyle's already been transported to the hospital. He's conscious, so the Officers on scene are asking him questions."

"I trusted Kyle once," I huff still confused by Kyle's part in all this. "I don't think he attacked me in April. But I don't understand how he knows who did it but didn't stop him or tell you, or- Detective Mathers? I'm honestly losing my mind I think," I end my little rant to his silence.

"She's his girlfriend," Selena suddenly points breaking up Mathers and my conversation as a bloody nurse rushes for me ripping off her surgical gown.
"Mr. MacNeil is being prepped for surgery, but we can allow a minute for you?" She asks as I freeze.
"*Saige!* Move your ass and go see him," Selena yells at me again as I stand quickly with Mathers' help.
Following the nurse just feet inside the busy triage I'm astounded by all the blood and instruments and chaos around Malcolm's stillness. The room seems so loud and chaotic, but Malcolm is so still he already seems like a ghost in the room.
"You need to prepare for the worst."
"Oh, I already have," I respond quickly. "I know he's going to die," I choke the words as she looks at me sadly. "It's okay, they always die on me," I touch her forearm briefly before walking through crap all over the floor, and bloody clothing and shit everywhere.
Leaning over Malcolm's huge body, grey and bloodied with patches and wounds all over him I can't understand what's been done to him. His whole upper body looks shattered like glass, bleeding from everywhere in ragged lines still pouring over his sides. I can't even tell if he's alive anymore though all the noisy machines and people waiting suggest he is for now.
Kissing his bloody forehead just once, ignoring the breathing mask and his closed eyes, I whisper everything left of us.
"I'm sorry I didn't trust you sooner or love you better. I'm so sorry I loved you, but if you survive this I promise I'll never love you again." Taking his cold hand, I beg him for everyone else. "Listen to me, Malcolm... everyone loves you because you're so beautiful, and so *so* special, so they need you to get better now," I gently kiss his head again. "Yer a fine wee lad," I brogue softly in his ear with a little grin for us. "And I'll never love another," I finally sob as a nurse touches my back to move me away. "Good bye sweet, sweet, Mallie," I whisper against his chest before he's wheeled away from me forever.

In my silence, doctors say things and nurses reassure. People talk and police watch. Everything continues as they take Malcolm away from me for the last time.

And still I stand as all the noise fades with Malcolm. I stand through my horror and I stand through my agony. Malcolm is gone, in life or in death, and I swear to any god listening if Malcolm survives this I will never love him again.

*****

"Saige?" Selena whispers holding my shaking body from behind where I stand frozen in silence. Crying snotty, soundless tears, I let her know I did what I should've always done. "I let him know I loved him... and I said goodbye to him."

Squeezing me tighter, Selena cries louder than me. She cries and shakes until I hold her hands against my chest to comfort her. I hold her holding me until there's nothing left of Malcolm's life in the cold bloody room we died in.

I know he's gone because he's faded away from me totally. And it was so quick- from love to death in a heartbeat it seems.

Feeling his life faded from mine, it's time for me to leave.

"I need to leave now, because he's gone," I whisper when Selena's crying calms.

"I'm going to the police station to make a statement, and you're having a police escort until they find whoever did this, Saige. You're going to be set up in a hotel temporarily until they find him."

"And you?"

"I'm going to Dave's parent's house in Lancaster for a few days."

Nodding against her chin, I'm relieved. "That's good, Selena. You need to be safe and you need to keep Griffin safe."

"We'll be safe."

"Okay. Um, what do I do now?" I pull away from her arms finally. Looking at Mathers and another officer by the door, I don't know what to do anymore.

"Come with us, Saige. Selena's going to the Precinct and we'll take you to a hotel," Mathers offers gently as I nod silently.

*****

Following Mathers out a short hallway with Selena and the other Officers, we push through a set of doors to another nightmare.

Leaning against the wall Tatum jumps forward and Moira cries loudly beside her husband looking at Selena covered in blood.

Actually as I turn quickly to Selena I wonder absurdly if she tried to keep Malcolm alive until the paramedics arrived. I'm sure she did and that explains why she's covered in his blood, but I didn't think to ask, and I didn't understand why she was so bloody until now.

"Saige?" Moira cries walking toward me until I raise my hand for her to stop.

Looking at her then over to Tatum, my heart is absolutely broken. "He's going to die, and I'm so, so sorry. I begged him to stay alive for you though, then I said goodbye for you all. I told him he was special and I kissed him goodbye..." I whisper holding my aching heart with my hand.

"Saige, what happened?" Tatum asks walking towards me leaning down low. "Are you okay?"

"No..." Looking up at Tatum the pain of their loss hits me so hard I actually stagger forward under the weight of it. They all love Malcolm so much this is going to destroy their entire family.

"Are your parents coming?"

"Alec's on his way. And Dan's picking up my parents."

Nodding, I have only one thing left to say as the pain overwhelms me. "I'm so sorry, Tatum. For you and for the rest of your family. I wish I had never met Malcolm so none of this would've happened to him. I wish-"

"Aw, Saige," Tatum tugs me right into his arms lifting me from the floor for the world's biggest hug. "Malcolm doesn't wish that, and even if he dies," Tatum chokes in a broken voice as he places me back on the floor, "He wouldn't regret one single day with you- even if this is his last. You're his fiery wee leprechaun, and he loved you-"

"To the death," I finish for Tatum as Moira sobs an uncontrollable sound that shatters my heart. "I have to go. Please extend my apologies to your parents and to the rest of your family. I'm so sorry," I cry turning before Tatum can hug me again.

Begging Mathers with my eyes he nods subtly as we start moving quickly down the hall through another waiting room filled with people. Ignoring all the stares at Selena, I follow closely behind Mathers to my freedom from Malcolm's death.

*****

After making the report about everything Kyle said and did to me I was left alone until tomorrow.

Walking toward the shower in my hotel room, I'm so cold my bones are chilled. I couldn't eat the food brought to my room, and I didn't want to talk to anyone before I was unceremoniously locked in.
I only want to shower quickly and sleep forever.
Honestly, I just want this nightmare to end the minute Malcolm's does.

Wrapping myself in the thick heavy bathrobe I sit on the tub ledge and sigh a weary heartache so powerful I can no longer move. I'm stuck in my agony and drowning in my sadness waiting to hear of his death.

Finding the strength to get to the bed, I shut off my phone and wrap myself in every blanket I can find. I know I'll never be warm again, but I need to at least try. I have to try until I'm officially told there's no longer a reason to try.

Unable to cry any more of my misery, I imagine Malcolm holding me tightly in his arms for the very last time. I imagine his warmth and weep wishing I had told him everything he was, and everything he'll always be to me before it was too late.
I now know and truly understand, the biggest regret I will always have, the deepest *sorrow*, and the only thing I'll never forgive of myself in this life- I wish I had loved him sooner so he had all my love at his end, like I had his love all along.

CHAPTER 38

Waking again, I don't want to try anymore. My moments of sleep are filled with blood and agony, and my body is suffering from them. I keep gasping away, or suffering the falling sensation as I lurch awake on a gasped cry. No matter how many times I try though, I can't forget Malcolm's hand hanging awkwardly off his deathbed in his driveway.

I felt his cold, and I knew his death first hand. I felt the end, and I felt the very absence of him squeezing me back since the moment of our first non-date date.

He always squeezes my hand or my leg. *Always.* It's Malcolm's thing, and something I'm going to miss for the rest of my life.

It's something I always knew with Malcolm but didn't appreciate when I had it. It was Malcolm- squeezing me to let me know he was always there for me.

It's such a funny little thing. It wasn't cheesy roses, or constant confessions of love. But it *was* love. Honestly and innocently.

Malcolm was love for me, and I didn't know enough to appreciate his little squeezes when I had them. It's only now in their absence that I see Malcolm so clearly.

And he really was love.

Malcolm was huge to my small, and strong to my weak. He was dark to my light, and relaxed to my intense. He was my Malcolm to his Saige.

Rolling over again, I reach for water and wipe my eyes again.

I'm not going to survive this, I know. Like knowledge you can't understand the source of, I *do* know this to be absolutely true. Both Malcolm and I are going to die soon, one physically and one emotionally, but twin deaths nonetheless.

There is nothing left. And no one to love. And I don't want to live anyway.

Flipping back over, scrubbing my eyes and face, I can't feel this anymore. I can't do it, and I won't.

My mother is fine with her Scottish Rite friends, and Selena and Dave are slowly working their way back to each other with sweet Griffin in between them. Even Mike is still young enough to find love once he settles down a little.

Holy *fuck*... If I thought Tyler's betrayal was painful- THIS is an agony I can't even explain.
This pain lashes at me and steals my breath. It rips apart my skin and claws away my mind. It imprisons me in its constant intensity.
This is unequivocal, and unequalled, and unimaginable pain.
This is death taking me slowly.

Reaching for my phone, I shouldn't do this but I can't stop myself. I need his words, and I need his humor.
Even angry and scared our last night alive I know Malcolm somehow gave me his humor to bring me home to him. I *know* he did, because he always has.

Scrolling to my 2nd last text, I read his replies one after another before my heart actually stops beating in my chest.

'I have to meet someone, but I'm safe. I can't talk now, but I'll tell you everything soon. I'm sorry if I've worried you but I have to do this.'
'WHAT THE FUCK ARE YOU DOING?'
'WHERE THE FUCK ARE YOU?!' Reading Malcolm's frantic reply, it still makes me smile slightly. He was never that insane with me unless he saw me hurt or believed I could be.
'I'll text you both soon. I'm shutting off my phone now. But I'm safe, I promise.' After I shut down my phone, Malcolm send one more text I didn't know about but now read in agony.
'Please, Saige. Tell me where you are so I can come get you?! I'm dying here. I'm not mad, I just want you safe. PLEASE come home now. PLEASE come home to me, and we'll do whatever you have to do together so I know you're safe. I won't argue with you and I'll stay quiet if you want but PLEASE COME BACK TO ME!'

After that last text when I was dealing with Tyler in my car, Malcolm sent many more texts to me.

'Saige. Please baby. Selena and I are scared to death. Where are you? Please tell me and I'll come get you.'

'Saige… When you get home I'm going to spank the shit out of you. We never really discussed bedroom kinky before, but I think now is as good a time as ever. I hope you like it, because when you walk through my door, ass meets hand. Oh, and Selena says she's going to spank the shit out of you, too, which is kinda hot. 😆 Come home, Saige. Please?'

Picturing Malcolm threatening me with a spanking is too funny. I think even if I *was* into that, he couldn't do it. Malcolm's belief in a man never, *ever* raising a hand to a woman is too strong I think to participate in spanking kinks. Almost laughing, I can't even test the theory now even if I wanted to.

'Saige, I'm still waiting for you. Please come home to me. I'm so scared you're hurt and need me. I love you.'

Reading his last reply while he waited for me, I feel the fear and pain Malcolm must've felt. I understand how selfish I was, and I know I hurt him. Though unintentionally, I can actually read the pain in his words until I texted him again.

'I love you, Malcolm. I'm so sorry if I worried you, but I needed to be sure, and now I'm sure. I want you to know I trust you totally, and I'll be home soon. xo'

When I shut down my phone again frantically driving to Malcolm, I had no idea he was still texting me. I didn't know there were so many, and I didn't know how beautiful they were.

'You love me? Well, that's awesome to read. Just an FYI though, confessions of love in person are wayyyy better. Like now. Please come home. I miss you, and I need to know you're safe.'

Reading that sentence makes me smile. Even desperate he could still tease a little. *Just an FYI?* Too funny.

'Where did you go? We called Mike but he hasn't heard from you, and we even tried the last number Selena has for Tyler but it didn't pick up.'

'I'm going to keep texting since you can't freak out and ask me to stop like you would if I was speaking to you.'

'I love you Saige. ♥ ← cheesy heart, I know.'

'I love you so much, I may need alcohol and medication after how much you've scared me tonight. But when I'm sober and no longer stoned I'm going to pick you up in my arms, sit in our fireplace chair, and I'm going to hug you until you trust me and BELIEVE me. I'm going to hug you in my arms until you finally believe IN me, Saige.'

'I love you so much I'll wait for you to finish school so you can have the life YOU want. Then I'm going to ask you to be a part of the life I want WITH you. I told you before I would wait for you, and I meant it. You are so worth waiting for, Saige.'

'I look like such an ass right now. Selena's sitting near me watching me text almost crying I'm so desperate for you to come back to me.'
Reading his text, he's not the only one crying. Holy *SHIT*. This hurts so badly, I didn't think it was possible for me to hurt any more than I've been hurting waiting for his death.

'Last text, I promise. When you get home, I'm going to kiss you right against the door, Saige. I'm not mad anymore. But even if I was, I'd get over it as soon as I see you again. I want to kiss you breathless so you never again forget who loves you like you want to be loved. I'm going to kiss you until you believe I'm never going to leave you baby, because I'm NOT them and I'm NOT leaving you.'

'I want to kiss you because I want you to be my fiery wee leprechaun for the rest of my life. And I want to kiss you so you finally understand I want to be your sweet, sweet Mallie for the rest of yours.'

'Come home to me Saige so I can love you forever. xo'

And that's the end of everything Malcolm.
Oh my *god...*
I may as well be dead in a burning hell with all this pain I feel destroying my soul.

Coding multiple times through the night and following day, Selena kept sending me updates I didn't want. She kept asking for me to go to the hospital by Tatum's request, and she kept begging me to call Tatum by Dan's request.

Everyone wants me to go to the hospital- but I can't. I made a promise, and I'll keep to my bargain as long as Malcolm lives.

Whatever happens to Malcolm, nothing is going to change for me regardless. I'll never eat or sleep again, and I'll never live or love again.

Nothing is going to change no matter how many days I wait in this excruciating purgatory. Nothing is going to change the end for us no matter how many texts and phone calls I ignore.

I am alone, and my sweet, sweet Mallie is forever gone.

(mis)TRUST

CHAPTER 39

It's funny how life has a way of continually shocking the shit out of you when you least expect it. It's funny when you think there can be nothing darker and nothing sadder than what you already know, life finds a way to hand you more darkness. It's amazing to me that the lows can always get lower.

This isn't my lowest day though. My lowest day happened 8 days ago.

Honestly, I can't even imagine there can be lower for me, or less peace to be found in this life. Yet life continues destroying me much more slowly than I would have chosen for myself.

Sitting in the police precinct, I finally have all my answers to the insane.

Malcolm managed to shoot his assailant in the stomach before he succumbed to his own injuries. Malcolm managed to turn the gun on the bad guy though the bad guy did get away temporarily. Knowing he would be caught if he went to a hospital though my attacker curled up in his little motel room- MY old motel room I rented near campus and slept in for just one night months ago- and he died.

The sick Fuck allowed himself to slowly, apparently quite painfully, bleed out for 3 days alone in my old motel room until he was traced to the room by his rental car and found dead among all my things this morning.

Like a sick fucking psycho he died holding my stolen panties tightly in his hands against his chest among all my photos from my now empty photo albums which he plastered all over the hotel room walls. He wore my necklaces around his neck, and my rings stacked one on top of the other on his baby fingers. He surrounded himself in everything Saige Masters as he slowly bled out over 3 days dying alone in my old hotel room 5 days ago.

And no one noticed the smell of his death, or questioned the Do Not Disturb sign that didn't change on his door for 8 days until this morning.

Harvey Murphy, my brother's old cell mate and murderer died because he loved my brother.

Harvey Murphy, who I barely recognized from 7 years ago, knew *me* quite well though. He knew me and hated me for getting him convicted and sentenced to more time. And apparently he also loved me because I was the last thread to Alec he could have.

Harvey Murphy, who loved Alec Masters so much he killed him, loved me too. Whether by accident or because of what Alec did to himself doesn't really matter- Harvey Murphy never recovered from the loss of my brother.

So he came after me.

For whatever reason a sociopath sees his own reasons justified Harvey Murphy thought by fucking me, or rather *raping* me like he did my sweet brother, he still held Alec close. I was the last piece of Alec he could have, and after being released from jail in early April, he came for me a week later.

He came for me because he couldn't have Alec, and he came for me because he blamed me for Alec's death.

Unbelievably, according to the diaries he left in my old hotel room, Harvey Murphy blamed me for not only lengthening his prison sentence, but for not helping Alec continue living.

In the darkest twist of irony I've ever known, we both actually agree with each other. I, too, have always felt I didn't do enough, or say enough to make Alec live. And Harvey Murphy agreed with me.

Staring at the blank walls of the room I'm in alone, I'm waiting for my mum to come get me. Mathers and another detective whose name I can't remember have shown me the photos of my old hotel room, shown me pictures of Harvey Murphy 5 days dead in my old bed, and shown me photos of all my stuff everywhere around him in death.

They let me read a few excerpts from his diaries, and they told me about the chronological events as best as they've pieced them together quickly as to what he did over the past 3 months since I was first attacked.

Strangely, though he's dead now I still find myself scared shitless.

Harvey Murphy was everywhere around me, all the time. He ate at D'Vecseys when I was working, and he followed me to Blenders when I stood freaking out holding Malcolm until I calmed. He was everywhere always, and the thought of that alone can still make me panic.

Thinking of how close he was to me always causes such a deep freeze, I feel ice slowly crawling through my veins at the thought of all the *what ifs* and *oh my gods* that was my life for 3 months totally unaware.

After each insight Mathers explained, though obviously they're nowhere near wrapping up the investigation, I felt the ice continue slowly travelling through my veins until a shard of ice actually punctured what was left of my beating heart.

And still the lows get lower.

Harvey Murphy is the father to both Kyle and Kaitlyn Murphy- my old classmate and semi-friend, and Tyler's whore.

No one knows yet how involved they were, or if they knew about me and Alec but we all assume they did. It was no secret at school that I was Alec Masters' little sister, and it was NEVER a secret that I helped put Harvey Murphy away for an extra 10 years, reduced to 7 at the young age of 16. It was no secret everything I accomplished for Alec after his tragic death.

Nothing about me was a secret, so we all assume they knew, and even as I stare at these blank walls waiting for my mum, Kaitlyn is being picked up by the Detectives handling mine and Malcolm's case for interrogation.

We know Kyle knew, and thankfully he's already in custody because of what he did to me 8 days ago. Admitting everything he did, Kyle actually justified kidnapping me and attempting to rape me. He justified what he did, because in his sick what the fuck world *he* was the better alternative to his father- who he knew was on his way to Malcolm's to kidnap and hurt me. Kyle honestly believes he saved me that night, which is another *are you fucking kidding me* I have to live with forever.

We also assume Kaitlyn knew about me as well, though I know the truth. The filthy looks Kaitlyn gave me in my own home and the hatred she showed me I remember at the time thinking was completely misplaced. I remember thinking this bitch is crazy for hating me when I'm nothing to her. I remember thinking she was completely out of line, and totally fucked in the head hating me when she was the whore caught with a man in another woman's bed. But it all makes sense to me now.

The detectives don't yet know how or why I even met Kyle and Kaitlyn Murphy- did they follow me here to school, or was it the World's biggest coincidence? What is the likelihood I left New Haven, went to school in Midland, started a job in a restaurant nearly 3 years ago and I just happened to work with Mike, who was a friend of Kyle's. Or did Kyle befriend Mike when he saw Mike and I were friends? Or did Kaitlyn only realize I was the Saige Masters she hated when she slept with Tyler? Or did she fuck Tyler *because* she hated me? Or, or, or?

See...? Head. Fuck.

Incidentally, the timing makes sense, too- one week after her daddy was released from prison my life imploded. So I know she knew who I was, and I know Mathers knows, though he still has to investigate by the book as he said, to nail their asses properly.

As another low that had the impact of a sledgehammer against my old Saige's heart, this one reads on paper almost comical.

Tyler doesn't love Kaitlyn. They broke up he insisted to the police when they interviewed Tyler looking for Malcolm's attacker. Tyler has had nothing to do with Kaitlyn for over a month, but he did confirm he watched his whore pee on a stick that quickly turned double blue lines in front of his eyes.

So my ex-boyfriend is going to have a child with the daughter of my rapist and with the daughter of the man who murdered my brother, whether indirectly or not. Tyler is going to be a dad to the grandchild of the man who raped both me *and* Alec, which is just too funny to me to shock me any further.

I mean seriously... where does Tyler even go with that?

Holy *fuck...* I'm done.

Waiting in this quiet room playing on my phone, I'm desperate to get away and get out of here. I'm desperate for my freedom though it was offered to me, and I'm desperate for my mum though that's weird, I laugh a little stupidly.

God, I hope these aren't two-way mirrors.

I'm exhausted from the last 8 days of my life, and really from the 7 years, or if you count my dad leaving- from the last 9 years of my sad life.

I'm so mental and emotionally exhausted, I can't even get past level 81 on candy crush, I burst out laughing again.

And crying.
And moaning.
And dying.
Slowly.

*****

"Saige? Your mother is here," a police officer says just as my mum
pushes through the door.
"Ye. Daft. *Cow!*" My mum yells shocking the cop but making me laugh
again. "Why didya no tell me wha's bin happ'nin?" Grabbing my face in
her hands, she continues yelling at me through my giggles. "Didya no
think I'd help ye?!"
"I didn't know," I admit honestly as I stare at the same green eyes I
inherited.
"Well, tha's fer crap! Yer comin' home wee me, and ye better no start
any shite. Ye hear'in me?"
Looking at her, I'm just... "*Mum...*" I manage to whisper before
everything implodes inside me again. Collapsing in tears, my mum just
catches me as she slumps down in a chair to pull me into her chest. "I
can't h-handle this any m-more..." I choke dying in her arms.
"Awww... wee Saige. I've got ye now."
"They all fucking die!" I scream as the pain slashes my skin and tears
apart my soul. "They all die on me..." I choke my final words before I
silence.
"Awww...love. List'en to me. Alec died because he was afraid t' live,
and your father died because he fell asleep behind the wheel. But this
Malcolm, well, he loved ye, and fought to pro'tect ye. And from wha I
hear, it was real love tha made the fella do wha he did."
Pulling away, I'm stunned she would give any credit to Malcolm or his
love at all. "But you don't believe in love, so how could you think Mal-"
stopping myself, I can't even say his name it hurts so much.
Grinning suddenly, my mother shocks me once again. "Saige, I'm just a
bit'ter ol' hag. Dunna list'en to a word I say."
Looking at her, I'm stunned. "But you screwed with my head, and
made me think love was bad. You kinda fucked me up."
"Aye. An I'm sorry fer tha. I dunna know love, but ye have. And ye
should treasure tha fella and tha love for the rest of yer days."

Exhaling my newest head fuck, I know I'll love Malcolm for the rest of my days. I know there will never be anyone like Malcolm for me again- no one like Malcolm period. He will always remain a treasure to me.

"Can I go home with you?"

"Aye. I think it's time fer ye to come home and decide wha you want ta do wee the rest of yer life now. You've got ta let them go, love. And ye have'ta figure out how ta live now fer yerself. Thur no com'in back, Saige. To either of us."

When my mum uses my own line against me I realize she wasn't the only one holding onto ghosts. "I know they're not coming back..." I cry.

*****

After a quick goodbye to a few of the police I spoke with, I passed along a goodbye to Mathers though I'm sure to hear from him later.

Sitting beside my mum in her new car, I think she's forgetting she's Scottish and supposed to be tight with her money as she's always said. Then again, maybe by finally living a little this is her own way of saying goodbye to her ghosts now. I don't know, but it's a really nice car, and my mum seems happy.

Driving in silence, my mum lets me have my quiet. She ignores my frequent tears, pauses in tears, then more tears. Other than handing me Kleenex from her purse halfway back to New Haven she seems content to just let me do my thing- whatever the hell that is.

Thinking about everything I've learned and still don't understand, my brain is gone. My mind was lost 8 days ago, so at this point I'm just a walking zombie trying to figure out the little step by step things I need to do to simply function.

I know I have to make some decisions, and I know changes have to be made. I'm not even sure if I want to be a lawyer anymore now that I let my sweet Alec go. I don't know if I'll ever return to Midland, or if I'll just make a clean break from whoever is left.

Selena won't be easily deterred though. Just the 400 texts from her the last 8 days alone lets me know she's going to force herself to be a constant in my life whether I like it or not. Though I do still love Selena and Griffin, and even Mike, I think I need the distance and the break from Midland now.

After everything that's happened, I can't easily return, and really there isn't anything to return to. I lived at Malcolm's, and my old apartment was packed and stored 2 days ago by Selena and Dave. My old job is over because of my memories of that place. And yeah... there's nothing untouched or unbroken in Midland for me.

Dan has texted me a few times, and though very kind and even generous offering his and Karen's time, I can't engage them. I know they're heartbroken over this, and whether they actually blame me or not, I don't know how they can't feel at least a little resentment toward me for what happened to Malcolm. God, I do. So why wouldn't they?

And then there's Tatum. Huge, adorable, funny Tatum who begged me to come back so his family can see me, and who eventually wished me well when I told him I couldn't face his family. Tatum finally texted to let me know I was always welcome at his mother's table, as Mrs. MacNeil extended the invitation that broke my heart yesterday.

So that's it. I don't know what to do, what I'm doing, or even who I am anymore. The extent of my ability to acknowledge the world around me suggests I go to my mum's and sleep in my old bed. Just sleep for the first time in 8 days, and maybe try to eat for the first time in 8 days.

Then maybe I'll deal with the horror of my existence tomorrow. Or the next day. Or whenever I can breathe past this continuous agony that is my life without Malcolm in it anymore.

*****

An hour from her home, still silent but for the radio softly playing, my devastation is complete.

When 'Ho Hey' by the Lumineers starts, I gasp and reach for the volume. Blasting the song, I picture Malcolm singing to me and my heart actually shatters a little more.

He may not be here, and I will never again have him yell sing a song for me, but right here, right now, I'm surrounded by Malcolm singing I'm his sweet*heart.*

I have Malcolm wrapped around me, holding me warm in my mum's car, and I actually feel a little warmth for the first time in 8 days.

Listening, I realize Malcolm is everywhere and nowhere at all.

Crying at the beautiful memory of him singing at the top of his lungs during Tatum's party, 'Ho Hey' is the best memory I'll ever know at the worst time in my life.

Just when I know I have to let him go, I'm reminded of everything Malcolm I'll never let go of.

And it breaks my heart more than I ever thought possible.

Looking at my mum's radio display, I sync my phone quickly and wait for the end of the song so I can start it again. On repeat through my phone, I imagine Malcolm singing for me everything he knew was true from the beginning for us.

He always knew what I didn't know until it was too late for us. But now I know he was right along.

There really was something special between us, and that will be my biggest regret until the day I finally die.

Ours was the forever kind of love I finally trusted with my sweet, sweet, Mallie, but didn't enjoy before it was too late for us.

Sobbing my pain, I'll sing softly for the rest of my life

"I belong to you. You belong to me. You're my sweet-heart."

CHAPTER 40

This is life,
And it's brutal.

This is love,
And it's horrible.

This is purgatory,
And it's hateful.

This is death,
And it's painful.

Nothing stops, but nothing moves.

There is no peace or even rest.
There is nothing but a never-ending cycle of decay.

And I *am* decaying.
Before my own eyes I see my life ending.

And it hurts so much.
I don't even speak of the pain anymore.

I am silenced by the slow moving death that still taunts me.
I am bludgeoned by the agony of the death that haunts me.

I am beyond fractured and shattered.
I am decay.

*****

"*SAIGE!* Ye canna keep doin' this," I flinch when my mum yells at me from my bedroom doorway. "Yer fella's awake, love. Selena just called and said he's awake."

Gasping, I cry, "What?" as I fall from my bed. "When? *WHAT?!*"

"Yester'day apparent'ly. And he's already speakin' and- why ye lookin' like tha?" My mum stops speaking and walks to my bed to help me back up. Sitting beside me, she whispers, "Why ye cryin, wee Saige?"

Oh god... I'm *dying* again. When he's almost dead I'm dying, and when he's alive I'm almost dead.

And I would do *anything* for all this pain to stop.

"Saige, it's time to go back ta see this fella. Ye have ta. It's time, love."

Trying not to scream from the promises made, I can't do it. I can't go back on my word and hurt him again. Not being with him is my penance to pay and my agony to live with knowing he's alive without me.

Shaking my head, I refuse. "I can't go back, mum. I promised god if he helped Malcolm live, I would give him up. So I can't. But-"

"*That's* what ye bin hold'in onto? That's why ye no bin eatin or sleepin? That's why ye dunna talk to anyone any'more?"

"Yes, I-"

"I'm gonna give ye a wee bit of advice, Saige. Are ye list'nin?" She asks holding our green eyes locked as she waits.

No part of me wants this, and everything that's left of me wants to run screaming from another piece of my mum's advice. Everything in me wants to run like hell, but sadly, I can barely stand I'm so weak from this month-long nightmare through hell.

"Saige?" She asks again actually squeezing my hand tightly until I exhale a hard breath and nod for her. "Yer a book smart genius- giv'in. But yer one of the stuuupid'est stubborn arses I've ever met in me life. Yer Agnostic, for Christ's sake- so who the bloody hell was ye praying to? And even if there was some god list'nin to yer prayers, do you really think he would hold ye to yer word when ye was desper'ate to see yer fella live? Every'one makes those promises and begs like tha when they feel desper'ate. Any god list'nin knows that and takes these promises with a grain of salt."

"I- *what?*" Shaking my head again, I'm WHAT?! "I think I thought you kinda had to keep to your word about life and death things when you prayed for them. I mean, don't you?"

"Not if ye dunna believe in god, Saige- which ye don't. Ye do finally believe in lovin' yer fella though, right?"

"I do- I mean I did, but..." Can this actually happen? Can I actually go see Malcolm? "Holy *shit*. What do I do?" I beg as my chest starts beating erratically I'm so confused.

"Ye get yer arse up, and get a bloody shower. Then we get in my car and drive to see this man who loves ye. And that's all."

"But what if-"

"Shut up, Saige. Yer friends are dying to see you, and from wha I understand of this man, he's dying to see ye too. I'm gonna call Mary ta tell her where I'll be headin' and *you* get yer shite together. Times a wastin'," my mum smiles, pats my hand, and walks to the door like I have no choice. Which I actually don't.

There was NEVER any choice with Malcolm- it just was.

I love him so much I can't breathe from his absence in my life. There *is* nothing without him in my life.

Oh my *god...* I'm going to see Malcolm. Standing up slowly as I sway a little, I find myself smiling for the first time in a month.

*****

Driving, my mum is still horrendous. She's also a scary as shit lead foot, which under the circumstances I'll take. Though honestly, I'm starting to question whether she and I will actually live to see Malcolm alive.

Pulling up to the hospital, my mum drops me at the doors and leaves to park. Offering to go with me, I shake my head as the excitement and nerves settle in deep. I'm so excited to see him, but I'm scared shitless to see him, too.

There are so many reasons he might resent me for what happened, and for what *almost* happened to him. Yet I'm going in anyway.

I have to.

There is no life without him, and until I hear he doesn't want me in his life I have to go to him.

Asking at reception for his room, I'm told 5th floor, room 516, and visiting hours are ending in 2 hours in the ICU ward. I'm told something else as well but I ran for the elevators too quickly to hear.

I can't wait, and I don't want to wait anymore.

I love Malcolm MacNeil, and I need to at least tell him that.

Slapping the door release to the ICU, I practically yell Malcolm's name and room number to a nurse at the receiving desk. When she takes too long I look over her shoulder to the room numbers and start run-walking to Malcolm. Rounding the corner I see Dan and Karen, and with a quick moment of relief I smile at Dan, then flinch away from the deadly look Karen throws at me.

Stopping me in my tracks, I'm winded and so goddamn afraid suddenly that before I throw up or pass out I manage to gasp, "Is he still alive?"

When Dan kindly says yes to me I moan my relief hunching over my own knees to breathe.

"Why the fuck are *you* here?" Karen seethes at me, and once again, though I expected people to blame me for what happened to Malcolm, I'm still shocked by her anger.

"I, um, I wanted to see him. I miss him," I choke up a little trying to keep it together. "I'm sorry... does he hate me?" I beg before Dan huffs a no quickly when Karen opens her mouth to speak.

Watching Karen stiffen beside him, she shakes her head and simply walks away. Without a word, or a backwards glance, Karen walks away without speaking another word to me.

"Go see him, Saige. It's about time," Dan nods to a door a few down walking away before I can say anything more to him.

Shaking harder, I hate that Karen hates me, but I need to see Malcolm more. Sucking up my shock and sadness at her reaction to me I walk to the door to Malcolm.

Holding my breath, I don't know what I'll see, but I don't care. Malcolm will always be Malcolm to me. So pushing open his door, I wait for...

Oh *god.*

Lying on his side, Malcolm is so pale and sick-looking. He's also way smaller than he was. I know it's been a month since he was hurt, but I can't believe how much weight and muscle he's lost in only a month. His skin looks sallow and his arms look half the size they used to be.

And he's just so beautiful to me.

When he suddenly opens his eyes though, I die.
There's nothing there. There's nothing between us, and no love left.
 I can actually see it all.

"Why are you here?" Malcolm asks in a voice I don't recognize, but will
never forget.
 Holding my stomach, I gasp a breath so painful, I feel like my lungs are
in as much agony as my heart is.
 "Oh, *Malcolm,*" I burst into tears.
 "What do you want, Saige?" He asks again in a tone filled with such
hatred I'm momentarily speechless. Looking at me, there's no crinkly
eyes or cheeky grin. He actually looks like the intimidating bastard I first
remember before he spoke to me at D'Vecseys.
 And I'm heartbroken.
 "I'm so sorry," I cry as his dark presence washes over me. "I'm sorry I
came. I just thought-"
 "What?"
 "I thought maybe I could see you," I whisper hoping, *praying* he
doesn't hate me.
 "Well, you've seen me. And now you can go," he huffs again, moving
himself painfully to his back. Actually throwing his arm over his face, I
can't believe this is what's left of us.
 I can't believe this is our end.
 Bursting into tears, I don't even try. I'm exhausted from all this shit,
and fed up with life totally.
 Lowering his arm, Malcolm watches me cry but doesn't reach for me or
even speak. He's looking at me totally unaffected by my heartbreak and
its breaking me further. Staring at each other, Malcolm looks dead in
the eyes and completely broken by me.
 Pulling myself together as best as I can for this goodbye, I say
everything left between us. "I'm very sorry you were hurt because of
me, and I'm so sorry you ever met me. I never meant for you to get hurt
that night. I was trying to get back to you so-"
 "I don't give a *fuck* about that night!" Malcolm yells then quickly
silences when I flinch. Reaching desperately for his own chest the
machines all around him are suddenly beeping so loudly they nearly
strangle me with sound.
 Breathing deeply as I panic at his pain and upset, *he* breathes the

unimaginable. "I can't believe you left me. I can't believe you didn't care enough about me and us to stay here with me when I needed you," he cries so sadly I move to him immediately.

Grabbing his hand, Malcolm rips it out of my own until I collapse on his stomach instead. Grabbing his sides, I hold him to me even as he fights my hold. Growling at me, he tries to tear my arms off his stomach while I cry my eyes out all over him holding as tightly as my weak arms will allow.

"I *didn't,*" I moan. "I promised. I begged and prayed, Malcolm."

"Saige, get the *fuck* away from me," Malcolm growls again so darkly I hold him even tighter.

"I said goodbye to you, and I kissed you, and I begged you to live. I told you I loved you and I begged the doctors and nurses, and I said goodbye to you."

"Fuck off, Saige."

"Malcolm, I was so desperate for you to live I did everything I could. I prayed for you. I begged whoever or whatever god there is to let you live. I begged and prayed and I *promised-*"

"I don't fucking care. Let *go* of me!" Malcolm yells angry enough that the machines start beeping loudly again.

Crying over his anger, I plead so he understands. "I prayed for you to live. And I promised if you lived I would let you go. I *promised,* Malcolm. And you were alive but not awake, and I was so scared."

Shaking his head he growls my name as I continue trying to explain away his sadness. "I promised if you lived I would let you go. That was my punishment and my penance for getting you hurt. So I left, Malcolm. I left so you would live. I needed you to live for all your family and friends. *I* needed you to live," I sob and cry and hold onto his waist as hard as I can. "I promised to let you go so you would live and then you lived. So I had to leave. It was my promise so you could live."

"Saige?" Malcolm moans. No longer ripping at my arms, Malcolm is suddenly calmer. "What the hell are you talking about?"

Risking a quick glance at his eyes, they're so dark and bruised looking I wish I could kiss them. "I didn't want to go. I *never* wanted to leave you. But I made a promise because I would rather you live without me then die because I loved you. I couldn't have you die like Alec and my father did." Gasping, I finish this for us. "I didn't want to leave you for even a second, but I knew if I loved you you'd die like Alec and my father did. So I made a promise to live without you so you would live."

"But... that's stupid," Malcolm says so deadpan, I laugh, and cry, and shake, and almost throw up beside us.

Gagging as my stomach turns again, I'm so exhausted from life I feel like ending it again. Just like I have every minute of every day for a month, I feel the overwhelming urge to end it all I'm so exhausted.

"I'm really tired, Malcolm," I whisper. "Like so tired of all this shit all the time." Sitting up and nearly away, Malcolm reaches for my arm before I can leave him for good.

"You gave me up so I would live?" Malcolm asks quietly. Barely hearing his words, I *do* feel his sadness inside me. Nodding my head, I'm wordless. Staring at my eyes still Malcolm asks the question for the ages. "Why?"

"Because I love you. And I didn't care how much it hurt me to let you go- I wanted you to live."

"So why are you here now?"

"Because my mum told me I don't believe in god, and god wouldn't hold me to that promise anyway. She said that was a promise everyone makes when they're desperate for something good to happen, so whoever or whatever god takes those promises with a grain of salt. Oh, and she said I'm really stupid and stubborn for sticking to it."

"She's right," he says again sounding so funny under the circumstances and desperation I'm feeling, I laugh another sad, hard laugh-cry straight from my broken heart.

After a few moments of silence while I get my shit together Malcolm asks, "So you didn't just leave me when things were bad?"

"No... I left so things would get better for you. I didn't leave you- I left *for* you. I promise."

"But you-" Cutting him off, I need to explain so he finally understands.

"I'm sorry for everything, Malcolm. For *everything.* I'm so sorry you were shot and have to feel all of this pain because of me." Inhaling deeply, I plead, "I don't have any other words, even though they don't feel close to enough. I love you, and I never want you to hurt because of me again. I *never* wanted you to hurt because of me."

"What happened to you?" Malcolm asks choking up in front of me.

With his eyes swimming in tears, my heartbreak is complete. "I'm going to go. I can't see you sad because of me anymore. I can't-"

"Saige? Look at me, baby. What's wrong?"

"I'm just tired," I huff trying to pull away from his hand holding my wrist.

"Tell me..." he moans. "What happened to you?"

"Nothing. I just haven't really functioned or exhaled or anything in a long time. But I'm so happy you're awake, I don't care about any of that. I wanted you to wake up and now you have, so it's all better now. You're alive and I can let go now."

"Of?"

"Us. You. Everything I wanted with you. I can finally let go now. I couldn't when you wouldn't wake up, so I was just waiting. But now-"

"Now you're leaving me because I'm awake?"

"I don't want to," I shrug. "But I don't know what to do anymore. I stubbornly held onto my promise so you would live, and now you're alive and hate me- which is okay," I nod so he understands I understand his hatred. "So now I can let go of you."

"Saige... I don't hate you. I just didn't understand. No one could tell me where you were, or why you left. So I thought you simply ran when things were tough. I was hurt because I didn't understand why you weren't here with me," Malcolm says softly squeezing my hand.

Looking at our hands I feel him squeeze mine, and I know everything Malcolm. He really is alive, and I love him.

Looking at his eyes, I feel a tear slide down my face as he watches. "What is it?" He whispers making a sob burst from my chest.

"I told you I loved you in your driveway, and you didn't squeeze my hand back. You were just lying there, and your arm was hanging off the gurney, and I held it and kissed it, and I told you I loved you. I held your hand and I waited, but you didn't squeeze me back." Choking on my words, I tell him everything. "You've always squeezed me, and I've always known you were there for me. But in that one moment, an endless second that lasted an eternity- I told you I loved you and you didn't squeeze me back." Wiping my face on my shoulders I let him know what I knew. "You didn't squeeze me back for the first time ever, and I felt your death, and then I felt mine. Ah, I knew I lost you so I died beside you in your driveway."

"But I didn't die, Saige."

"I know..." I moan my dark reality. "But I didn't think you would live."

"But I did live."

"I know..." I nod taking my first huge breath since the moment I said goodbye to him in the hospital.

Squeezing my hand tightly, Malcolm smiles and asks, "Would you do something for me?"

"God, yes. *Anything.*"

"Could you say, 'I'm just a girl, standing in front of a boy, asking him to love her'?" Looking at his crinkly eyes, I'm totally confused until he laughs, "Notting Hill. Julia Roberts. Wanna see me bawl like a baby when the girl gets the guy?"

Crying my eyes out, I look at Malcolm and feel nothing but love for him. Every part of my entire world feels my love, and everything I am wants him back.

"I *need* to love you, Malcolm. For the rest of my life, if you'll let me?" I beg him desperately.

"Okay, that was *way* better than Julia's line," Malcolm teases. "Come here. Come up here, Saige," he begs still tugging my hand until I gently climb on his bed. Against his side, I move one thick wire from his chest right over my head, carefully navigate around his IV, and lean into his side as he pulls me against his chest.

"Are you mad at me for getting you hurt?" I ask finally.

Squeezing my side to him closer, Malcolm breathes, "Never," as I exhale deeply all my fear. "I'm mad at so many things, but never that. I know what happened to you before, and I understand you left to help me. Mathers explained what that fucking dick said about me being hurt if you didn't go with him?"

"Yes."

"So you actually left with him?"

"Not by choice. He forced me to my car, but I didn't care. I didn't want you to get hurt, and he said you would if I didn't go so I would've gone to save you anyway. But then he just took me," I huff thinking about Kyle and that night again. "I don't really want to talk about that, Malcolm. It's all warped in my head, and heavy, and just awful. But I barely remember anything that happened before I was dying in your driveway, and then-" Shaking my head I don't want to cry anymore, and I don't want to feel anything but this for the rest of my life.

"Okay, I'll let this go. For now," Malcolm squeezes my side again. "But we *will* talk about what you went through that night. And this time I'm making you go to counseling, okay?"

"No, I-"

"This is non-negotiable. I couldn't force you to counseling after you were raped in April, but I'm forcing you to go this time. You need it, Saige. You have too much stuff unsettled and overwhelming between your past and your present. There's just too much for you to handle by yourself, and I need you to do this for us. I'll be and do anything you want, but I need you to get all this shit out with someone who can help you so we have a solid chance. Because *I* need to love you too, Saige. For the rest of *my* life."

Smiling, I agree because it's non-negotiable, and because Malcolm wants me to. "Okay."

"Ah, there's my wee lass," he brogues making me shiver. "I've missed you so much this past month, Saige."

"You only woke up yesterday," I smile.

"I know, but I missed you when I was unconscious. I know I did. I *felt* it."

"I missed you every moment of every day. I sang Ho Hey in my head constantly, and I cried all the time. I was just destroyed when you-" Stopping myself again, Malcolm doesn't need to hear anymore. I'm sure he understands what I was going through without him.

"Tell me, Saige. *Talk* to me."

"There's nothing to say. You were almost dead, and I *was* dead. Um, that's what the last month has been like for me," I whisper again so he doesn't feel hurt by my sadness.

"You look terrible, Saige. You look so thin and awful, and just so sad. I'm so sorry you went through this alone."

"*I'm* sorry. And you look way worse, Malcolm," I respond as stubborn as usual which makes him laugh a little against me.

"So we'll get better together?"

"Yes."

"Will you come home now?"

"If you'll have me?"

"Saige... nothing has changed for me. That last night, before everything happened you were coming home to me. You loved me, and you said your goodbye to Tyler and to your past. So I was waiting for you. Before I was shot you were supposed to come home and that hasn't changed. Nothing has changed for me and I still want you. I still *love* you. I've been unconscious for a month so everything picked up for me yesterday where it left off that night until I thought you ran from me and us, and-"

Sitting up to stare at his eyes, I tell him my absolute. "I *never* ran. I just gave you up to save you."

Nodding, Malcolm breathes *our* absolute. "You don't have to give me up, and I'm not leaving you. *Ever,* Saige."

"Okay," I exhale happily.

Understanding what I always mistrusted and couldn't accept, I trust and accept it now. Malcolm is not leaving me and I don't have to give him up. *Ever,* apparently.

"I love you, sweet, sweet, Mallie," I tear up a little but smile against his chest when I feel him squeeze me closer to his side.

THE END

(mis)TRUST

Epilogue

Turning to Malcolm shuffling through the kitchen, I reach for his hand to squeeze. "I thought you'd sleep a little longer?"

"Nope. I've got a Thanksgiving to prepare for. And this is the only meal I cook well. So get out of my kitchen, Saige," he smiles and kisses me quickly.

"Thank god," I grin. "The potatoes are boiled, the yams are made, and, ah, that's about the extent of my culinary skills. I'll set the tables while you get your chef on with 2 friggin' turkeys. *Honestly,* Malcolm. *2*?"

"We have 19 adults coming over, plus kids. So I'd rather have too much turkey than not enough. Plus, I don't know how much your mum and her date will eat," he smirks again as I swat his arm.

"I guess she *reeeeealy* didn't like cocks, did she?" I ask as Malcolm howls with laughter.

Finding out my mother was a lesbian was a complete shock, though a total relief as well. I actually welcomed the news because it took all the anti-male pressure out of the equation for me. Not that it would've continued anyway- Malcolm charmed the bitter old hag right out of my mum *and* her lovely Scottish girlfriend Mary.

Still grinning Malcolm turns me toward him before I can walk away to set the tables. "Wait. I need to-" Lifting me on the breakfast bar, Malcolm scooches between my spread legs and pulls me to his chest. "This is going to sound so cheesy," he grins placing my face against his chest. "But I'm so proud of everything you've done and *are* doing. And honestly, I'm so thankful for you in my life, Saige. But I thought I better say it now before the Thanksgiving toasts so I don't make a weepy ass of myself in public."

Pulling away to look at his eyes, Malcolm takes my face in his hands and kisses my lips so softly I melt right on the counter. Pulling away, I look at his bright blue eyes and feel all his love surrounding me.

"You did all of this, Malcolm. Without you supporting me, I never would've turned down Harvard. I wouldn't have finally decided I didn't want to be the old Saige anymore. I wouldn't have applied at the University or talked to Handle about what I wanted to do. And I *never* would've accepted the teaching placement he pulled off without you telling me I could do it. Everything I am now is *all* you," I whisper before he kisses my lips again softly.

411

"I love you, Saige."

"I know," I grin before he kisses me again. A little harder and deeper Malcolm kisses the humor from my lips as my body heats up for him.

"I need you," he groans as I nod.

Tearing at Malcolm's jeans, I rip down the zipper as he lifts my ass off the counter. Yanking my track pants down one-handed, he pulls away quickly to push his jeans to his knees before I'm pulled right to the edge of the counter.

God, he still turns me on and gets me going just from his strength alone. In only 3 months he's put back on most of the weight and muscle he lost in the hospital, and he's been back to work for a month now. Due to his twice weekly physiotherapy appointments his left arm is even back to functioning at 85% from the nerve damage he suffered from one of the 4 bullets he took that horrible night.

Stopping to look at Malcolm completely still in front of me, I'm overwhelmed again by how close we came to ending, how close he came to dying, and how close I was to never knowing this happiness with him.

When I see him like this, sexy as hell, with his intense growly face towering over me it can still overwhelm me that I not only live with this man but that he loves me *to the death* as he says now on a regular basis to remind me of his love.

"Baby... don't. I'm fine, and you're fine. We're safe and today is going to be a very fun, very *loud* celebration with all our family and friends."

"I'm not-"

"I know that look, Saige. And I know when the fear and sadness overwhelms you. I know you cuz 'you're my sweet-*heart*,'" he gently sings against my ear as I moan in his arms.

Breathing against my mouth Malcolm whispers, "Never again, Saige. Your ghosts have finally passed on, and the bad people are out of your life either in prison or dead. Kyle is still in jail for a long time, and Kaitlyn is awaiting her trial for accessory after the fact and hindering a police investigation. They're *gone,* Saige. And- "

"But Tyler- "

"Will deal with whatever happens to Kaitlyn and that child, between them. But *I'm* always going to be here with you. Okay?"

"Okay," I breathe on a quick exhale as Malcolm kisses me deeply back to our present.

Sarah Ann Walker

(mis)TRUST

ABOUT THE AUTHOR

Sarah Walker is a Scottish Canadian living in Canada with her son.

In her real life, Sarah is a devoted mother, and an absolute junkie for coffee, dark chocolate with sea salt, and high heels.

www.authorsarahannwalker.com

Sarah can be found on Facebook
www.facebook.com/SarahAnnWalkerIAmHer

Amazon
http://www.amazon.com/author/walkersarahann

Goodreads
https://www.goodreads.com/Sarah-Walker

and
Twitter
@sarahannwalker0

(mis)TRUST